SKINNED

Books by Joanne Clarey

Fiction

The Hummingbird Falls Mystery Series:

The Mysteries of Hummingbird Falls
Riddled to Death

The Dr. Christie McMorrow Thriller Series:

Twisted Truth
Skinned

Non-fiction

I.A.M.G.R.E.A.T. (GROWTH THROUGH RESOCIALIZATION, EXPLORATION, AWARENESS TRAINING)

I.A.M.P.O.O.W.E.R. (PROMOTING OCCUPATIONAL OPPORTUNITIES FOR WOMEN THROUGH EXPERIENCE AND RETRAINING)

SKINNED

Joanne Clarey

Published by Alabaster Book Publishing
North Carolina

This is a work of fiction. Names, character, places, and incidents either are the product of the author's imagination or are used fictitiously and any resemblance to actual persons, businesses, events, or locales is coincidental.

Published by Alabaster Book Publishing
P.O. Box 401
Kernersville, North Carolina 27285

Book design by
D.L.Shaffer
Cover Concept by Joanne Clarey
Author's Photograph by Joan Seidel Photography

First Edition

ISBN-13: 978-0-9790949-0-3
ISBN-10: 0-9790949-0-9

Library Of Congress Control
Number: 2007925089

In our 21st century world, where freedom and democracy are spreading to every continent, it is appalling and morally unacceptable that hundreds of thousands of men, women, and children are exploited, abused, and enslaved by peddlers in human misery.

Trafficking touches many countries across the globe, including my own. An estimated 800,000 to 900,000 people are trafficked every year. Nearly 20,000 of these victims enter the United States. The transnational character of this crime means that countries of origin, transit, and destination must work in partnership to prevent trafficking, protect its victims, and prosecute those who are responsible for trafficking.

Using force, fraud and corruption, coercion and other horrible means, traffickers prey on the powerless, the desperate, and the vulnerable. Girls as young as five are sold into prostitution, boys as young as 11 are being strong-armed into militias to serve as child soldiers or to perform labor for the combatants.

The United States stands prepared to help countries that demonstrate a determined commitment to strengthen their domestic capacities for combating trafficking. Working together, we can help the victims of trafficking escape bondage and allow them to live in dignity and freedom. Working in partnership, we can spare countless thousands the pain that others have suffered.

U.S. Secretary of State Colin Powel

Adapted from his remarks following the release of the 2003 Trafficking in Persons Report on June 11, 2003

THIS BOOK IS DEDICATED TO:

Those who work to free victims of human trafficking.

Those who protect the dignity of the human body, whether alive or dead.

Those victims who suffer exploitation, abuse, enslavement, and indignity.

ACKNOWLEDGEMENTS

First and always I give thanks to my friends and fellow authors in the Triad Writers Roundtable for their unwavering support: David Shaffer, Dixie Land, Helen Goodman, John Staples, Kathy Fisher, Lynette H. Hamilton, Emogene Joyner and Larry Jakubsen.

I have been gifted with fabulous readers who helped me immeasurably through the many versions of Skinned: Larry Jakubsen, Candace Crowell, Anne Garland, Ruth Ann Brown and editor extraordinaire, Nancy McCallum.

My gratitude goes to the many researchers and workers in the field of human trafficking, human rights, illegal harvesting of body parts and global exploitation of children who shared their expertise with me personally and through writings on the internet.

I thank David Shaffer for his design work, photographer Joan Seidel for her portrait of me and Alabaster Book Publishing for their commitment to my work. I appreciate the others who contributed to Skinned, in one way or another, so numerous that I cannot include all their names. You know who you are.

Love and thanks to Anne Garland for providing me a warm and creative writing environment and the encouragement to work at what I love.

As always, any errors or mistakes are my own.

"Trafficking Humans: Problem in U.S. poses elusive target for coalition combating it. Victims of American style human trafficking have had very different venues for ordeals as bad or worse-brothels and bars in New Jersey, slave labor farms in Florida, a small tree cutting business in New Hampshire. 'Human trafficking is so hidden you don't know who you're fighting-the victims are so scared. They're not going to tell you what's happening to them.'"

From the AP, David Crary, National Writer

Baby trafficking arrest sparks protest, concern. A 56-year-old woman was sentenced to 15 years in jail for leading a gang that sold abducted babies, over 78 in one year alone.

From the Greensboro News Record, March 7, 2006

Skin, skinned: a swindler, cheat, a fleecher; to strip money or belongings; to defeat; to slip away; to strip off skin, to flay; relating to pornography as skin magazine; one's life, as in to save her skin.

Webster's Dictionary

The *Dance of Death* by Hans Holbern and *Human Corpis Fabrica,* by Andreas Vesalli are both bound in human skin. They may be found in Brown University's Hay Library. Their covers are tanned and polished to a smooth golden brown, like fine leather. In fact, a number of the nation's finest libraries, including Harvard's have such books in their collections.

From the Associated Press, January 11, 2006

A 300 year-old book that appears to be bound in human skin has been found in northern England. It was not uncommon around the time of the French revolution for books to be covered in human skin. The practice, known as anthropodermic bibliopegy, was sometimes used in the 18th and 19th centuries when accounts of murder trials were bound in the killer's skin.

From the *London Times,* February, 9, 2006

Some headlines from 2006:

"N.C. Patients Notified of Stolen Tissue."

"Body Parts Scandal Spurs First Lawsuit."

"Patients Blame Viruses on Stolen Body Parts."

"List of Patients Receiving Stolen Tissue Grows."

"Authorities: Bone tissue Came from Funeral Homes."

Give sorrow words; the grief that does not speak
whispers the o'er-fraught heart and bids it break.

William Shakespeare

Perhaps everything terrible is in its deepest being
something helpless that wants help from us.

Rainer Maria Rilke

We shall draw from the heart of suffering itself the means
of inspiration and survival.

Winston Churchill

When it is dark enough, you can see the stars.

Ralph Waldo Emerson

1

He's right behind her. Creeping closer. Soon he'll reach out and touch her. He'll grab her red wool coat. His fingers will seize her long brown hair. He'll pull her close; her endless nightmare turned into grim reality. He'll bury her in his sinister madness and then she'll disappear forever into his shadow.

Christie knows who he is. He's not a crack head, hiding among the cars in the underground parking lot, waiting for an easy mark to get money for his next fix. He's not a car-jacker admiring her sweet red Saab. He's not a sexual predator attracted to her classic beauty, her slim athletic build. He's not a stranger.

She's been waiting for him. She looks for him everywhere: in dark corners, in reflections from her rear view mirror, under her car, behind the bathroom door, outside her windows. And now he's here, barely an arm's reach behind her. She pushes her already exhausted legs to move faster. She imagines his warm breath streaming out, white wisps in the cold air, flowing close enough to stroke her skin.

She can't outrun him. In seconds he'll be on her. Christie debates turning and facing him. She could try to scream him away. But what if his icy eyes lock onto her sky-blue eyes, freezing her rigid? She'll be powerless, easy prey. Then he'll have her. So she stares straight ahead and calls on all the inner strength she can marshal. She limps as fast as she can toward the elevator, using her single crutch to propel her.

The dark form drops back a little, as if he doesn't want

to end the chase too soon. Christie understands he's enjoying his pursuit, playing with her. She remembers how he smiled last fall when he pushed her fear to the breaking point. How he toyed with her, a predator obsessed with tormenting his victim. That's what he's doing now. Using her fear as his most potent weapon, waiting for her terror to betray her.

Christie strains to move even faster. The elevator's so far away. What if the door doesn't open? What if it's stopped on another floor? What if he reaches out and touches her, as she focuses on the numbers flickering slowly from Level 1 to 2, to 3?

A whimper trembles in her throat. She tries to cry out, but her mouth is so dry only a faint whisper for help quivers in the air.

She looks for someone to help. Powerful lights illuminate the concrete parking garage. Shadows between the tightly packed cars push into the narrow driving lane, but none of them move. None resembles a human form that might save her.

Should she forsake the elevator and run? What will happen if he traps her in there? In that tight shiny box, where the air's so thin? She'll never escape from that suffocating coffin once the doors lock them inside together.

He'll stop the car between floors. The elevator will imprison them together. Breathing the same stale air, smelling her sweat and his mingling together, fusing them forever. How long can she survive in that terror filled space?

Christie reaches the elevator and pounds the buttons with her fist. Both buttons. Up and down. Down or up, it doesn't matter. Desperate, she beats them again. Nothing happens. The door doesn't open. She can't wait. He's too close. She'll have to try to escape through the parking garage.

She turns from the elevator, bends low and limps down a row of parked cars, deeper into the underground garage. She doesn't hear his footsteps behind her, but then, she didn't hear them before, either. She doesn't need any sounds to know he's still shadowing her.

She runs faster than she knew she could. Adrenalin's fueling her aching muscles. Ahead she spots a large SUV and ducks behind it, squatting by the left rear tire. Maybe he won't see her in the deep shadow the big vehicle casts.

She smells gas fumes and wet rubber, feels grit and water under her hands. She tries to quiet her gasping breaths. She looks around for a weapon, a rock, a stick, anything. She scoops up a handful of sand and gravel. Her only defenses are a small ball of grit, her briefcase and crutch. Christie envisions her gun lying in the drawer of her bedside table and wishes she had put it in her briefcase today. She scans the driving lane, waiting for his silhouette to loom toward her hiding place.

What can she do besides cower here in her hidey-hole? For a second, she wishes for the huge forsythia bush that sheltered her when she was young. Way inside, no one could see the little girl bent over, hoping she was invisible. She clings to this image as she waits for him to find her.

She hears the sound of a car engine. The driver hesitates at the turn, deciding whether to head left or drive up the ramp toward her. Christie holds her breath and prays. The car continues up the ramp, increasing speed. She takes her chance. She limps out of her hiding space and steps directly in front of the oncoming car. It's now accelerating, moving very fast. She closes her eyes, this time praying the driver will stop the car before it hits her.

2

Brakes screech. The sound echoes against the concrete walls, screaming. The black Audi's lights assault Christie. The chrome bumper stops, cold against her legs. The driver's window rolls down and a sequence of curses fly out. Christie stands shaking until the car door opens and a man jumps out.

"What the hell's the matter with you? I could've killed you. What are you doing?"

Christie tries to answer, but her voice trembles so much she can't articulate her words. She licks her lips and tries again.

"There's a man. He's following me. He's going to kill me."

The driver of the car looks around the garage. Seeing no one, he asks, "Where?"

Christie points back up the ramp.

The man walks up the ramp, looking under and behind the cars. He turns and studies Christie, then looks around the garage once more and walks back to her.

"I don't see anyone. Are you sure someone's following you?"

He looks at her as if she might be crazy, one of the many mentally ill people who walk the streets of Portland, Maine now that the Bangor Institute for the Mentally Ill has closed its doors.

"Yes, I'm sure. He was right there." Christie points toward the elevator.

"Well, he's not there now. Maybe he ran down the stairs

when he saw me coming. Or maybe he took the elevator. I'll call for help."

Tall and handsome, the man wears a blue wool business suit covered by a long black wool overcoat. His dark hair is cut short, suitable for his athletic look and his thirty-something craggy face. He reaches into the front seat of his car and picks up a cell phone. He speaks for a few moments. Then he walks over to Christie, pulls out his ID folder, flips it open and shows it to her.

"I'm Detective Tom Wilder. I'm the associate director of the Maine State Task Force on Violent Crimes. I called security and they're on the way. I'll stay with you until they get here. No one seems to be around now; so I think you're safe."

"Thank you," Christie murmurs. "I'm so glad you came when you did. He was just about to grab me." Her eyes sweep the parking area, searching, not believing the man is gone. "Oh God."

Christie breaks into tears, shaking with relief. Tom hands her a lightly starched white handkerchief and she covers her face as she sobs. After a few minutes, Tom sees her struggling to pull herself together. She wipes at her eyes and gulps huge breaths of air. By the time the security guards arrive, she has stopped crying and is starting to explain what happened.

Two guards search the floor thoroughly and then approach Tom and Christie.

"I'm Security Officer Bob Sanders and this is Officer Brown. I've posted extra security at the exit to check everyone leaving the garage. We searched on our way to this level, but didn't see anyone suspicious."

"But you must have missed him. He's probably hiding," Christie says.

"Camera surveillance scans the parking levels, the elevator and staircase 24/7. An officer ran the tapes for the last half hour and no one used the stairs. All the elevator passengers had checked in. The tape for this parking level shows several people leaving their cars and walking to the elevators, but they all work here. He saw a woman hurrying to the elevator on the tape; Miss, which must have been you. However, you were alone; nobody was chasing you. We'll search this level again, just to be sure, but it's possible you thought you saw a man walking behind you and you got scared. Tell me what happened. What does this man look like?"

"Well, I didn't actually see him," Christie says. "I felt him behind me. I could tell he was following me."

"You didn't see him? You mean you didn't see him at all? How do you know someone was there if you didn't see him?" Sanders asks.

"Officer Sanders, please don't yell at me."

"Sorry, Miss, but I'm trying to understand. How did you know he wanted to kill you? Did he have a weapon? Did anyone else see him?"

"Please stop drilling me. I know it sounds odd, but I don't need to see him to know he's there. I know this man. I'm familiar with how he operates."

"You know him? Well, who is he?"

"Hold on, I'm trying to tell you. I was the only one, besides him, up here. I looked for other people, but no one else was around. I know it's hard to understand, but even though I didn't actually see him, officer, I swear he was here. He was right behind me. His name is Stephen Scott."

Tom stared at Christie. He opened his mouth to speak but before he got a word out Sanders asked, "And who are you?"

"I'm Dr. Christie McMorrow. I'm the consulting forensic psychologist for the Maine State Task Force on Violent Crimes, which has offices on the third floor of this building. I have an appointment with Detective William Drummond, the director. I checked in when I arrived."

"Yes, I'll be able to verify that. I know you, sir, are

Detective Tom Wilder. Do you know this woman?"

"I'm sorry, but I don't. I can't identify her as Dr. McMorrow. I do know a Dr. McMorrow used to work here and is coming in today to consult on a new case."

Officer Sanders asks, "May I see some identification, Miss?"

"Why are you wasting time questioning who I am? Why aren't you looking for the man following me? He wants to kill me. He's Stephen Scott, the serial killer who escaped from the Portland police last year. He's come back to kill me."

A silence falls as the two officers glance at each other and then look at Tom.

"Stephen Scott? Stephen Scott was following you?" asks Tom.

"Yes. Now, will you stop asking questions and look for the bastard?"

"Take it easy, Miss. We've got everything under control. Just let me see some identification please."

Christie digs out her task force ID and thrusts it at Sanders.

He studies it closely then hands it to his partner.

"So, you're the one Scott kidnapped? I thought you looked familiar," Sanders says.

Brown looks up from Christie's ID. "That's her. I remember seeing her picture in the paper last November when the whole thing went down."

Sanders says, "Sorry, Dr. McMorrow. Your description of what happened sounds, well, a little strange, especially since the tapes don't show anybody following you. I apologize if we've upset you."

"I understand the need to check identities. What I want to know is how Scott got by you. Certainly he couldn't pass the entrance scan."

Sanders answers, "Nobody's gotten past us yet, Dr.

McMorrow, but I suppose there could always be a first time. I'm sorry about what you said you experienced."

"It's not what I said, damn it, it's what happened. Why can't you get that?"

Brown interrupts. "You want us to believe that Stephen Scott was here stalking you? Look Dr. McMorrow, no one showed up on the cameras. How did he manage that? And exactly how do you know it was him if you didn't see him?"

"I can't believe this. You're insinuating that I'm a liar, crazy and hallucinating. Right? Well, I resent your implications. I don't know how he avoided the cameras. I don't know how he got by you. But I do know Officer Brown, Stephen Scott was here, following me, intending to kill me. After what I've been through with him, I'd know when he was near even if I were blind and deaf."

"Well be assured, we're going to double check. Officer Brown means no offense, I'm sure," said Sanders. "We'll escort you and Detective Wilder to the task force floor and then continue our search. We'll report our findings to Detective Drummond."

"Thank you, Officer Sanders," says Tom.

"Maybe you shouldn't be driving around by yourself, Dr. McMorrow, if that killer's out to get you, like you said. It's not safe," Brown says.

"You infuriate me, Officer Brown. There's no 'ifs' about it. He's out to get me; you can count on that. Okay? Understand? And since I was coming to a so-called secure garage, I didn't think I'd need a guard to escort me. Next time, I'll have one. Can we get out of here now?"

"An escort's a good idea," Tom says as he and the guards walk Christie to the elevator, looking around as they go. "I'm sorry I didn't recognize you, Dr. McMorrow. I started to work with the task force in late November, after you left for rehabilitation. Of course, I'm familiar with your excellent reputation. Bill told me you were coming back to consult on this new case. Welcome. I'm glad to meet you. Wish it were under better circumstances."

He studies her face as they walk. He finds her a striking woman, beautiful in the classic sense, with high cheekbones and large blue eyes framed by thick shoulder length light brown hair. He notices dark circles under her eyes and the beginning of worry lines forming around them. He wants to know more about her. What happened when Stephen Scott kidnapped her? Why did she choose forensic psychology and what does she like to do on her time off?

"Thank you. Me too," Christie murmurs. She hates that what happened last fall turned her life into a public event. It's common knowledge that Stephen Scott tortured and almost killed her. Although law enforcement personnel kept the horrific details private, she can imagine people gossiping, guessing what atrocities she'd endured. The news she's back at the task force is spreading fast, evidently. If she gets one look of pity from anyone, she'll scream, maybe even quit. She isn't sure she should be back working with the task force so soon anyway.

They enter the tiny elevator and as the doors slowly close, Christie panics. Locked in an elevator. Not enough air. Not enough room. She thinks about Stephen Scott trapping her in here. She has trouble breathing and beads of perspiration break out on her forehead.

She wants to punch a hole in the shiny steel wall, kick down the thick door. She needs out of the slow moving canister. However, as frenzied as her panic makes her feel, her analytical mind dominates. "Stay still," her mind commands. "Look composed." If she reveals her terror, the men riding the elevator with her will surely believe she's off her rocker.

The tension brings her to the verge of passing out. Just in time, she recalls the calming routine she has used so many times over the last five months. As she slowly counts to ten in her head, she takes a breath on every even number. When she gets to ten, she counts backwards, breathing in on the odd numbers. As she starts counting again from the number one, the doors slide open and she stumbles out onto the third floor of the building, the offices of the Maine State Task Force on Violent Crimes.

Bill Drummond's waiting in the hall. "I heard," he says as he takes Christie into his arms. Then he whispers, "Are you okay?"

Christie pushes him away. "Yes, I'm okay. I had a bad scare downstairs. Why didn't you tell me Stephen Scott's back?"

3

Christie sat in the large black leather chair in Bill's corner office. She put her aching feet up on the matching ottoman and stared out the windows at the dark clouds hovering over Portland, threatening to blot out the setting sun. Already a gloomy dusk was settling over the city and lights were blinking on in office buildings. Meteorologists had predicted snow and temperatures had barely climbed from the below-zero lows of last night. Frost etched the windows and the baseboard heaters struggled to keep the office at the 65 degrees dictated by the state. Christie could see sea smoke wisping up from the waters of the harbors and bays that surrounded the Eastern Promenade.

"You owe me a Goddamn explanation, Bill."

"Christie, listen. If Scott were back, you'd be the first person I'd notify. I promised you that and I mean it. You know I check constantly with Dave Hadley, our local FBI liaison officer, for updates on Scott's whereabouts. I just talked with him while you were in the rest room. He said he's pretty positive Scott's not in Maine."

"Pretty positive doesn't do it for me. Why only 'pretty'? Why not just 'positive'? And he is here. He followed me in the garage. Hadley doesn't know anything, obviously."

"You're as familiar with how Scott operates as we are. He hits one place and then moves on. Never kills more than one woman in a single location. I told you we've tracked him down South, zigzagging around. The FBI positively identified fifteen women as his victims. His ritual killing methods remain consistent. However, he has stayed in the South. No sign of him anywhere else."

"That you and the FBI know of, you mean. It's been two months since they found his last victim. Since then not one sign of him, right? So where is he? I'll tell you. Here. Right here in your secure garage. How do you know that a copycat didn't kill the fifteen women? After all the media attention, everyone knows exactly how Scott kills and what he does with the bodies."

"We've held some evidence back, you know that. We're positive Scott committed the murders down South. No doubt about it. No one else could possibly replicate each detail. Every murder was executed exactly the way Scott carried out his previous 129 murders."

Christie stared at Bill. "He was in the garage. I'm not crazy."

Bill leaned toward her. He looked into her eyes, searching. Then with a sigh he said,

"I know you're not crazy. No one's saying you are. But a lot of bad stuff has happened to you. Some people with Post Traumatic Stress Disorder develop unusual behaviors; you know that. They experience extreme sensitivity, they imagine things or reenact their trauma. Almost anything can trigger a panic attack. Like a backfire triggers a Viet Nam vet into thinking he's back in the war. Maybe you had a panic attack in the garage."

Christie started to stand up. The touch of her feet on the floor sent a sharp pain up her legs. She sat back down. She glared at Bill.

"Goddamn you. Stop patronizing me. I didn't have a panic attack. For God's sake, Bill, I'm still a psychologist no matter what Scott did to me. I do not need a lecture from you. I know what a panic attack is. I know what PTSD is. Most of my clients are survivors of trauma and diagnosed with the disorder. I treat survivors; I'm a survivor. I refuse to be treated as a victim.

I survived that monster's best effort. So stop suggesting I'm imaging things. I didn't have a panic attack in the garage. Stephen Scott was stalking me."

"Let's look at the facts. You and I both have to deal with facts in our work. The security force reported no evidence of anyone in the garage who didn't belong there. They checked every car at the entrance. No one on foot could get inside without being processed. He didn't show up on any of the tapes. And you admit you didn't really see Scott, so you can't be positive he was there, can you?"

Christie rubbed her forehead as if she wanted to scrub away the afternoon's events. She knew without tape evidence or an eyewitness, her story was hard to believe. She found it difficult to believe herself. Why hadn't he appeared on any of the surveillance tapes? Christie gave up. She just didn't have the energy to put into a long drawn-out battle with Bill about what really happened.

"I'm not going to argue with you. Either you trust me and have faith in my judgments or you don't. I want you to think about that. You need to trust me 100% if we're going to work together. I don't want my work questioned. I don't want you second-guessing me. And I don't want to work with a colleague who's wasting his time assessing my every move instead of concentrating on doing his job."

"I hear you. Listen, I trust you. I know you. I don't need to think about that. You've been there on every case we've worked. I trusted you before Scott and I trust you now. I want you working with me on this case. I need your help."

Christie's eyes strayed toward the window again. She wondered if Bill was mixing up the feelings of trust and love. He had confused loneliness with love last fall when he asked her to marry him. She turned him down gently, and with some regret. Bill hadn't finished grieving for his wife Emmy who had died of breast cancer two years before.

Bill broke the silence. "I care about you. You're special to me, more than you realize. I want you around."

Her thoughts confirmed, Christie paused. She smiled at Bill. He looked so earnest, almost boyish. She felt her fondness for him warming her.

"I've told you I'm not ready for a serious relationship. I'm not sure you are either. I feel honored to have you as a close friend and colleague and that has to be enough for right now. If I'm going to work with you, it has to be because I'm the best forensic psychologist for the job, not because you care for me."

"I know. I'm sorry. I didn't mean to bring the subject of us up. Even my therapist warned me to respect your boundaries. I'm afraid, I guess. Afraid you'll quit. Afraid I won't see you. Afraid you'll decide I'm not the one for you."

"Don't Bill. I can't do this now."

Bill rushed on. "Afraid for you, too, and all you have to deal with." He paused. "However, you are the best forensic psychologist I know. I want you on this case and I do need your help. Will you work with me?"

Christie looked out the window and saw the dusk dissolve into night. The twinkle of lights poked holes here and there through the dark. Bill switched on his desk lamp and the room brightened as the scene outside the window faded. She looked back at Bill and nodded yes. She needed this job. Moreover, she did not want to walk away from Bill.

"On two conditions. No more personal talk about us, especially on the job. And from now on I want an escort to meet me at my car and walk me back to my car each time I come here."

"I agree to both conditions. And, I'll be glad to escort you myself, if it helps you feel better."

"Nothing makes me feel better these days. Until I hear that Scott's apprehended or dead, I'm living a nightmare that doesn't get better."

"What can I do to help? You only have to tell me and I'll do all I can."

"Find Stephen Scott. Put me to work. I don't want to think about him, about what he did to me or about what he wants to do to me. Work helps me more than meds and therapy. Start by telling me what you know about this new case. I understand the autopsy's tomorrow. Fill me in on what to expect."

Bill smiled. This was more like the old Christie, a dedicated, hard-working professional with a talent for understanding the criminal mind and a need to right the wrongs in society. In the past, he had kidded her about being a work-aholic. Sometimes Bill believed some inner demon drove her to work so hard. Certainly, Stephen Scott was evil enough, the devil who drove her now.

4

Christie pulled into the driveway of her two-hundred year old farmhouse and quickly pressed the remote to open the garage door. After the door closed behind her, she exited the car and unlocked the steel fire door leading inside. Once inside, she slipped the three dead bolts into place and keyed the security box to alert. She dropped her briefcase on the floor by the coat rack and placed her hat and coat on the rack.

Using her crutch, she walked directly from the family room into the kitchen without glancing at the antique furniture and decorations, which used to give her such pleasure. The material things she had collected with care over the years meant little to her now. She had more important matters on her mind.

"Hi," Alex said as she smiled at Christie. "Welcome home. I bet you're tired. How're your feet holding up?"

"They're sore. It's been a long day."

"Are you hungry? Come sit down. I made some vegetable soup, a loaf of whole wheat bread and a tossed salad."

"Sounds good. Thanks. I'm not very hungry, but I could eat a little soup. I haven't had much to eat today, I guess."

Alex looked at Christie. "You guess? I bet you didn't eat at all. Christie, you have to eat more. You've lost so much weight; your clothes don't fit you. Come on. Sit down. Have some bread with your soup."

Christie acquiesced and Alex lit the candles and set two places at the pine kitchen table overlooking the wooded back yard. Christie jumped up and closed the curtains. She sat back down without commenting and managed to eat a bowl of soup and one slice of bread before she folded her napkin and leaned back in her chair. Alex continued eating. She chatted about her newest painting and the gallery in New York City that expressed interest in showing her work. She carried the conversation, a monologue, as she had done since Christie returned home two months ago.

Alex shared Christie's house and had been her friend for the last four years. They were compatible in many ways and had grown very close over the years. When Christie returned from three months of rehabilitation and informed Alex that she didn't have the energy and no longer had the interest in developing a more intimate relationship with Alex, Alex had not protested. She had expected Christie would make that decision. She respected Christie's need for space and because she cared so much for her, Alex stepped back into her supportive housemate role.

"So what's up with you? Did you and Bill decide to work together on the new case?"

Christie hesitated. She wanted to tell Alex what happened in the parking garage today, that Stephen Scott had returned, but she held those words back.

"Yes, I'm going to do it. I need to get back to work and the case sounds challenging. The autopsy's tomorrow. It's going to be a tough one."

"Tell me about it. I love hearing about your work with the task force."

"Maybe another time. I don't know much about the case yet, except that the victim is a young Jane Doe found in the woods in Cumberland County. Besides, I'm spent. Today's been a hard day for me. I'm just going to read a bit to relax and then go to bed."

Alex nodded, got up and started clearing the table.

"Okay, let's make it another time. Actually, I was planning to go out tonight, if that's all right with you. Do you mind? I'm meeting Frannie over at her place and we're going to try to devise some more activities for the domestic abuse workshop. You'd think we'd have it finished by now, but we get to talking and before we know it, the evening's passed."

Christie's alarm siren started to wail. She wanted to cry out, "No, don't go. I need you. I'm scared to be here alone. He might come."

She longed to let Alex know that Scott had found his way into the secured garage today and terrorized her. She wished she could tell Alex that no one believed her. They thought she was crazy, a victim seeing things. Alex would believe her. Alex had always believed in her. And Alex believed, as she did, that Stephen Scott would find her and try to kill her. Christie wanted Alex to stay home and keep her safe from the lunatic who was stalking her.

But she couldn't tell Alex. Christie loathed her own vulnerability and considered her fear an unacceptable weakness. She had learned when she was very young that displaying vulnerability or fear was dangerous and attracted those who preyed on the weak. She still had the deep inner scars from her mother's scalding verbal abuse. Her thoughts slipped into the past. She saw her mother reading, drinking her scotch. Before she continued down that old rutty dead-end road, she snapped herself back to the present.

She had discovered early on that denial was the only way she could safely cope with her fear when around others. One way to deny fear was to pretend she was perfectly fine and in control. Since she'd returned to Maine from the burn clinic, she'd tried to behave in ways that demonstrated how well she was recovering from her trauma. She kept others ignorant of the pain, terror and despair she was really experiencing. Expressing rational thoughts, organizing her plans, and returning to her normal life patterns reassured most of those around her that she was emotionally healthy once more. That the old Christie had returned.

She knew she should not show the excessive fear and sensitized over-reactions that often dominated her. Look what had happened to her today when she lived her fear and expressed it. The security guards thought she was crazy. She needed to keep her external behavior divorced from her hidden inner reality. Even though that meant she was living, in essence, as two separate beings in one body.

"Sure," Christie said. "Go ahead. I'm fine here. You don't have to baby-sit me."

"I know. I didn't mean it that way. You're sure? I won't be too late or if I am, I'll call. Okay?"

"It's okay, Alex. Do what you want. You don't have to ask my permission every time you want to go somewhere. And stop worrying about me. I don't like it. I'm just fine. I'm going to have a cup of tea and read my book by the fireplace. Maybe I'll take a nice long hot bath. Then I'll go to bed. No problem. Go ahead."

Alex washed the dishes and got ready to leave. "I'll take Tashie out now and then when I get home I'll let her out again. Don't open the door to let her out while I'm gone. Okay?"

Christie picked up the novel she was reading and her cup of tea. "Yes Alex, I hear you. I won't open the damned door, even if poor old deaf Tashie begs to go pee. I'll stay safely locked inside. Now leave me alone."

Christie walked into the living room and knelt by the fireplace. She crumbled yesterday's paper into tight balls and placed kindling over them on the fire grate. Then she placed two pieces of split apple wood on top. She struck a match and carefully ignited the paper. She placed the screen in front of the fire and watched the kindling catch fire, sending their tiny flames up to scorch the harder wood. Then she turned and sank into her overstuffed chair and opened the novel to the place she had left off reading. She picked up her tea and sipped it as she stared at the fire.

Suddenly she jumped to her feet. The book fell to the floor. The teacup overturned in the saucer and splashed tea on her blouse. She ran to the window, lowered the shade, and pulled the heavy drapes. She did the same for the other four windows in the living room and then moved through all the other downstairs rooms, pulling shades and closing drapes.

Alex sighed as she watched Christie go through her routine, but made no move to stop her or help her. She had figured out that Christie needed to shut out the world this way to feel safer and that doing it herself gave her some sense of control. However, she was worried about Christie's continuing fears. Stella, Christie's oldest and best friend, had said it would take time for Christie to feel safe again, but Alex didn't think she would remain in such a fearful state for this long. Five stress-filled months had passed since Christie had fallen victim to Stephen Scott. She had been home now for two months. Long enough, Alex thought, to begin to enjoy her home and friends again.

But it hadn't happened. Christie was a mess. She was anxious, jumpy and cranky. She wasn't eating or sleeping well. She never went outside with Alex to walk Tashie. And every night since she'd come home she had performed the same shade-pulling routine. Alex had hoped that when Christie returned to work for the task force she would get better. Nevertheless, tonight Christie was still frantically shutting out the world.

Alex had to admit that the last two months hadn't been fun at all. She and Christie hardly ever talked and they never went out together. Christie read by the fire, stayed in her room upstairs or met with Stella or Celeste, her therapist.

Satisfied that no one could see inside, Christie returned to her chair by the fire, picked up her teacup, settled it in the saucer, and started to read her novel as if nothing had happened. When Alex came in to say goodbye, the sight of Christie posed in this cozy peaceful scene brought tears to her eyes, which she hurriedly blinked away.

"You're sure you don't mind? You know how to reach me if you need anything. I won't be late."

"Have a good time," Christie answered. "Say hi to Frannie for me. And drive carefully. The weather report said we might get some snow tonight."

"I'll be home long before the snow accumulates. Well, then, so long. See you later."

Alex patted Tashie, curled up on the floor next to Christie, and then left. Christie heard the door slam closed, the garage door raise and lower and the sound of Alex's truck pull out of the driveway. Except for the crackle of the fire, silence settled all around her.

5

The draped body lay spotlighted on the stainless steel autopsy table in the Maine State Bureau of Investigation's basement morgue. The tiled room echoed every sound emitted from the group of investigators, law enforcement, and medical personnel standing around the autopsy table. After a few minutes of light talk, most sunk into silence, awkward about disturbing the antiseptic sterility and quiet that this place seemed to demand. The unmistakable stench of decomposing bodies further chilled the atmosphere of the death-filled space.

Christie's shoulders slumped as she pulled her beige wool cardigan sweater more tightly around her. Cold had seeped into her bones and the disinfectant meant to mask the smell of the dead was coating her face like a layer of rancid grease. She wondered if she was ready for the medical examiner's mechanized deconstructing of the young girl who waited under the white drape.

Bill leaned over and whispered to Christie. "She looks so small."

Christie nodded, wordless in this room where the dead were the ones who spoke the secrets and told the truth.

Bill continued, "The field team initially identified her as a young child. She isn't even five feet tall." He paused. "Actually, she may be a teenager. We'll know soon."

Dr. Helen Atwood, Chief Medical Examiner, entered the room and looked at the attentive faces. "I believe all of you have attended autopsies before and are familiar with the process. If you feel the need to leave the room at any time, please do so quietly and without comment. Just so you know what to expect in this case, the preliminary external examination revealed that Jane Doe's eyes, scalp, 80% of her skin, tendons, cartilage and several bones are missing. I believe a number of her internal organs are gone as well."

The group shifted nervously around the autopsy table as Dr. Atwood paused, giving time for any who wished to escape. No one left. They stared transfixed as Dr. Atwood removed the white drape and revealed the nude body of a young girl. Tears gathered in the corners of Christie's eyes as she looked at the hideously disfigured corpse. Christie dreaded witnessing the slicing and evisceration of this young girl, robbed of her life and now her dignity.

The killer had severed the dead girl's scalp and hair from her skull. A jagged cut ran from the forehead, around the back of her ears and down to the base of her neck. The top of her skull, already cleaned in the routine pre-autopsy prep, presented no visual evidence of trauma.

The murderer stripped the epidermis from the face, chest, abdomen, and thighs, much like a hunter would skin a rabbit or a deer, leaving the meat, subcutaneous tissue and muscle mostly intact. Christie imagined he had skinned the girl's back as well. The raw flesh no longer bled but the pinkish red color of the body's tissue stunned her. Christie was more accustomed to observing bluish white or ashy brown corpses.

Dark cavities gaped where Jane Doe's eyes belonged. Her killer had removed her left arm bones and right leg bones and the remaining flesh puddled shapelessly on the table. Stitched up rents in her abdomen and chest highlighted the depressions where tissue sagged, lacking the mass of underlying organs, now gone.

Christie grappled for something to distract her from the

girl's grisly remains. She had attended many autopsies before in her capacity as forensic psychologist for the task force, but never one as repugnant as this. And never when she felt as fragile as she did now. Her mind skittered about, trying to grab onto any solid thought that would distance her from the cruel reality that murderers kill young girls who end up on autopsy tables in front of a crowd of strangers.

The sharp clang of metal on metal startled Christie. She jumped, grabbing Bill's arm. Christie's face was pale; beads of perspiration broke out on her forehead.

"Are you all right?" Bill whispered to her. "Can you do this?"

Christie nodded and let go of his arm. She watched Dr. Atwood pick up the scalpel that had dropped from her hand onto the stainless steel table.

"Sorry. The scalpel got away from me. Not a good time for butterfingers, is it?"

Several in the group tried to laugh, but their nervous anxiety mutated their chuckles into hollow groans.

Atwood clicked on the taping equipment and faced her audience.

"For those who don't know me, and for the record being taped on video camera, I'm Dr. Ellen Atwood, Chief Medical Examiner for the State of Maine and I'll be conducting the autopsy on Jane Doe, #5667, today, March 12, 2006, 10:00. Assisting me are Dr. Tom Sheldon, Chief Resident in Pathology and Residential Intern, Dr. Leslie Conley.

"Those present are involved with this case and informed about the circumstances of where the body was found, by whom and when. However, for the record I'll commence with a brief summary of the facts as we know them at this time."

The observers shifted their feet and several crossed their arms over their chests. They were clearly uncomfortable and try as they might, they could not hide that fact from each other.

"At 2:30 yesterday afternoon, March 11, 2006, three young men called 911 and reported finding a body wrapped in a sheet in the woods where they were snowmobiling. The dispatcher contacted EMS and the Cumberland County Sheriff's office. Sheriff Wood, present today, has jurisdiction of that area."

Dr. Atwood gestured toward Sheriff Henry Wood, a tall man with a ruddy face and a bulging belly, standing with two men in similar brown and beige uniforms. Sheriff Wood raised his hand and smiled at the others like a candidate acknowledging a group of voters.

"The boys led paramedics, Sheriff Wood and one of his deputies to the site where they found the body. Sheriff Wood sealed the area, initiated forensic scene investigation, and secured the body until the local coroner released it to us. He also informed the Cumberland County District Attorney, Frank Sampson, who called the Attorney General. The AG assigned the case to the Maine State Task Force on Violent Crimes, headed by Detective William Drummond, present today."

Bill nodded to everyone in the room. Gray hair at his temples and the beginning of lines around his lively gray-blue eyes only enhanced his handsome face. His six-foot frame was lean. Christie thought he looked attractive in his brown tweed sports jacket, a tie that matched his eyes and charcoal gray wool pants.

"Dr. Christie McMorrow, present, consulting forensic psychologist to the task force, will be aiding in the investigation."

At the sound of her name, Christie also looked around the room and acknowledged the others: a state police investigator from the State Bureau of Investigation (SBI), Cumberland County Sheriff Henry Wood, his two deputies, two staff members of the State Medical Office (SMO) who would record and monitor the findings, as well as the two autopsy assistants.

After Dr. Atwood introduced the others in the room, she put on her mask and faceguard, checked that the recorder for voice and video was functioning properly and turned to stand over the body.

"When we received the body, it was frozen solid. The autopsy assistants completed routine initial procedures. They thawed her, printed her and scraped under her nails for any latent evidence, finding none, and then clipped the nails for preservation of evidence. They took measurements, x-rayed the body and teeth. They conducted a careful search of her external body for trace elements, fibers, foreign hair or any other evidence. They found nothing. They washed the body to prepare it for autopsy. She has not yet been identified. The purpose of this autopsy is to determine the cause of death and to look for information to help identify the victim and find the perpetrator of this crime.

"As you can see, the perpetrator harvested the body for hair, skin, eyes, organs, and bones. Unfortunately, that seriously limits recovery of evidence of Jane Doe's health status and eliminates certain tests that could reveal evidence of certain toxins or poisons, but I'll proceed with the autopsy, keeping as close as possible to the prescribed routine. I will now begin."

Dr. Atwood bent to make the initial Y incision, describing her actions precisely and recording her findings.

Christie stood dazed as the autopsy continued. She thought Dr. Atwood was never going to stop. She seemed to go on and on, cutting, slicing, drilling, and sawing. As the autopsy and Dr. Atwood's monologue slowly moved forward, Christie wondered why Dr. Atwood's voice started to fade in and out. The scene in front of her grew blurry. She felt lightheaded. Her mouth filled with salty saliva as her stomach twisted with nausea. Her dizziness intensified. She knew she was close to vomiting or fainting. She had to leave the room before she embarrassed herself and the task force.

To avoid drawing attention, she took a short step backward and paused. She waited for the vertigo to ease and then stepped back again and turned toward the door. It looked miles away.

Leaning on her crutch, Christie slowly made her way toward the door. Her flat brown leather shoes clicked unevenly on the tile floor as she painfully shuffled forward. Every head turned to follow her progress and then one by one quickly refocused on the autopsy as if they didn't want to be caught staring at the retreating woman. Christie knew they were curious about her physical condition.

Eventually, she reached the door. She felt their eyes on her again as she pulled it open with her white gloved hand and disappeared into the corridor outside.

6

Alone in the empty hall outside the autopsy room, Christie leaned against the cool tile wall and forced herself to breathe deeply. She wanted to run home and leave all this horror behind. If she could have moved right then, gone to her car and sped away, she would have. But she couldn't. She didn't have her car, she was too dizzy to drive, and her job was to help find the killer of this young girl.

Gradually, her vision began to clear and the dizziness slowly released her. Even as she began to calm down and think more rationally, she knew she wasn't ready to return to the autopsy.

Christie's physical wounds, inflicted during Stephen Scott's vicious attack, had healed after three months of intensive treatment and physical therapy at the North Carolina Burn Clinic. Rehabilitation workers encouraged her to overcome her debilitating injuries and she had struggled to get on her feet again, first with a walker, then with two crutches, specially designed to reduce pressure on her hands. She used just one crutch now, mostly for confidence, as her coordination remained inconsistent and her range of motion was restricted. These limitations were painful reminders of the loss of her former gracefulness and athleticism. She still experienced sharp pain and swelling in her feet when she had to stand for an extended time, as she had this morning.

When she was feeling a little better, Christie limped into

the bathroom across the hall and removed her gloves. Christie usually hid her scarred and shiny hands. They drew attention and looks of curiosity and pity. She didn't need the horrific reminder that their raw red appearance and agonizing stiffness brought to her. Therefore, Christie covered her hands with white cotton gloves, justifying them as medically advised to protect her tender new skin and numerous skin grafts from infection.

She rinsed her face with water and slurped a handful of the cold water into her mouth. The water helped to dissolve the acidity produced by her anxiety and she felt her stomach settle a bit. She drank a little more water and leaned on the sink, taking some of the weight off her legs.

Christie raised her head and gazed in the bathroom mirror. She didn't like what she saw. She was pale. Dark circles loomed under her eyes. Her clothes hung on her thin body. She still had a hard time believing that she was the one who had experienced the trauma which continued to torment her body, mind and soul. What she suffered at the hands of Stephen Scott had altered her forever.

Christie delayed leaving the women's room as long as she could. However, she needed to reenter the autopsy room and face the reality of another female's physical trauma. In addition, she had to stare down the pity and disdain of those who stayed through the autopsy. She wanted to show them she could handle her job, even if she wasn't so sure herself.

She took another drink of water. Then she tried to brighten her face by pinching her cheekbones until they flushed with some color. She bit down on her lips to darken their dull red. She slowly walked out of the bathroom.

As she entered the hallway, the door to the autopsy room opened and the observers filed out, talking quietly among themselves. Several turned and glanced at her as they passed, but made no comment. Bill said goodbye to them and hurried over to her.

"Are you all right? When you left, I didn't know what to do. Is everything okay?"

Bill studied Christie closely. She had aged ten years in the last five months. Her light brown hair, usually shining with gold highlights, lay flat and dull, robbed of its previous sheen. Her large blue eyes had lost their hypnotic beauty and instead glinted with pain. Weight loss gave her face a pinched look. Her high cheekbones stood out, gaunt now.

"I'm fine. Don't worry. How did the autopsy go after I left?"

"Let's talk about it in the car. I need to get out of here and I think you need to sit down. I can't stand breathing this sordid air another second."

"What I want is fresh air, a hot cup of tea and to put my feet up," Christie said as they moved slowly toward the exit. "I'm sorry about walking out on you. I was just coming back, but I guess I was too late. I hope I didn't mess things up by leaving."

"No problem. The autopsy was shorter than normal because so many organs were missing. Atwood didn't have to weigh and slice as much or make as many specimen slides. Anyway, you'll be able to read the full report tomorrow and I'll fill you in on anything you want to know."

Bill helped Christie into the black Ford SUV with the MSTFVC logo emblazed on the side doors. When he started the car, he looked over at her.

"How do you think Atwood does it day after day? She's good at what she does, but my God, what a horrific job. Well, where to now? Want to get something to eat or go to your office? Or I could tell about the part of the autopsy you missed. We could discuss the case files that have come in and get a head start, if you feel up to it."

Christie shook her head and grimaced. "I couldn't eat or be around food right now, sorry. It's been a long morning and you're probably starved. You could drop me off at my car if you want to grab some lunch. I don't want to go to my office."

Shortly after she returned from the burn clinic, at the insistence of her colleague and friend Stella, Christie rented a new office for her private psychotherapy practice, which specialized in treating survivors of trauma. She couldn't bear to return to her old office where Scott had initiated his torture. She sold all the old office contents to a used furniture dealer. She transferred files and forms to her new address, a high security building with a guard stationed at the door and security cameras mounted on every floor. Best of all, Stella's office was just one floor down from Christie's new space.

She furnished the office with the basics and didn't add art or personal touches. She ordered new business cards and installed a phone. However, she hadn't taken any referrals, contacted former clients, or advertised that she was available for new clients. She didn't know if she would ever be ready to take clients again. Psychotherapy with traumatized clients requires a practitioner psychologically healthy enough to handle intense emotional intimacy and stress.

Christie, still in recovery from trauma herself, had little to give to anyone. She used most of her energy struggling to climb out of the abyss of depression and fear that lurked within her. Coping with the stress of everyday life was a job in itself. What little strength she had left she put into maintaining the pretense that nothing was wrong with her. Working this new case would help her distance from her own agony. She would have to concentrate on forensic information. Focusing on factual details, psychological assessments and profiles would provide an escape from her pain. She welcomed the relief of hard work, even if the reprieve was only temporary.

"I'm not hungry either," Bill said. "Hard to work up an appetite after watching Atwood do her stuff. Let's go to my office. We can get some tea or coffee there and I'd like to start planning our approach for this case, now that we have some preliminary information from the autopsy. Are you all right with that? Feel up to it?"

"That's fine. Let's do it."

Christie leaned back into the seat and let Bill chat. He was good that way. He liked to talk and didn't require much response. She could count on him to keep the conversation going even though of late it often turned into a monologue as she blanked out or found herself thinking of other things. As they drove and he chatted about his kids' college antics, she tuned him out.

She was relieved Bill had not pressured her regarding the state of their relationship. Christie told him as soon as she returned that she needed all her energy to recover and could not get into intimate issues with him. Small talk and task force work were all she could handle right now. Bill had understood and had supported her decision without crossing any boundaries, at least until yesterday afternoon. He hadn't mentioned moving their friendly alliance to a more intimate relationship as he did before Scott's attack on her. She was grateful that he had stepped back, removing that pressure on her, but sometimes she felt lonely and missed his touch, the closeness they had begun to enjoy with each other.

Christie had detached herself, in fact, from most of her previous activities and the people she usually saw. She turned down speaking engagements, workshop offers, and mentoring opportunities at the University. However, she had agreed to continue to consult for the MSTFVC, knowing that the intensity of hard work always managed to disconnect her from the private pain in her life.

She learned the coping mechanism of separating from her own problems by working hard when she was young. Christie spent as much time as possible at school. She tutored other kids and participated in many extra-curricular activities and sports.

She'd take the long route home, often walking instead of riding the late activity bus, to delay her return to her house. She babysat at night. She'd study long and hard at the library. Anything to keep away from home. Home. The place where she tried to escape notice. She would hide in her room or behind her sisters and brothers. However, her mother would eventually notice her. Somehow, Christie triggered her mother's disease. She would cut into Christie with her razor sharp tongue, slashing Christie's soul to bits.

Later on, after college and graduate school, Christie met Ted and they were married a year later. Two years after the wedding, Christie's marriage started to flounder. When she and Ted finally divorced, she disappeared into her work, demanding so much from herself that she had no time to think about personal difficulties or the failure of her relationship.

Christie chose to speak of her pain and struggles only with her therapist Celeste and with her friend and long-time colleague, Stella. Sometimes she wished she were more intimate with her brothers and sisters. However, years of separation had reduced the sibling closeness to an acquaintance level; they were people who shared past history and cared about each other. But Christie did not want to share her traumatic experience with them.

Bill and Christie checked in with security at the garage entrance, passed the scan and drove into the secured space reserved for task force personnel. They parked next to Christie's Saab. Christie took a long look around the garage before she opened the passenger door and got out. Bill found himself nervously imitating her as they waited for the elevator that took them to the third floor, where his corner office was located.

In the lobby Jenny Johnson, the receptionist for the task force, greeted them. Pretty, young and capable, she sat behind a pine counter with the MSTFVC logo painted on the front and two banks of phones on either side of her.

"Hey Jenny, you remember Dr. McMorrow, don't you?

She's working with me on the Cumberland County case. We're going to need some hot drinks as soon as you can get them to us please."

Jenny stood and stretched out her hand to shake Christie's but quickly jerked her hand back when she saw that Christie was wearing white gloves.

"Oh, I'm so sorry, Dr. McMorrow. Forgive me. I forgot."

Bill spoke up. "It's all right, Jenny. Dr. McMorrow can shake hands."

Jenny glanced at Christie. "Oh, I'm sorry."

Awkwardly she extended her hand again and very gently shook Christie's gloved hand.

"Of course I remember you from that case last summer. It's good to see you. I'm very sorry about what happened. Everyone's so enraged about what that maniac did to you. We're happy you're okay now and back at work. Oh, forgive me for going on. Can I get you some coffee or tea, Dr. McMorrow?"

Bill started to answer when Christie interrupted him.

"I can speak for myself, Bill." She turned to Bill's receptionist. "Yes, thank you, Jenny. I'd love some hot tea with lemon, if you have it. And I'd rather forgo the formalities. Just call me Christie."

Jenny smiled. "Coming right up, Christie."

"No sugar, just lemon and hot, Jenny, thanks," Christie said as she limped toward Bill's office. She really needed to sit down and raise her feet to reduce their swelling and stop the throbbing. With relief, she sank down in the black leather chair. She removed her shoes and put her sore feet on the black ottoman. Under her stockings, Bill could see the white wrapping covering her toes and feet.

After Bill and Christie sat down and Jenny delivered their tea, they looked at each other.

"What do we have, Bill?"

"First, Dr. Atwood says cause of death was asphyxiation.

The killer strangled Jane Doe. Crushed the hyoid bone. Tissue around the neck shows contusions. The body was mutilated and dismembered. Bingo. Homicide."

"That doesn't surprise me. How'd we catch it?"

"The township of Cascade Hills, where the body was found, has no police force of its own and is located in Cumberland County. Sheriff Wood covers that county and normally would head the investigation, with co-responsibility shared by the state police and SBI. However, it got complicated. Wood has no formally trained investigators right now, only two patrol deputies, and the state police have suffered massive cutbacks in investigative personnel. Because of the heinousness of the crime and the expertise of our staff, the Attorney General assigned the case to us. We'll get forensic support from SBI, on-call staff and backup from state police and Sheriff Wood. This Jane Doe is definitely our case. Now the state cops and SBI might not like that. Sheriff Wood might not like it. And quite frankly, I don't like it either, but it's ours."

"So we have to watch whose shoes we step on?"

"No," said Bill. "We have to be careful not to step on anyone's shoes at all. These territorial dogfights make me sick, but they're serious. Everyone wants to be the hero, get on TV, and pile up points for promotion or election. They all want the extra funding and manpower that comes with a big case."

"So Jane Doe be damned, it's a political field day?"

"I've seen it happen before. Sheriff Wood's one person we have to tiptoe around. The public has elected him sheriff for as long as I can remember; he knows everybody and has a lot of power. Remember the problems he gave us last summer during the investigation of that Jane Doe whose body was burned and dumped in his county?"

"Oh yeah, I remember. He was unbelievably controlling, demanding to know everything we discovered and getting in our way more than he helped. I hope he stays clear of us this time."

"Me too, but I doubt he will. Anyway, two others to watch are Skip Preston and Frank Sampson. Skip's chief of the state police. He's a career man, while Frank is the Cumberland County District Attorney. He's appointed. They and Wood are the holy trinity as far as power, politics and cronyism goes. The top man, Roger Banthrop, III, Attorney General, who gave us the case, is somewhat of a mystery lately. History would say he goes by the book, but I've seen some cases he's let fall through some big cracks. We have to make friendly with them all or we could find that getting reports, more investigators, evidence, or tips might become very difficult."

"You mean they'd obstruct? They can't do that. It's against the law."

"They are the law, Christie. Don't forget that. Sheriff Wood has ties everywhere. Sometimes it's hard to tell who's on what side. Maybe they won't exactly refuse to deliver evidence, but they could take their time about it, and that could affect the way we carry out our investigation. Nevertheless, let's hope for the best. It's in everyone's interest to find the bastard who's doing this and find him fast, before he does it again."

Bill looked at Christie and asked, "You do think he'll do it again, don't you?"

7

Five months ago, doctors in the Portland Memorial Hospital Emergency Room treated Stephen Scott for two bullet wounds he received when a Portland police detective shot him to stop his ritualistic, murderous assault on Dr. Christie McMorrow.

Days later, when doctors declared Scott out of danger and released him from the intensive care unit, three Portland police officers entered his room to transfer him to the Cumberland County Jail infirmary. One officer unlocked his handcuffs while the others stood guard. In a flash, Scott stabbed him in the neck with a syringe he had hidden under his sheets, grabbed his gun and shot him and his two companions. Scott ran from the room, leaving three bloody bodies behind. He ducked into a room across the hall, three doors closer to the nurses' station and waited until hospital personnel responded to the gunshot sounds. During the ensuing chaos he slipped out of the room, ran to the doctor's lounge where he grabbed a pair of scrubs, shoes and a coat, exited the hospital by the staircase and headed directly to his stash of money and false identity cards hidden in a shallow hole behind an old grave marker in the city cemetery. Scott always secreted a back-up kit, filled with cash, the necessary documentation for several additional identities, and pain and antibiotic medication where he could find it in an emergency. Stephen Scott became Robert Cummings, with a Maine driver's license, social security card, credit cards and cash.

He holed up in a dingy hotel near the wharfs on Commercial Street, frequented by transients and fishing boat deck hands on down time. After a week, the stubble of facial hair had altered his appearance; he was strong enough to visit a Goodwill store and purchase used clothes that completed his change of persona.

All his adult life, Stephen played chameleon around others. Disguised by wearing the clothes and using the accent that blended with each location he visited, he drew little attention. His demeanor was quiet and polite. He was civil to those who engaged with him, but avoided conversation. Camouflaged, no look or behavior alerted people about his sordid history, severe psychopathology, or his programmed compulsion to kill women.

Stephen learned how to behave from his Uncle Luke who adopted him when he was eighteen months old. Luke's estranged brother Matthew and his wife Candy had severely abused their only child Stephen since his birth. One day the couple disappeared, leaving their furnished apartment trashed and their baby nearly dead in the middle of the mess. Doctors hospitalized the child and turned his well-being over to the Bureau of Foster Care. Social workers located Stephen's Uncle Luke, eventually certified him as an approved guardian and brought the toddler to him. Stephen's education began that day.

Uncle Luke began by teaching Stephen the necessity of following orders. He demonstrated when necessary the painful consequences of disobedience. When Stephen didn't do as he was told, his uncle would plunge a long silver needle into his flesh. He called the needle his persuader. Uncle Luke established discipline in a very short time.

Then he started a rigorous home-schooling program, thus effectively isolating Stephen from all outside influences. Stephen was bright and painful emotional and physical punishments fostered success in his studies. He learned the required educational curriculum, passing each year's mandated home-schooling examination with honors. Thus, Uncle Luke avoided all direct contact with educational personnel and put off social workers' dictated visits.

Uncle Luke also taught Stephen life skills and social necessities. On training trips outside his home, Stephen gradually learned to conduct himself as a well-behaved child his age would. No one could suspect the life the boy was really living.

However, Uncle Luke's most important influence on his nephew's development was the mind control programming that he constantly drilled into Stephen. For hours, Uncle Luke would preach about the evils of women. He would rant about how Eve had betrayed God. How all humanity suffers because of women's innate evil. Then Uncle Luke would leave Stephen, dress in women's clothing, and return. He called himself Mother Luke and demonstrated to Stephen how cruel a mother, a woman, could be. Demeaning him verbally and punishing him for no reason, Mother Luke showed the child no warmth or love, only disgust and rejection. She repeatedly instructed him that her behavior was a woman's way. Gradually, Mother Luke added sexual assault to the verbal and physical abuse. If Stephen objected or showed distress, she punished him with physical pain. If he failed to perform to her satisfaction, she would threaten to call in Uncle Luke. When Stephen did perform sexually, Uncle Luke would later appear and terrorize him for fornicating with the devil-woman, always using pain to bring the confusing message home to the young boy.

Cut off from all others and entirely dependent on his Uncle/Mother Luke, Stephen initially survived by dissociating from the terror and torture. He would leave his body and watch what was happening to him from a corner of the basement ceiling. That way he wasn't the one who felt the pain inflicted by his Mother and Uncle Luke. After a few years, he joined in the behavior with his torturers willingly. He actively participated in the sexual acts, linking pain with sex until his brain accepted that sex and pain were one.

He came to believe that his mother and uncle worked for God, helping Stephen to earn the position of God's chosen one. He was grateful to them for their mentoring and admired them for believing in him and preparing him to be the one selected to do God's work.

By the age of eight, Uncle/Mother Luke had programmed Stephen to believe that women were evil and the cause of all sin and immorality in the world. He understood God chose him to rid the earth of women. He learned the ritual of release and practiced using the ritual knife to perfection on cloth manikins. He excelled at sexual torture. He used the long silver needle attached to the leather band on his wrist, identical to his uncle's, to remind him of the need for discipline. At the first sign of loss of control, he would plunge the needle deep into his flesh and continue stabbing himself until he activated the programmed discipline once again. The silver needle was a painful, but perfect trigger.

Accompanied by his Uncle Luke, Stephen killed his first woman when he was twelve. He soloed when he was fourteen. By the time he could officially drive a car, he had released over twenty women. He kept fastidious records and photographic proof of his accomplishments. His program demanded that he provide a model through the notes and evidence he kept in scrapbooks and journals for others enlightened enough to follow him.

Stephen celebrated his graduation at sixteen by killing his uncle/mother. He took the box documenting the vast financial investments, now in his name, grown over the last twenty years from the large life insurance payment made to Luke when his father and mother died, the folders containing the stolen, forged and purchased alternative identities, and the large amount of cash his uncle had been amassing for him. He tucked the ritual knife into his suitcase with his journals and scrapbooks. Then he incinerated the house, destroying all evidence that

Stephen Scott or his uncle/mother had ever existed. He set off to follow the program that controlled his every moment.

After eighteen years and over one hundred ritually released women, Stephen had arrived in Portland, Maine last November and randomly selected psychologist Dr.Christie McMorrow as his next mission. Although he failed to release her and the police now knew who he was and what his mission demanded, he would not stop until he completed his duty by releasing Dr. McMorrow.

With his altered look and his new identity, within a week of his escape Scott felt secure enough to walk into Rent-a-Wreck, lease a sub-compact car and drive south down Route 1. He would return.

Never before had one of his selected victims lived to tell about the ritual or about him. Now the police had all his journals and scrapbooks as well. He felt a quiver of fear mix with the thrill of danger.

The world knew all about him now. People would read the details of his sacred missions and learn that God had chosen him to spread the truth about the innate evil of women. The media would broadcast warnings that he lurked somewhere, ready to select and release another sinful woman from her degradation.

He had come to believe that God initiated the breakdown of the mission with Dr. McMorrow in order to grant his chosen one some gifts. The first gift was God's warning to be more careful, especially when he returned to Portland to finish the mission with Dr. McMorrow. God's second gift ensured that the truth about the evil of women screamed from every headline worldwide. God's third gift was designing Stephen's failure so the truth the world needed to hear would spread more quickly and efficiently than ever before. Stephen loved the irony that his failure bred success and was excited that God enjoyed irony as much as he did.

With his strength renewed, Stephen Scott returned to Maine in February. His bullet wounds had healed, leaving raised red scars. He had completely changed his appearance. Gone was the neat and well-dressed handsome young man with his blue oxford shirts and smart black wool pants. Instead, Stephen now resembled a man approaching middle age with a salt and pepper beard and a little paunch around the belly. He wore wire-rimmed glasses that hid the intensity of his large blue eyes and a red and black checked wool hunter's cap that covered scraggly, unkempt hair. He bought his clothes from flea markets, Goodwill stores and yard sales. Flannel shirts and corduroy pants, wool socks, scuffed work boots and a ragged down-filled jacket transformed him into the typical working-class Mainer. A set of identification cards protected Stephen's newest character. He carried the Social Security card, Maine driver's license and credit cards in the name of Henry Wilson of Randolph, Maine, age 44.

He bought an old beat-up Ford truck with a For Sale sign in the front window that he found on the side of a back road. He paid cash and received the title, promising he would register the car the next day and turn in the old license tags. He drove north into the lake country, about one hour from Portland.

February in Maine is the weather god's punishment to all Mainers for their sins of the last eleven months. Temperatures dipping below zero are common and Maine residents expect the storms that dump twenty to thirty inches of wet, white snow. Convoys of snowplows clear the main roads first and then the secondary roads before starting over again on widening the paths they opened on the major roads.

Most Maine lake and pond residents desert their vacation homes during the winter. Many of the cottages along the shoreline are seasonal and owners close them before the first hard frost in fall can freeze exposed pipes or early snow fill dirt lanes that never feel the scrape of a snowplow. Back roads around camp sites, summer tourist areas and lakes used only seasonally are left pristine, touched only by prints of birds, rabbits, squirrels, fox, deer and an occasional snowmobile, snowshoe or cross country ski track. The few ice anglers drive their vehicles onto the lakes from public boat launches or leave their cars near easy access to the lake and their ice shacks. No one bothers to walk off the ice and check the shoreline camps. They are too busy watching the red flags that pop up when a fish takes the bait and drinking their hot toddies to keep warm.

Using a detailed Maine map, Stephen spent two days investigating unplowed roadways, especially those leading to a quiet pond or lake whose shores held boarded-up cottages sprinkled privately among the evergreens. He parked the truck on a secondary road. Then he walked through the woods just off to the side of the unplowed road, often following the deer paths which already flattened the snow, until he arrived at the road that snaked around the lake's frozen edge. He checked out the cottages, assessing each carefully. When he didn't find what he was looking for, he walked out in his own footsteps. He carefully swept the track as clear as possible with a telescoping ice scraper and brush used for clearing windshields of ice and snow. The snow looked dented in, but the cause of the depression in the snow was difficult to discern. Stephen would make his way back to his truck, drink hot coffee out of his thermos and drive away, looking for another road that might better serve his purposes.

On the third day of searching, he found the perfect place perched on the shore of a medium-sized pond whose shoreline held only a few isolated cabins. The old log cabin had seen better days. Cedar and hemlock trees crowded close together, opening only a little for the path to the back door and one off to the right to the outhouse. The wooden back door had an uncovered glass window set in the top. The small piece of plywood that originally protected the window lay covered with snow by the back step.

Stephen looked inside. He saw one room furnished with several wooden chairs, a kitchen table and little else. One wall held a stone fireplace and against another wall stood a wood cook stove. A large front window looked out over the pond and next to it, a door led onto a covered porch. Stephen trudged through deep snow around to the front of the cabin facing the pond and climbed up the four stairs to the covered porch. Split hard wood lined the walls of the porch, over a cord as far as he could tell. More than enough for his needs. He looked around. No other cabin was visible. The fir trees stood tall, well above the roofline of the house, hiding the cabin from the air.

He continued his walk around the small cabin, noting that faded and warped plywood covered the windows on the side of the cabin. Only the door and the front window were left exposed. He completed his tour, satisfied he had found the perfect place to live while completing his mission with Dr. McMorrow.

His desire was for closure. Dr. McMorrow had made a fool of him by surviving. He would not tolerate that outcome. When the time was right, he would finish what he had started. She would not escape this time. Stephen would kill her as the plan dictated and complete his mission. Then he could continue on the chosen's path.

Not that he had stopped ritually releasing other women over the last five months. In fact, he had chosen fifteen and successfully completed their releases in a swing through the South. Repeatedly he used his long silver needle for discipline and punishment, trying to slow and control his need to carry out another mission so soon after the last. However, even this time-tested persuader, firmly attached to the leather band on his wrist for as long as he could remember, failed to keep him from his addiction of mutilating and killing. He would plunge the silver needle repetitively into his thighs and buttocks, piercing and ripping his skin, as his Uncle Luke had done to him as a child to teach him to obey. However, Steven found he could not stop searching for, selecting and ritually releasing women. His obsession with spreading the truth had intensified. He was worried about his loss of discipline and the growing compulsion to increase his missions, afraid he might become careless. He felt spurred on by a deep and developing need that was growing stronger everyday. Sometimes he feared that Uncle/Mother Luke were taking possession of him, reaching out from hell, whispering to him, demanding that he do their bidding.

Stephen retraced his steps from the cabin, brushed out his tracks and headed back up along the unplowed road toward his truck. As he neared the plowed secondary road, he noticed an old weather-beaten garage sitting about ten feet from the road. It tilted raucously to the right, looking like another foot or so of snow on the roof could bring it down, but Stephen immediately saw its possibilities. He walked to the double front doors held by a wooden bar resting between two metal loops. He slid the bar aside and one of the doors moved a little, enough so he could step in. The dark, dank empty interior was big enough to hold his truck. Stephen stepped out, refastened the doors and smiled. Everything was falling into place. He had a garage to hide his truck and a cabin to live in, all within an hour of Portland and Dr. Christie McMorrow.

8

Bill looked at Christie. Christie raised her tormented blue eyes to meet Bill's eyes. A tender, sad look passed between them before Christie looked away. When she glanced back at him molten fury had replaced the tenderness.

"Bill, we both know that he'll kill again, and again, until we catch him. This kind of killer always repeats his crime. He's sick with the need to kill. Killing consumes him. He's killed before."

"Maybe there's a link to that Jane Doe from last summer. We never closed that case. I'll get out those files and let's do some comparisons," said Bill. "If I didn't know Scott's MO so well, I'd guess he might have killed these two girls. But, he doesn't victimize young girls; he doesn't take body parts, or burn his victims' corpses, as far as we know."

"Nope. It wasn't Scott. Our Jane Doe doesn't match his MO. She has no internal knife wounds; we didn't find any neatly folded clothes, or a cross carved on her chest. Scott needed the vic's skin to make his mark. He would always mutilate the breasts and genitalia, but other than that, he left the bodies intact. So, I'm sure he isn't our killer. However, the MO of this unsub indicates he's a serial. I'm willing to bet more bodies are out there somewhere waiting for us, ready to tell their stories. Let's hope we can move fast enough to stop him from slaughtering again. Now tell me what else Dr. Atwood found."

Bill looked at his notes. "Well, Jane Doe was twelve to fourteen years old, according to bone and teeth maturity evidence. Never visited a dentist, but needed to. Physically small for her age, probably due to malnourishment. Her eyes, scalp and hair, heart, liver, kidneys, pancreas, lungs, cartilage and bones were surgically removed, post mortem. Why the killer bothered to stitch her up is a question for you, I guess."

"He sewed her up? Oh God. Thank goodness the poor child was already dead."

"Tox screens, DNA, other lab work are on rush, but won't be ready for a few days. X-rays show signs of recent broken bones in her left hand. No signs of treatment. The bones healed, but improperly. She must have had limited use of that hand."

Christie shook her head. "What happened to this poor girl? What monster did this?"

"That's what we have to find out. My gut feeling is that someone used her for body parts."

"Body parts? You mean like for sacrifice in devil worship or satanic cult rituals?"

"No, I was thinking more about the huge market for organs, skin, tendons, corneas, bone marrow, and more. People in need pay big money for the right part. In the U.S., corneas sell for up to $3000; skin goes for $1,000 a square foot. A femur costs $3,800. When bone's ground up for teeth implants, an ounce costs more than an ounce of gold. A patella tendon can cost up to $4,000."

"And that's legal?"

"Yep. Legitimate companies handle donated cadavers and body parts and obtain family permission for post mortem donations. Then they screen for any possible disease or infection and sell hospitals, doctors, and clinics what they need. I was surprised to find out that over one million procedures a year involve implants of cadaver tissues. All on the up and up, for the most part."

"Bill, I am one of those patients."

Bill stared at Christie. She was looking at her gloved hands. She slowly pulled the gloves off and put them in her lap. She held up her scarred hands and showed them to Bill before she turned them around and inspected them herself. Tears started to well in her eyes.

"Christie," Bill started. He wanted so badly to put his arms around her and hold her. It took all his strength to stay in his chair. He willed his eyes to stay dry and his mouth to keep shut.

"I've had at least ten skin grafts on my hands. More on my feet. At first, I didn't think about where the skin actually came from. One doctor showed me the skin he was preparing to graft on my hands as he explained the procedure to me before my first operation. He just peeled the skin off a piece of paper. The skin looked like a manufactured product. I never let myself acknowledge the skin that was going to be a part of me came from some dead person."

"I'd guess you were somewhat emotionally detached at the time. After all, you were in shock, in a lot of pain, and taking heavy-duty pain meds. And who would want to analyze where the skin came from just before it was about to be attached to your body?"

Christie shuddered. She pulled the gloves back on and crossed her arms over her chest, hiding her hands under them.

"I was in a legitimate burn clinic, a hospital. They serve thousands of patients from all over the United States. That's a lot of skin and many skin donors. Are there that many people who sign a donor card before they die?"

"Unfortunately, no. Legitimate donors can't supply enough of all the body parts that medical facilities demand."

"So, that's where the black market comes in?"

"If you can't get the part you need legitimately in the U.S. or have to wait too long for the proper donor, those with enough money search alternative routes to get the part they need. In the U.S., unfortunately, some of the legitimate companies are working out the back door, hiring people to find donors or body parts that they desperately need. Then they sell those parts privately or to legitimate customers as if they had obtained them by routine legal means. The companies don't solicit thieves, but they don't question their free-lance suppliers enough, either. Others seeking a matching body part may travel to China or North Korea or any number of other foreign countries where body parts are for sale. In China, for $6000 you can buy an eye, no questions asked. $20,000 for a kidney, $40,000 for a liver and $60,000 for a heart."

"Are those parts stolen from dead bodies, too?"

"Some. But human rights groups have discovered that in China, for instance, guards are killing prisoners for body parts. If the supplier requires a heart or body organ, prison guards shoot the prisoner in the head. If they need a cornea, the guards shoot the convict in the chest. They cover up the real cause of the deaths, reporting death as the result of a prison riot or attempted escape. It's evil."

"It's hard to believe. I've heard of poor people selling one of their kidneys for cash, but to actually kill someone for their body parts?"

"We haven't run into it in Maine yet, as far as I know. However, they have in Massachusetts, New York, New Jersey and Pennsylvania. There have been multiple cases of organ theft, skin and bones taken from bodies in funeral homes, even bodies stolen out of fresh graves."

Christie was quiet for a moment. She stared out the window before looking back at Bill.

"When I was in the clinic and after I had received several skin grafts, I decided to read up on the subject, just to educate myself. I was shocked to find that many patients unknowingly received poorly screened parts. The articles said hundreds of patients undergoing procedures like bone, skin, tissue transplants, reconstructive surgery, teeth implants, and spinal fusions have contracted infectious diseases. Hepatitis, HIV, syphilis, even cancer have been spread from poorly screened body parts."

"I've heard that, too."

"I was freaked out for a while that the skin transplants I received could have been infected with something. I hounded the doctor until he showed me the lab records that listed all the screening tests the skin I received underwent. I was relieved to see the lab reported completing every required test. I think it was then that I finally realized that my recovery was dependent on someone else's death, someone's generosity to donate their skin, as well as the quality of lab work and the honesty of the companies supplying the skin."

Christie looked down at her hands. She slowly stripped off the gloves and ran her fingers gently over her new skin.

"I'm very grateful, really. I guess hiding my hands has been a sort of self-pity. I should be proud to be the recipient of a gift from one of the good people in this world."

"I'm so sorry you had to be the one hurt. I would have gladly taken your place if I could. I blame myself for being so slow to find you. If only I'd gotten there sooner."

"Stop it. You did the best you could. If you hadn't showed up when you did, I'd be dead. You saved my life. Now let's move on. What else do you know about this body parts business?"

"I can always count on you for finding some good in the bad. Thanks." Bill took a deep breath. "Anyway, many donors' permission forms are forged by these thieves. Sometimes they just break in or pay off the funeral homes, never checking the medical history of the cadaver. All without the family's or the legitimate companies' knowledge. Right now, that's where the big bucks are."

Christie closed her eyes for a moment. She slowly placed

her hands together as if in prayer. When she looked up, her forehead wrinkled into a frown.

"So do you think this girl was murdered and then later robbed of her body parts while she was in a funeral home? Is it possible someone killed her so they could take her body parts and sell them?"

"Could be, Christie. Young body parts go for a high price. On the other hand, someone might have murdered her and her family gave permission to remove the parts, thinking they were helping someone in need. But if that was the case, why wasn't she buried?"

"Of course. The fact that her body wasn't embalmed or buried means it never made it to a funeral home or that it was stolen from the funeral home before it was readied for burial."

Bill got up and started pacing around the room as they talked, excited to be forming theories on the motive and method of the Jane Doe's death.

"Or the family might not have known that she wasn't in her casket when they buried her. Maybe they never gave any permission to remove the parts. The thieves could have forged the papers or in a case of a false burial, they didn't need any signed forms. The thieves could have stolen the body from the casket prior to burial, removed the parts and wrapped the remains in a sheet. Later they could have disposed the body in the woods where animals over time would take care of it, eat the tissue and scatter the bones. No more Jane Doe."

"But this body wasn't disturbed by animals, right?" Christie asked.

"No, you're right. Dr. Atwood said there were no signs of animal bites. In fact, the body was not decomposed. She suggested the killer froze the body immediately after skinning and dissecting it. The ice crystal evidence should tell us more about that."

"Whew. This case so far is just about more than I can

take. I can't imagine the butchery body thieves are capable of. Somehow, it seems even worse than murder. And to think of all the poor sick and hurt patients who get these parts, not knowing where they came from, not aware that they might come down with some terrible disease later. I might have been one of them."

Bill didn't know what to say. Nothing he could say would change the fact that Christie had someone else's skin on her hands and feet. He wished he could assure her that her transplanted skin was legitimate, was free from some hidden infection. He chose instead to lead the discussion into a more analytical direction, one that would distract Christie from her own situation.

"I know what you mean. It's one thing to kill in passion. It's something else entirely to cut up a body to sell its pieces. Who would do that?"

Christie answered quickly, "Someone who values money more than human life. That's whom we're dealing with if our proposed scenario is correct. A sociopath."

"Okay. A sociopath. That's not surprising. Been there before. Actually, we've managed to create quite a series of scenarios. That's a good start and gives us a wide range of possibilities to explore. But let's get back to the business of hard facts. We have to collect and organize all the facts we have in this case to date. I have piles of folders already that we need to go through. And most important, we need to identify our victim."

Bill settled back into his desk chair and looked at the pile of folders in front of him.

Christie said, "Yes, we need to know who she was and I think the place to start is to research all female deaths under the age of 15, whether accidental or natural, because the family or officials might not have known the girl was murdered, right?"

"Right. They may have just found her in her bed and the officials they called may not have detected strangulation. It's happened before. We have to look at all deaths, natural, accidental, homicidal, suicidal."

"So, we investigate funeral homes and mortuaries for records of girls between twelve and fifteen, in case the homicide was not reported. Bill, we'll have to examine any suspicious action reported in funeral homes and hospitals, and graveyards as well, given the stolen body parts angle. That'll take forever. How far back do we have to go? When did Atwood determine the time of death to be?"

"Three months ago. I guess you missed that part."

"Why three months? Her tissue didn't show decomposition matching that length of time."

"That's because her body was probably frozen right after she died and was mutilated. Atwood determined three months because that's when she figured the baby was born."

"The what? What baby?"

9

Christie stared at Bill. Again, she asked, "What baby are you talking about?"

Bill closed his eyes for a moment as if he were trying to block out the information stored in his head. He glanced over at Christie, not wanting to say the words, but remembering that she had demanded he stop protecting her. He decided to tell her the facts just as he had heard them at the autopsy.

"Atwood found that Jane Doe gave birth to a baby three months ago. In December. There's no question that she'd been pregnant and delivered a child."

That's horrible," said Christie. She pictured a twelve year-old girl lying on a dirty mattress somewhere, screaming as she forced a baby from her childlike body. She quickly brought herself back to the present. "She was too young to be having sex and getting pregnant."

"Well, anyway, we know she was alive in December, at least until the second week or so. She could have survived the birth and continued living for a period after that. There's a possibility she might have died delivering the baby, but Atwood didn't find any evidence of that. The ice crystal evidence will take a little time to process, so we won't know the exact time of death for a while yet. But it looks like three months is pretty close."

"A baby. My God. What else happened to this poor

kid? So, she was pregnant for nine months until December. That puts conception around this time last year? She must have been only twelve or eleven when she got pregnant."

Christie took a drink of tea and looked out the window. "Too young, way too young. Something was very wrong in this child's life."

She looked back at Bill. "What about hospital reports, homes for unwed mothers, school records showing truant girls, runaway and missing children websites, mid-wives' and ob-gyns' records for the past year? We'll need to put someone on that."

"We should also check social services for underage or unwed teens' records. Maybe she or her family checked in at a clinic or with the state for help," Bill added.

"Or, if she's a runaway we should check police records for missing children, too. If she was living at home, someone must have reported her missing in December or earlier. Someone must have known Jane Doe was pregnant. Someone must have cared for her. Someone must have known of her existence."

"And obviously, someone wanted her dead," said Bill.

"Maybe her family was involved in the murder. Then they might not have filed a missing person report or maybe just simply reported her as a known runaway, or reported her dying of natural causes so that the police wouldn't need to be involved."

Bill added, "Or the father of the baby might have wanted to get rid of her. Maybe he was married and had a family already. Maybe the pregnancy was the result of incest and Jane Doe's father killed her so she wouldn't report him."

"Well, those are good theories. There are probably a dozen other possible story lines we could develop. If we can determine her identity and why she was killed, I think we'll find the murderer," said Christie.

"That's true. Finding out who this girl was may turn out to be an impossible problem, but it's key. First, we have to identify her. So far, nothing we have matches anything in the database. We'll have to keep checking other data files. She has no identifying marks, no prints, no tattoos or scars left after the killer removed her skin. There are no clothes to help trace her. Surprisingly, she hasn't had any dental work, although she has evidence of extended tooth decay. We can circulate an artist-enhanced picture of what she looked like based on skull size, facial bones, and the tissue remaining on her face. We'll mention the broken hand and use the media to get the news out about her age and the possibility of a child born to her, but we have nothing else helping us ID her right now."

Christie said, "Let's hope we get a break when the news hits the papers and TV. Hopefully one of the calls will give us what we need."

"Yeah. It should be a headline story tomorrow. That can only help us."

"I'm thinking," Christie mused. "Jane Doe's baby would be no more than three months old. I'm wondering where the baby is or if the baby's alive. We'll need an extended search of the woods to see if the baby's been left somewhere out there too."

"Or maybe other bodies," Bill said.

Silence fell like a deep velvet curtain. Bill stared out the window at the snowflakes that drifted slowly down. Christie bent over and started putting on her shoes.

"What harm could a thirteen-year-old pregnant girl or a young girl with a new born baby do? What threat was she to her killer?" she mumbled.

"Maybe none. Maybe they just wanted to make money off her," Bill said softly. "There are some real bad people out there, Christie. You know that better than most."

Christie stood up. "Then we'd better start working fast and get rid of as many of those bastards as we can. Especially those who prey on kids."

"I agree. Hey, Christie, before you go, can we quickly

review the files we have received from the investigation so far? It'll only take a few minutes."

They bent over the files. Photos of the crime scene, the boys who found the body, the snowmobile trails and machine tracks spilled out of one folder onto the desk. Another folder held typed reports by officers at the site, forensic information gathered at the crime scene, detailed reports of the interrogation of the three boys who found the body, plus their background histories and family data. Other files contained computer printouts mapping the area and information from Sheriff Wood detailing six months of criminal behavior in his county and a list of possible suspects. A file from the SBI detailed known felons in the area who in any way matched the psychological typology or had a history of using the methodology involved. The last file contained a list of all registered births for the last year in Maine, a list of all reported missing children and a list of all missing women.

"Looks like Wood has provided us with a lot of good information. Maybe he's changed since last summer. That would be a break."

Christie nodded, leaning on her crutch.

"I'll walk you to your car. A breath of fresh air would do me good and I have copies for you of crime scene reports, witness statements, photos, everything we've collected so far. If you have time to look them over at home tonight, we can share our reactions tomorrow. How's a 9:00 start for you?"

"That's fine. I want to get on this as fast as we can. And thanks for carrying the box for me."

Christie smiled at Bill and then quickly looked away. She didn't want to encourage him and felt awkward with him. Would a smile give him hope? Yet, she was reluctant to discourage him too much. She wanted to be more than just a colleague to him. She missed the easy banter, long talks and movie nights they had shared before. Sometimes she despaired of getting anything right anymore. Everything in her life had changed so drastically. She felt like Alice after she fell down the rabbit hole, living in an unfamiliar and very frightening world, with no one, including herself, who knew who she really was.

Both Bill and Christie knew that the offer to accompany Christie to her car and her acceptance had nothing to do with the box of reports. They knew no one had apprehended Stephen Scott since he escaped from Portland five months ago. They knew he must have been the one who killed the fifteen women found ritualistically mutilated throughout the South during the first three months he had disappeared. They also knew that no one had reported any activity from him in the last two months. They knew he was out there somewhere. In addition, they both knew that sometime Stephen Scott would return to Maine to get Christie. She was convinced he had followed her yesterday. Even now, he might be watching for her to leave the task force building. Alone.

10

By the second week in March, Stephen Scott had lived in the small cabin on Yardly Pond for almost two months. He chopped a hole in the ice every morning for water to boil for cooking, washing and drinking. Outdoor temperatures supplied all the refrigeration he needed for perishables. He used the outhouse for his toilet. The hardwood stacked on the porch fired the woodstove and kept the cabin warm enough most nights. He would heat the stove until it was cherry red, cook his meals and heat his water on the top surface. He usually slept on a stained, straw-filled pad he found in the cabin, dragging it up close to the woodstove.

He didn't build fires during the day, afraid someone might spot the smoke. If he became too cold, he would back his truck out of the ramshackle garage and drive his mapped-out route with the heater blazing. He practiced his plan for the release of Dr. McMorrow repeatedly on these trips, working to perfect each detail.

He continued covering his footprints by brushing them out, but he had seen no one at all since he started living in the cabin. He took to the isolation well, using his time to think and plan. He built up his physical strength and endurance, lifting wood as weights, chinning himself on the low beams, repeating push up after push up until he collapsed on the pine floor. He practiced his patience and strengthened his discipline as well. He used the silver needle as needed if he felt his impulsive desires sneaking up on him. His thighs bled steadily from his obsessive maiming, the scar tissue growing thicker and the rawness a constant reminder of his purpose in life.

His discipline had held so far and he had kept his compulsion under control. He killed no women in February or in the first two weeks of March. He prepared to begin the mission with Dr. McMorrow. He wouldn't be able to hold out much longer.

11

After her meeting with Bill, Christie drove to her therapist's office. She and Bill had managed to identify all the files they had access to, make a list of investigators needed to get additional information and put a plan of action into place. Tomorrow they would interrogate the boys who found the body. They were hoping to uncover something the boys had noticed or knew, that they hadn't yet revealed. Then in the afternoon, they would study the autopsy report and photos. It would be a full day.

She parked her car and used her cell phone to call Celeste.

"I'm outside now. Will you have the security guard come out and meet me? Is it Charlie today? The red Saab. Right. Thank you."

Christie watched Charlie Dowd, the building security officer, leave the brick building and walk to her car. He looked around as he passed by the parked cars and glanced inside each car. Christie waited to unlock the doors until he smiled and said, "Should be safe now, Dr. McMorrow."

Charlie accompanied Christie to the second floor office of Celeste McHale, LCSW.

"Call down when you're ready and I'll be up to meet you," he said.

"Thanks Charlie. I'm glad I can count on you."

"You're welcome, Doc. Anytime."

Christie opened the door and walked into the waiting

room. Celeste was straightening magazines. She looked up, walked over to Christie and gave her a warm hug. Then she locked the outside door.

"Glad to see you, Christie. Come on in and I'll make you a cup of tea."

Christie was tired. She sank into the soft couch and watched Celeste as she poured hot tea from a china pot into two mugs. They sat quietly for a few moments, enjoying their tea together.

"I'm glad it's March, even though I hate March. At least the temperature's above the freezing mark some of the day and the snow's melting off the roads. In a few weeks, thank God, daylight savings will be here. At least we'll have more light."

Celeste nodded, listening to Christie as she eased her way into the therapy session.

"I think about my gardens, the crocus and daffodils struggling to find their way to the light through the snow."

Christie paused and sipped her tea. She looked up at Celeste.

"But going back to my house is still so hard."

Christie paused. She wiped a tear from the corner of her eye with a tissue.

"Alex did wonders with the house while I was in North Carolina. She turned the downstairs guest room, where he kept me, into her artist's studio and her former studio upstairs into the guest room. That helps a little, but I just don't feel like I used to feel at home."

"How are you feeling when you're there?"

"Nervous. I can't relax. There's a new security system, unlisted phone, motion lights and surveillance cameras. Even all that doesn't help much. I can't seem to relax."

"Why is that, Christie? Why can't you relax?"

"Because he's out there. He's going to kill me. He followed me yesterday. I know it was him. I could feel him behind me, getting closer. I thought at any minute that I would feel his hands around my neck. I was terrified."

"Oh, Christie. I'm so sorry. Tell me what happened."

Christie related the events that occurred in the garage the day before.

"I was devastated when I realized no one believed me. None of them. Not even Bill. They all thought I was just overreacting, having a panic attack, experiencing PTSD, imagining Stephen Scott was in the garage and coming after me. I could see it in their eyes. They felt sorry for me. I'm now an object of pity."

Celeste nodded and then asked, "That's a lot, Christie. You say they don't believe you. Instead, they pity you. How does that make you feel?"

Christie mumbled, "Perfect psychotherapist question, Celeste. Couldn't do better myself."

Celeste didn't respond. She waited for Christie to calm down and continue.

"It makes me feel Goddamn pissed off, if you want to know. Just because Scott almost killed me doesn't mean I'm no longer a viable, believable and trustworthy person. They act as if I've lost my mind. I haven't lost my mind, only my peace."

Christie thought for a moment. "And I feel sad. I'm sad everything in my life changed. Everything's different. Everyone either feels badly for me or gets uptight and nervous around me. They don't know what to say. I don't know what to say either. I don't want to talk about what happened to me. It's not as if it's an interesting piece of conversation, for God's sake. I just want things to go back where they were, that's all."

"That makes sense," said Celeste.

"But nothing's like it was. I'm not like I was. My life won't ever be like it was before. I don't even want to go home now."

"You started to talk about that earlier. Tell me about that, not wanting to go home."

"I guess it's because so much happened there. It reminds me of him."

Christie looked off into the distance. A minute passed. Her face blanched. She bit her bottom lip. She picked at a hangnail. She ran her gloved hands up and down her arms.

"I can see his face looking down at me. I'm tied to the bed in the guest room, both my hands and feet. The rope is so tight. They hurt so much, as if they're burning. My hands and feet are freezing, but searing hot, too. I don't know what's wrong with them. I can't lift my head up far enough to see my feet or my hands. I don't know what he's done to me and I'm scared. He's taking his clothes off. He's climbing up on me. I feel his weight pressing my body down into the mattress, his skin's hot against my cold flesh. He's staring down at me. I can see the pores in his skin, the hair in his nose. His eye lashes. His huge blue eyes bore into me. I try to look away, but he holds my head so I can't turn. His eyes. They're so blue and he doesn't blink at all. I'm afraid to look away. I think that maybe he'll get mad if I don't keep staring at him. I don't know what he wants or what he's going to do to me. His smile, his expression is so sick, so perverted. I know whatever he's going to do will hurt me, make me want to die."

Christie shivered and wrapped her arms around herself and sank back on the couch. She cleared her throat and blinked back her tears.

"That was weird. It was like being back there again. Ugh. Just thinking about it makes me feel sick."

"Stop a minute and take a drink of your tea. That might help," Celeste suggested.

Christie complied. She sat a few moments sipping tea and looking out the window.

"Anyway, before that, he'd already shown me all the pictures in his scrapbooks. He made me look at them. If I looked away or closed my eyes, he'd jam a long needle in my arm or leg. So, I had to look at them. The pictures were so horrible. I didn't want to see them. Those poor women. What he did to them. So awful."

Christie looked up at Celeste. "I haven't talked with anyone about what was in the pictures. I couldn't. The pictures come in my nightmares now. That's why I dread going to sleep. I see all those pictures."

"Tell me what you'd suggest to a client if she told you what you just said to me."

"You mean about the nightmares, the pictures, not wanting to go to sleep?"

"Yes, exactly. What would you say to her?"

Christie sat still. Then softly she said, "I'd tell her sometimes talking about the horror you've experienced releases it. That telling someone else opens a door so you're not alone with all that you endured. That telling helps."

Silence filled the room.

Then Christie began to talk. So softly, Celeste had to lean forward to hear her words.

"He bit their breasts, their nipples. He ripped their nipples off with his teeth. Every single woman had her nipples ripped out."

Christie started to cry softly. She wiped at her eyes with a tissue, but the tears rolled down her cheeks and dripped slowly off her chin.

"I was so afraid he was going to bite me, too. I imaged how it must feel to have your nipples ripped off. Somehow, at the same time, I almost wished he'd just do it. Get it over with. I thought maybe I'd offer them to him in exchange for my life. I'd be almost happy to trade my nipples for my life. That's when I really got it. He was going to kill me no matter what. He was going to bite me, rip and stab me to pieces, just like all the pictures."

Celeste intervened. "Christie, that had to be so awful

for you. To be so afraid of what might happen, what he was going to do to you. I'm so sorry you had to go through that. However, you're here now with me. And he didn't bite you. He didn't rip off your nipples. He didn't kill you. What you imagined, what you expected, didn't happen. Somehow, some way, you stopped him. You may not know how, but you did."

"But I couldn't do anything. I was tied. He wouldn't listen to me. I didn't know how to get away or get him to stop."

"And yet, he stopped. You aren't a picture in his book. You did do something to save yourself. Focus on that."

Christie shifted in her chair. "Well, at least I tried. I tried everything I knew. If I did stop him or change his plans somehow, at least that's something, I guess. More than those Goddamn cops, FBI and all those other agencies are doing. I'm so mad. I can't believe that nobody's caught him. How can that be? That man's killed over a hundred women, all over the country. His face is on every post office wall. Most Wanted featured him. Every newspaper on the globe has put his picture on the front pages. But no one can catch him! Can you believe it? I can't. He's still out there. And I know he'll come back to finish what he started with me. I know he's out there somewhere. I'm so scared."

Christie broke down sobbing. Celeste fixed them both another mug of hot tea and let Christie cry. She patted Christie's shoulder as she put down the mug.

"Take a sip of tea when you're ready. You've gotten past the hard part."

Gradually, Christie's sobs eased. She blew her nose and looked around the comfortable room, warmly lighted by Tiffany-style lamps and green with lush healthy houseplants. Antique bookcases filled with multicolored books brought the colors of life to the soft white walls.

"I don't even feel safe here. God, I have to have an escort or I don't dare to get out of my car. No new locks and other security mechanisms can change the fact that Stephen Scott, a delusional psychopath obsessed with bringing his twisted truth to the world, has failed only one mission. I'm the only woman Scott's attacked who's still alive. I know he won't stop until he kills me."

"How are you doing with all this pressure?"

"Not too well. Lately I've felt an ominous presence, as if an evil spirit was moving toward me. I don't see anything suspicious, just feel it. Sometimes I think I see him. Like I'm in the grocery store and see a man in the aisle ahead of me. I'm sure it's him. Then he turns and he isn't Scott. Or a car pulls up next to me at a stoplight. I look over and it's him. Then he looks at me and it's someone else. Sometimes I just sense some dark coldness coming closer to me and know it's him. Like yesterday in the garage."

"You've been through so much, Christie. It's normal to have fears and dark fantasies about what could happen."

"Don't patronize me, Celeste! Don't try to reassure me. You and Stella listen to me but are too damn quick to dismiss what I feel. You both tell me that my senses are still in high anxiety response modality, normal for Post Traumatic Stress Reaction. In time, you both tell me, the feeling of evil will fade and then disappear. Well, I'm not going to bother to argue with you anymore, but I don't agree with you. I may have PTSD, but this evil thing I sense is more than just a heightened response. It's real. So real that my hair rises on the back of my neck. Goosebumps pop out on my skin. My peripheral vision's on overdrive. My sleep's so light that my own breathing wakes me dozens of times each night."

The rest of the session passed quickly. Celeste would gently remind Christie of her strengths and encourage her to talk about the coping mechanisms which would most help her during this difficult time. Christie would resist, insisting angrily that if the law enforcement world would do what it should and catch Scott, she wouldn't have any problems. Then Christie would burst into tears of frustration, fear, sadness and loss. Celeste would comfort her while respectfully witnessing her turmoil and pain.

When the session time ended, Christie made an appointment for the next week. Celeste hugged her goodbye and called Charlie to walk Christie to her car.

12

When Christie returned home after her therapy session, there was a note on the kitchen counter from Alex.

> "Hi Christie. Hope your day went well. Salad in refrig. Warm up some bread and soup. Eat please. I'm down at Frannie's again. Didn't get enough done last night. Under deadline now. Won't be too late. Call if you need me to come home. See you soon, Alex P.S. Exciting. Heard from gallery in NYC. They want me to come down ASAP!"

Christie crunched the note up and threw it into the wastebasket. She looked in the refrigerator at the soup and salad. She just was too tired to bother heating up the soup. She slammed the refrigerator door shut. She cut off two slices of bread and spread them with peanut butter. She poured herself a glass of Chardonnay and sat down at the kitchen table.

Suddenly, she jumped up, pulled the drapes together, turned on the overhead light and sat down again. She started munching the bread and sipping her wine. She wondered what she should do. Alex had always been here when she got home. The silence in the house seemed overwhelming.

Then she heard it. Someone was in the living room. Someone was moving around. The thick Persian rug hid the sound of footsteps, but the old wooden floorboards under the rug creaked with each move. The sound was coming toward the kitchen.

Christie grabbed the bread knife. She backed up against the wall behind the door. She waited.

Clicking noises started, just about where the rug ended and the pine floors were exposed.

Before Christie collapsed on the floor, she put the knife on the kitchen table. Then she opened up her arms. Tashie limped into them and started to kiss her face with her tongue. Christie hugged the old dog, patted her head, and then scratched her chest. After a few minutes, Tashie whined.

"You want to go out, girl?" Christie asked even though she knew Tashie had been totally deaf since her stroke three years ago. She no longer could serve as the watchdog she once was. She couldn't even hear Christie's car when she drove in the garage. In addition, she was still limping from the brutal treatment she received last fall from Stephen Scott.

Christie liked talking to her dog. Since there wasn't anyone else to talk to tonight, she continued.

"I'd like to take you out, sweetie, but to tell the truth, I'm a little scared to go out in the dark these days. You remember, don't you girl? Oh, how I love you."

Christie hugged Tashie again. "But I'll tell you what." The old dog looked up, trying to understand. "I'll let you out. When you want to come in, you bark. Okay?"

Christie got up off the floor and made the "up" sign to the dog. Tashie got up too. Then Christie gave her the sign for "out." Tashie headed for the front door. Christie peered out the window. The outdoor spotlights shone brightly, reflecting off the snow outside and chasing darkness into deep shadows where the light couldn't reach.

She looked down at the dog. "Now when I open the door, you hurry out. I'll wait here until you bark." She gave the sign for "bark" and Tashie replied with a series of gruff barks.

"Good girl. Here we go." Christie looked outside again and then quickly undid the three dead bolts and opened the door. Tashie cooperated and walked quickly outside. Christie slammed the door shut and slid the dead bolts into place. She sighed deeply and looked outside. Tashie was squatting down, doing her business. When she finished she walked around sniffing for a few moments then headed back to the front door. She stood there and let out a series of barks. Christie obeyed. She slid the dead bolts back again, opened the door, let the dog in, and then secured the door again.

"Now, that wasn't too hard, was it, girl? But I think I need some more wine to calm me down now that everything's okay."

Christie and Tashie walked to the kitchen and then to the living room together. As Christie performed her ritual of closing all the drapes downstairs, Tashie followed right after her. When they got back to the living room, Tashie lay down in her fleece bed next to Christie's chair while Christie lit the fire.

"Well, here we are, just us two ladies in front of the fire. I'm glad you're here, Tashie."

The only sound was the crackling of the fire and Tashie's little snores when she fell asleep. Christies leaned back and watched the fire as she sipped her wine. Alex would be home soon. Then she could go to bed.

13

Alex kneeled down and hugged Frannie hello. Frannie's wheelchair created a challenge for a good close hug, but Alex managed to snuggle into her embrace.

"Good to see you, hon. How're things at home?"

"It's like walking on eggshells, as usual," Alex sighed as she stood up. "I'm worried about Christie; you know that. I care so much for her and I don't think she's getting any better emotionally. Maybe she's getting worse, if that's possible. She did another one of those pull-all-the-drapes-down numbers again last night."

Frannie nodded as Alex talked. Alex had spent a lot of time with her in the last five months. Frannie had listened to her as she grieved for Christie and helped her explore new perspectives about her feelings about Christie. She rolled over to the refrigerator and got out two Rolling Rocks. "Want a beer? How about some crackers and cheese?"

"Sure, fine. Thanks. I'm doing it again, aren't I? Talking about Christie instead of focusing on my own life. You must be bored. Anyway, we're supposed to finish the plans for the workshop tonight. Let's get to it."

"No, it's okay. I'm not bored. I like listening to you. I find you quite interesting. You intrigue me."

Alex laughed. "Well, that's a new one for me. Intriguing, I'll have to think about that."

Frannie looked at her. "Why wouldn't you be intriguing? You're sexy, beautiful and tall, with a gorgeous body. You dance better than anyone I've ever seen. You could win that dance contest on TV hands down."

Alex laughed. "Come on, Frannie, quit it."

"I've hardly started. You're smart, quick, alert. You're an accomplished artist. God, you have your art in all the best galleries and the Boston Globe featured you in an article. You're on your way to big times, girl. New York City wants you."

"That's enough."

"One more thing," Frannie said as she rolled over to the table and passed Alex a beer. "You're a survivor. You got through that awful childhood, several disastrous affairs, and the Stephen Scott thing. And you're surviving your crush on Christie."

She took a swig of beer and grinned. "Of course, I also like the way you dress. Especially the white shirts, tight jeans and boots. But the smoking has got to go."

"Okay, okay. I'm intriguing. Now will you stop?"

"I forgot one thing. You're one hell of a loyal friend. I really respect you for that."

"Thanks. I'm doing the best I can. Sometimes I just don't know what to do."

"But you hang in anyway. That's so good. I know it's hard. I know Christie must be scared. I would be, if someone who tried to kill me was still out there free. You must be scared, too."

"You got that right. We're both afraid. She's frightened, even though she doesn't admit it to me. She acts as if everything's fine, although it's obvious that she's terrified. I wish she'd talk to me. She's so Goddamned protected about her feelings. Sometimes I don't think I know the real Christie at all. I don't think too many people do. Maybe Stella and Celeste get to see more of who she really is. I used to think I did, but not anymore."

"Look, why don't you two move? That would be the first thing I'd do, if I were in her situation. After all, he knows where she lives. He was in the house, for God's sake. If he comes for her, it's logical he'd go there."

"I know. I've tried to convince her to move. Everyone has. But she won't. Says she won't be driven out of her home that she worked so hard to restore."

"But you could rent a secured condo or stay in a residential hotel for a while, at least until he's caught. Wouldn't that make you feel safer?"

"Moving would make me feel better, sure. I looked that monster straight in the eye that morning in the woods. He's pure evil. He's more like the devil than anyone I've heard of. A guy as depraved as he is won't just let her go. He'll be back. And she knows it. But Christie refuses to move and I'm not going to leave her there alone. What else can I do? It's even worse because she shares so little with me these days and bites my head off if I ask her anything personal. Oh, she tries to be pleasant, and we do chitchat about stuff, but not about how she feels."

"She's keeping to herself a lot more, isn't she?"

"Yeah. She's really isolated herself, except for work with the task force and Stella and Celeste. She doesn't let many people in. Christie has been a giver, but she has a hard time receiving. Right now she's so reserved I don't think anyone could reach her heart or soul."

"What a shame. She's changed so much."

"Oh, I don't know. Maybe she's always been that way, only she's more so now. I think she just doesn't want anyone to reach her that deeply. Maybe she avoids intimacy by working so hard, giving so much to others. She's never revealed much about her early life or emotional self to me. And, she hasn't had a relationship since her divorce and that was years ago. I don't know why she's that way, but I sense that it's easier for her to stay in the world of work and good deeds than risk the vulnerability that an intimate relationship demands."

"Sounds like someone else I know," Frannie laughed.

"Yeah, I've been pretty scared myself about letting my walls down. I admit I have tremendous trust issues. I've been hurt a lot and don't want that pain again. Christie and I aren't the only ones who are afraid. I think many people are afraid of being hurt and feel they're not worthy enough to be loved and adored. You know what I mean?"

"Yep. Especially with those we care the most about, unfortunately," sighed Frannie.

"Isn't that the truth?" Alex sighed too.

"Let's have another beer if we're going to get seriously philosophical here."

Alex tipped up her bottle and drained the remains. "No thanks. I think I should go. I've left Christie by herself two nights in a row. Talking about Scott makes me nervous. Actually, I'm spooked. What if he does come to the house? We haven't heard any reports about his whereabouts for months now. It's as if he just dropped off the face of the earth. And, that makes me really nervous."

"Maybe he died from his wounds. That could be why there haven't been any reports."

"The devil doesn't die, Frannie. He just goes on and on forever. The FBI had reports he was killing women down south a couple of months ago. Then, nothing. Where is he?"

"What are you going to do if he does come? Do you have a plan?"

"Yes. We have a security system, phone link to the cops, patrols going by night and day. Plus, I bought a gun."

"A gun! Oh no, Alex. Not a gun. People are killed with their own guns. Or they kill innocent people thinking they're intruders. I don't think a gun's a good idea."

"Bill suggested it. Actually, he picked out guns for both Christie and me. I've been training at the shooting range. I've really learned to shoot the damned thing. I think Christie's practiced too. At least we'll have two guns between that animal and us."

"A gun. Oh my God, Alex. Be careful. It scares me that you both have guns."

"I know. It scares me too. I don't like having guns in the house either. But the gun helps me feel safer. If he comes back, at least I'll have something to even the odds. Oh, let's not talk about this anymore. It's giving me the creeps."

"Okay. Want to work on the schedule for the workshop?"

"I think I'll head back home, if you don't mind. I don't want to leave Christie alone there too long."

"Just be cautious, Alex. I worry about you two out there. Maybe you guys should get another dog with specialized training. You know, a guard dog. Tashie's so old and so deaf now she can't hear a thing. With a guard dog, Christie might feel safer by herself, or you might feel safer leaving her by herself. You have to live your life too, you know."

Alex shrugged into her parka. "I know, Frannie. I know. Things will get better with time I'm sure. Then I'll get on with my life, too."

She gave Frannie a hug and turned to go. Then she stopped and turned around.

"I've got an idea. I told you that the NYC gallery called today and wants me to come to the city and talk about a show. I sent them the slides of my work months ago. Well, I was going to tell them I couldn't come, that we'd have to do all our negotiating on the phone or by email.

"But what if we do go to New York? Christie's working now and she's going to be so busy she won't even notice I'm gone. I know how she is when she's on a case. The rest of the world disappears. I'll ask her, of course, if it's okay. Maybe I'll set up someone to stay with her at night if she wants. But wouldn't that be a blast? You and me driving down to NYC and doing the town, seeing all the galleries and hopefully signing a contract for my own show? Wow that would be so fine."

"It would be a good first step to getting on with your life. It looks like Christie is trying, why not you, too?"

"Right. So you'd go with me?"

"In a heartbeat, baby. New York. Here we come."

"Hold on. I have to be sure that it's okay with Christie and line up a helper for Tashie. I'll call you tomorrow and let you know."

14

The phone rang, shattering the silence in the old house. Christie walked into the kitchen and looked at the caller ID. A blocked number. The answering machine picked up and Christie turned the sound on and listened. At first, she heard nothing. Then she froze. The sound of heavy breathing pushed out of the speaker and into the kitchen. She stepped back as if the breather could grab her if she was too close. She stood rigid and listened until the caller clicked off the phone. Then she doubled over and wrapped her head in her arms.

He was back. Stephen Scott had called her. He was letting her know that he was out there in the dark, waiting for her.

Christie dialed 911 on her cell phone and gripping the phone, ran to the doors and checked the locks and the security alarms. She made sure to activate all the motion lights. She rushed back to the kitchen, still waiting for 911 to pick up. She looked at her cell. It wasn't dialing. The battery icon was blinking. She threw the cell phone on the counter and reached for her landline. Just as she reached out to pick up the receiver, the phone shrilled out again. She jerked her hand away from the phone as if it were on fire.

"What do you want?" she screamed at the phone. "Go away. Leave me alone." Then she burst into tears. The machine clicked on.

"Christie, are you there? It's Bill. I have some news about our case. Pick up."

Christie ripped the phone off its base.

"Bill," Christie screamed. "He called me. He knows where I am. He just called. What should I do? I think he's here. I'm all alone. Help me. I don't know what to do."

"Hold on, Christie. Stay calm. First, activate all the security measures."

"I did. I did, but that won't stop him. Nothing can stop him. What should I do?"

"Christie, listen to me. You're safe in your house. He can't get in."

"You don't know him like I do. He can do anything he wants. He's going to kill me, Bill."

"Christie, I'm notifying the patrol in your area. Hold on a minute."

Christie heard Bill's voice talking in the background.

"They're only three minutes away and will be coming down your driveway with their bright lights on. Watch for them. They'll signal you by blinking their lights two short and one long so you'll know it's them. Let them in. They'll take care of you."

"But what if he gets here first? What do I do?"

"Calm down and listen. First, go get your gun. Put down the phone and get your gun."

"Okay, but don't hang up. Stay there. I'll be right back."

Christie climbed the stairs without bothering to grab her crutch. She grabbed her gun from the bedside table. She hurried back down and picked up the phone.

"I've got it."

"Is it loaded?"

"Yes. I left it loaded."

"Switch off the safety but be careful. The gun will be ready to fire."

"I switched it off. Now what?"

"Move to the front window and watch for the state police."

Sobbing, Christie stretched the phone cord to the front window and pulled the curtain aside just enough so she could peer out. It took all her courage to do that much.

"I don't see anyone."

"Good. They won't be there for another two minutes. Talk to me. What did Scott say to you?"

"That's just it. He didn't say anything. He just breathed at me."

"Wait a minute, Christie. How do you know it was him?"

"I just know. The number was blocked. Nobody said anything. Then came this terrible breathing and then he hung up."

"Christie, you have an unlisted number. Maybe the caller dialed incorrectly and then realized it and hung up. Maybe some kid was calling random numbers to scare whoever answered. What made you think it was Scott?"

"I just know, Bill. I know. Just like the other day, I knew. Look, even though I have an unlisted phone, somehow he got my number. He wants me to know that he's coming to get me."

"I'm in my car now, Christie. I'm on my way up there. Keep talking to me."

"I don't know what else to say. I've been feeling like he's around here. Just some second sense or something keeps warning me. He'll never let me go. You know that. I'm the only one who got away from him. He can't tolerate failure. He's going to come back and finish his 'mission'. He's going to kill me."

"Christie, I'm on the highway now. Twenty minutes tops and I'm right there. You should see the state police patrol car any minute now."

"Someone just pulled into the driveway. They stopped. Oh, thank God, they're blinking their lights. Two shorts and there's the one long one. It's the patrol. It's the patrol. Oh, thank God. I'm going to the front door. Two state troopers are getting out of the car. They're here."

Bill listened as Christie unlocked the dead bolts and welcomed the troopers. He heard them introducing themselves as they came in. He heard them ask Christie to please place her gun on safety and put it away.

"Christie, let me talk to them for a minute."

Christie handed the phone to Walter Tate, the officer who stood closest to her. She reset the security alarm and invited the other officer, Peter Billings, into the kitchen. While Tate talked with Bill, Christie put her gun in the drawer with the knives and started to make a pot of coffee.

"Well, Dr. McMorrow," Walter Tate said as he walked into the kitchen, "Detective Drummond should be here in about fifteen minutes. If you don't mind we'll stay until he gets here."

"Oh thank you. I appreciate you coming so fast. I'm so afraid. I didn't know what to do. I'm making coffee. Will you have some while you wait?"

"Love to, but while it's brewing, Pete and I'll take a look around, if you don't mind. We'll check the yard, around back, just to be sure that all's secure."

"Oh thank you. I know I keep saying that, but I'm here all alone and I didn't know what to do. I panicked."

"That's pretty normal. That's what we're here for, to help people feel safer. We'll just check everything out, come around to the front door, and knock when we're finished. Please reset the alarm system behind us."

Christie saw them out, sank down into a kitchen chair, and watched the coffee drip down into the glass carafe. As some of her fear seeped out and her adrenaline stopped surging, she felt an overwhelming exhaustion. She wondered how she could possibly keep going. If one phone call triggered a major panic attack, how was she going to cope with all the possible threats that existed out there in the world? She put her head down on the table and wrapped her arms tightly around her body.

15

Stephen Scott drove slowly by Dr. McMorrow's house with his headlights turned off. He saw the state police car pull into her driveway, stop, and then the driver blink the lights quickly two times and then once longer before the officers exited the vehicle. He smiled. He had a knack for being in the right place at the right time.

He continued on his way. He was pleased with the result of his call to Dr. McMorrow. He had learned several important things. One, the number he had acquired by paying an internet investigative service was indeed hers because she had reacted by calling the police. Two, Dr McMorrow was scared. She was very scared. She must be thinking as much about him as he was thinking about her. Three, the state police responded so quickly that they must be closely patrolling her area. He would need to curtail some of the drive-bys that had been giving him so much pleasure. Just knowing Dr. McMorrow was inside that house, so close, filled him with excitement and anticipation. Four, a signal had been arranged to inform Dr. McMorrow when someone safe had arrived at her home. Now he knew that signal and could use it when he was ready. Stephen Scott had found his way in.

16

Bill held Christie in his arms. She sobbed on his shoulder. In between sobs she would gasp, "What am I going to do? How can I live this way? I'm so scared."

Bill just comforted her and didn't try to answer. He couldn't. He didn't have any answers. He didn't know what she could do to feel safer. He didn't know how someone stalked by a psychopath like Stephen Scott could live a life with any quality. He didn't know how to take away her fear, or his own, for that matter.

Finally, Christie slipped out of Bill's arms, grabbed a paper towel, wiped her eyes, and blew her nose. She sat down and covered her face with her hands. Bill sat next to her.

"How about some coffee, Christie? We're going to be awake for a while anyway, so we might as well let some caffeine tromp around in our systems."

"Yes, that would be good. I need something, that's for sure."

While Bill poured the coffee, he wished he could chat about the light snow that had just begun to fall and the weather warnings about frigid temperatures for the next couple of days. He wanted to tell Christie about one of his young assistants who was a dog owner for the first time and had lost two pairs of shoes to his pup's sharp teeth. He yearned to steer the conversation away from that evening's events, Stephen Scott and the horrors that overwhelmed Christie. But all he could think about was Christie's fear and the danger she was in.

"When's Alex coming back?"

"She said she wouldn't be late. What time is it now?"

"Just after ten. I'm going to stay here until she comes. If you want me to stay longer, I will. Just let me know what's best for you."

"I'm feeling a little better now. I didn't realize how fast those troopers could get here."

"You did everything right tonight, Christie. You secured the house first and dialed 911. The dispatcher has a special hook-in to your number and when you call, a direct link goes to the state police patrol, to my cell, to the local sheriff. So, just remember how many folks are out there to help."

"But I thought they wouldn't ever pick up. Then I saw that my cell battery was too low. I had forgotten to recharge it. So, the call never got through. Anyway, last time I dialed 911 it took them forever to answer. What the hell's wrong with them?"

"I have that on my list. I'll be checking with them on my way home. We've had trouble with the dispatcher in this town before. She thinks nothing of going to the coffee room and leaving the phones untended for a few moments. That's going to stop, as of tonight."

"I hope so. If you hadn't called, I don't know what I would have done. I just stood there with the dumb cell phone in one hand and the land line in the other." Christie's eyes welled up again.

"Well, I did call and everything's all right now. No sign of a trespasser outside. And think of it this way. It's like we had a test run. I contacted the state police and they got here fast. I got here quickly, too. We've just had a dry run in case there really is an emergency some time. So, we're all set on that. If there's a next time, you know you have to get your gun."

"Yes. I didn't even think about the gun. Thanks. Thanks for being here."

"You can count on me, Christie. I'm not going to let anything happen to you. Now, if you feel up to it, the coffee's ready and I'd like to talk with you about the Cumberland County case. I've had some new ideas that I'd like to toss around with you. I was going to talk to you on the phone, which is why I called in the first place, but being here with you is even better."

Bill smiled at Christie as he poured their coffee. He offered sugar and milk to her, even though he knew she took it black and then sat down and fixed his coffee with two teaspoons of sugar and a healthy amount of milk. At another time and under another situation, sitting in this warm kitchen sharing a nighttime coffee with Christie would have been romantic. Bill struggled to rid his mind of this train of thought. Romance was not about to happen now, maybe never. Christie interrupted his dreaming by laying her hand on his for just a moment. Then she removed it and picked up her coffee mug. She smiled at him.

"I'm really glad you're here, Bill. Thanks. I mean it. I wish I could let you know how much it means to me that you're always here for me. You've never let me down. You're one of the few people that I can rely on, really trust. Trust is everything to me, especially now. Thanks a lot."

Bill blushed and blurted out, "Christie, you know I'd do anything. I wish I could kill that bastard for you. I'm so sorry he escaped. If only I'd been more cautious."

"Stop it, Bill. It wasn't your fault. And there's something you can do for me now. Tell me what you've come up with. I need to get my mind off Scott right now or I'll go crazy. I want to work. I want to think about who our Jane Doe is. I want to go over case notes. I want to hear what you were calling me about. So, what do you have? "

"Well, let's do it then." Bill sipped his coffee, put down his mug and began. "I was thinking about that case we worked on last summer. Jenny mentioned it several times today and it's stuck with me. That Jane Doe was an unidentified young woman, burned beyond recognition. There were reports of cult activities, fire circles at night, missing pets. Someone called about that farmer, Oscar Little, remember?"

"How could I forget? I was closed in the interrogation room with that horrible man for hours. I was certain he was the killer, everything pointed to it, but he wouldn't confess. He managed to get an air-tight alibi and the D.A., Sampson, wouldn't bring the case to trial because he said the evidence just wasn't there."

Bill could tell that Christie was feeling stronger. Work was like a healing tonic for her. Once her mind was involved in analysis, deduction, and intellectual challenges, the other part of her, her emotional side, just disappeared. He decided to pressure her to put all her energy into the Cumberland County case. Then she wouldn't have time enough to slip back into her emotional sinkhole of fear and worry.

"Well, we never identified that Jane Doe. I think we should have Atwood take another look at her to see if she can determine if she had ever been pregnant or if she had any body parts removed before she was set on fire. Maybe try for some DNA evidence. As I remember, the autopsy was completed while Atwood was on vacation and was rather sketchy. Maybe the substitute missed something."

"Great idea. You're always coming up with some new angle. I like this one. You think the Cumberland County murder might have something to do with cults or Oscar Little? A cult or commune could account for babies being born without records. Babies and women too, for that matter, disappear and often no authorities are notified."

"Yeah, some of the really alternative communes have many transient members. People come and go all the time. A young runaway girl, like Jane Doe, might have hooked up with one. Maybe not such a nice one. Could be someone took advantage of her and she got pregnant. Later the baby's born with the commune's mid-wife's help and then the group takes the baby."

"What happened to Jane Doe, then?"

"That's the part that doesn't fit. I can't imagine why they would kill her. And stealing body parts is definitely not a communes' or cult's usual pattern. So maybe my idea really doesn't make much sense."

"We never got anywhere with the cult idea last summer, either, as I recall. Other than a few night fires and some nasty gossip, nothing turned up that looked suspicious. Just some hippies out camping and drinking the night away. Cult killings, like Manson's and that Mexican group's do happen, but they're rare. Thank goodness. Of course, numerous cases exist where bodies were dismembered both by groups and individuals."

"Yes. What about a satanic cult? Could one be operating up there in Cumberland County? You've had some experience dealing with cult victims in your practice, haven't you?"

"Some, but the diagnosis can be difficult. Satanic cults are very rare, usually highly secretive. I doubt that a satanic cult would be so careless about body disposal. They're efficient and well organized. The research on satanic cults doesn't indicate that they've been involved in selling body parts. Involving outsiders by contracting to sell body parts would be too risky. Secrecy is paramount for their security."

"I don't know much about these cults and so called satanic circles. Much of what I read about them is just rumor or tabloid sensationalism. The ones I've investigated turned out to be naturalists, greens, pagans, environmentalists or just plain ordinary people who wanted to celebrate nature, solstice, the equinox or traditional holidays of the past. They're harmless and usually oriented toward preserving peace and ending global pollution. We could use more of those kinds of cults, if that's what some want to call them."

"I agree. But we've gotten off track. Let's get back to Oscar Little. He lived with his sisters on some dirt-poor farm, didn't he?"

"Yes. If I remember correctly, we always interrogated him at the sheriff's or state police facilities. I never saw his farm or his sisters. But the record states he lives with his sisters on an old farm in Cumberland County, somewhere close to Cascade Hills, as a matter of fact."

"That's interesting. He's really close to both crime scenes, then?"

"Too close. And I recall he actually butchers his own cattle, sheep and pigs. Runs a small butchering operation for hunters, too. So, he has the experience of slicing up bodies."

"Well, this forensic psychologist will bet money that Oscar Little's a real possibility for the killer. We thought he was good for that homicide last summer and he could be responsible for this Jane Doe. That scum would do anything for money, I think. Even cut up cadavers to steal body parts."

Just then, Bill and Christie heard a car in the driveway.

"Stay right there," Bill said as he moved to the window.

He peered out through the softly falling snow and saw a truck in the driveway.

The sound of the garage door opening hit both Bill and Christie at the same time.

"It's Alex," they said in unison and then laughed together with relief.

"Hey, what's up?" Alex asked when she saw Christie and Bill in the kitchen.

Bill walked with Alex into the family room and related what had happened that evening while Christie cleaned up the coffee cups and prepared the coffee machine for the morning. He reminded Alex about the emergency routine that they had gone over repeatedly in case Scott contacted Christie or showed up at the house.

"I remember the routine fine. But I'm terrified that Christie's so vulnerable here. He can call her. He can drive here. He can follow her. We have to do something. Can't you get her to go somewhere safer?"

"Wait a minute. Remember, we don't have any evidence that Scott actually called. It could have been anyone. The patrol hasn't seen any suspicious cars. And no, I can't get her to move. I've tried. You've tried. Stella practically threw a fit trying to convince her. She won't go and I can't make her. We have to deal with the situation as it is. She has plenty of outside support, the patrols, and the security. She's actually safer here than most places."

A cold feeling of dread enveloped Alex. "He's coming," she said. "I know it."

"We don't know that. We've no indication that Scott's in Maine."

"Don't pull that reassurance bit on me. I don't buy it. Be honest. He's going to come back to kill her, isn't he?"

"I don't know, Alex. I'm doing all I can to prevent that. I need you to help me keep her safe."

Just then, Christie came into the family room. Bill turned to her.

"Well, it's up to you Christie. I'll stay here tonight if you want me to, or I'll drive back to Portland if you two are set for the night."

"I'm all right now, thanks," said Christie. "I just panicked there for a minute. I'm over it now. I just want to go to bed and sleep for about eight hours. We're meeting at nine tomorrow, right?"

"Yep, the three boys are coming in. I really want you to question them, if you feel up to it."

"I'll be there. Really, I'm fine now. Alex, you can show Bill out when you let Tashie out for her night business, can't you? Remember to lock everything up tight and set the alarms. I'm really tired and heading upstairs now. See you tomorrow. And again, thanks for all you did tonight, Bill."

"Sure thing. Good night," said Alex as she walked with Bill to the door.

"Night. See you tomorrow," Bill called.

As they stood outside with the snow swirling all around them, dancing brightly in the surveillance lights, Bill spoke softly to Alex.

"Today, she seemed to handle things pretty well, at least after the autopsy. However, she really freaked out tonight. Got me scared, too, I have to admit."

"Scared, you?"

"Not about the call. But yep, when I saw how broken up Christie was, I got scared. Worried about her. She seemed to bounce back when we started working on the case again. She seemed just fine."

"She can do that. Cover up her feelings by switching away from them into solving a problem or helping someone. Are you two going to be working together everyday? Long days?"

"That's how it usually goes. Especially at the beginning of a case like this. We'll be busy, running around, interviewing, gathering facts and so on. Why?"

"That's good for Christie, a lot of hard work. I guess it might be bad timing, but I was hoping to leave for a few days. I have to go to New York City. I thought if the case tied Christie up with work, she'd be too busy to miss me. I won't be gone long and I have someone to take care of the dog. I thought I might try to convince Christie to stay in town with Stella. Or maybe have someone come out and stay with her."

"Hmm. I don't like her being here by herself."

"To tell you the truth, there's so little interaction between us now, she might as well be here alone. She just reads or goes to bed when she comes home."

"You know what I mean. Someone here just in case."

"I don't like the sound of that. Do you know something you're not telling me?"

"No. No sign of trouble. Even the FBI's certain Scott's still in the south. But Christie thinks he's here. If she were alone for three or four nights, even though she's exhausted from working the case, she might… well, I don't know what she might do."

"So, you're saying I shouldn't go to New York?"

"I certainly can't tell you what to do. However, I think it would be a good idea for Christie to stay in town for the nights you're gone. It'll be hard to convince her, I know. She doesn't like to look needy."

"That's for sure. Look. You think she's safe right now. Right? I wouldn't think of going if she's in danger."

"I don't think there's danger right now. Nothing points to Scott being in Maine. Nothing. I'm not so sure Christie's recovered enough to feel safe, though. That's what I'm concerned about."

"I'll ask her how she feels about me leaving. If she gives any indication she wants me to stay, I will. If not, then I'll try to get her to stay in town or have someone stay out here. How's that?"

"Good. That's good. That should work. Well, I have to get going. Let me know if you're leaving, when and where I can reach you, please. And Alex, I'm glad you've stayed here with Christie these last months. She needed a good friend like you."

"Thanks. I wanted to be here. I want to help in anyway I can."

"You've got your gun, right?"

"Yes," Alex answered.

"You feel all right about using it? You still practice at the range, don't you?"

"Yes." Icy cold shivers ran up Alex's back. She stared

up into the falling snow, blinking as the flakes landed on her long lashes.

"Keep it handy, will you? You never know when you might have to use it. I feel better knowing you could shoot the son of a bitch if he does show up."

17

The world was white and untouched. Snow had covered everything with a sparkling white blanket that hid the brown mud and slush. Evergreen branches dipped toward the ground, occasionally dumping a clump of snow and springing up released from their burden. The skeletal outlines of maples and oaks were clothed in white, dressed for the day. Thick giant clouds, remnants of the storm, huddled on the horizon to the east, moving slowly away. Although spring was officially only a few weeks away, Maine was still mired in winter.

By the time Christie got to the task force offices, plows had cleared the roads, workers had shoveled sidewalks and trucks had spread salt over the streets. A security guard followed her car up to the third level and walked her to the elevator. He rode to the third floor with her, tipped his hat, and rode the elevator back down. Christie was pleased that he completed the process in a quiet and professional manner.

"Hey there, Jenny. How're you doing today?"

"Fine, Dr. McMorrow, umm, I mean Christie. Sorry, it's going to take me a while to get used to calling you Christie. Bill's already in the conference room. He's expecting you."

"Thanks, Jenny." Christie walked toward the conference room where they would meet with the three boys and their parents this morning.

"Hey Bill," Christie said. Bill was reading a report at the large conference table. Christie found this setting much more comfortable and informal than the police interrogation rooms where they usually did their interviews. Setting was important when interviewing witnesses or potential suspects. Today the intention was to gather as much information as possible from the three boys who found the frozen Jane Doe in the woods. A pleasant setting, away from the intimidating police headquarters, would help the boys relax. A relaxed witness remembered more details and usually felt more willing to please the questioner. Christie hoped that would be true today.

Bill looked up. "Hi there. Good to see you. Did you get any sleep?"

"Actually, I did. I was so tired I just dropped off the minute I took my meds and fell on the bed."

What Christie didn't mention to Bill is that she awoke about an hour later and was unable to get back to sleep. Insomnia haunted her. Most nights she lay awake alertly listening for any unusual sound that might indicate that Stephen Scott had managed to invade her home. She wanted to be ready for him.

Bill wondered what meds Christie was talking about. He had never known her to take medication. As far as he knew, a vitamin and an occasional aspirin were the only medications that ever passed her lips. He decided to let her comment pass. If she needed something to help her sleep, he couldn't blame her. She had been through hell and was still lingering near its border.

"Glad you could get the rest. You certainly deserve it and will probably need more after we get through our schedule for today. Sam Grover will be here in a few minutes. He's the kid who actually discovered the body."

"How's he doing? He must have been pretty shook up."

"I think he's going back to school today after the interview. Therefore, my guess is that he's fine. We'll see in a minute. Let's look over his file before he gets here."

Bill read the pertinent facts about Sam Grover aloud. "He's an only child, age 16, two professional parents. His mother works as a dental hygienist; father manages a small box-making business in town. First marriage for both. Sam's an average student, a sophomore in Cascades Regional High School. Fairly good recommendations from teachers who think he could be a better student if he applied himself. Plays junior varsity soccer and baseball. No previous contact with the law. Has a girlfriend. Jim Foster and Brad Philbrick, the other boys at the scene, live close to him and seem to be his best friends. That's about it."

"So no police record. No obvious reason to think he's lying. Any chance that he knew or had something to do with the murdered girl?" Christie asked.

"I don't think so. These boys don't seem the type to do something so heinous. Of course, three boys together could have spotted a young girl and harassed her. Maybe they went too far, got scared and killed her so she wouldn't tell anyone. That's too common an occurrence these days, unfortunately. But skinning her body and taking out her bones and organs? It's very unlikely these boys would do something that brutal. The boys couldn't possibly identify the girl, either, even if they knew her. They couldn't see her face, since it was skinned and disfigured. They all have denied knowing her. No girls are reported missing from their high school or any of the other local schools either since December. Nothing has turned up yet that looks suspicious about these boys. I'm counting on you to decide on whether they're lying or not. We haven't requested a lie detector test. If you think one's justified after talking to them today, we'll request that they each submit to a polygraph test. Of course, they're minors and under no obligation to cooperate."

Bill and Christie looked up as Jenny knocked and poked her head in the door. "Sam Grover, his mother and father and their lawyer, Benjamin Durkin, are here."

Bill groaned. "Complete package. I was afraid of that. Well, we'll just have to make the best of it. Show them in, Jenny, please."

Benjamin Durkin strode through the door briskly, his hand stretched out to shake whomever he reached first. He was an imposing figure, six-feet-five, at least 250 pounds, with bright white hair pulled back into a ponytail that fell halfway down his back. He wore his fifty years well, although Christie was willing to bet that Botox and perhaps some surgery helped retain his youthful looks.

"Good to see you again, Bill. Sorry it's under these ridiculous circumstances, though. I can't understand why you're harassing my client. He and his family have gone through a terribly traumatic time. For God's sake, let them have some peace. This is his fifth questioning in three days."

As he paused for breath, Bill took the opportunity to deflect his aggression and introduced Christie to him. Durkin barely nodded at her and turned back to Bill.

"Well, let's get on with it now that we're here. But you only have thirty minutes. Sam's due back at school today and I don't want him too late. By the way, this is Mr. and Mrs. Grover. They wish to remain with their son during the questioning. Of course, I'll be at his side to advise him."

Bill and Christie introduced themselves to the Grovers and invited them to sit at the conference table next to their son, who had already slumped down in one of the upholstered chairs that lined the table.

Sam Grover was a few inches over six feet tall and his lanky body hung over the edges of his chair, as if he wished he could slide on down under the table. Short brown hair on the sides of his head contrasted with the three-inch long bleached-blond locks that adorned his crown. He wore an earring in his left ear, a stud in the form of a cross, a silver necklace over his black t-shirt, black jeans and a pair of expensive looking Nikes. He looked down at the table, avoiding eye contact. Acne spotted his long face.

"Do you mind if we tape record this meeting?" Bill asked.

Durkin answered quickly, "No recording."

"All right, then, let's get started," Bill said. "My colleague Dr. McMorrow will ask the questions. If you don't object, I'll be taking some notes and may have a few questions of my own. Please, let's not be so formal, so serious. We're not accusing Sam of any crime. He's an important witness who may have crucial evidence that could help solve this crime. We just want a chance to discover all that he knows."

Sam's parents visibly relaxed after hearing Bill's explanation. Sam's mother patted her son's arm, which Sam instantly jerked out of her reach. She smiled at Christie and said, "This has been a horrible experience. Sam's a very sensitive boy and finding that woman's body has really upset him."

Christie leaned forward and smiled at Mrs. Grover and then at Sam. "Of course, this has been very hard on you all. We have just a few things we want to ask and I promise it won't take very long. We want to go over exactly what happened, the precise order of events. Can you tell us, Sam, why you, Jim and Brad decided to go snowmobiling that day?"

Sam glanced at his lawyer. Durkin nodded at him and said, "Go ahead, Sam. If there are any questions I don't want you to answer, I'll let you know."

Sam continued to look at the table as he mumbled, "Just to do something, I guess. We were bored."

"And why did you choose to ride that particular trail instead of another?"

"I don't know. No reason. It was just there."

"Had you been there before?"

Sam hesitated. "No, not really. I mean I haven't snowmobiled there before."

"What do you mean, 'not really'? Had you been in those woods before?"

"Well, yeah. A couple of times. Jim, Brad, and me. Just fooling around. Last summer and sometimes last fall."

"What were you doing in the woods, Sam?"

"Just hanging out. We weren't doing anything wrong. Just walking and talking."

"Just the three of you each time? Anyone else out there with you?"

Sam looked at Durkin. "Do I have to answer this crap? What does any of this have to do with finding that body? I don't see why I have to tell her what I'm doing on my own time."

Durkin said to Christie, "Can't we get on with it? The boy has to get to school. Let's just stick with what happened the other day. What he does with his time is irrelevant."

Sam's mother jumped into the fray. "Stop harassing him, Dr. McMorrow, or we'll just walk right out of here. You have no right to badger him this way."

"I'm sorry," Christie said to the sulky teen. "I certainly didn't intend to scare you, Sam."

"You don't scare me, lady. I could…"

Durkin interrupted Sam before he could say any more. "Let's cut to the quick, Dr. McMorrow."

"Sure," Christie replied. "Tell me in your own words, Sam, what happened that day you found the body."

Thirty minutes later, the Grovers and their lawyer left the office. Bill moved over next to Christie.

"Well, what's your read on this kid? As far as I can tell, his story's consistent. He's said almost the same thing in each interview. His story matches the other boys' reports. And I didn't hear anything new that can help us."

"I don't know. I agree his story seems straightforward and holds together tightly. But there's something else going on with this kid. What's with his attitude? Why was he so nervous about telling us he had been in those woods before? Why so reluctant to talk about what he and the other boys were doing there last summer and fall? Why is he all lawyered up? I think he's hiding something."

"They were probably smoking weed or drinking. He wouldn't want to admit that in front of his parents. But I noticed his tension rate go way up, too. Maybe there's more going on in those woods than he wants us to know."

Christie nodded. "When we talk with Jim, let's play him a little. I'll tell him Sam came clean about what went on in the woods. If Jim thinks we know about it already, he might agree to talk about it."

"Good idea. Worth a try. Let's see what Jim and Brad have to add when they think that Sam has spilled some beans."

"I want to look at the map before we talk to Jim. Where's that aerial photograph of the crime scene?"

Bill looked through the folders and produced a map of the area and the aerial photograph taken by the task force crime scene photographer. Christie and Bill bent over to study them.

"The surveyor I talked to yesterday told me these woods have been owned by the same family for years. Other than cutting off some of the soft wood for the mill and harvesting some of the hardwoods for fuel, they've been left pretty intact. Look, you can see the skid trails in the aerial. They make perfect snowmobile routes in the winter. Right here, at the tip of my pencil, is where the body was found."

"What's this over on the right side of the woods?" asked Christie.

"Oh, that's a private pond. The surveyor thinks the same people own it. See that island in the middle of the pond? I believe that's where the local Boy Scouts' summer campsite used to be. It's very isolated. You can barely make out the dirt road that runs around the pond to a small boat launch. The pond's pretty shallow and the surveyor said it's posted with no trespassing signs."

"And what's this on the other side of the pond? It looks like a small farm."

"Yeah. I didn't ask about that place, but it looks vaguely

familiar. I can check that out later. And then there's state-owned land here, the town well site, and this last bit you can see is a pine forest watershed that grows into the next county."

"The rest of the woods look solid with trees. I can't see any trails there. The trees run right up to this housing development."

"I see that. What are you getting at?"

"Well, if those boys were hanging out in the woods last summer or fall, they most likely were on the trails or near the pond, don't you think? They probably weren't bushwhacking through thick forest. That wouldn't be much fun. They could have run an ATV or bikes down the trails in the summer and fall."

"That seems reasonable. But I don't get your point. I'm not following you."

"They could just be having fun outside, fooling around," Christie began. "But why was Sam so reluctant to tell us? I have a feeling this area might be a regular hangout for kids, maybe drug dealers, maybe worse. It's accessible by the main road to the trails or by the dirt road around the pond and back to the trails. It's private and the police probably never patrol back there. The kids could park their cars on the dirt road and walk in, or bike in, or just party on the road. And the Jane Doe had to get onto that snowmobile trail somehow. Maybe she was brought up the trail that leads from the pond."

"Wait a minute. Wait just a moment. I've just remembered something. I've got it. Hold on just a minute."

Bill turned back to the pile of folders at the end of the conference table. He rustled through a pile of papers in one folder and pulled one paper out.

"My God. I thought something rang a bell. That small farm you pointed out? The one on the other side of the pond? That's where Oscar Little lives with his sisters."

18

Bill and Christie stared at each other. Oscar Little had evaded them last summer when they were investigating him for the murder of a young woman found burned and mutilated. Not enough evidence had emerged to convince the county D.A. to seat a grand jury to indict Little and hold him for trial. Now he had popped up again, living within a few miles of where the boys found the second Jane Doe.

Jenny knocked at the door to announce that Jim Foster and his mother were outside.

"Tell them we'll just be a moment, Jenny, please," Bill said. He turned to Christie.

"We'll have to deal with the Oscar Little factor after these interviews. Can you believe this? I'll bet you dinner he's involved with this Jane Doe in some way, too."

Christie nodded, remembering the snide sneers and dark dead eyes she had encountered last summer during her interrogation of Oscar Little.

"I know you're right. He's a killer. I knew it then and I know it now. This time we'll nail him. Maybe these boys know him. I'll try to work his name into the interview with Jim Foster and see what reaction we get."

Jim Foster arrived at the task force office accompanied only by his mother, a pleasant middle-aged woman who agreed to wait outside while Bill and Christie talked with her son. Both Jim and his mother appeared calm and cooperative and while

Jenny brought coffee to Jim's mother, Bill led Jim into the conference room and closed the door.

Christie smiled at Jim and shook his hand. Jim was good looking, with short dark hair trimmed neatly, thickly lashed brown eyes and a well-toned athletic body. He was dressed neatly in jeans and a buttoned up shirt. He was an "A" honors student, active in student government and described by all his teachers as a gifted and enthusiastic student. His mother was divorced from his father who had remarried and moved out of state. Jim's mother had worked as a bookkeeper for a local business for almost eight years. Jim's record was clean.

"Nice to meet you, Jim," Christie began. "Thanks for coming in and talking with us. I know you have been through questioning several other times and must be pretty bored with the subject, so I'll try to keep it short."

Jim smiled at Christie. "Oh, that's okay. Actually, it's been interesting being involved in a real homicide case. I've watched CSI, Law and Order and all those TV shows about investigating murders. I never thought I'd be a part of one. I'm glad to help. What do you want to know?"

Christie asked him to detail the day the boys went snowmobiling and found the body. His story matched Sam's and was consistent with his other testimony. There were no surprises. Then Christie decided to switch gears.

"Jim, Sam told us you guys spent quite a bit of time in those woods last spring and fall. He told us you all had some pretty wild times out there."

Jim looked shocked. He coughed and looked around the room and then coughed again.

"Could I have something to drink?"

"Sure." Bill walked to the end of the table and poured a glass of water from the pitcher that sat next to the coffee urn and placed it in front of Jim. Jim drank some water, coughed again and then drank the rest of the water. He looked up at

Christie.

"Excuse me. What did you say?"

"I said Sam told us about what went on last summer and fall."

"He did? He told you what we did? I can't believe that. He said that we went with him? What did he actually say?"

Christie knew Jim was trying to delay the questions, side step them so he could figure out what to do. She honed in on him quickly, not giving him the time he needed.

"Jim, he told us what you did. He gave details."

"He told you? I can't believe it. We swore we wouldn't ever say anything. I promised I'd keep my mouth shut."

"Maybe Sam felt it was the right thing to do."

"Geez. I don't know. What did he tell you?"

"I'm not at liberty to release a witness's statement. But it might be a good idea for you to get your side of the story on the record, just in case what you have to say differs from what Sam told us."

"Oh God. I thought I'd never have to tell anyone about this. I wish it had never happened. I don't really trust Sam all that much anymore. Maybe he lied to you."

"Then tell us your version."

Yeah, I guess I better. Sam probably told you that it was Brad and me that knew about the island. But it wasn't. It was him."

"That's what I'm talking about. It's a good thing to get your side of the story down, so there's no confusion about what you did, what you knew. You know what I mean?"

"Yes. But, I don't want to break my promise. I really don't want to talk about what happened at all. It's embarrassing. Really awful. But if Sam already told you, then I guess I better tell my side of it, like you said." Jim put his head down on the table and covered it with his hands.

Christie and Bill waited, knowing that silence would

eventually help Jim to speak out. People with secrets would often hold on to them when questioned, but spill them in the anxiety of long silences.

"It was all his idea. Sam's. Brad and me, I mean, Brad and I, didn't even know what he was up to. We just thought we were going to the pond to fool around. Swim, catch frogs, throw stuff. You know what I mean?"

"I do. You thought you were just going to hang out, play a little. But it turned out differently, didn't it?"

"Yeah. We didn't know what went on there. If I had known, I wouldn't have gone, I swear. I'm sorry I ever went. I don't know why I ever went back the second time. I only went twice. I refused to go back after that. I'm pretty ashamed of myself."

Christie waited, giving Jim a chance to continue. He looked devastated, remembering whatever had happened last summer and fall. She didn't want to push him too hard, afraid that he would either clam up or fall apart.

"You didn't go back, so that's a good thing, right?" she encouraged him.

"I think Sam went back again, though. I think he'd been there lot of times before he took us. I don't know about Brad, but I'm pretty sure he hadn't ever been there either. I doubt he ever went back after the second time. I never talked about it with either one of them after last fall. When we snowmobiled we stayed away from the pond and only used the woods' trails. When we found the body, I was afraid that maybe it had come from there."

"From where?" Christie urged.

"From the pond, the island. Where the girls were."

Bill intervened. "Go back a few steps, will you Jim? You're doing a good job, but I missed a few things. You, Sam and Brad visited the island last summer and then again last fall, right? There were some girls there. Then what?"

Jim said, "As I was saying, one night Sam said he had a surprise for us on the island. We rowed out there and in the clearing near the old Boy Scouts' camp, a big fire was roaring. Some girls drinking booze invited us to join them. I swear I didn't know the girls were going to be there or who they were. They weren't from our school. I thought they might be from another town, having a slumber party or something. We thought it would be cool to have a few drinks. It seemed like fun, at least at the beginning."

"Then what happened"

"Well, do I really have to tell you everything? It's kind of embarrassing."

"No, but if you don't fill us in, then Sam's testimony is the only one on record."

"Okay, but this is really hard."

"Take your time, Jim. Do you want some more water?"

"Yes, please." Jim drank another whole glass of water and then ran his fingers around the rim of the glass as he talked.

"I guess I just better get it over with. My mother can't hear through that door, can she? She doesn't have to know, does she?"

"No, she can't hear and what you say in here is confidential unless we need to use it in court or to indict someone. So don't worry. Your mother won't hear anything from us."

"Okay. Here goes. Well, we drank a lot, more than I realized at the time. The next thing I knew I was alone with four girls. Sam and Brad had disappeared and so had the other girls. I was really drunk. I remember wondering if they had put some drug in my drink, 'cause I was so dizzy and sleepy, too. But I was too messed up to do anything about it. Later, I thought maybe they put that date rape stuff in my drinks because of what happened next."

"What happened, Jim?"

"Well, the girls were all over me. It was crazy. I was so

drunk I could hardly move. I've never had anything like this happen to me before. They took off my clothes. I tried to stop them, but I couldn't even raise my arms. They felt like lead. And four girls were stronger than me. Then, I remember that they started touching me, messing around with me. I can't remember it too well, but I think I had sex with some of them. I don't know how many. It's all fuzzy. Then I must have passed out. When I woke up, Sam, Brad and I were off the island and back at the launch dock. I don't know how we got there."

"So you were off the island. What happened next?"

"We stumbled back to our bikes and rode home. We didn't talk about it at all, not that night and not the next day, either. I was too embarrassed. Maybe they were too. I don't know. I wondered what happened to them. If it was the same thing hat happened to me. But they never said anything, so I didn't either. It's kind of hard to admit that some girls took control of you."

"You said you went to the island twice."

"Oh God. I can't believe I went out there again."

"What happened the second time?"

"Sam told us the girls would be there again. I didn't want to go because I hated what had happened the first time. Don't get me wrong. I like sex and all that, but it felt so wrong somehow. What those girls did to me. And in the fall, I had a girlfriend I was pretty serious about and didn't feel right having sex with someone else. But Sam said he would tell my girl I cheated on her if I didn't go, so I went. I didn't want to take the chance of losing her."

"And what happened this time?"

"The same thing happened as before. Except maybe, I wasn't so drunk as before. I didn't want to pass out like last time. After all the sex, I just lay there, pretending to be asleep, and watched the girls. They didn't seem very drunk. They were huddled around the fire and they looked so, I don't know, unhappy or something. They weren't having a good time like I had thought before. I remember thinking maybe they were just pretending to have fun."

"What made you think that, Jim?"

"Well, some of them were crying. Then I noticed that they were younger than I thought. At first they had looked like older girls, you know, my age or older, all made up and dressed real cool. But when I paid attention to them that second night, I could see they were only kids, just like 10 or 12. I couldn't believe they were so young. I felt sick to my stomach. I couldn't believe I had sex with such young girls. I was so ashamed."

Jim put his hands over his face and bent down, crying. "I'm so sorry. I wish I had never gone."

Christie said, "Jim, you didn't know. You had too much to drink and you didn't expect your friend Sam to get you involved with such a bizarre event."

"But I went back again. I knew then what was going on, only I didn't know those girls were so young. If I had known I never would have gone back, no matter what Sam threatened to do."

"I believe you, Jim. What did you do that second time when you discovered that the girls were so young?"

"I wanted to tell them I was sorry, but I didn't know any of them. We were never introduced, like by names. When I went over to them, they backed away from me. They looked scared and they didn't seem to understand me. I don't think they understood much English. I heard some of the girls speaking some other language. Not French or German, because I take those languages in school. Maybe some Slavic or Russian language."

Jim paused to take a breath. The information had exploded out of him like lava gushing from a red-hot magnum core. He started to cry again.

"I didn't know they were so young. My little sister is

older than some of them. I couldn't tell anyone. I feel so bad."

"Did you ever go back?"

"No! No. The next time Sam asked I refused to go. My girlfriend and I had broken up, so Sam didn't have any way to make me go and I wouldn't have gone anyway, no matter what he threatened me with or what he called me. I didn't care. I wasn't going to do that again, not with little kids. We, Sam, Brad and I, aren't really close anymore. I feel creepy around them now."

"Did you see any other people out there? Any adults?"

"No. Just the girls around the fire. But I passed out the first time and was pretty drunk the second time, too. I don't remember everything that happened. Someone got us to the launch, the first time, so there could have been other people. The second time, we made it to the launch ourselves. It's just a small island and there are only a couple of buildings on it. I never thought anyone used it except the Scouts. I don't know how the girls got on and off the island. There weren't any boats at the launch except the one we used."

"Do you know a man named Oscar Little?" Christie asked Jim.

"No. There's a kid name Jeremy Little in the ninth grade, but I don't know anybody else named Little."

"Jim, you've been very helpful," Bill said. "Thanks for helping us out. We might have to call you back later, if that's all right with you."

"Yeah, that would be okay, I guess."

"I would strongly suggest that you keep what you said here to yourself. Don't tell Sam or Brad what you have told us, please. I'm telling you to keep your testimony confidential. If you tell anyone about it, it may leak back to the press and I don't think you want that to happen. If you don't tell anyone, you might be better protected from stories appearing in the papers about your behavior last summer and fall."

"Oh God. What would I do if that happened? Everyone would know. That would be so humiliating. My poor mother would die or maybe she would kill me. I won't tell anyone, I promise."

"Besides, we don't want to release this information publicly because we're not sure it's relevant to the crime. It may be helpful, but we just don't know. Please be assured we won't use any of this information unless we have to. If you think of anything else that might help us, please call the number on this card."

Jim stood up. "I'm not in any trouble am I? That body didn't come from the island did it? I didn't get anyone pregnant, did I? I know I didn't use anything, you know, condoms or anything. That's the first thing I thought about when I woke up the next day. Well, actually it was the second thing. My first thought was what if I got some disease from those girls, you know, AIDS or warts or crabs? I was really worried for a while. I even went for an HIV test. Thank God that turned out okay."

"You're not in trouble, Jim. We're just trying to identify the body you boys found and looking for any information that can lead us to what happened to her and who she is. You've been a great help. Thank you. You can go now."

19

Stephen decided he had waited long enough. Spring was on its way and people who summered on the lakes and ponds would be returning soon to open their camps, even though the ice still hadn't melted off the pond. The little hole he had chopped to get his drinking and wash water barely froze over at night now. The snow had receded and bare spots were growing in size everyday. It was time to move on.

His plan was perfect. He had every detail worked out. He had the timing down. He had finalized his escape route. He would release Dr. McMorrow as she deserved and be on his way to his next mission. By this time next week, he would be tanning in Florida and looking for a woman walking on the beach to select for his next mission. He was back on track.

He had read about the girl's body found frozen in the woods not far from the cabin where he was staying. The Portland newspaper had mentioned that Dr. McMorrow was working on the case with Detective William Drummond, the same man who had bullied him in the hospital, trying to get him to talk. Stephen contemplated killing them both and placing their bodies in sexually explicit positions to validate his truth about the sinfulness of women. The media would report Dr. McMorrow had seduced the detective on the job. Stephen's letter to the editor of the Portland paper would report statistics on the rise in the number of work-site affairs, now that women filled offices and every business employed them. He would make his point clear. Working women caused faithful hard-working men to forgo their marriage vows and jeopardize their careers. The community would remember Dr. McMorrow as a seducing harlot rather than a reputable psychologist. Only one small jump from that conclusion to the next, that Dr. McMorrow deserved to die for her sins. He would validate God's truth once again.

Stephen drove to the Portland library on Congress Street. He went to the bank of computers and slipped on a pair of double latex gloves. He wrote his letter to the editor of the Portland Press Herald. He signed the letter Jack Kittering, from Grant, Maine knowing the paper required signatures before publishing a letter. He printed a copy, retrieved it from the printer, signed it, and stuffed it into the self-seal envelope he had already addressed. He affixed an adhesive stamp and mailed the letter at the mailbox outside the library front doors.

Satisfied, Stephen tore off the gloves and strolled down Congress Street until he located the family restaurant he had frequented last fall. He was looking forward to a crusty chicken potpie, a tall glass of ice-cold milk and a piece of apple pie with a scoop of vanilla ice cream. Then he would do some shopping for items he would need for the mission.

Stephen enjoyed his dinner and felt very pleased with himself as he walked down Congress Street toward his old truck. He was excited about the upcoming event and confident once more. For a while after the police shot, arrested and hospitalized him, his confidence wavered. After his escape from the hospital and Portland and while he was recovering in his safe place in the Atlanta area, he slowly regained his belief in his ability to carry out the missions for which his uncle had trained him. Now he had all the optimism and faith he needed. He was working for God again.

The first part of his plan was simple. He went over it in his mind often. He would not be using a journal to record his detailed plans. He would not record this mission with photographs pasted in scrapbooks as he had previously. The selection and releasing of Dr. McMorrow and Detective Drummond was the finalization of an old mission, not a new one. He would begin journaling and photographing again on his first mission in Florida.

He knew the headlight flash code to gain access to Dr. McMorrow's home. He knew her unlisted number. He knew what car she drove. He followed her to the task force building and knew where she parked her car. Although guards and cameras secured the parking garage, Stephen knew ways around all types of security devices. He also knew where Dr. McMorrow's new office was and where she parked there. He had bypassed the tight security in the lobby of the building and had taken the elevator to the floor where Dr. McMorrow rented her office. He knew everything he needed to know about her routines: doctor's visits, physical therapy and psychotherapy sessions, the grocery store where she shopped, the address of her friend Stella, the time the post office driver delivered mail to her roadside mailbox and everything else that might be relevant to the satisfactory completion of this mission. Uncle Luke had trained Stephen to be thorough. Attention to detail and obsessive planning had enabled him to successfully complete over one hundred missions so far. Although he had made some necessary changes, he had kept true to the basics he had learned.

He stopped in Home Depot and purchased ten 2"x 6" boards, nails, a coil of nylon rope, a roll of wire, a 4'x 4' piece of wire mesh, duct tape, several heavy-duty large batteries and a battery operated halogen spotlight. He drove to True Value Hardware and obtained some paint rags, straps with tightening devices and hooking latches, and several long-handled butane lighters. He bought five white rats from the Pet Smart Supermarket store near the Mall, along with a cage and a bag of pellets to feed them. Then he headed back to his cabin.

20

Bill and Christie waited until the door closed behind Jim and then both started to talk at once.

"My God. What's going on out there?" Christie asked. She was pacing around the conference table.

Bill answered, "If it's what I think it is, the pieces are starting to come together." He started gathering up the piles of folders.

Christie stopped walking and stared at Bill. "Jim said they were just kids, pre-teens some of them. Drinking, drugging and having group sex."

"I know and I'm pretty sure that what he's describing may be a child sex ring operating over at the pond site. Very young girls, speaking a foreign language, servicing men with alcohol and sex, in a secluded spot. It sounds like a brothel set-up using victims of human trafficking."

"Human trafficking? Here? I thought that happened mostly in Asian countries, not here."

"Unfortunately, the trafficking of humans happens here, too. I read a report from the State Department recently that estimates that over 20,000 people, mostly women, young girls and boys, are smuggled into the U.S. illegally each year. The traffickers purchase, lure or abduct their victims and force them into prostitution, pornography, and other labor. They make a lot of money from selling their services."

"That's inhuman, Bill! It's modern day slavery! Imagine

having your child stolen and knowing that traffickers will force her into sexual slavery!"

"I can't even begin to. If anything like that happened to my two kids, I don't know what I'd do. Things like that aren't supposed to happen. But they do and are happening more every day. The human trafficking industry is growing fast. It's third highest on the global list of criminal acts. Based on Jim's description, these girls meet the criteria of extreme victimization."

Christie started to put on her coat. "I don't want to believe it could be happening here. Those poor girls. However, unlike our Jane Doe, at least they're still alive. Let's go out and find them before it's too late."

"Hold on. We can't just run out with the task force and raid the island on the word of one teenage boy. And what Jim reported happened last year, then three or four months later. That's a long time ago. A lot could have changed since then. Maybe they aren't there anymore. We need evidence. We need collaboration of Jim's story. Maybe he's not telling the truth. And there's something about his story that bothers me."

Christie finished buttoning her coat and started to slip on her leather gloves. "But he could be telling the truth and every minute we do nothing about it, those girls are suffering, maybe dying. It hurts to think of what they're going through. We can't wait. We have to do something."

"Wait. Think a minute. Those boys weren't charged money. Why would they get away without paying? That doesn't make sense. Brothels and prostitution rings are out to make money, especially if they offer very young girls or virgins. Why did the boys get free liquor and sex?"

Christie stood still. Then she pulled off her leather gloves. "I don't know, but I'm sure there's a reason. You realize our Jane Doe could have been one of those girls?"

"Yeah, I was thinking that same thing. If it's a child sex

syndicate, maybe she wouldn't cooperate or tried to run and they killed her. Sometimes the ring leaders select a few of their victims to kill in front of the others, as an example of what would happen to them if they don't do what they are told."

Christie slumped down into a chair and started to unbutton her coat. "I knew our Jane Doe suffered at the hands of some monster. These traffickers are the scum of the earth."

"If Jim's story is true, we're going to be facing off against the bottom feeders of the criminal world. Stolen body parts, child sexual exploitation, human trafficking, murder of a young girl, maybe two if we find reason to include last summer's Jane Doe as a part of this investigation."

"What about contacting the FBI?"

"I'll do that right away. Let's see if they know about any trafficking cases in Maine."

Jenny knocked on the door and announced that Brad Philbrick and his parents were outside.

"Tell them it will be just a moment. We're almost through here," said Bill. When Jenny left he turned to Christie. "Let's see if Brad tells us the same story Jim did. If he does, that will support Jim's testimony and strengthen our case for FBI cooperation. Just do what you did before. You were brilliant."

Christie stood up, removed her coat and flung it over the back of the chair. "Thanks. It feels good to be working again and to see that I haven't lost all of my old skills."

"You haven't lost anything. It's all there. Just needs some working out and some time."

Christie nodded. "Thanks again. I appreciate you saying that." They exchanged smiles. "Now let's call Brad in."

An hour later, the questioning completed, Christie and Bill determined that Jim's story had been true, at least based on what Brad had reported. Jim and Brad cited similar experiences. Both were either drugged or ingested large quantities of alcohol. Both recalled being barely conscious and overtaken by several girls who engaged in sex with them. Both boys reported that the girls were very young, between 10 to13 years old. Brad didn't remember how they got off the island the first time, either, nor had he seen any other people there. The girls didn't ask him for any money. Brad thought the girls were just partying, not soliciting, since no one asked him to pay. He, too, worried about the ages of the girls and refused to go back when Sam invited him the third time. Neither boy had remained close friends with Sam and only occasionally hung out with him, as they did on the day they went snowmobiling and found the frozen body.

"That's enough for me. I'm calling the FBI now." Bill called Dave Hadley, the task force liaison with the FBI and arranged a meeting with him for tomorrow.

"Well, we have several choices now. Grab lunch and go over the final autopsy report that Atwood just faxed over or grab lunch and try to set up another session with Sam Grover to see if we can get more information out of him. Obviously, he knows more than he indicated to us. But, his lawyer could be a problem. Or we could head up to Oscar Little's farm and talk with him. What do you want to do, Christie?"

"No question. I want to look that bastard in the eye and see how he reacts to us. I have a feeling he's in this up to his neck."

"My choice as well. We can stop at the Cumberland Diner in Grant on our way up. Cheap and fast."

"Perfect," said Christie. "Some nice hot food to energize us for our discussion with the butcher of Cumberland Country."

21

During the ride to Grant, Christie and Bill discussed the weather and road conditions. The day was gloomy. Occasional showers of sleet and snow spat down, making driving difficult. They passed several cars which had fishtailed off the highway.

"Pretty dangerous out here," Christie commented as they hit a stretch of ice and the car slid sideways.

Bill steered into the skid and the car straightened out. "I've seen a lot worse. Now, if it were really snowing and blowing, with these cold conditions, we'd have us a blizzard. Then driving gets to be quite a challenge."

"I don't mind the snow, but I hate the cold. Winter seems too hard when it gets this cold. What is it, anyway? 10, 12 degrees?"

"Colder, last time I heard the weather report. The temperature's supposed to drop even lower when the sun sets. We'll be well below zero tonight."

"Brrrrr. Glad I have a warm fireplace to sit in front of at home. Do you want to…?" Christie's voice stopped. Then she asked, "How far to the restaurant?"

She had almost broken her own boundary. She was going to ask Bill if he wanted to come to her house after work and sit in front of the fire with a glass of wine. Just in time, she had caught herself. For a moment she had envisioned herself and Bill together, talking and laughing, enjoying being inside where they could ignore the freezing cold outside.

"Just a few miles. What were you starting to say?"

"Nothing. Just wondering what you were going to order at the diner."

"Oh, I thought... Well, I don't know, maybe a big burger. What about you?"

Bill took his eyes off the highway and looked at Christie. She was looking out the window now. He was struck again by how much he was attracted to her. It wasn't just her classical beauty that drew him. He liked the way they fit intellectually and how they could laugh one minute and then switch to analytical problem solving mode the next. However, sometimes, a silence would stand between them, pushing them each into their own space. He hadn't been able to get to know that silent Christie, but he wanted to. Only rarely could he predict what Christie was going to say or do, for that matter. That was part of what intrigued him.

Communication with his wife had been different. They knew each other so well they would finish each other sentences. Sometimes, they didn't even need to do that. He'd hand her a book or a gardening tool and she'd say, 'Thanks, how'd you know I was looking for that?'

After eighteen years of marriage and two children, they were still in love when doctors diagnosed her with breast cancer. It had been almost three years since Emmy's death and he still missed her immensely. He missed the smell and feel of her and resented the changes that came with being a widower. He hated living alone. He'd been in therapy the last five months, working to put closure on his grieving and starting to understand the importance of moving on with his life. He wanted Christie to be part of the moving-on process. But he had learned in therapy that he needed to be patient while Christie moved through her own recovery. His therapist suggested he work on his own issues and wait until she indicated she wanted more. He hoped that day would come soon. He had thought she was going to ask him back to her place just a moment ago, but she had cut her words off and him, too.

When Bill couldn't stand the silence any longer he said, "If you feel up to it, I'd like you to take the lead with Little and help me get a read on him. We both feel he's involved with this case somehow, but as of now, the only link is his proximity to the crime scene. The police haven't pulled him in for anything since we talked to him last year. He's stayed clean, not even a traffic citation."

"I'll lead. Not that I want to get that close to his ugly face and those eyes again. But if he's linked to abusing and killing kids, I want to be in on getting him."

They stopped at the Cumberland Diner and then drove on to Dalton, where Oscar Little lived. Bill had the car heater humming and the defroster blowing to keep the windshield clear of ice and still Christie shivered in the front seat as they approached the turnoff to Little's.

"No one's been here before, right? Didn't we make Little report to task force headquarters for interrogation?" Christie asked.

"He came to Sheriff Wood's office and state police headquarters. But you're right that nobody's been to his farm. That's why I didn't recognize his location on the map right away. I knew his farm was up here somewhere. When we visited the crime site last summer, we were less than a mile from Little's, but on another route. I can't wait to see what kind of a place he lives in."

"How do you want me to approach him? I could play him several different ways."

"Yeah, I've been thinking about that. The tough cop approach I used last year got me nowhere."

"I didn't do any better with the 'let's clear our conscience and confess' angle either. Stroking his ego didn't help. I couldn't reach him. I think he's an emotionless sociopath, no conscience, cares about no one but himself."

"Then how should we deal with him?"

"I'm going to try undermining his ego, his accomplishments, and his intellect. Treating him as if he's too stupid to have committed such a crime. I'm thinking I'll say something like we just want to talk to him because he's been in this area so long, he might have heard something."

"That's a plan. Maybe he'll get mad and start to boast a little and give something away. You start and I'll jump in if you need me. Just give me a glance and I'll pick up where you leave off. Okay?"

Bill slowed the SUV as they turned off Route 33 onto a roughly plowed driveway marked by a shot-pocked mailbox tipped almost to the ground. Faded letters spelled "Little".

"Sounds good. God, this driveway's bumpy. What's under all the snow? A boulder belt, moguls for snowmobile jumping?"

Bill was gripping the wheel, trying to keep the big four-wheel drive SUV on the narrow winding road that led to Little's farm. "I think he might be trying to discourage visitors. They'd need a tank or a Hummer to get through here any season other than winter. At least the snow fills in some of the holes."

Christie gripped the armrest and tried to keep her head from bumping the ceiling of the vehicle when the SUV bounced from one pothole to the next. Sometimes they landed on two or three wheels after plunging into a hole or jerking out of one.

"We aren't going to tip over are we? Can't you go slower?"

"If I slow down any more, I'll lose our momentum and we could get stuck. I don't want to be on foot around here. We must be almost a mile from the main road. His house has to be up around that next curve. Just hold on."

"Believe me, I am. At least I've forgotten how cold I am. I'm actually working up a sweat."

As they fishtailed and bumped around the next curve, they could see the Little farm in front of them. An old two-story farmhouse sat in the middle of a clearing, white paint adhering only in little strips and patches here and there over weatherworn wooden clapboards. The front porch sagged and needed repair. A rusty chain mesh fence stretched across the front yard and angled toward the back of the house, surrounding it.

Like many old New England farmhouses, a long ell attached to the house joined the huge barn set in back. At one time, the barn had been red but now the red had faded from seasons of sun and harsh winters had stripped the paint off most of the warping boards. The barn was beginning to "lean towards Sawyers" as the old expression went and several windows on the second and third floors were broken and stuffed with cloth. The huge barn doors looked like they would never slide open again.

Rusted farm machinery, parts of old pickup trucks and cars, corroded oil barrels, piles of snow-covered twisted, rusted out iron and other debris littered the space around the house and barn. A new Chevy Silverado sat shining in the driveway.

Bill stopped the SUV, but left the engine and heater running. "They built big houses in the old days. There must be fifteen rooms in that place, if you count the ell. Look at that, five chimneys. Three of them are working; smoke's coming out. At least there's some heat in there."

"It sure could use some help. Terrible to let an old place like this get so run down. What a mess of junk."

"Look, don't get distracted. Keep your eyes open in there. See what you can pick up from stuff that's around."

Just then, the front door slammed open and four barking dogs, two huge pit bulls and two massive Rotweillers, came charging toward the car.

"Thank God for that fence," Christie said just before all four dogs squeezed through a cut in the fence and raced toward the SUV.

"Get away, down, get down," screamed Bill and Christie as the dogs jumped up, clawing and gnashing their teeth at the windows. Their claws scratched at the glass and sides of the doors, making loud screeching noises that added to the chaos of the non-stop barking and growling. Two dogs jumped up on the hood of the car and came snarling at the windshield, teeth slashing, foam and drool dripping from their jowls. They wore thick leather collars with long metal barbs sticking out. They thrust themselves against the windshield again and again.

"They're going to break the windshield! The silver things on their collars are chipping the glass. Do something. Put the car in gear. Let's get out of here," Christie yelled.

"The car's running, but we aren't leaving. No pack of dogs is going to scare me away. I'll shoot them if I have to."

Bill hit the horn and the siren at the same time. The dogs stopped for a moment and looked around. Bill took his gun from its holster and slid in a clip. Before he finished, the dogs renewed their attack on the front window with even greater fury. They were determined to get in.

"Bill, do something. That window isn't going to hold much longer. There's a crack starting over here."

"Hold tight. I'm going to back up, then go forward, and try to shake them off. Maybe I'll run over a few if I'm lucky."

Bill jammed the SUV into reverse and with tires spinning, gunned the gas. The backward movement shook two dogs to the ground. Bill quickly slid into drive and rammed the car forward. Instantly, the dogs jumped back on the hood.

Bill slammed into reverse again. One dog grabbed a windshield wiper in his jaws and held on. The other fell off to the side and they felt a bump as the SUV rolled over it.

"Oh God, I think you hit it," Christie yelled. The dog holding on to the windshield wiper was only inches from Christie's face. His yellow eyes glared into hers. They heard squealing and yelping from the dog they had hit.

The dog on the hood jumped off. The other two dogs ran to the side of the injured dog. All three dogs started snarling and nipping at the wounded dog.

"They're going to kill it. What kind of dogs are these? They're going to kill one of their own."

"At least they're not trying to kill us right now," Bill answered. "Better it than us."

The door of the house opened again. A medium-sized man, dressed in a grimy red and black checkered jacket, an equally foul matching wool cap, stained farm overalls, and big filth-covered work boots, stepped out. Dried blood splattered his face and spotted the ratty stubble on his chin and neck. He was holding a shotgun aimed at the windshield of the SUV.

22

"Git off of my property. Git now or I'll shoot them windows out and the dogs'll take you."

Bill rolled his window down no more than two inches and yelled, "I'm Detective William Drummond, Maine State Task Force on Violent Crimes. I'm here on official business to see Oscar Little. I'm warning you. Put down that gun. If you assault a state officer, you'll be in very serious trouble."

The man continued to point his gun at Bill and Christie. "I'm Little. You hurt one of my dogs. You'd no call to do that. I'd kill you just for that. Up around here, someone kills your dog, they don't live long enough to brag about it. I'm not feelin' too inclined to do what you said, Mr. Detective dog killer. How do I know you're who you say? Show me some identification. Come out with your badge where I can see it."

Bill pulled his identification folder out and flipped it open. He turned off the car's engine and rolled up his window.

"Bill, don't be foolish. Don't go out there. He might shoot you. The dogs are all around the car. They're so worked up they'll attack you like they attacked that other dog, if you get out."

Just then, one of the dogs jumped up on Bill's door, dirty yellow fangs scraping the glass. Bill leaned back toward Christie and stared at the enraged dog.

"I think you're right. I'll have to get him to call off the dogs."

Bill rolled his window down one inch. He could smell the rancid breath of the dog as he leaned toward the crack in the window and yelled,

"Call off the dogs. Put them inside. Then I'll come out and show you my identification."

Oscar Little watched as the three dogs renewed their attack on the SUV. He stood smiling as the dogs thrust themselves against the car doors harder and more furiously, working up into a foaming rage. Then he slowly lowered his gun and gave two short whistles to the dogs. Instantly the three dogs leaped on the hood of the car and starting attacking the windshield again. They ripped the wipers off the car. The crack inched its way across the glass from the passenger side toward the middle as the dogs scratched, banged their bodies against the glass, and tried to chew it open.

"Do something. Shoot them. They'll be in here in a minute," cried Christie.

Just then, Little let out a long shrieking whistle. The dogs leaped off the car, ran for the chain-link fence and squeezed back in. They jumped up on the front porch and surrounded Little, wagging their tails and panting. Little whistled one more time. Bill and Christie watched the fourth dog limp toward the house, dragging her back leg on the ground. Slowly, she crawled through the fence and then on her belly inched her way up to the porch steps and lay there exhausted.

Little bent down and looked the dog over. He kicked her once lightly, turning her on her side so he could examine her leg. The dog whined and looked up at Little. Little stood back up, aimed his gun and shot the dog in the head. He stepped back up on the porch and let the other three dogs into the house. Then pointing his gun at the SUV he yelled,

"Now git out with your badge held high so I can see it."

Bill unzipped his parka, slid his gun into the back of his pants, and opened the door, holding his hand up with the identification folder.

"Okay. I'm coming out. Don't let those dogs out and put that gun down now, please. I'm not here to cause trouble. We just want to talk with you."

Little stepped down off the porch, kicked the dead dog aside and walked toward the gate in the fence. He bent and punched some numbers into a metal pad next to the gate. Then he flipped a switch connected to a steel box. Bill heard a buzz and then a click. Little opened the gate and closed it behind him. He stood there and waited for Bill.

Christie opened her door and stepped out of the SUV. She stayed close to the side of the vehicle while she watched Bill close the distance between Little and himself. He walked slowly on the slippery icy surface of the rutted driveway, but kept moving his eyes between Little and the front door as he walked. When he was just out of reach, Bill stopped and handed his identification toward Little. Christie waited for Little to acknowledge Bill's authority before she started walking toward the men.

Little hesitated and then took a step forward and grabbed the folder. He looked at it and back at Bill.

"Git her over here, too."

"She's got bad legs, an accident. She doesn't do too well on ice or snow."

"Well, if you want to talk to me, she's got to come over here. I want to see her face."

"All right. But you have to guarantee, no dogs. I swear if you let them out, I'll shoot them. I'll go back and help her over."

Bill walked back to the car and stood looking down at Christie.

"He wants you there. He remembers us from last summer. I don't like this situation at all. Too many variables, the dogs, no back up, he's got the gun. Someone in the house could let those dogs out. I could probably shoot a couple of them before they reach us, but I'm not sure I'd get them all before one of them got us. Little's sure to shoot back if I gun down his dogs. I don't want you to come over. I'll handle the questions, or we can come back another time with back up and a warrant."

"Stop it Bill. Stop protecting me. We're here now and Little's standing right there. He's lowered the gun. The dogs are inside. He seems to be calming down a little. I'll be fine and we agreed that I'd take the lead. I'm better at getting him to talk than you. After all, he doesn't think women are good for more than, well you know, so he isn't as defensive with me. If all hell breaks out, if those damn dogs get out, shoot them. I'll go for Little's gun. At the least, I can keep him busy until you finish with the dogs. Two's better than one, in this case. Let's go."

"I've got a bad feeling about this. I don't want you to get hurt."

"If we're going to work together you have to trust that I can back you up, that I'm strong enough to handle myself. If you don't, then I shouldn't be working with you like this."

"I trust you, Christie, you know that. It's just…"

"Just what, Bill?" Christie's voice hardened with anger. "My scarred up hands can't hold a gun well enough? My swollen feet can't outrun mad dogs? You don't feel safe with me? Tell me, Bill? What's your problem?"

Bill looked over at Little. He looked back at Christie. "Nothing, no problem. Come on. Be careful; it's slippery."

Bill and Christie walked slowly over to Oscar Little.

"Well, howdy do, pretty Doc. You just standin' over there by that big car, I thought maybe you don't want to talk with me even though you'd come all this way out here. And after all those nice long talks we had last summer. I'd not set the dogs on the car if I knewed you was in there. How're you doin', Doc?"

"I'm just fine, Oscar. How are you?"

"Well, just now I'm pretty pissed, excuse the French, Doc, over losin' one of my dogs. Them dogs is trained from birth. Took a lot of work and effort. Now I got to find me another one. I just think maybe the state should pay me for killin' my dog, whadda you think, Mr. Detective?"

"Mr. Little, we just have a few questions to ask you about a case we're working on. Do you think we could get out of the cold and go inside? I think we'd all be a lot more comfortable," Bill said.

"I don't know about that, Mr. Detective. Better think twice on that idea. My dogs is in there and I think they might not like havin' them's sister's killer comin' in and all. So, we'd better just stay put out here. What do ya wanna know?"

Christie started. "We'll keep this short, Oscar. Down the road a bit, in the woods over in Cascade Hills, some boys found a young woman's body. She doesn't have any identification and we're trying to find someone who might know her or know of a missing girl, around 11 to14 years old, five feet tall, thin, some bad teeth. Does that sound like anyone you know?"

"You tryin' to pin this on me, too?"

"Not at all, Oscar. We believe the killer of this girl was very smart, well organized and very exploitive. We just wanted to ask you if you might know of any girl who's missing or heard anyone talking about the killing."

"You sayin' I ain't smart enough to kill some girl?"

"Well, Oscar. I don't know, but the condition of this body indicates that her killer had some sophistication."

"I might be smarter than you think, Doc. I don't know nothin' 'bout that sophistication stuff, but with all your education and fancy degrees, you didn't git very far with me last summer, now, did you? So, I might just be smarter than you, right?"

Little laughed, a high sneering chuckle, his breath making fog puffs in the frigid air.

"It's true you didn't confess to killing and burning that

victim. Of course, that doesn't mean you didn't do it. Nevertheless, I'm not here to talk about last summer. Today I'm looking for information about this latest killing. Do you know anything about this murder?"

"No Doc. I'm not 'sophisticated' enough." He chuckled again, showing broken black stubs where his teeth used to be.

Christie bit her tongue to keep from spitting out her frustration.

"Well, have you heard anything about a missing girl?"

"Nope. Sure haven't. Gotta picture?"

Bill pulled the enhanced photo from his pocket. "This is an artist's rendering of what she might look like." He handed it to Little.

Little studied the picture. "Nope. Never seen her. What all happened to her?"

Christie answered, "She was murdered. We can't give out any more information than that. We think her killer may be from around here. Have you heard anyone talking about hurting a girl, or heard of any girl that has gone missing or ran away, say in the last three to five months?"

"Hmmm. I guess you're just gonna keep askin' that same ol' question until I git you an answer or we all freeze to death. You better be puttin' some warm overalls on them pretty legs of yours, Doc. You gotta be feelin' mighty cold."

"Thanks for your concern, but I'm just fine. Could you answer the question?"

"Well, there was that tart Nancy Lee Jones who rode off with that vacuum salesman two years ago. But she wasn't thin, no sir, not thin a'tall. Other than that, I don't know nothin' about no missin' girl. Bad teeth you said. Up here, we all got rotten teeth. Not a dentist except down Portland way and who'd want to go there? Why'd you come here to ask me? Ain't there folks closer to Cascade Hills than me?"

"Oscar, you told us last summer that you and your sisters

have lived out here a long time. We thought you'd probably know everyone or know who to ask. Do you think we could talk with your sisters?"

"Nope. They don't talk to no strangers. I'm the one you ask, you're right on that, pretty lady. And if I don't know, then no one does, 'cept the killer who'd be keeping it all to hisself or be long gone by now. I bet he skipped town. Maybe you should be lookin' for missing killers, don't you think? You already got that missin' girl, why waste time on her?"

While Little laughed at his own cleverness, Christie glanced at Bill. He nodded and said, "Mr. Little, thanks for your time. Since you've been somewhat cooperative today, I'll see what I can do to get some compensation for your dog. Probably won't be too much, but maybe a cash payment will help you to think of someone else we could talk with or remember someone saying something about a missing child, a girl."

"That bitch were a genuine registered guard dog, bred and trained. Trained her myself. Worth a lot. Wouldn't a sold her for less than $500.00. And that's not countin' the pups I coulda sold off her, neither."

"I'll see what I can do, Mr. Little. I'd like my identification back."

Little looked the identification over, slowly closed the folder and handed it out toward Bill, leaving just enough distance so Bill couldn't reach it. Bill paused and then took the necessary step to reach the folder, took it and placed it back into his pocket. He stepped back, watching Little all the while.

Christie asked, "By the way, do you have any children, Oscar?"

"You know I don't, Doc. It's all in them files you had last summer. Why?"

"I was just wondering. Some of the clothes on the line back there look like kids' clothes. Do your sisters have children?"

Christie pointed to the clothesline that stretched across the side porch of the ell. Short dresses, skirts, knee length socks and pastel-colored underpants filled the line.

Little stared at the clothesline. "None of your business what I got on my line. But, I'll tell you this, Doc. My Christian sisters is washin' clothes collected by the church for needy families. They do good deeds like that when they're able."

He smiled at Christie, the leer she remembered from last summer. The same flat eyes that hid the truth that lay deep within him stared at her. Involuntarily, she shuddered and broke eye contact.

"I'm pretty cold, Bill. Any more questions?"

"No, we're all done here for now. We'll be in touch, Mr. Little."

Oscar Little watched as the SUV turned around and then drove down the bumpy driveway and around the curve. When it was out of sight, he turned toward the house, released the gate, walked inside and reset the code. He flipped on the electrical switch that activated the current that ran through the metal fence. Then he yelled.

"Junie. Betty. Git out here and git these clothes off the line. How many times I told you stupid bitches to be careful? Git out here now or you'll end up like old Nelly, deader'n a doornail."

Little kicked at the dead dog again, moving its body away from the steps. Then he put down the shotgun, picked up the dog's body and heaved it over the chain link fence.

"Come and git it," he yelled. "Free food for all you vultures, crows, fox and what have you."

23

Oscar Little scratched the top of his balding head, jammed on his wool hat, and pulled the tattered earflaps down. He tugged up the collar of his old checkered jacket while he stared at the state trooper standing in front of him. Walter Tate was frowning and shifting uncomfortably from foot to foot, all six feet and two inches of him. His state issued troopers' boots couldn't keep out the frigid air and his feet were freezing. The glacial air stiffened his leather jacket. His nose was running and his eyes watering. The two men were out in Little's calf barn, a dilapidated wooden shed behind the big barn. Below zero wind gusted through the wide cracks between the vertical boards. A cow and her new calf were huddled in a corner stall piled high with hay. Smokey breaths from the animals and the men rose in the air toward the bare light bulb hanging from the ceiling, its electrical cord wrapped with dusty cobwebs and old spider eggs.

"I'm telling you. We have to shut down for now. The task force's investigating. The Goddamn attorney general gave them the case instead of Wood. What's with him? Isn't he on the payroll? You know what happened last summer. They almost got us."

"Well," said Little smiling, "they didn't quite git us now, did they? I'm standin' right here. You're standin' there. Wood's still sheriff. Preston still runs the state police and Frank Sampson's still the district attorney. Ain't one of us in jail. The attorney general don't know shit. The task force got no evidence and they ain't gonna find any. They didn't git nowhere last summer. They won't git nowhere this winter. Don't go all shaky on me now."

"But if they find out what we're doing, the girls and all? We'll all go to death row. What if those boys talk? They could ruin everything. We never should have used them in the first place. That was a stupid idea, too risky. We didn't get any money from them, just headaches. Why didn't we just stick with the regulars?"

"You know why we used them boys. A couple girls was ready and we had orders comin' in for babies. Had to act fast. There wasn't no time to put out the usual notice."

"We could have done it ourselves. We have before. Then we wouldn't have gotten into the trouble that these boys are probably going to get us into."

"You're such a Goddamn stupid ass, Tate. I told you and told you. Can't you git it in that thick head of yours? Or do you just miss your kiddie sex romps?"

"Come on, Little. I wasn't the only one, you know. Preston, Wood, Sampson, you, George Parks, Mel LeBlanc, and I don't know who all were getting their rocks off. It wasn't just me."

"Listen Tate, and remember. We had to stop breedin' them bitches ourselves for safety reasons. It got real clear when that girl ran off two years ago. Our DNA could'a been traced. If we hadn't got her before she made it to someone not in our game, we could'a all gone down. So, we sell it now. Make good money from the suckers who come. It's their DNA and not ours in the baby, if some girl escapes."

"Whatever, Little. Look, I'm begging you to stop the operation now. It's just too risky. We could just postpone everything until the investigation dies down. Just for a few months."

Little picked up a hayfork and pushed the sharp metal

tines against Tate's chest. The tines made deep dents in Tate's leather coat as Little pushed hard against Tate. The trooper's face blanched as Little backed him up against the rough gate of the new calf's stall. The Holstein cow and her newborn baby moved to the far corner of the small enclosure and the cow's eyes grew wide in alarm as the tension grew. She mooed at the men but they ignored her.

"You'd better listen to me Tate, and listen good. I don't want no mouth off you or no thinkin' either. I'm runnin' this outfit and what I say goes. We ain't stoppin' nothin'. That kid Sam knows what'll happen to him if he says anything and them other two kids don't know nothin'. They were doped and dead drunk. The schedule's set and goin' forward. A new shipment of bitches comes in the next week couple of weeks. It's too late to back down."

"But Drummond's too good. He can't be bought and he's going at this case like wildfire in a hayfield. He's got the media sticking their noses into everything, too. The Cumberland County Daily editor, Larry Davis, called Preston three times for an interview."

"Look Tate, and listen up. God, I'm sick to the death of you. Everything's ready to go. There ain't nothin' to fret about. Preston'll handle his end of things. He's got somethin' on Davis that'll keep him quiet. We got too much money at stake to stop things now and no good reason to. Drummond's an ass and rumors say that Doc workin' with him went bonkers since she almost got burnt to a crisp by that sicko serial killer guy last fall. I talked to them both this afternoon and they're dumb as sticks. They got no idea what's goin' on."

"But, can't you see…"

"Shut up Tate. You do just what I tell you. I'm sick a listenin' to you yappin' your mouth. Cooperate or I'll send the tape showin' you playin' with them girls to the TV folks. I'll send those lovely pictures of you screwin' them girls to your wife, parents and the papers. You'll be the one caught. All the evidence I got will implicate you and you alone. You'll be the one on death row and I'll still be doin' my little farmin' business with my sisters, just like before. Got it?"

Little moved the tines from Tate's chest to his throat. He pushed hard enough to draw pin picks of blood from the thick neck of the trooper. Little was enjoying his display of power and smiled as he watched the sweat pop out on the state trooper's face.

"Okay, okay. I hear you. Get that stinking fork out of my neck. I'm not going to do anything or tell anyone. I'm going to do just what you tell me. You're in charge. I know I'm up to my ears in this shit. Now back off. Please."

Tate whined as he begged for Little to release him. The huge man cringed before Oscar Little, who stood almost a foot shorter than he did. Little lowered the hayfork and then pitched it to the side.

"Now that you understand me, Tate, there's a little somethin' I need you to do. I got to get rid of another package."

"No, Little. I don't want to do that. It's too dangerous."

"Fine, Tate. The envelope's in the mail first thing in the morning."

"Shit. I ought to kill you, Little. We'd all be better off without you."

Tate's hand went to his gun holster.

Little stared at him. "You're outa your freakin' mind, Tate. You kill me with your friggin' state police bullets, they'll find out everything and in no time they'll be on to you. At least, if you're goin' to try to kill me, use your own Goddamn hands. You'd stand a better chance of gittin' away with it. You're so Goddamn stupid. How'd you git so dumb?"

Tate hesitated. Little jumped at him and caught him in the stomach hard with his elbow. When Tate bent over, Little kicked him in the groin. Tate went down moaning, holding himself. Little stood over him. He kicked him again, this time in the kidneys. Tate screamed.

"No more, Little. Stop. I didn't mean it. I wasn't going to kill you. I just wanted to scare you, so you'd stop all this crap."

"Yeah?" said Little as he kicked Tate again hard. "You gonna take the package and git rid of it?" He kicked Tate again. "You gonna shut up and keep that dumb mouth of yours shut?"

"Yeah," Tate groaned. "Stop. I'll do it. I'll do it. Don't kick me anymore."

Little stepped back. He reached down, pulled Tate's gun out of his holster, and stuffed it in his coat pocket. Then he grabbed Tate's arm and tugged him to his feet.

"Git up. Don't be shamin' yourself, lying in that cow shit. Git up."

Tate slowly brushed himself off. "I'll do it; I'll take that body, but just this one. I'm telling you. I can't do this anymore. I've got a wife and kids."

"Stop bellyachin'. It's too late for you to quit. Why didn't you think about that when you was enjoyin' them girls and earnin' the big fat bonuses for drivin' them 'cross from Canada?"

Tate didn't answer.

"I'm sick of you. Go do what I told you. Go into the butcher shed. The key to the freezer's in the lock box up on the third beam from the door. Open up the freezer in the back and take the package marked "4" out. Make sure you relock the freezer and put them keys back in the box. Hide the box back on the rafter. Take the package with you when you leave. Drive to the dump just past Homer's woods. You know the one them honey dippers use to empty that shitty sludge after they've sucked a tank? They pay Wood a damned lot to use that illegal site. Drive down like you was patrollin' and when you get a chance and no one's around, throw that package as far as you can down into the pit. Then leave. Do you understand?"

Tate nodded. "Why don't we just burn them like before? It's safer and easier."

"Idiot. Because sometimes they don't burn all the way, like last summer. Goddamn George Parks got scared and left after he set her afire. The freakin' fire went out before it burnt up all the body. That's how the task force got called in. They found what's left. Weren't supposed to be nothin' but ashes. Lucky they couldn't pin anything on us. But, I can't risk that again. If I ever see that Parks he's a dead man."

"But they found the one Mel put in the woods. Maybe they'll find the one in the dump."

"Not if you throw it far enough. Someone's bound to dump garbage or septic shit on it tomorrow and cover it up. Mel messed up the body dump in the woods. Said he saw bear tracks and left it next to them. Said the bear would eat it. He's an idiot, too. Stupid fool forgot that in December bears go into hibernation. Not a chance it would eat that body. Plus, the body was frozen stiff. Ain't no odor to attract no bear. I got to work with such fools, sometimes I just can't stand it. And you're one of them. If you don't want to suffer what Mel's sufferin' right now, do what I said and do it before midnight. Do you git it?"

Tate mumbled, "Yes, I understand."

"Then," said Oscar, "we're done here. Git goin'. I don't want see you here again. If you need to git in touch with me, and I mean, if there's an emergency and you need, really need, to git hold of me, then follow the rules and leave a message in the box by the boat launch. I check it twice a day, morning and night. Other than that, stay away. You hear me? If you show up here again, that fork'll be all the way through your damn throat and out the other side. Now take your gun and git out."

24

William Tate drove directly to Sheriff Wood's house. Although it was close to midnight, light glowed from a first floor window. Tate knocked on the door. The sheriff opened the door and squinted at Tate.

"What the hell are you doing here? I told you never to come here. Now, get the hell out."

The sheriff moved to close the door. Tate stuck his foot in it.

"You've got to listen to me. There's trouble. Big trouble. We've got to do something."

"Be quiet. Wait a minute. Go back to your car. I'll meet you there in a minute."

Reluctantly, Tate removed his foot. Wood slammed the door. The light went off. Tate walked back to his cruiser and waited. Shortly, a bobbing light came toward him. Wood jumped into the car.

"Turn your heater up. It's colder than a nun's tit out here. And make it quick, Goddamn it. You want to blow it for all of us? You're not supposed to make any contact unless it's scheduled. You know that. What is it? And it better be good."

Tate started to grumble. "Little wants me to dump another one. This whole thing's going down. I can feel it. The task force will get those boys to talk and then they'll be onto us. They're just too close. We've got to stop and clean it all up before it's too late. I tried to tell Little, but he won't listen. He told me that you and me'd go down for it before he does and he doesn't care. He told me he has tapes on you that he could show the TV people if you try to interfere. He's got stuff on me, too. He said he's going ahead with the plan no matter what."

"He said what? That I'm going down for it? That bastard. I knew I shouldn't trust him."

"What are we going to do?" moaned Tate.

"Shut up. I'm thinking," said Wood. "You're sure he said he would take you and me down? Not just you, Tate, because you're giving him a hard time?"

"Yeah, he said both of us would end up on death row, but he'd still be farming."

"Well, let me think this through. We don't have to worry about two of those boys. They don't know anything about our operation. All's they know is that a couple of times they went out to the island, got loaded on drinks some girls gave them, had sex, and passed out. That rape drug the girls added to their drinks insures that they won't remember much of anything anyway.

"Now that other kid, Sam, he's another story. He's tough, but I suppose he could get scared into telling what little he knows, which is not much. Just that some guy saw him out by that pond one day and invited him to have some fun. So, he saw Little and could identify him, I suppose. Little swears he gave him a phony name. Little called him a couple more times and asked him to bring some buddies with him who could keep their mouths shut. That was because some of the girls were ready and we hadn't set anyone up to do them and we had orders to fill. Sam might have figured out Little's more than just a friendly guy offering drinks and sex to kids. Maybe he might guess that he's running some regular sex party out there and he could tell the cops that. But that's all he knows. And Little's the only one he knows about. But telling could hurt Sam, too. If it gets out he's been drinking and having sex with underage girls, his reputation will get damaged and make it tough for him to get recommendations for college. So I don't think he'll talk. But if he's not real careful he could slip up and mention the island and what went on. Then the task force might start nosing around there and get on to Little. Maybe we'll have to eliminate him."

"You mean kill him, Wood? Then we'd be in more trouble."

"Shut up. Let me think. Little can take care of himself with the task force, I'm sure. He was really hassled last summer and got out without a problem. He didn't give them anything. So if they come after him again about this last body, he'll handle it just fine. They've no reason to hold him. I made sure his record's all cleaned up."

"But what if he's pressured? Would he tell on us to get out of trouble? Make it seem like we're the ones running it?"

"I'd be surprised if he turned anything over to them. I didn't know about those tapes showing us, damn it. I know we taped the VIPs, so we could get money from them, but I didn't think he had tapes of any of us. He's a sneaking weasel. But Little turning over tapes to the task force doesn't make much sense. Having tapes would only implicate him more. He's not stupid. No, I think he was just threatening you. He likes to be a mean son of a bitch. But he'll stay solid. He won't say anything to them. Like last summer. He just hung tight. He can do that. He's cold. The more someone bothers him, the colder he gets. Then later, he takes care of it in his way. I've seen him do that. And he likes the money too much and he likes the partying too. And none of us have crossed him. Word to the wise, Tate. Just do what he says. Don't cross him or he'll get you."

"I know. He almost put a hay fork through my neck tonight."

"Yep, he's dangerous all right. Maybe crazy. If he's been making tapes behind our backs, he's in big trouble with me. No one told him he could do that. So, maybe he's doing some operating on his own and I don't like that. And threatening that he could turn the task force on to us, that's going too far. I don't want him thinking he can intimidate any of us like that. We might have to do something about Little. I hadn't planned on that."

The two men sat tense and silent in Tate's car. The air inside was cooling fast in spite of the heater running on high and both men puffed out frosted breath.

"I don't like this one bit," Tate said. "I have a wife and kids and a job I want to keep until I can collect my state pension. If this blows open, I can kiss all that goodbye."

"Look Tate, if this blows open you might as well shoot yourself in the head. You'll be in jail with all those scumbags who'd love to kill you and worse for sending them up there to Thomaston. You won't last a week."

Tate groaned. "I think we better kill them both. The kid and Little."

"Not we, Tate, you. You'll have to kill them."

"Why me? What about you? You're in this as deep as me."

"No, actually I'm not, Tate. You brought the girls over the border. That's smuggling, human trafficking, and an international crime. If it starts to go down I'll say I got an official call to bring some immigrant girls down from Jackman to Little's farm to board while they got medical care. That's not a crime in anyone's book. Actually, one could say I was helping some foreigners out. Preston will back me."

"But you knew what the girls were for. You knew about the babies. You made sure all those important and wealthy guys got up to Little's. You were paid big bucks for your part."

"Try to prove it, Tate. For all I knew, I was just helping out, moonlighting, providing safe transportation for men who had too much to drink at a private party. I dropped them off and picked them up. What proof is there that I knew anything?

Or what happened to those girls later after they had those babies? In fact, what proof is there that any of them even had babies? Or where the babies ended up? I'll tell you. None."

Tate said, "Well, we all knew, Wood. Any of us could tell them you were involved."

"Oh, yeah? Who would they believe, Tate? You? Little? Or me, the sheriff with the best county record over the longest time in this state? Who would your boss, Preston, stand up for? A rotten apple in his barrel? Or me, his friend for over twenty years? Who's on a first name basis with the governor and almost everyone else who matters up in the capital? Me, Tate. Come on, asshole. Start thinking right."

Tate started to panic. "Those body-parts guys from Boston know what's going on. They could squeal on you, Preston and Sampson. After all, you're the ones making money on that deal. Whose idea was it, anyway, to use the girls' dead bodies, skin them and sell every bit of them? How'd we get mixed up with those Boston guys in the first place? We were just supposed to be doing a simple sex and baby business. I bet it was Sampson, with all his connections in Massachusetts, who made that deal. Then, the Boston gang probably furnished all that special equipment for Little to use so the body parts would still be good when they picked them up at Little's butcher shop. That whole scheme's sicker than anything I've done."

"Just shut up about that, Tate. You don't know what you're talking about. You don't go messing with those guys or we'll all be giving our body parts away. I'm telling you. Stay clear of it."

"But I have one of those bodies in the trunk right now, Wood. Do I follow Little's orders and dump it where he told me? I don't know why we don't just burn them all like last year. If we had burned that body to ashes we wouldn't be in this mess. Why's Little dumping them where they might be found, anyway? That's crazy, if you ask me. We should be burning them or taking them out of state. Maybe back up to Canada."

"No one's asking you, Tate. You get paid to do what we tell you. Now shut up and let me think some more."

Silence descended on the car once more. Outside the dark sky started to spit small snowflakes and soon the front windshield was dotted with little white crystals.

Finally, Wood opened the door, got out and leaned down, looking at Tate. "Just keep cool for now, Tate. Dump the body exactly the way Little told you to. Make sure no one sees you. I'll figure something out and get back to you in a few days. Don't call me. Don't come here. I'm warning you. If you screw up, I'll be the first to rat you out."

Wood slammed the door and hurried into his house. Tate started the car and drove out of Wood's driveway toward the hidden dumpsite. Soon, his car vanished in the falling snow.

25

Bill was reading notes from a file when Christie knocked and peeked in.

"Come on in. Good morning. Have a quiet night?"

"Yes. Eventually everything was fine. I sat in front of the fireplace for hours after our escapade with Little. I couldn't stop shivering for quite a while. Images of those hideous dogs kept coming back to me. Their yellow teeth and mad eyes. Drooling and frothing all over the car. Trying to rip us to pieces. How hideous."

"Yeah, it took me a long while to get to sleep, too. Two brandies helped. I kept thinking about those collars! They must have weighed a ton with all those metal prongs."

"What were those things? They looked like two-inch studs, with razor sharp points. They kept whacking the windshield, using the collars like hammers. If they hit a person that way, they would have sliced him open."

"Well, they did a job on the SUV. I just talked to the shop; the damage is going to cost the taxpayers over $4000 in bodywork repairs, and then the car has to be painted. There are huge dents in the hood and sides. Those beasts clawed all the way through the paint and into the metal on the doors. They totally destroyed the windshield wipers, the rearview mirrors and spotlight rig too. The mechanic at the shop asked me if anyone was injured in the accident. He thought the car had been hit and rolled over into the woods."

"Understandable. That scene was horrific, not something I ever want to repeat. But those dogs keep Little protected from anyone snooping around his place."

"And from anyone escaping."

"Right. If those girls are imprisoned at his farm, they'd be scared to death of those dogs. I wouldn't want to try to outrun them. Plus, that fence arrangement. I bet he's got that whole place booby trapped or electrified."

"I'm trying to get a warrant to get in there. I have a call in to the judge now."

"Good. We have to do something and soon. How long will it take to get the warrant? I'm ready to go back there now and look for those girls."

"I have to wait for the judge to get back to me. I called Frank Sampson, the district attorney, too, to see if he can speed things up. Meanwhile, FBI agent Dave Hadley will be here in 10 minutes. You remember him, don't you?"

"Of course. I'm not going to forget the man who's in charge of keeping me safe by monitoring all leads to the whereabouts of Stephen Scott."

"Right. Well, I'm hoping he has information about any human trafficking that might be going on across the border into Maine. I also asked him for anything he's got on organized sexual exploitation of girls in Cumberland County."

"He should be up on that."

"Then after Hadley, we have the final autopsy report to go over. It came in yesterday. And look at this pile of files we need to go over. Also, we need to discuss some strategies about softening up Oscar Little."

"That sounds like a full morning. I'm having lunch with Stella at noon, so I have to be out of here before then."

"Fine. After lunch, we'll talk with investigators and see how they're doing with funeral homes, reported deaths, missing kids' reports. However, if our Jane Doe was smuggled into

Maine from Canada or another country, there wouldn't be any family, reports, or funerals to find. We'd be wasting our time on all that leg work."

"Let's wait until after we talk with Dave to make the decision of whether to keep working the funeral homes angle. I agree with you, though, on the smuggling scenario fitting this case. I'm feeling more and more that Little's running the show. I think those girls are being held prisoners at his farm. Those clothes on the line sure didn't look like the kind of clothes that church kids would wear. Too many sequins, spaghetti straps and bikini underpants."

"God, you've got a sharp eye. I was too busy watching Little's gun, the front door in case someone opened it and those monster dogs ran out, and Little's ugly mug to notice a clothesline. That's just one of the reasons I want you working right next to me on the task force."

Christie smiled. "Any others reasons?"

Bill just looked at her.

"Sorry. That didn't come out exactly as I meant it. Please just forget I said it."

Bill could see that Christie was blushing. He hoped her slip of tongue was a sign she might be starting to loosen up with him, letting down her walls a little. He wanted that familiar closeness so much. However, he knew enough not to push. He decided to just side step the comment and give Christie time. Without pressure from him, maybe she would gain the courage to open up to him more.

Christie broke the awkward silence. "Do you agree that Little's the one to focus on?"

"Yes, for now. However, I doubt he could put a whole international smuggling ring together. He might be lead man here, but I have a feeling others, higher up, are pulling the strings in Canada and overseas. Little's just a local boy. What would he know about running an international operation? He's not that sharp."

"Right. But who would he have ties to? How would someone like him become involved with the big fish in this sewer?"

"I don't know. Maybe Hadley can help us with that."

Jenny knocked and opened the door. "Dave Hadley's here."

"Send him right in, Jenny. And please, could we have coffee for three?"

"Jenny, make mine tea with lemon, please."

"Sure thing, coming right up. Agent Hadley already has his mug of coffee."

FBI Agent Dave Hadley stepped into the room, carrying a large stainless steel travel mug of coffee. Only thirty, he was already balding, but he was in fine physical shape; clearly, he spent time at the gym.

"Hey there, you two. How's it going?"

Dave stuck his hand out to Christie and then to Bill. He plopped down at the conference table and looked around at all the piles of files.

"I see you've been busy. Catch me up."

Bill ran though the case of the Jane Doe, the possible connection with last summer's Jane Doe, Jim and Brad's description of what had happened at the pond site, and the interview with Oscar Little. He finished by listing some of the theories he and Christie had developed.

"So you think these Jane Does may be victims of human trafficking and were part of a prostitution ring in Cumberland County? In addition, there's a group selling body parts from dead girls who have been used as sex slaves? Wow. When you call me in to consult, you certainly do it in a big way, Bill. Christie, is he always this generous?"

"We're a little overwhelmed by it, too, Dave. That's why we wanted to pass it by you. Do you have you any information that could help us out?"

"Did you get any collaborating evidence from the first Jane Doe? Was she missing organs and skin, eyes, too?"

"Her body was pretty much destroyed by fire. A substitute for Atwood handled the autopsy and it looks like he didn't do a very thorough job. I've asked Atwood to re-examine the remains of the first Jane Doe. Maybe she can determine an alternative cause of death and whether skin was taken, bones, organs, or eyes were missing. She said she'd get to it tomorrow. So we should know have her report by the day after tomorrow," Bill said.

"That'll be helpful. If there's evidence that body parts are missing from both bodies, then there's reason to believe that the two murders are connected. So, let's see. If the same person killed both girls, then we could be dealing with a serial killer who uses the body parts for his own perverted purposes, like Dahmer, although the M.O. of the dispersal of the bodies differs. One burned, one frozen and left hidden in the woods. Or a body-parts seller killed both girls. That's pretty unusual. Most body-parts thieves steal from cadavers. Or a prostitution ring murdered two of its victims and then sold their body parts. That's not common either. You've got to have special facilities, medical supplies, and a way to keep the parts cool and viable. I haven't heard of any prostitution operations with that kind of set-up. You have to have hard evidence to support any of those hypotheses. All you have now are two unidentified dead girls, one dismembered, the other questionable, and two teenage witness reports to substantiate girls are supplying alcohol and sex, free. Could be some teenage fad, I suppose."

"But the boys said some of the girls were younger than teens, maybe as young as ten. Have you heard of any child sex rings or child smuggling in Maine?" asked Christie.

"Yes, we've had several cases over the years. Nothing as big as what you're suggesting. It's relatively simple to move anything or anyone over the border between Canada and Maine. Drugs, cigarettes, people; it doesn't matter. When the customs people toughen up, then the smugglers just go cross country a few miles, pick up a snowmobile track or timber company road and sneak in that way."

"But haven't customs geared up since 9/11?" Christie asked.

"Not really. Not enough. Usually customs regulation and inspections on the Canadian border have been very laid back, even after 9/11. Most illegals get right through the border check if they know how to do it. False walls inside of moving vans can hold twenty to thirty people. And if they're hauling little kids, even more. Some of us think the Canadian border situation is more dangerous in terms of possible terrorist invasion, than the Mexican border. Especially given the length of the border, the wilderness areas abutting it and the small number of border guards in the north. In Mexico, it's mostly poor and starving people stealing across the border with hopes or promises of jobs. And they still get through even with all the thousands of border police, National Guard and local authorities. So, what would you expect on the Canadian border where there are almost no border troops and hundreds of miles of unwatched land?"

"I would expect that they'd do a better job. Kids' lives are being destroyed," Christie said.

"They do the best they can do with what they have. But I agree with you. More funding is needed to beef up U.S./ Canadian customs. Once the traffickers cross the border, they seem to disappear. They move south to the big cities, Boston, New York, New Haven, Atlantic City, Philadelphia, Baltimore, Washington, DC and on down the east coast. They don't consider Maine a big enough market to produce the money they want, so they move where the bucks are. That's another reason this supposed ring up in Cumberland County doesn't ring true. Not enough money for the risk. Unless they're doing something else, too."

"Something else besides prostitution and selling body parts?" Christie asked.

"Well, if they're stealing and selling body parts, they'd make money. It's easy enough to move body parts to outlets in New Jersey or New York. But remember, usually these body parts operatives are not killers, just robbers."

"What else, Dave?" Bill asked.

"The obvious, drugs."

"One boy thought the girls put some drug in the drinks. He said he couldn't move his arms and legs right and later passed out. He thought the girls wanted to be sure he was cooperative when they started being sexual with him."

"I'm talking a bigger drug operation than individual participation, Christie. Like a syndicate that sells wholesale to dealers in large amounts. That's where the money is. However, it's interesting to me that these girls might have drugged their customers. Why? Usually, clients have to pay for extras like drugs. And these kids paid nothing, not for sex, drinks, or drugs if they were used? There's something else going on here that we're not getting. Or nothing's going on at all and you just have a bunch of horny girls partying at a slumber party."

Christy shook her head. "It doesn't sound like that to me."

"Like what else do you think could be going on?" asked Bill.

"I'm not sure, but it has to be a big money-maker if they don't charge for anything else."

Christie said, "Maybe blackmail. They take pictures and later confront the clients and demand payment?"

"Did your two boys get hit for money?"

"They didn't mention it, but then we didn't ask, either. We can follow up on that," said Bill.

"The prostitute ring would have to cater to more lucrative

clients than teenagers to make the kind of money they'd want. They'd have to bring in wealthy men with lots of disposable cash to pay blackmail demands. Maybe they stage sex parties, confidential and private, and then later hit the guests with the bad news that they're on tape or in photographs. An operation like that would make good money. However, it's highly improbable. Too hard to cover up and keep quiet. Too many comings and goings. Rural Maine's too far out of the mainstream. Customers would have to fly in. People would start asking questions. No one's tipped us about a sex ring or blackmail that I know of. And if it were that big, we would have heard of it."

"But why did they risk using the boys?" asked Christie.

"We seem to keep coming back to that question, don't we?" asked Bill.

"Look folks, I think I've heard enough. I'll go back to the office and start searching our databases for human trafficking, smuggling children, sex rings in operation and who's running things in the eastern part of the States. I'll also check out body parts operations, blackmail schemes. Let's see what I come up with."

"Thanks Dave, that would help a lot."

"Glad to help, if I can. If something is going on, I don't want it in my jurisdiction and I'm sure my superiors will give me permission to come in and help. It's still your case, understand, but if we get into smuggling, violations of U.S. statutes, then I may have to step in a little further."

"Understood, Dave. Thanks again."

"I'll call you when I get something. You do the same. See you later, Christie, Bill."

After Dave Hadley left, Christie and Bill sat quietly, lost in their own thoughts and theories.

"I don't know about you, but I feel better having someone like Dave and the FBI working with us," Bill said.

"Me, too, in a way. They can tackle things we can't touch

and their investigation ability, computer technology and databases stretch further than we can go. If something's going on around here, I'm sure they have some knowledge about it."

"What did you mean by, 'in a way', Christie?"

"Did you get the feeling Dave downplayed our ideas of what could be going on?" asked Christie.

"No. I think he's cautious before he has any facts in front of him. And, we don't have much in hard facts right now. Don't tell me you're suspicious of him, too?"

"Something just felt funny. He didn't give us any details on the cases he said he'd run into. He kept giving excuses why this wouldn't be happening here."

"He's just being realistic. You don't suspect the FBI is conspiring with the likes of Little, do you? That's a pretty ridiculous conspiracy allegation, if you ask me."

"I don't doubt the FBI. I'm just wondering if Dave isn't protecting someone or something."

"I'm sure he knows many things that he can't or won't share with us, Christie. Give him a break. Remember I worked for the FBI for years before I moved to Maine. I understand there are just some things they can't talk about, even with local authorities. Their focus is broader than ours is. They have to look at the big picture. I have a lot of respect for people like Dave. We aren't all crooks and bad guys, you know. You'll just have to trust what Dave says."

"Why? Why do I have to trust Dave, or anyone for that matter? I'm right to be suspicious of the men who hold so much power. Maybe you're one of the good ones, but look at the record, why don't you? From Enron to Medicare, to Iraq, greedy men are screwing someone. Why not Dave? If the FBI knew something, why didn't they alert us? If this has been going on for as long as two years, and they knew, why didn't they tell us?"

"Christie, stop it. You're overreacting. Calm down. Don't get all hysterical."

"That's insulting. Don't you call me hysterical. I'm just doing my job. I'm assessing the personalities and motives of people who might have something to do with abducting and violating little girls, and those who might be protecting those scum in exchange for money or power. And if knowing these horrid things go on and believing that they might be going on in front of our noses protected by some two-bit official makes me loud or upset, than I think I'm reacting appropriately. Maybe you ought to get a little hysterical yourself instead of stuffing all your feelings inside in a tight little ball."

Christie leaned back in her chair and closed her eyes. Bill looked down and studied the file in front of him. Neither spoke for a while.

"Sorry, Christie. I was out of line. I apologize."

"No, you were right. I got carried away. I'm sorry I said what I did about you. Forgive me?"

"If you forgive me, partner. Let's just chalk it up to the tension of this case and the massive amount of unknowns we're dealing with."

"And to ugly dogs, that horrid Little, and that agonizing autopsy, not to mention everything else."

"So, we're all right?" Bill asked, his voice soft.

Christie smiled at him, liking the way he looked at her, and the gentle tone of his voice.

"Yes, partner, we're all right. This might be our first argument, but I'm sure it won't be our last. We're going to disagree and argue about some things, and that's okay. But hitting low and hurting aren't acceptable. We have to watch that, both of us, especially when the tension gets high. If we can treat each other with respect and forgive each other for our mistakes, then we'll be okay."

26

After a short break, Bill and Christie sat close to each other at the conference table, looking over files and discussing their plans for the rest of the day. The sun was breaking through the clouds and the gloom of the last several days was lifting. Bright sunlight streamed through the office window, warming their backs as they bent over the piles of papers.

Bill said, "Let's skip the autopsy report for now. I read it earlier and there's nothing more in the final report that's particularly helpful to us. Same findings: cause of death, asphyxiation; method, homicide by strangling. No alcohol or drugs in her system. Brain normal size, no aberrations; body dismemberment was post-mortem. Other than some signs of neglect, tooth decay, and malnutrition, the girl seemed healthy enough. Of course, Atwood couldn't examine the major organs, so there could have been something there, but she's pretty sure it's not likely. No evidence of any foreign matter in or on the body."

"Then that's it? That's all we have to go on? No other indicators of who she might be?"

Bill skimmed over the notes at the end of the autopsy.

"Oh, I forgot this. One note at the end is curious. Atwood added that the person who skinned the Jane Doe and removed her organs had some basic surgical skills and used a fine instrument, probably a scalpel or very sharp knife. But, Atwood reported, the stitches were not professional. In fact, they looked more like sewing or darning stitches to her. They used a waxed thread, rather coarse and most likely they stitched her up using a regular sewing needle. Definitely not the kind surgeons or doctors use."

"That's fascinating. That little detail might just help us a lot."

"How so? What do you mean?"

"First, we have the question of why they bothered to stitch up the victim at all. Why didn't they just get their parts and leave the body as it was? The fact that they closed the incisions indicates some kind of guilt, maybe remorse, or need to make the body look better. We're dealing with someone who isn't totally dedicated to what he's doing. He tries to put the body back together. In a sense, make it better."

"That isn't typical of a sociopath's behavior, is it?"

"Nope. So on first thought, we'd have to eliminate Little as participating in stealing the body parts, although that doesn't mean he didn't kill the girl and cut her up. Only that he wouldn't have sewed her back together again."

"Maybe they had a deal with some of the people down south who steal body parts and they came up and took care of it."

"Could be. But the stitching is the kicker, I think. Body part thieves wouldn't bother to stitch up the body, anymore than Little would. We have skilled surgery, but amateur stitching. Sounds like two different individuals may have been involved. One cuts; the other cleans up."

"Maybe the cutter doesn't know the cleaner is doing the stitching?"

"Or, maybe the cutter is both the killer and body part thief and the stitcher feels guilt or shame about what the cutter has done."

"Hmmm. That's interesting. A team effort, but with different emotional reactions to what they're doing."

"Yes, so we can put Little back on the suspect list for killer, cutter and body parts thief. He has butcher skills, but we know as a sociopath he wouldn't have remorse. But his sisters might."

"His sisters? Oh my God. The sisters. Of course. They'd have to be in on it, too."

"They'd have to know what's going on if the girls are locked up there. Especially if the sex parties are held in the winter. The girls can't work outside on the island, too cold. So, people would come to the house or barn, or somewhere on the farm. And the girls would have to eat. I can't see Oscar Little cooking at all, let alone for a large group. So the sisters are probably taking care of them, washing their clothes, feeding them. Then what if one of the girls disappears and they suspect Little's to blame? Maybe they sneak over to the butcher shed and see what he's doing and come back later and sew the girl up with that waxed cotton string I use to sew up my turkey at Thanksgiving."

"Thanks, I'll never be able to eat turkey again."

"We have to go out to the farm again. We have to talk to those sisters."

"No go. I talked with Judge Howe while you were in the rest room. He finally got back to me. He wouldn't give me a warrant for Little's premises. He said kid's clothes hanging on a line wasn't enough. Attack dogs are within the rights of the homeowner, so that didn't work. And since none of the boys who participated in the sex party admit they know Little, or even heard of him, not enough evidence exists for the judge to issue a warrant."

"Damn. Then we can't get in to question the sisters and check out if the girls are there, or were there. We can't even look for a scalpel or knife with blood evidence or matching string."

"Nope. And we have to hope that Little didn't get so edgy after our questioning that he moves the girls and any incriminating evidence before we get our warrant. That's why time is of the essence."

"Isn't there some way to convince the judge? What do we need to get a warrant?"

"Hold on. The good news is we did get a warrant to examine the pond site and the Boy Scout camp on the island. The boys' testimony was enough to get the judge to agree that we could look there. So, are you up for it? We could leave right after lunch."

"Wow. That's great. We're sure to turn up something on the island. The snow last night didn't amount to much and the base snow has melted down a lot. There might even be some bare spots. They must have left something behind from those parties last summer. I put my winter gear in the car, this time, just in case. I learned my lesson yesterday up at Little's when I nearly froze to death. I'm ready for any weather now."

"I'm hoping we'll find something that will implicate Little. Judge Howe said if we could connect him to the island and therefore to the boy's testimony, that would be enough to secure a warrant to examine his house, barn, outbuildings and grounds."

"Then we better look really hard. Can we get some more people to go with us? Would dogs help?"

"Yes, dogs would be great for finding drugs or dead bodies. If we had something with Little's scent on it, the dogs could tell us if he'd been out there. I called Herb, but he's on another case with his dogs today. So, since we don't have Little's scent to use anyway, the dogs couldn't help us connect the sex party to him. When I go back to Little's to pay him some compensation, call it bribe money, for that dog of his, I'm going to try to get his prints or scent on something for the dogs to use."

"You're actually going to pay money to that man? I don't believe it. He should be paying you for the damage to the SUV."

"Well, I mentioned money to him for a couple of reasons. One, it's a way to get back on his property and look around, if we can't get a warrant. He'd let me in if he thought he was going to collect some cash, I'm sure. Second, I figured a little money might motivate him to tell me something that could help. And, if I can get out there, this time I'm going with a gang of big guys, plenty of guns and in a Hummer. Those dogs won't stand a chance. I just have to figure out how to get his scent on some material."

"Put the money in a canvas bag with a hard plastic handle. He'll open it to see the cash and count it. You know he won't trust you've given him enough. Then ask for the bag back. You'll have the prints and scent."

"That might work. Good idea. Anyway, this afternoon, we won't have his scent and we don't have the dogs, either. I don't imagine we'll find any bodies over there, but anything's possible. I'd be surprised if they left drugs. They'd want to keep expensive drugs secured and close by in order to move them quickly to a dealer. We can call Herb's dogs in later if we get Little's scent or see something suspicious on the island, like newly filled holes."

"I want to look at the buildings. I don't think they would leave those girls out there by themselves. Too risky. So probably someone was on guard in one of the buildings. With all that activity, someone must have left something. A cigarette butt. A bottle. Maybe one of the girls left a clue of some kind, hoping someone would find it. Maybe we'll get lucky. By the way, I've been meaning to ask you. What do we have on Little's background? Anything in addition to the old files from last summer? I'd like to go over that information before we go out there. We still have some time."

"Sure. Tom Wilder's been looking for anything we might have missed about Little last summer. Here's the updated file."

Christie took the manila folder from Bill and opened it.

An 8" x 10" photo of Little's face was the first page. Christie stared at him.

"He even looks like one."

"Like one what?"

"Like a sociopath serial killer, although there really isn't any way physically to distinguish a sociopath from anyone else. But his eyes are so flat, like many of these killers. You can't see into them. They just reflect you back like you're nothing. Like you can't get into them, in where their truth lies. They give me the creeps. They don't care about anyone or anything.

"Look at the way Little killed that dog. A vet could have fixed that dog's leg up. But Little just saw something that was broken and therefore of no use to him, so he shot it. Cold. I'll take a good old psychopath anytime. At least they let you know what's going on with them, even if it's delusional or obsessive-compulsive wackiness."

Bill didn't respond. He wondered if Christie realized what she had just said. Was she so distanced from her emotions and past experience when she was working that she was able to forget Stephen Scott and that he was a psychopath? He felt uneasy about her ability to switch so easily from a vulnerable terrified victim, to a cool rational professional. Sure, it helped her to cope and she certainly functioned effectively, but he worried about what might cause her to flip the other way, and when. She had been fine when questioning Little, even after the dog attack. She didn't crack under those very stressful conditions. And when she wasn't working? When she didn't have her major coping mechanism working for her? What happened to her then?

The whole question was alien to Bill, who during his years of working with the FBI and then as director of the task force, had Emmy. When work got too stressful, he talked or cried with her. When he was angry, she soothed him, by touch, with good cooking, by humming one of his favorite songs. When Emmy wasn't available, there were the children, who by their very ages and natures pulled him into fantasy, fun and outdoor adventure.

He didn't really understand Christie's addiction to work. He was always so eager to get home to his family. If Christie and he did restart their relationship, would it ever grow to resemble what he had loved so much before? Or would she stay married to her job? Was it possible that his love for her could help her to find some inner peace and allow her to open her heart?

Christie continued to scan the folder, turning the pages one by one.

"This is interesting. Little's the oldest of three children. He has two sisters, Betty and June. We knew that. However, I didn't know that their parents died in a freak farm accident, overturned tractor, when Little was 19, Betty 17, June 15. The parents left the farm to the children. There wasn't much else, not even life insurance, according to the will. None of them ever married. They've lived together on that farm for over 45 years. That's how old Little is now."

Bill said, "Yeah, if you look at the tax reports, you can see that they've never made enough money to pay income taxes. Just barely paid property taxes up until the last couple of years, when they paid the full amount and on time."

"That's ties into the time-line we're looking at for the prostitution ring beginning."

"Yes, and the new Silverado was bought just about six months ago. Where did the money come from? I'm willing to bet not from the fresh eggs the sisters sell at the farmer's market."

"Or from the butchered sheep, steers, and pigs," Christie added.

"Don't forget that he dresses bear, deer and moose during hunting season, Christie. He probably makes some money from that."

"Enough to buy the Silverado with cash? I don't think

so. This guy has another source of income."

"I mentioned that to the judge. Still not enough to get a warrant."

Christie closed the folder. "Except for our interrogation of him last summer, Little has not seen the inside of a jail. He doesn't even have a record of parking tickets. This guy is clean. Too clean. It's as if his file has been erased or cleaned up or something. Everyone gets a speeding ticket sometime, even me, I admit. Little doesn't even have a speeding ticket citation."

"Strange, isn't it?"

"Very strange. Here's a sociopath who cares nothing about anyone or anything. And he's never been in trouble for bothering anyone, or picking a fight, or disregarding authority or rules? Where are his school records, by the way? Maybe they'll show us some truth about Oscar Little."

"Good point. I guess Wilder decided they wouldn't be relevant. I'll have him get them for us."

"Great. What time is it?"

"Hey, time to go. I'll walk you out to your car. I'm meeting Skip Preston for lunch. I wanted to pick his brain about how the state police look at this case. We'll meet back here around 1:00. Eat hearty; it's going to be cold out there this afternoon."

27

Stella and Christie met for lunch in a cozy sandwich shop in the West End. They had ordered their food and Stella was commenting about the décor, finding it acceptable, but a little clichéd.

"I hope the chef's better than the decorator," Stella said, picking at the vinyl tablecloth. "At least it's clean in here."

"Yeah," Christie mumbled in reply. She hadn't really been listening to Stella's fashion faux-pas commentary.

"Well, since my decorating know-how doesn't grab ya, what do you want to talk about?"

"Sorry, I was in another world. I'm thinking about going back to work."

"Work? Aren't you working with Bill on that dreadful Cumberland County case?"

"Oh that, yes. I'm working the case with him, but so far mostly strategy, interviews and reviewing backgrounds. Creating a few scenarios. We don't have much to go on, yet. We did have one wild scene with killer dogs yesterday, though, that would get your heart beating."

"No kidding. Tell me about it."

"Well, I'll skip the details. Just think about Steven King's Cujo and you'll get the picture. Don't want you to have bad dreams. But the outcome for me was significant."

"Yuck. That book was scary. Tell me, what outcome?"

"Well, I was really scared of the dogs, afraid they were going to kill us. But later, when the dogs were put away, I was more eager to get out of the car than I expected."

"Yeah, why?"

"We were assessing a major suspect in the Cumberland County case. The same man I spent so much time interviewing last summer trying to get him to confess to that Jane Doe murder. The burned body? Remember?"

"Oh yes. I remember. We don't usually have burned women's bodies turn up. That was spooky."

"The suspect's the one who's spooky. Sociopath. Tricky and slick. Shot his dog to death in front of us because it had a broken leg. Then kicked it."

"Wow. I'd have been scared silly."

"I was and then I wasn't, Stella. All of a sudden, I felt so strong. I just wanted to walk right up to him, look the bastard in the eye, and play him. And I did. I kept my cool and asked him whatever I wanted whether he liked it or not. I didn't run. I stood my ground. I didn't get much out of him, but somehow that didn't matter as much as the fact that I had the courage to face him."

"Oh Christie, that's wonderful. Oh, I'm so glad. That's really something."

"You bet it is. I've been scared for so long I began to think fear would never let me go. Terror was my constant companion. Yesterday, I recovered a feeling I haven't had for a long time. I felt capable, confident, full of myself. I was doing my job and doing it well. And I wasn't scared of that horrid man. I felt so strong."

"This sounds like a turning place for you. You're definitely getting better, aren't you?"

"I think so, at least yesterday and today, I think so. I do have my ups and downs. But after yesterday, I feel different, more like me."

"Besides strong, and confident, how else like you?"

"I think I want to go back to work."

"Work? You're already working."

"No, I mean going back into practice."

"Tell me more. I was wondering when you might begin to feel ready to see clients again. Heaven knows, I can send you a bunch right now. I'm head over heels with Seasonal Affective Disorders right now. If spring doesn't come soon, all of Portland will be on my couch complaining about SAD."

"I thought if I saw one or two of my former clients, just to begin with. You've told me several are over the critical phase now. I could pick up on the work you've done, support it and then terminate with them as they ease out of therapy. That way, we'll have closure and the work wouldn't be too emotional for me to handle. What do you think?"

Stella grinned. "I think that's a great idea. How about Roberta? She's worked hard and is just about ready to finish her individual work. I'll keep her in my incest survivor's group for a while yet. She would love to see you again. You helped her a lot."

"Yeah, I like her too. I think it would be good for both of us to get back together for a couple of sessions. Why don't you talk to her about meeting with me when you see her again? Give her my number if she wants to see me."

"Sure. Then there's Sherry. She still has a way to go, but she's stopped crying through the whole session and is beginning to look at some of her issues of grief and loneliness. Why don't you take her on too? That way when Roberta finishes up you'll still have Sherry coming in."

"OK. Talk to her about it and tell her I'm available. What about Jean? I think she might want to come back and work with me again."

"Hey Christie, all your clients want to come back. According to them, there's no one like you. And I agree. Better to start with just one or two longer-term clients and some short-term clients just in case you realize you aren't quite up to it yet. Give yourself a chance to ease into work. Jean would be good. She can shop now without too much anxiety, but she's just becoming aware of the subconscious motivations that produced the behavior."

"Yes. I think so. Yes, three clients, Roberta, Sherry and Jean. Run it by them this week, will you? Tell them I'll be available, say in two weeks. That gives me two weeks to think about it and get ready. Then give them my new number. I hope I'm ready."

"What's stopping you? What's not ready?"

"One, being in an office alone again. It spooks me to go there, even though it's a new office. I keep thinking Scott will be outside the door waiting for me."

"Oh, Christie. That's awful. I'm so sorry you're still so scared. You must keep telling yourself that you're protected in every way. And, Scott's smart. He won't come near you when he's sure to be caught. Everyone has his description and picture. All law enforcement personnel are on the alert for him. You know that. And our office building has brand new, top of the line security."

"I know, I know, but I can't help thinking he's going to come back no matter how hard I try to erase that idea from my mind. But, there's another reason I'm worried about seeing clients again."

"What reason?"

"I'm not the same as I was before. You know that. My confidence has been broken. When I needed to, I couldn't do anything to save myself. And I tried everything I know. God, I tried to talk him out of it, to psyche him out of it, to guilt him, fight him, scare him, shame him, befriend him, listen to him. Nothing worked. Everything I had learned as a psychotherapist failed to turn him around. I failed. What if I fail with my clients?

Then what would I do? Stella, I'm scared I won't be an effective psychotherapist again."

Christie wiped at the tears rolling down her face with the napkin from the table setting. As if on cue, the waitress arrived with their sandwiches. She put the food down and discreetly returned with more napkins before disappearing.

"Christie, you just told me the story of how yesterday you felt so courageous and strong. That's how you'll be working with clients again. You're going to feel like you did before. You're going to be the wonderful listener and guide that you've always been. Of course, you're nervous about starting again. But you're going to be all right. Better than before because you have survived a terrible trauma and know more fully how your trauma survivors feel. Your sorrow and pain will turn into a gift."

"Thanks Stella. I hope so. Thanks for having such confidence in me. It means a lot to hear you say you think I'm ready. I needed to say what scares me out loud and you responded with just what I was looking for. Thanks."

"Good. So we have a plan then? I'll talk to Roberta, Jean and Sherry this week and get back to you with their reactions. Now, let's stop talking about work and serious matters and eat our lunch and do a critique of the chef before we head back to work."

The two women nibbled at their roll ups and made small talk for the rest of the meal. They left a large tip for the server and walked outside into the freezing cold day under an ice-blue cloudless sky.

"I'll be in touch. Call me anytime you want to talk, Christie. Don't let so much time go by before you call next time. Okay?"

"I'll try, Stella. Sometimes it's hard for me to reach out, but you know that by now, don't you?"

"Yep, I know you. And I love you. Take care."

Stella watched while Christie limped over to her car, got

in and locked the door. Then she unlocked her own car and drove off. Neither paid any attention to the old truck parked across the street from the restaurant that pulled out after them and followed Christie's car.

Christie glanced around as she entered the task force garage and keyed in her card allowing her access. Only one security guard was on duty.

He walked over to her. "Dr. McMorrow. Sorry. You'll have to wait a few minutes before I can follow you to level 3. My partner's taking a bathroom break. He should be back in five minutes or so."

Christie smiled at him. "Officer Brown, isn't it? Look, it's fine. I'll be okay on my own today."

"You sure, Dr.? It'll only be a few minutes."

"I'm sure. Don't worry. See you later."

She drove up the ramp and parked as near to the elevator as possible. She looked around and seeing no one, quickly grabbed her briefcase and got out of the car. She locked the doors with her remote as she hurried to the elevator. The door stood open and the elevator was empty. She held her breath while the door slowly shut and then leaned on it, breathing fast. Her panic started to rise. What if he stopped the elevator? What if the door opened and he was outside it, waiting for her?

She had to admit to herself that she was still terrified to be outside on her own. She had done a good job of fooling herself after confronting Little yesterday. She could talk about being brave with Stella. She could pretend she was well enough to go back to her private practice. She could tell the guard she'd be fine on her own.

However, every car, every stop, every man she saw, even this elevator seemed like a potential danger. She still looked behind doors. She watched for movements behind her in bathroom mirrors. She listened for every sound, wondering if he had finally come. She froze at shadows and hated walking down long halls filled with closed doors, thinking maybe he was behind one of them. Sometimes she just wanted to stay in bed with the covers over her head. Her fear had only gone into hiding for a while. And getting out of her car and into the elevator had whipped the fear back in full force. She realized the only time she felt safe was in the task force offices themselves. Even the garage with its heightened security still put her into a panic. How could she go back to work? How could she tell clients to do something she couldn't do herself? Christie's spirits plummeted into the dark place waiting inside.

28

Stephen was right behind her. His security card scanned perfectly at the entrance to the task force parking garage and the security guard smiled at him, glanced at his identification and wished him a good afternoon. But his truck stalled out as he was making the turn onto the second level. By the time he got the truck going again and drove up to the third floor parking area, he saw the number above the elevator registering 3. Dr. McMorrow had made it to the task force office.

He seethed at his loss. Today was supposed to be the day. He set his plan to begin this afternoon. Now he had to change everything. He wanted to finish his mission. His anger grew into a rage. He thrust the silver needle into his thighs repeatedly until he finally regained control.

He sat in the old truck and thought about how he could take the elevator and ride up to the third floor. He could start the mission in Detective William Drummond's office. That would show them all how powerful he was. Omnificent enough to kill them both right in the task force director's office. What fun. What publicity.

He would position the bodies on the director's desk. Fornicating on the job. He would have to change the ritual to accommodate the new plan, but his Uncle/Mother Luke would most likely approve, if they were here. If they were alive. If Stephen hadn't killed them so very long ago. Maybe they were watching him, reading his mind. He listened hard. Nothing.

They weren't communicating with him yet. They would, he believed. They would come to him soon, whispering in his ear that he was forgiven, that he was doing what he had been chosen to do.

Stephen sat in the truck and waited, trying to decide if he should embark on this new plan. He started his engine to run the heater. He was getting cold and he was afraid the white rats he had stashed under the truck seat in their cage would get too cold and die before he had a chance to use them.

Waiting gave him a chance to rethink his new plan. There was extraordinary risk involved in actually entering the task force building. He might get in fine, but escaping after he completed the mission might be more difficult. He didn't know Detective Drummond's schedule or who might have access to his office, a key. He didn't know if cameras and security forces monitored the floor. He heard his uncle's voice. "Not now. Soon."

Startled, he looked around, but saw no one. He nodded and gave up the idea of beginning his mission today. He would return to the cabin, consult his notes and make a new plan for tomorrow or the next day. Perhaps his Uncle/Mother Luke would speak to him again, give him some advice. But no matter what, he couldn't wait any longer. The time had come.

29

Bill saw traces of smudged eyeliner below Christie's eyes and wondered if she had been crying. Perhaps lunch had been difficult for her. But he didn't say anything. His therapist had suggested that he wait for Christie to bring her issues to him, when she was ready, on her own timetable. Asking her if she were okay might bring up memories that Christie didn't want to deal with. So, he held back and didn't question her, even though it was hard for him to resist trying to help her.

"Hey, you didn't call for me to meet you in the garage."

"Didn't need to today. I was careful."

Bill deliberated whether he should argue that point with Christie, but decided not to. Christie was showing a little independence and confidence. That was a good thing, as long as she didn't take it too far. He hoped her newfound courage wasn't the result of a regression into denial about the danger Stephen Scott presented. Stella told him trauma victims often used denial as a defense mechanism.

"Ready for a ride to the country?"

"Yep, I'm ready to go. I'm so bundled up that I can't bend, so don't expect me to move too fast. By the way, what did you learn from Preston?"

"Nothing. It was a waste of my time. He wasn't current with the case, doesn't know any more than someone would from the newspapers. In fact, he seems totally disinterested. Kept changing the subject to his shortage of funds and labor. He'll send us the State Crime Scene Mobile Unit, its operators and equipment when we need it, but he's turning all the rest of the investigation completely over to us. Just wants updated information and reports."

"That's good isn't it? He's cooperating, but not controlling. Just what we hoped for."

"That's true. But Preston doesn't usually operate that way. He's not a 'hands off' kind of person. Either he's really pressured by not having enough troops to handle his case load, or…"

"Or what?"

"Or something funny's going on."

"Now, you're the one with the conspiracy theory. Haven't we already gone through that drama once today?"

He laughed. "Yes we have and don't need to repeat it. Let's get ready to head out to the island."

"I'm ready."

Bill turned and took a good look at Christie. She looked twenty pounds heavier, padded with layers of clothes, topped with a fluffy down jacket.

"You look like a little kid overdressed by your mom so you won't catch cold. Did you ever have so much on that you were too stiff to play? I remember that."

"No, not really. My mom wasn't the overprotective type. Just the opposite. At least I'll be warm and if vicious dogs show up they'll have to chew a while before they get to my flesh. I'm prepared for anything."

The phone rang.

"I'll get that and then we'll go. Take off your mittens and hat. You'll get too hot."

"I can't bend enough to do it," Christie laughed.

"Yes, Detective Drummond speaking. When? Where? Who's there? Keep a tight lid on it. I'll be there in twenty minutes."

"What is it? You look white as snow."

"They found another one. That was the Cumberland Country emergency dispatcher. They got a call from a man who saw a body at a dumpsite. Anonymous caller, but they sent the paramedics out to check. Do you want to come with me?"

"Sure. Let's go."

30

Ice slicked the deep ruts of the winding dirt road to the dumpsite hidden in the woods on the north side of Cumberland County. As Bill and Christie drove down the treacherous lane, they could see indentations in the snow where other vehicles had skidded off the road into the ditches. Long deep furrows of dirty gravel flecked snow indicated where trucks had backed up and then moved on. Even though it was mid-afternoon, dusk was already falling and the woods lurked, dark and dangerous, close on either side of the road.

They arrived at the dumpsite clearing and pulled in next to a sheriff's patrol car. No crime tape was in evidence, but the paramedics had arrived; their lights cast a dim reddish color as they reflected against black tree trunks and white crusty snow.

"Where is everybody?" Bill asked. "I got the call twenty minutes, no twenty five minutes ago. I'm the most distant responder. Where are the state troopers? Their office is right up the road. Where are the forensic people? Where's the Mobile Crime Scene Unit? What's going on here?"

"Let's get out and find the paramedics and the deputy. Maybe they know something. Or maybe it turned out to be a false report," said Christie.

Bill left the engine running and the heater on. He and Christie climbed out of the vehicle. Bill held on to Christie's free arm to give her additional support in the rough and rutted icy roadway while they headed for the edge of the dump hole.

They looked over the side. Two paramedics were standing in the dim light on the bottom of a slight decline, up to their knees in newly dumped sewage. They were dragging something out of the muck.

"Hey, I'm Bill Drummond, Director of the Maine State Task Force on Violent Crimes. Who's in charge here?"

The paramedics looked at each other and shook their heads. One yelled up to Bill.

"Don't know, sir. We got a tip, anonymous call, that someone saw a body down here. We followed up. When we got here, a sheriff's car was already here. Must be Bobby Hamlin, but we didn't see him. We called out but no one answered. So, we started looking in the dump for a body. Didn't want to waste too much time in case there was still a chance of resuscitation."

"Stop what you're doing now. Have you moved the body?"

"Just a little, trying to find it in all this shit. Uh, excuse me sir, in all this gunk. We needed to determine if the person was alive."

"Well?"

"No, sir. Dead. No pulse, no heartbeat. And cold, seems frozen solid. Been dead a long time, I guess."

"Come up out of that mess. Leave things as they are until the forensic unit gets here. You should have on biohazard equipment. That liquid stuff you're in must be lethal. I can smell it from here."

The paramedics slowly made their way up the slime and ice-encrusted slope to the top of the dumping area. Smelly waste covered them from head to toe.

Bill went to the back of his vehicle. He pulled out a duffle and opened it. He handed large antiseptic wet-wipes and towels to the two men.

"Here. Strip off your clothes and uniforms. Stuff all the

dirty clothes into this biohazard bag. Stand close to the open door of my car. The heat's on full blast. That'll keep you from freezing. Clean yourselves off as well as you can. Then apply this antiseptic cream everywhere. You know the routine. Do you need clean clothes, outer garments?"

"No, we keep a change of clothes in the truck and we always strip down to our uniforms when we have to go into something messy like this dump."

"What is this place? It can't be a town facility. There are no signs or regulations posted."

"No sir. We're sure this is an illegal dumping ground. Costs a lot to drive a load of septic waste to the official station. Price's too high for some of the small honey dipper outfits. So, they find places to unload. Looks like this dump has been in operation for quite a while."

"God help the environment and the wells around here. Well, start cleaning up. Stay in your truck after you've finished. I'll come back and talk with you in a few minutes."

Bill turned to Christie. "Go look for Bobby Hamlin. He must be around here somewhere. He's not in the patrol car. Maybe he's following some tracks. Wear a pair of these booties over your boots. Watch where you walk. There may be footprints or tire tracks, other evidence that we don't want to mess up."

"What are you going to do?"

"After I call Sheriff Wood and Skip Preston and ask them where the hell they are, I'm going to change into a biohazard outfit, go down in that muck and see what I can before it gets totally dark. Damn, we should have those halogen lights set up and the scene secured by now."

"It's awful down there. Why don't you wait until the crew comes? It'd be safer that way."

"Nope, I want to see it right now. When you find the deputy, quiz him on what procedure he's following, how he got here, what he knows. I'll be back soon. Take a flashlight with you. There's a couple in my glove compartment. And be careful out there. It's easy to slip and fall. If you get into trouble, call out or use your phone. Do you feel up to it?"

"Yep. The crutch actually gives me a little more advantage in the snow. Sort of like a hiking stick."

"Okay then. When you find the flashlights, bring one back for me, too."

Christie followed a small trail that led from the dumping area into the brush and then into the deeper woods. It was darker under the hemlocks and spruce and colder, too, but she could make out tracks heading down the path. She was glad she had dressed so warmly, even though the layered clothing slowed her movement. She moved the flashlight back and forth, as she stumbled down the path. She called out Bobby Hamlin's name. She stopped to listen, but heard nothing but the dim sound of the engines running back at the dumpsite.

She reached the end of the little path. A thick wall of scrub pine and spruce that looked impenetrable faced her. She doubted that Hamlin would have gone any farther than this, if he came down this trail at all.

Christie turned around. She flashed the light in a circle around her. The second time around, she saw it. A brown boot jutted out from under the lowest branches of an old drooping hemlock. Above the boot, Christie could see the wet and muddy cuff on the bottom of a brown pair of pants, the same brown that the sheriff and his deputies from Cumberland Country wore.

Using the crutch, she pulled aside the branches. A man lay there face down. Christie slowly panned the flashlight up his body. When the light reached where the man's head should have been, she gasped. The back of the head was blown away. Bits of skull, teeth and brains lay scattered in and under the green hemlock.

31

Christie walked as fast as she could back to the dumpsite clearing. She slipped once or twice, but didn't fall. She thanked God she was still using the crutch. When she got back, she didn't see Bill, but the two paramedics were changed and sitting in the front of the ambulance, drinking out of a thermos.

Christie knocked on the window. "I need your help."

The door opened and the paramedic said, "Hi, Doctor McMorrow. I recognize you from some of the cases we've both worked on. I'm Danny Souza and my partner here is Tim Desmond. How can we help?"

"I found a body. I think it's Sheriff Wood's deputy, Bobby Hamlin. He's hurt. Follow me."

"Right with you, Doc. Let me get our pack and you lead the way. Tim, grab the big flashlight. It's almost totally dark out there now."

They retraced Christie's steps down the path. When they reached the spot where Hamlin's body lay, Christie stepped back, but kept her light shining on the boot. The two paramedics moved forward, lifted the drooping branch and shone their lights underneath.

Then, they bent down and started to check for vital signs. In a few minutes, they stood up and walked back to Christie.

"He's dead. Looks like a bullet smashed into the back of his head. Probably exited through his face."

"Is it Bobby Hamlin?"

"Yep, sure is. Name's on his badge, clear as day."

"I think we'd better leave things just as we found them and wait for Bill's instructions, fellows. He should be coming up out of that smell hole by now, I hope. He can tell us what to do."

"I can go back to the truck and radio it in," Tim said. "Maybe that'll help get those forensic folks out here faster. I can't imagine what's holding them up."

"I'll tell you what's holding them up," said a voice as a man walked out of the dark and into the light from their flashlights.

"God Bill, you scared me," Christie said. "Don't sneak up on me like that. I'm already shaking like a leaf. It's terrible. I found Bobby Hamlin and he's dead. Someone shot him in the head. It's horrible. He's back there under that tree. We tried not to touch anything, but three of us walked on the trail. Only I had booties on. Sorry. We were in a hurry. Oh God, I can't seem to stop talking. He looks so bad."

Bill put his arms around her. He could feel her trembling. He wished she hadn't been exposed to such a brutal scene, but all he could do was give her a bit of comfort.

Danny asked, "What's holding them up, sir? You said you heard something?"

Bill let Christie go and turned to the paramedic. "Yes, it came in over the radio. It was on your radio, too. I heard it while I was cleaning up and changing."

"What is it?"

"There was a huge accident on the turnpike. A tractor-trailer hit a state trooper's vehicle. The truck driver's fine, just some scratches and a broken arm."

"What about the state trooper?" Christie asked.

Bill sighed. "Dead, instantly, they said. It was William Tate."

"Oh no," Christie cried. "Not William Tate. He has a wife and two kids. He's been wonderful to me. Oh, how terrible.

I can't believe it. Are you sure it was him?"

"Yes, I'm sure I heard the report right. It's a tragedy. Just out doing his duty and wham, dead. And now Bobby Hamlin."

Bill walked over, pulled the hemlock branches aside, and squatted next to Bobby Hamlin's body. After a moment, he shook his head slowly and stood up.

Tim spoke up. "No wonder no one made it down here. They must all be dealing with the accident on the highway. I wonder if they need us there, too. I'll call in. We can't do any more here. It's up to the coroner now and the forensic guys."

Bill said, "Yes, sure. Call in. You can go on over to the accident if you're needed. All I'll want from you people is a statement about the call you received, time it took you to get here, what you saw when you got here. By the way, did you talk with Bobby Hamlin at all?"

"No, and that was strange. When we got here, his patrol car was parked right where it is now, but no one was in it. As I said, we called out a couple of times and got no answer. So, we just looked into the dump where the caller said he saw a body and right away we saw something partly wrapped in a sheet, sticking out of the goop. We didn't wait for Bobby, just got down there as fast as we could, in case she was still alive. She wasn't."

Bill looked at Christie and nodded. "Thanks guys. I'll get back to you if I need more."

The paramedics walked back to their ambulance followed by Bill and Christie. Tim called the dispatcher on the radio. A few minutes later, he opened the ambulance door and called,

"They could use us on the turnpike. Couple of fender benders occurring due to backed up traffic and the slippery road. So, we're out of here and heading over there. You two okay here? Want us to call for someone to come out?"

"No thanks, Tim. You go on. I've contacted Sheriff

Wood and the state police. They're splitting up the equipment and sending some up to us as soon as they can. They don't really need the Mobile Crime Scene Unit down at the accident any longer, so they'll be over with it in awhile. We'll be fine."

The ambulance backed up, turned around and drove out. Bill and Christie jumped into their SUV and pumped the heater on high.

"God almighty. We're right in the middle of a monster nightmare, Christie. That body down there? Skinned, just like the other one. So another skinned girl, a dead deputy, and William Tate, a decorated state trooper, killed. This is unbelievable. What more can go wrong?"

32

Three trucks parked next to each other had their engines on, headlights out, and tail pipes sending frosty plumes into the freezing cold night. Only the sliver of a quarter moon lighted the road by the pond. Glitters of ice crystals shone from the pond's surface. The crusty snow, unmarked except for the tracks of the trucks, reflected brittle diamonds.

The interiors of two of the trucks were dark. The third glowed dimly from the tips of two cigarettes in the front seat of the large red Dodge Ram with a crew cab. The interior brightened and subsided as the two men inside pulled the smoke into their lungs.

From the backseat growled the voice of the third man. "God, put those things out or go outside. I can't stand that smoke."

"Nothing doing, Preston. It's too damn cold out there. You get out if you don't like it," Wood growled back.

"I don't like anything about this Goddamn fiasco, Wood. First, you're careless with the bodies and then your deputy, Bobby Hamlin, almost ruins everything. What were you thinking? Now everything's going to blow up."

"Cool down, Preston. It's not all me. Little takes care of the girls and getting rid of the bodies. It's on him that three bodies have been found. I've got my part under control. Hamlin had to go. He spotted Tate dumping the body. What the hell Hamlin was doing in that area is a mystery to me. I specifically told him to patrol in the southern part of the county last night. I knew Tate was dumping that body. It could be Hamlin was on to something, I don't know."

Frank Sampson said, "He was your deputy, Wood. If he was suspicious, that's your fault. How would he be on to us anyway?"

"I don't know, Frank. He's always been a snoopy type, getting into every case whether it was his or not, looking things up on the computers. Asking a lot of questions. He's one of those good officers, never willing to bend or look the other way. He once arrested someone trying to slip him a twenty to avoid a ticket. You know. That kind."

"Why'd you ever hire him, if you knew he was like that?"

"Had to. His father backed my campaign, donated a lot of money. Only asked that I give his son a job."

"So, what happened with Hamlin?"

"The only thing I can think of is that Hamlin had seen Tate come into the office, maybe more than would be normal. I told Tate to stay away, but he was scared. Wanted to whine about us stopping. Maybe Hamlin thought it was strange that Tate came to see me. Maybe he had his ear to the keyhole. So he must have suspected something and followed Tate. Anyway, last night he disobeyed my order. Instead of patrolling south, he went up north. He must have picked up on Tate somehow and trailed him. He probably watched Tate toss the body into the dump and confronted him. Bad move on his part. Only one thing Tate could do. So he shot him and then ran to me. I called you and Sampson right away."

"How are you playing it?"

"Big press. Today the Sheriff's Department has expressed sympathy for the deputy and his family and mounted a fund-raising campaign. We've called on the community for help and information and we've promised follow up on every lead. We've conveyed our regret about the lack of witnesses and evidence at the scene of the crime. Eventually it'll die down."

"Wood, they found the girl's body there. How's that going to die down?"

"There's no connection between that body and us or Tate. None. No one knows Tate was at that dumpsite. The only one they know was there is Hamlin. They can't identify the body and never will. Drummond will chase down leads the same way he's done with the other bodies. He'll get nothing. He might think Hamlin dumped the body and then got taken out by one of his partners. That would work for us. I'm going to suggest to Drummond that Hamlin was acting weird and that I'd been worried that he was doing something illegal on the side, but couldn't prove it. The dispatcher knows I told Hamlin to patrol south last night. So, why'd he end up north? That's evidence of a deputy with something secret to take care of. That'll help throw them off the track."

"Wood, Drummond's been coming down hard on Little. He's working to get Judge Howe to issue search warrants for the farm. That scares the shit out of me. If I didn't know the judge so well, I'd be on a plane for South America right now."

"Maybe he's sniffing Oscar's way, Frank, but he's got nothing on him. He's too tough to crack. I've cleaned his record. Little's more likely to shoot Drummond than tell him anything."

Frank replied, "I talked to the judge twice today. He finally agreed he wouldn't issue a warrant to the task force to go onto Little's property until he's got the girls out of there and cleaned up everything else. Howe's in no hurry to have the task force nosing around, finding photos or videotapes."

"Good thing. None of us wants those Goddamned tapes and pictures to get out. That would put an end to everything. You handled Howe well, Frank. Now how are our Boston partners taking care of the move and when?"

"During the funerals for Tate and Hamlin, practically every law official in Maine, including the governor, will be in

Portland. The tractor-trailer's scheduled to arrive in Grant the night before. The driver will stop at that motel on Route 100 and park around back. He'll leave the back of the truck unlocked. Little just has to move all of the girls to that location and stick 'em in the box in the truck. Next day, while the funerals are taking place, the truck pulls out and heads to Boston. Little's going to destroy all the evidence at his place. So, problems over."

"Money's over, too, unfortunately. We won't be able to run this show again for quite a while. Hope you guys put some of it in the bank."

They laughed. Wood and Sampson lit up cigarettes again.

"Not more smoking, Goddamn it," said Preston. "I'm going to leave. We're through, aren't we?"

"Not quite, Preston," said Wood. "We're going to have to deal with Little after all the girls and evidence are gone. He's going to be trouble when the money stops flowing, I think. Plus, he crossed us making tapes with us in them. He wasn't supposed to do that. Probably thought he could use them for insurance in case something went wrong. We need to make sure he doesn't keep any of those tapes. He needs to go. Who's going to do it?"

"Shit, Wood. Do it yourself," said Sampson. "Let the big Boston boys do it; they make enough money, a lot more than us. I don't care who does it, but I can't be seen going to Little's farm. How would I explain that? A district attorney visiting a low-life like Little? I don't have any connection to him, or even know him, as far as anybody knows. And I don't want one. I'm not doing it."

"Look, Sampson," said Preston. "I've got to lay low because of the Tate thing. I took the risk getting him out of the way, so I've done my part. It's up to you, Wood. You'll have to do Little."

"Okay, okay. I can't say I'll mind shutting him up now that we don't need him anymore. He's a stinking weasel. The way he enjoyed skinning those girls? Not natural. Treated them just like they were deer or sheep carcasses. Made me sick. I had to leave. Anybody who'd get his rocks off that way is probably better off dead."

"That's settled then. We'll count on you to do it right, Wood. And then we have to find another place for the next start up. Be thinking on that. I'm off then. See you, Preston, at the funeral. You'll be there, too, Wood, right?"

"Wouldn't miss it for the world. Lots of press'll be covering it. I'd never miss a chance like that. The elections will be here before we realize it. See you then."

Two men got out of the Dodge Ram, walked over and climbed into their own trucks. Without turning on their lights, they slowly drove down the old road. When they arrived at the turnoff, they waited until no traffic was coming either way, switched on their headlights and headed in different directions. A few minutes later the big Dodge Ram pulled up and when the road was clear, turned onto the main road switched its lights on, then disappeared into the cold night.

33

Stephen Scott had his new plan in order. He had constructed the head trap and let the white rats familiarize themselves with it. They were hungry. He had fed them very little over the past days. They scurried around the head trap, excited to find a little peanut butter clinging to the mesh wire. He thanked his Uncle Luke for this idea. The trap Stephen made resembled the one his Uncle had forced him to wear so often when he was a little boy. He hoped that Dr. McMorrow and Detective Drummond would feel the same terror he had as the rats investigated his face, eyes, nose and mouth, nibbling here, nibbling there. He hoped having the trap locked onto their heads would help persuade them to do exactly as they were told. The longer they resisted, the hungrier the rats would become. And rats weren't fussy about where their food came from.

He planned to take both Dr. McMorrow and Detective Drummond. He would surprise them and then paralyze them with his taser gun long enough to secure them. Then he would take them to his cabin and the fun would begin. When they were ready, when they had confessed their sins and begged for redemption, and he was certain the ritual release was timed perfectly, he would finalize the mission.

Somebody would eventually find their bodies. Naked, wrapped around each other in a fornicating position, they would disgust everyone. Dr. McMorrow on top, of course. A woman dominating and destroying men. The truth must be shown to the world. Women are evil and to free the world, they must be stopped, released to the punishment of a higher power.

Stephen smiled at the image he had created. It was perfect. It was creative. It was, for the first time, his very own invention. He had moved beyond the simplicity of his Uncle Luke's ritual to a higher level, involving the complexity of a woman demonstrating her evil with a man. How delightful. How like his Mother Luke.

Closure would be his. He would free himself from Dr. McMorrow. Then he could continue to carry on as God's chosen one. He would be one-step closer to achieving the plan that God had laid out for him so many years ago. If he finished this mission well, perhaps he would no longer need to use the silver needle so much. If he regained his discipline, his control, he could stop plunging it into his raw and ripped skin, deeper and deeper, searching for the pain necessary to trigger his programmed brain to perform as God demanded.

34

Christie walked quietly into the kitchen. It was past midnight and she was exhausted, cold and hungry after hours at the dumpsite. Without turning on the overhead light, she opened the refrigerator door and stared at the contents. She was so tired she couldn't register what she was looking at. It all looked the same. She didn't know how long she stood there, leaning on the refrigerator door when she heard a footstep behind her.

She whirled around. In the dim light from the refrigerator, it was hard to make out the dark figure standing still, watching her.

"Christie, what are you doing?" Alex asked.

"Oh, it's you. God, you scared me. Don't creep up on me like that. I didn't know who it was."

"Sorry. I heard some noise, but I didn't know it was you, so I was quiet. Let's get some lights on."

Alex switched on the overhead. She was in her flannel pajamas and moccasins. Her hair was mussed and hanging over her face. She brushed it back with one hand.

"What's that in your hand, Alex? My God! It's a gun."

"I know. When I heard the noise, I was afraid so I grabbed my gun. I wanted to be ready in case…"

"In case, it was Stephen Scott. I know what you're thinking. I could have been Scott. So you got your gun. I'm lucky you didn't shoot me."

"I wasn't going to shoot. At least not until I saw it was

him. That's what the guns are for. To keep us safe. But I wouldn't shoot you. You have to know I'd be more careful than that. By the way, where's your gun?"

"Right here, in the knife drawer."

"Don't you think you should carry it with you? Especially with all that's going on?"

"I don't know. I hate guns. I'm scared of them. I'm afraid my gun might just go off by itself and I'd hurt someone or myself. But you're probably right. Maybe I'd feel safer if I kept it in my briefcase."

"I'd feel safer if you'd take it with you. You never know what's going to happen. And you're dealing with all those murders now. Bill carries his gun. All the investigators do. Why not you?"

"Okay, you've made your point. I'll put it in my briefcase tomorrow. Satisfied? Now, help me find something to eat. I'm starved, but I can't seem to find anything."

Alex fixed a sandwich of sliced chicken on whole wheat bread and warmed it in the microwave oven for a minute. She added some left over salad on the side and put the plate in front of Christie on the kitchen table.

"Something to drink?"

"Thanks, a glass of Chardonnay would be great. Sit with me, will you?"

"Love to. I'll have a glass of wine with you, but I'm not hungry."

The two women sat quietly while Christie wolfed down her sandwich and her glass of wine. Alex poured her a second glass.

"Thanks. A little food and a little more wine and I'll be ready for bed. What a day, but I don't want to talk about it or I'll never be able to get to sleep. I'm glad you got up. I've missed you. I've been so busy. The time just flies by and before I know it, I feel like I haven't seen you in days."

"That's good, isn't it? Not the missing part. I mean it's good that time is moving so fast for you. You seem really involved in this case. Like before. When you were on a case, you'd just about disappear until it was solved. I like seeing you so interested and picking up your old routines."

"Yeah. Me, too. It's about time, isn't it? I think I'm turning a corner. Even though this case is gruesome, it's challenging me. I want to get these killers so badly. So many people are being hurt. But, even though so much bad is happening, something good is happening too. Working hard is really helping me. I feel like I have some power again. I think I might actually be able change some of the evil in this world, if I work hard and solve these murders. Maybe I'll even save some lives."

"I hope so. But I don't know how you do it. I couldn't. Seeing the bodies of those poor girls. I'm sure these girls never did anything to hurt anyone. Yet, they're suffering so much. How unfair. Life sometimes is so unfair."

"I know. I agree. You know, traffickers buy and sell boys too. So it's not just girls, even though many more girls are abducted and exploited than boys. The fact that someone actually forces children into slavery for the money they generate appalls me."

Alex and Christie sipped their wine quietly, sharing their anger and sadness in a moment of silence.

"Let's change the subject into something a little lighter before bed," Alex suggested. "I'm thinking of driving to New York City. The NYC gallery asked me to come down and talk about a solo show. It's such a great opportunity and it would just be for a few days. What do you think of that?"

"Oh Alex. How exciting. Of course, you have to go. This could be your big chance. You could finally break through with your art. In addition, you deserve it. You've done such beautiful work. No wonder they want you."

"I'm pretty amazed they want me. It's hard to believe. I'd love to go. You wouldn't mind?"

"You've been here, watching over me for months and before that taking care of Tashie and the house while I was gone. You haven't been anywhere for over six months. You have to go. I want you to go."

"You're sure? And there's this great show at the Modern Museum of Art. It's ending this week, so I'd really have to leave tomorrow, or the next day. Impressionists' paintings in Normandy. I'd love to see it. Frannie and I could drive down, stay a couple of days, and then come back. We'd only be gone a total of four days. It would be such fun, getting out of here for a while. Change of scenery. I wish you could come."

"Go for it. I can't leave in the middle of a case. I'll be fine here."

"Are you sure? You could have someone come up here and stay with you. Or, you could stay in Portland in a hotel or maybe at Stella's. Then your commute would be shorter while you're working so many long hours and you wouldn't have to come home to a dark empty house. The tech down at Lisa's veterinary hospital already agreed to come and take care of Tashie during the day if you decide to go to Portland."

"I'm sure. Everything will be fine. You go. I'll be okay."

"Really? You're not just saying that, are you? Because if you would rather I stay, I will. I can go later on. There will always be another show and NYC gallery isn't going anywhere. Please tell me the truth."

"I did tell you the truth. I'll be just fine. I'm so busy with this case right now; I probably won't even notice that you're gone. I want you to go. I'll feel less guilty about all you've had to put up with from me if you go and have a great time. Really, Alex. I'd feel awful if you didn't go because of me."

Alex jumped up and hugged Christie. She chattered about where she and Frannie would stay in New York, the other shows they might see, the galleries they would visit, as she and Christie washed up the dishes. And while Alex talked on excitedly, Christie pretended to be thrilled for her.

However, Christie was really thinking about being alone with her fear. Alone in the house where Stephen Scott had tied her to a bed and done unspeakable things to her. Alone to deal with every creak of the old house, every slap of a branch against the window, every car that passed by on the dark road. Alone, walking into her house not knowing what she might find, wondering if he was behind her closet door, or lurking on the basement steps, or waiting for her in the next room. Alone, all through the darkness of the night, hoping that she would be alive to see the sunrise.

35

Christie didn't see the sunrise the next morning. Dark snow clouds killed any light from the sun. She had to switch on the lights inside the house and the Saab's headlights to see the road as she drove to Portland. A freezing cold wind bent stiff branches and whipped snow from the ground up in whirls that swept across the highway, causing whiteouts. Treacherous driving conditions tightened her already stressed body and she felt exhausted as the security guard escorted her to the third floor.

Chaos spread through the task force office. Folders, photos and papers were piled high on the conference tabletop. Investigators moved between the table and the bank of phones that lined the back wall. Secretaries delivering more folders and pink message slips, officers circling around the table and in and out of the doorway and phones ringing competed with the voices of the lead team huddled at the head of the table. Techs had set up computers, crowded together at the far end of the table. Three computer specialists were silently studying their monitors and punching keys as fast as they could. The wastebasket overflowed with Dunkin Donut's coffee cups and empty donut boxes. It was just 8:30 in the morning, the day after Bobby Hamlin and William Tate had died.

Bill and Christie started their workday by studying the preliminary report of Bobby Hamlin's death.

"He was shot in the back of the head with his own gun. Only prints on the gun are his. Only one shot. Scorching shows the gun was held next to or very close to Bobby's head," Bill read.

"Sounds like he killed himself. With only his prints and his own gun as the weapon, doesn't that raise the question of suicide?"

"I think we're supposed to think it's suicide, but the angle of the shot and the placement of the gun says different. Nevertheless, Atwood will have to be the final voice on that. If she calls a suicide, I might theorize that Hamlin dumped the body and then in remorse, killed himself. Murder-suicide is almost common these days, sad to say."

"So, you think he could be involved with the Little operation?"

"She was skinned just like the others. However, I just don't think Hamlin fits the picture. He's not a sociopath. I didn't know him well, but he's been Wood's deputy for years. And done a good job, according to the folks I've talked with."

"What if Atwood says he was murdered?"

"Then I'd guess that Hamlin saw the killer dump the body and confronted him. The killer somehow turned the tables and got control. The killer wanted Bobby's body out of sight, so he forced him to walk into the woods. That way nothing gives away the body in the garbage. If Bobby's body were lying on the road, someone would call it in. And probably during a scene check would find the Jane Doe in the trash pit. So, the killer covers the reason he was there and takes out the witness. Makes it look like suicide. That works for me."

"I guess we better wait until Atwood declares one way or the other."

"We're getting Hamlin's files from Wood. He reported that Hamlin disobeyed his orders last night and patrolled north instead of south. He also said that Hamlin has been acting weird the last couple of weeks. And he suggested perhaps Hamlin had something to do with the other Jane Does."

"Well, that certainly puts some weight on the theory that Hamlin was working with Little. We'll have to look into Hamlin's background and see if he had any connection with Little. Better check his computer and start asking questions about him."

"Yep, if what Wood says is true."

Christie's eyes widened. "What?"

"Let's just leave it at that for now. Until we get the final autopsy report, let's just do some background checks."

Christie nodded, but her frown remained fixed on her forehead. "Any evidence come up at the site? What about tracks?"

"At this point we have six set of tracks. Yours, mine, the two paramedics, a set that matches Bobby's boots, and a sixth pair, large, looks like size 12 boot. So, if the sixth set is the killer's and not just someone who walked down that path to take a leak, we're assuming the killer's a man, tall, about 210 pounds."

"What about tire tracks?"

"There were too many tracks leading to the dump to sort any single track out. So we have no leads on the killer's car."

"When will Atwood finish the autopsy?"

"She's been busy. We should have the report on last summer's Jane Doe right away. She's going to fax it over. She finished that this morning. She's doing the Jane Doe found last night in the dump next, probably this afternoon. We'll have preliminary results tomorrow. Then she'll do Hamlin and finally Tate."

"Why Tate? He died in an accident. That doesn't call for a required autopsy does it?"

"Not usually. However, forensic techs on the scene couldn't find any skid marks on the highway from Tate's vehicle. He should have stepped on the brakes hard and taken evasive action when he saw the truck crossing over into his lane. He would have left black rubber marks. He didn't. His tires should have shown the wear. They didn't."

"Do you think he fell asleep? Maybe he was focusing on something else and didn't see the truck in time to brake. Did he get a radio call at that time and lose his concentration? There has to be some reason a seasoned officer failed to control his car."

"Hell, I don't know. It could have been anything. Maybe his brakes didn't work. Maybe he had a coronary. That's what the autopsy will determine. It's unusual enough circumstances that an autopsy is required."

"Atwood's one busy woman lately."

"Unfortunately, yes. Let's hope this is the last of them she has to do for a long while. It's a shame about Tate."

"Amen to that. Tate was very helpful to me that night I got the phone call. He seemed like a nice man. I heard they're planning a funeral march to the cathedral on Congress Street and a combined service before separate burials," said Christie. "Every law officer in the State of Maine will be there and plenty from Massachusetts, New Hampshire and Vermont, as well. Probably representatives from other states. It'll be a huge event."

"Yeah, especially with the May elections coming up and next November's big vote. I expect we might get some of the bigwigs from Washington, too. Coming in to get their faces on local television. Police will go crazy with logistics. Thousands of people will mob Portland. Of course, regulations require the task force to participate in the funeral parade and service. That means you too. You'll be with us, I hope."

"Sure. It'll be an honor. Two fallen heroes. Reminds us all that our funeral could be the next one. Live is short and you never know when your time is up."

"Yep." Bill stood up and stretched.

"So while we're waiting for the reports, are we going to search the island? Or hit Little's? We have the warrant for his house, don't we?"

"No, not yet. The warrant we have is limited to the island.

Our forensic team's out there right now. Last night I set up the search for daylight this morning. I knew we'd be too busy to conduct it ourselves with all that's happened. They'll call as soon as they find anything, if they find anything. Let me see, they've been out there since daybreak, about two hours, now. No call yet."

"They've got to find something, Bill. We've got to get that warrant."

"I know. Judge Howe said he'd be in chambers all day, waiting to hear from us. We only have today because he's scheduled to fly to Chicago for a judges' conference. Otherwise, we have to start over with another judge. That will take even more time. So, we have to find something before he leaves for the airport tonight."

"That gives us all day, then. They should find something."

36

In spite of the cold and the fierce wind bringing the wind chill factor below zero, the forensic team combed the island in grids, covering every square foot, looking for anything that might be evidence of the presence of Little or the girls. They were searching for drugs, paraphernalia, tracks, prints or anything that indicated that the sex parties the boys had testified about had happened there. They needed evidence to help secure a warrant to search Little's property.

It was a dark morning, the sun blocked by storm clouds. The team used flashlights even though it was day. By noontime, they had nothing. The old buildings were empty and the grounds clean of foreign debris. There were signs of a campfire and charred pieces of wood within a circle of rocks. They bagged the ashes and small particles of burned material they found, but doubted that they had anything in the plastic evidence bag except ashes from burned logs. Just what should be there.

After the noon break, the wind calmed down and the sun managed to slip through the thick clouds. The men gathered for their instructions.

"All right. Everybody start again at the boat dock and cover every inch of ground again. Bend over and examine that ground, inch by inch. Crawl if you have to. Know that something is there. You're here to find it. Go," Forensic Chief Farnsworth shouted.

The searchers, spread arms width apart, bent and walked

inches at a time following the grid paths. After two hours, one of the searchers put up a hand and yelled.

"I've got something."

Everyone but Farnsworth froze in place. He carefully walked over to the searcher, stood behind him and said, "Point it out."

The searcher pointed at a small object that glittered in the sun. "I only saw it because the sun hit it and it sparkled."

Farnsworth patted him on the back and stepped up beside him. Then he carefully knelt and studied the object. It was silver. With his evidence brush, Farnsworth swept away a little of the crusted dirty snow next to the object, placed it into a plastic evidence bag and labeled it. The silver object grew in size. He brushed at the snow again, each time being careful to collect the debris in case it held some trace evidence. Finally, he leaned back.

"We've got it. Congratulations, team. I want the rest of you to keep working the grid. Find us some more material. The more we find the better."

The searchers bent over again and continued with the grid, leaving Farnsworth kneeling by the silver object.

Farnsworth called out. "We've found what we were looking for I think. I need Johnson and Wilkins over here with cameras and lights. Coster and Dean, bring your evidence cases over here."

After the silver object was photographed and the scene videotaped, Farnsworth carefully picked it up with a pair of tweezers, put it into a plastic evidence bag and sealed the bag with care. He labeled the bag with the date, time found, his name, the searcher's name and the coordinates of the location. Then he stood up.

He spoke to his assistants. "When the team finishes the grid, that will be all for today. If they find something else, we'll need you to stay and do the evidence collection. If they don't find anything, then we're set to go for today. We may have to come back tomorrow, but I won't know until later. I'm going to call Drummond now. Then I'm taking this evidence right down to him. Coster, you're in charge. Tell the searchers to treat themselves to a good meal on the way down to Portland. It's on me."

Farnsworth turned and looked over to the edge of the pond. With a smile on his face, he took out his cell phone and called Bill Drummond.

37

The conference door opened. "Hello. I stopped over because something has come across my desk that I think you ought to know about," Dave Hadley said.

Christie and Bill shook hands with Dave and then all three walked to Bill's office. Hadley closed the door and started talking in a low voice.

"My supervisor just let me know that it's okay to tell you what's been going on in our office regarding smuggling of children into Maine from Canada. It's been a top-secret operation for two years now and he needed some convincing before he released the file. He doesn't want our work jeopardized by your organization."

"It's no secret that the FBI's not especially cooperative with locals. Nevertheless, to have something of this magnitude going on and not letting us know? That's a crime itself," Bill said.

"Hold on Bill. There's a good reason for withholding the information. We've kept it quiet because some very important people are involved. Not in the smuggling per se, but as clients and as those who have convinced other agencies and institutions like orphanages in Bosnia, Afganistan, and Romania to look the other way."

"Clients? You're protecting the clients? And corrupt officials? I don't believe it. How could you?" Christie asked.

"Yes, we're protecting some people right now. Important

people, like judges, Congressmen, corporate executives, law enforcement personnel, politicians. Names everyone would recognize. Before you blow up, listen. There is a good reason for why we're doing this."

"Better be better than good," Bill growled.

"This human trafficking operation, Canada to Maine, is only one of the traffickers' entry points in the U.S. They have quite a few on the West Coast, primarily in Oregon and Washington. And on the East coast, Florida, of course, and on up."

"So, what's happening here is only part of the picture?"

"That's right, Christie. Actually, just a small piece compared to the other operations. That's why to take action here would be like shooting dragons with a peashooter. We could hurt them a little here, but they would keep right on firing up in other locations. If we took the Maine group out, we'd only be warning everyone else. They'd go deep for a while, maybe, or have to pay out more cash, but we'd do nothing more than temporarily stop the smuggling. More importantly, we'd lose our contacts, the surprise factor, and probably all the evidence we hope to find that could put the operation out of action in every state."

"Are you telling us that you don't want us to continue our investigation, Dave?" asked Bill.

"Please, keep your voice down. This is still top-secret. The information I shared with you is only for you two. If you were to announce it, or say I told you this, the FBI would call you liars. They would categorically declare that there's no such investigation, has been no such investigation and suggest you're just trying to improve your status, salary or planning a run for Congress or governor."

"Goddamn it, Dave. How can you do this to us? Why'd you bother to tell us anyway?"

"Because my supervisor doesn't want you stumbling into

a hornet's nest and stirring everything up, making everything public. That would just hurt and not help. When we're ready and we have the goods on all the big people, we'll go after them. Don't worry."

Christie said, "I'm already worried. How do we know that you and the local FBI aren't being bought off too? If all those so-called big important people are on the take, why not you? Why should we trust you?"

Dave looked directly at Christie. "Look, I'll tell you the truth. You shouldn't trust my supervisor, the FBI, or me. Or the sheriff of Cumberland County, the D.A. or the governor or the chief of the state police, or your judges, Congress or Senate. In fact, you can't trust the federal government any more than you can trust the state."

"Then what the hell are we supposed to do?" Christie demanded.

Dave shook his head. "I don't know. Go get a house in the woods in northern Maine and forget about trying to save the world. You know what Pogo said? 'I've seen the enemy and them is us.' Our government's way of doing things, of operating, has become so complicated that no one really knows what's going on. Maybe we're our own worst enemy. Maybe no one can really do anything."

"I refuse to believe that. Maybe I can't reorganize the government, but I have to believe that I can try to stop a twelve-year-old girl, imprisoned in my own state, from growing up as a sex slave. I wouldn't be doing this work if I didn't believe that," said Christie.

Bill added, "I'm with her. I'm not going to stop this investigation, no matter what you and your supervisor tell me to do. At the very least, I'm going to get the local criminals who are involved. I can leave the big people to you if that's how you have to have it. But I'm cleaning up the shit in my own back yard."

"I hear you. I told my supervisor that you'd respond that way. He said if you stick with the evidence you've discovered about the locals involved, and play it as a small prostitution ring, he'd stay out of it. However, if you go over the line and imply or disclose individuals who are involved at the state or national level, he'll come in and close you down. The FBI has too much at stake to allow you to interfere at this stage."

Bill and Christie looked at each other. Their eyes locked, fused together with their rage and resentment. Christie nodded her head at Bill.

He said, "Doing it your way corrupts the legal system. I don't know how you can keep working there when you know the victims of your supervisor's deceptive game are little girls. The ends don't always justify the means. But we're not stupid, either. We don't have the power to move against the FBI. So, as much as it kills me to say this, I'll agree to keep our investigation, indictments, arrests, and information releases limited to local involvement."

"Thanks for cooperating, Bill, Christie. Down the long road, you won't regret it. We'll get these bastards and get them good, but we have to set off a national sting that hits them all at the same time. And when we do, you'll know that you helped by what you've agreed to today."

"Thanks for the kind words, but excuse me if I don't give them much weight. When or if, anything breaks about a national exposure of human trafficking and child exploitation in the U.S., then I'll call you up and apologize. But if, as you say, our elected leaders, appointed administrators and judges, corporate big shots and national, state, county and city, town and village paid legal enforcers endorse and use human trafficking for their own purposes, I don't think they're just going to give up their lucrative games. Until they do, I guess I'm on my own, doing what I'm paid to do."

Dave rose to leave. He stuck out his hand to shake, but

both Christie and Bill remained in their seats, hands folded under their arms.

"Sorry it has to be this way. I'll be seeing you. Take care."

38

After Dave left, Bill got up and poured himself another cup of coffee from the carafe sitting on the desk.

"Ughh. Cold. Bitter. Evil tasting. That damn coffee is no good. Jenny. Jenny, get in here!"

Jenny appeared in the door. "Yes?"

"Brew some new coffee and make it fast."

"Yes sir," Jenny replied quickly. She had never seen her boss so angry or so rude. He'd never treated her that way before. She knew things were crazy today, but usually he handled chaos calmly and remained a gentleman. She picked up the carafe and without looking at him hurried out the door.

"You don't need to yell at Jenny. It's not her fault."

Bill started pacing back and forth. With each word, he gestured wildly with his hands.

"Look, I'm really pissed off. I know it's not Jenny's fault and I'm sorry I took it out on her. But when it comes down to the bottom line, the fault doesn't seem to belong to anyone, anywhere or anytime, does it? It's nobody's fault, is it? It just goes on and on, and on and on and no one's to blame. Bad people escape punishment and continue to victimize vulnerable children. What's the point? What's the point of anything? Look at the time. In a few hours, Judge Howe will be leaving and it will be too late to get the damn warrant. We might as well give up."

"Bill, please."

Bill stopped pacing and leaned on his desk, his face close to Christie's.

"Don't. Do not try to calm me down or make it better. Look, I fell in love and got married, had two kids, worked hard all my life doing the right thing and then what happened? She died. She died in agony. I had to watch the cancer slowly take her away day by day. I loved her so much. We were so happy. Then slam! What's the point? We just end up dead, one way or the other. We might as well go north like Dave said and watch the sun go up and down. At least maybe we'd have some peace."

Bill started to pace and continued his harangue. Christie listened to Bill rave. Gradually he stopped talking and slowed his pacing. He finally stood, gazing abstractly out the window.

"I'm sorry. I kind of lost it, I guess."

"Hey, buddy. It happens to the best of us."

"Thanks for letting me get it out. I guess I needed that."

"It's okay. I think I understand what you're saying. I haven't had anyone I love as you loved your wife, die. However, I can relate to having a life where everything seems to be pretty sweet and then getting knocked on my ass. Stephen Scott made me wonder what the point of life was, too. When one individual takes total control over another and makes you wish you were dead, you tend to think maybe you'd be better off dead."

"Yeah, I think you know what I mean. But, things do get better, don't they? Every day, I think of her, but some days I forget for a little while and things are good. The sun's shining, the fish are biting, the birds are singing and one of the kids calls just to say hello. That's when I'm glad I'm still here."

Christie smiled at Bill. "Yes, things do get better. Sometimes slowly, but I believe they eventually get better. You know the old cliché, things happen for a reason. We don't always know what that reason is, but if we wait, sometimes the worst things turn out to be one of our greatest gifts."

"Yes. Although I'm still waiting for that part. Haven't

got that reason figured out yet. Do you?"

"Nope. Can't say that I do. But at least I think there might be a reason. That's a step forward beyond what I thought yesterday," said Christie.

"Well, then, we're both making some progress. Let's see how we can make this damn case progress as well."

They walked back into the busy conference room. The fax in the corner started spitting out the autopsy report on last summer's Jane Doe. At the same time, the red hot-line phone on the table rang. Bill picked up the phone and Christie walked to the fax machine.

"Drummond here. Yes. All right. Bring it in as fast as you can. I'm calling Judge Howe now to alert him."

Bill slammed down the phone and picked it up again, dialing as fast as he could.

"They found something. They're bringing it in. I'm calling for the warrant now."

He dialed the judge's chamber number and started talking rapidly to someone. Christie hardly heard him. She was staring at the autopsy report and pictures of last summer's Jane Doe.

39

Bill phoned Farnsworth back. "What is it? I called Judge Howe's office, but he's in court now. He'll call me as soon as he gets out. Tell me what you found. I don't want to wait until you get here. You tell me and then I'll tell Howe on the phone when he calls. That way I won't have to argue every point in chambers."

"Bill. Don't worry. Tell Judge Howe to set a time to meet. We have what you need for the warrant. Took us a while, but it sure paid off."

"Are you going to tell me what it is, Farnsworth, or just keep me in suspense?"

"Sorry. It's a silver pen. It was partially hidden under some dirt and old snow."

Bill groaned. "A silver pen? That's all? How does a silver pen help us?"

"Would it help if it were engraved?"

Bill held his breath. "What does it say?"

"To O.L. from R.B. For all the f'n good times."

"That's it. God. Thanks Farns. I owe you one. Bring it in. I'm calling Judge Howe's clerk and telling him to set the appointment now. This will get us the warrant for sure."

40

Bill hung up the phone, stood up and whirled around, hands in the air.

"I've got it. The clerk put me right on with Judge Howe. He tried to argue finding the pen with the initials O.L. wasn't a direct link to Little, that it could be some other O.L. He was so Goddamn cautious; it makes me wonder about him."

"Maybe he's in on it, too. How did you turn him around?"

"I reminded him that if another little girl's body turned up in the next couple of days and the media discovered that Judge Howe had blocked the warrant that could have led to the perpetrators and prevented a death, he'd have a hard time convincing voters that he deserved to be re-elected. He thought that over and said he'd sign the warrant for us."

"Good job. When do we leave? Do we have time to look at this autopsy report on last summer's Jane Doe? Looks like Atwood found some pretty important information."

"I'm too busy for that right now. I have to get this operation up and running. It's going to be dark when we get to Little's farm as it is. I have to put the calls into the state for the Mobile Crime Scene Unit, the forensics teams, round up enough people to search the whole farm and make sure the K-9 units are set to go. Plus, I have to go meet with Judge Howe."

"The K-9 units?"

"Yep, we don't know how many dogs Little has or where he keeps them. I don't want to take any chances, especially after what we went through before up there. So, I plan to have the K-9 unit up front for canine control, so no one gets hurt."

"That's a great idea. Makes me feel better."

"Yeah. By the way, that brings up something I need to talk to you about. I don't think it's a good idea that you come tonight on the search."

"What? What did you say?"

"Now don't get mad. It's going to be pitch dark, slippery and dangerous. We have no idea of what we'll find or who's there. You're not so good on your feet yet, as you yourself admit, and I won't have time to watch out for you."

"I don't need you or anyone else to look out for me. I'm perfectly capable of looking after myself."

"You won't even carry a gun."

"So, if it makes you feel better, I'll carry one. I've gone through the training for the last two months. I passed the same test your officers have to pass. I'm a good shot. As a matter of fact, I have my gun right here in my briefcase."

"Indoors, you do all right. What about out in the cold? With two pairs of gloves on? With your numbed fingers and slowed reflexes?"

"God almighty, Bill. What are you trying to do? My hands were burned. I've had plenty of operations, skin grafts, and rehab. They're not too nice to look at, but other than being a little stiff, they work just fine. Moreover, it's a low blow, telling me you'd have to hold my hand so I can walk around tonight. What do you think I do when you're not around?"

"Look, I'm sorry. I didn't mean to demean you. I'm just calling it as I see it. I need a fully alert, physically fit and strong search and perhaps rescue team. I have to focus totally on the operation. A lot depends on how I handle things. Many lives depend on me. This is a huge operation and it could turn deadly. I'm saying it's too dangerous for you. I don't want you hurt. I don't know what we're going to run into and I don't have time to worry about you tonight. I'm telling you that I don't want you there. You can't go and that's it."

"Don't do something you'll regret. You know you need me there. Oscar Little's sisters may have valuable information for us. They'd most likely talk more to me than they would to a man. What will happen if you find the girls? They'll need psychological help. Come on, think this through."

Bill slammed his hand on the table. "This is a direct order. You may not travel with the task force tonight to Little's farm. I will fill you in later with any information you need. Then, when we secure the site and declare it safe, you're free to go there and do your stuff. That will probably be tomorrow at the earliest. Now I'm very busy and have a lot to accomplish. Do you understand?"

"Oh, I understand your orders perfectly, Director Drummond. I hear you loud and clear. You don't think I can handle a dangerous situation. You're afraid I'll freak out or have a PTSD reaction and cause a problem for you. According to you, I'm a handicap, a weak link in your chain of action. And you're ordering me to stay away from the investigation until you decide it's safe enough for me. You aren't discussing this with me or asking me if I can handle it. You're telling me.

"And you know what? You're wrong. You're going to need me tonight to talk to Little's sisters, to talk to the girls if you find them, especially if the situation turns dangerous. When it comes to figuring out how to approach certain situations, I do just fine. So, think about that while you're out there in the crusty snow under the stars at Little's. When you finally realize that you do need me after all, don't bother to call. I won't be available. I won't work with someone who doesn't trust me, has no confidence in my abilities and treats me like an incompetent. I quit."

Christie picked up her briefcase, crutch and coat and stormed out of the conference room. She rushed past Jenny's desk and pushed the outer office door open.

Jenny called out, "Christie, wait. I'll get someone to walk with you."

Before she could finish her sentence, Christie was out the door and limping quickly to the waiting elevator. She stepped in. After the doors closed, the elevator descended to the underground garage.

41

The elevator doors opened on level 3 of the underground garage. Christie, walking much slower now, headed straight for her car. She unlocked the door and threw her crutch and briefcase onto the passenger seat. She got in and just sat there, talking to herself, fuming with rage.

"The nerve of him. He's such an asshole sometimes. He knows I'm perfectly capable of being out there tonight. What got into him? I'm sick of his need to protect me. I can take care of myself. I've been doing it all my life. Just because...Goddamn it. Goddamn him. Goddamn it all."

Just as she placed the key into the ignition, she heard a click. The car door opened. A dark figure jumped into the back, grabbing Christie's hair and twisting her head against the seat. He touched her throat and then started stroking it softly. Gradually, he intensified the pressure. His hand became a vise grip. Christie couldn't move. She could barely breathe.

She didn't want to believe what was happening to her. Her mind moved to denial, the safety of believing something is not what it is. The hand holding her hair, the hand around her throat must belong to a carjacker, a mugger, a man desperate for money. Anyone but him.

"Please," she gasped. "I have money. You can have my car. Please don't hurt me."

The man leaned forward. "I wouldn't think of it, Dr. McMorrow. I'm not here to hurt you. I've just come back to release you from this world."

42

"Git moving. Now. Don't take nothin' with you. Just git up and form your line."

The girls stared at Oscar Little, trying to decipher what he was saying. Most of them did not speak English. Only a few had been able to learn a smattering of English terms and those mostly had to do with the services that they were forced to perform.

Startled, some girls began to mill around, trying to figure out what was happening, a couple with thumbs in their mouths, others wrapped in blankets. Their wide frightened eyes focused on their keeper. Most were skinny, some rail thin; tiny bodies still that of children, with just the hint of buds where their breasts would be. Only a few of the girls showed any signs of oncoming puberty. Lack of food robbed hips and thighs of curves. Their hair was long and unkempt and their clothing skimpy and insufficient for the cold temperature of the room that imprisoned them. Many girls looked grimy, nails torn and bitten, arms and legs marked with bruises. The little girls held their arms wrapped around themselves to help ward off the cold.

Some huddled on dirty stained mattresses and pads on the floor of a large room. Wrapped in old tattered blankets, church charity offerings or Goodwill bargains, groups of girls clung together for extra warmth and comfort. A few pulled the blankets over their heads and shoulders as if hiding from the cold. Others lay curled up on the dirty pads with only thin, ragged pajamas or nightgowns to protect them from the frigid chill.

Twenty-one girls, ages 6 to14, lived in the big room on the second floor of the ell, attached on one side to the old frame house and on the other to the barn. Plywood covered the window, nailed from the inside into the wood frame. A single dirty bulb hanging from the ceiling provided the only light. An old iron radiator standing in one corner supplied meager heat. It banged loudly day and night as if calling for more warmth. The room temperature hovered around fifty degrees.

Five plastic buckets stood along one wall. Four served as toilets and one for trash. Strips of ripped newspaper spilled over the floor, intended as toilet paper. Two boxes of Kotex sanitary pads stood next to the buckets. A big aluminum trashcan placed along another wall and filled with drinking and bathing water dangled a black and white chipped enamel dipper over its side. There was no food in sight.

The girls started to stand up, responding to Little's demands; those who had them, stayed wrapped in their blankets. They formed a line next to the door. Little counted off five of them, opened the door and shoved them out. Waiting outside in the hall was Junie, Oscar Little's sister. She led the five girls to the room across the hall.

Betty, Little's other sister, stood in the other room, surrounded by piles of clothes. She had sorted children's clothes into tops and bottoms, socks, underwear and shoes. As each girl stepped into the room, Betty grabbed her and pulled a shirt, a skirt or pants, a pair of socks and a pair of shoes from the piles. She thrust them into the girl's hands and indicated she was to get dressed. If some item did not fit, the girl would raise her hand and Betty would give her something else to try. When the first five were dressed, she pushed them back into the hall at Junie who walked them to a third room and locked them in.

This process continued, with Oscar Little yelling constantly for the girls to hurry up. Little slapped, pinched, and pushed if they moved too slowly. Clearly, something unusual was happening and the girls looked frightened and confused. Some started to cry.

In the final group, one girl wept and bent over, clutching her stomach. Little slapped her and yelled at her to be quiet. She bit her lip and tried, only to break out in moans and tears a few minutes later.

Little opened the door and spoke to Junie. "Git Betty and hurry. Junie, you stay in the clothes room and find 'em something to wear. Watch 'em closely."

Junie went into the clothes room and sent Betty over to Oscar.

Oscar turned to his sister. "What's the hell's the matter with this one? She's actin' funny. Holdin' her belly. She sick?"

Betty looked at the girl and gasped. "Oh my God, Oscar, it's Nadia. Oh dear. What can we do?"

"Nadia? Who's Nadia? You know I don't know no names. What's wrong with her?"

"It's her time, I think. I knew it was near. But she's a little early. She's got the contractions."

"Freakin' A. I ain't got time for this shit now. How long'll it take?"

"I don't know. This's her first. Could take all night."

"Well, I ain't got all night. I gotta leave now. And make her shut up. I don't want to hear her bawlin'. It'll just upset them others and they got to be quiet. Shit."

"Oscar, you know she won't be quiet. She's having a baby. That hurts, especially since she's so small and there's no painkiller. Maybe if you gave her some whiskey and aspirins, she'd go to sleep."

"I ain't got time for this crap. I gotta git out of here. The cops are gonna be here real soon. That judge ain't gonna hold them off forever. Look, I'll just take her out to the shed when the last group finishes dressin'."

"No, Oscar, please. Don't. She's so young and she's tried hard to do everything we've asked. She's never been a problem like some of them. Just take her with you. The other girls'll help her."

"Hell, no. Somethin' might go wrong. She'll make noise. Or she could die or the baby die, and then when they open that truck, I'll be in big freakin' trouble. They don't want no dead bodies. They want live girls. I ain't gonna be bogged down with her havin' a baby now. I'm on a time limit. You know that."

"Oscar, think of this. That baby's worth $10,000 to us. The new parents are ready for it. The money's in the bank. As soon as they git the baby, the money's goin' into our account. You don't wanna throw $10,000 away, do you?"

"Stupid bitch, no way do I wanna lose that money. But I can't git caught with them girls. If that cop shows up with a warrant before I git 'em all out, I'm dead meat. I seed 'em searchin' this morning out on the island. Maybe they found somethin'. I ain't waitin'. I gotta get rid of her. Goddamn. I could sure use that $10,000. They owe me. That's my money."

Betty said, "How 'bout this? Take them other girls tonight like you planned. Junie and me'll take care of Nadia and the baby. Then when you come back, the baby'll be born and you can take Nadia to the truck and take the baby to the lawyer. That way we'll git our money."

"Hmm. Maybe that'll work. I'm worried about how soon them cops'll git here. I'll phone up the judge and tell him to stall on the warrant as long as he can. They shouldn't git here before midnight anyways and I can drive down to Grant and git back long before then. At least we'd git the money that way. And the count would be right. If I kill 'er, then we'd be down one. That'd make them Boston boys madder 'n hornets."

"We wouldn't want to git on the wrong side of them,

Oscar."

"Right. Okay. I'll take the rest of them now. You see if you can git that baby born fast. Then you and Junie git everythin' out of here. Everythin', I tell you. No mistakes this time. Burn it all in the outside incinerator. Pour gas on it first and then burn every sign of them girls, baby bottles, clothes, and records of their periods, anythin' they can git us for. Make sure all them tapes and pictures is burned too. Put them buckets back in the barn with the calves. Clean out these rooms and take off the plywood. Turn off that radiator."

"I'll take care of it. I always do."

"Right. And the money that takes care of you comes from me. Don't forget, sister. I'm countin' on you two to do this right. I'll git back soon as I can. You got that?"

"Yes, Oscar. I've got it. We'll do it right. We're in this mess too far now to say no anymore."

Oscar Little looked sharply at his sister. He thought he detected a note of sarcasm in her voice where none had ever been before, to his knowledge. The sisters had always been completely subservient to their cruel and punishing brother.

Oscar pushed the pregnant eleven-year-old girl at Betty. "Take good care of this'n. She's worth $10,000 right now."

The little girl bent over her bulging stomach, groaning. Little walked across the hall and pushed the four girls who had just finished dressing over to the third room. He unlocked the door, herded the last four inside, and locked the door again. He ran down the stairs and outside. He backed the Silverado up to the porch and lifted the back door of the truck's camper top.

He ran back up the steps carrying a rope he took from the truck. He unlocked the third room door and yelled at the girls to line up. He tightly tied each girl to the length of rope until he had lashed all twenty girls together in a long line. Then he marched them down the stairs and put them into the back of the truck. He lowered the door and locked it.

He ran back into the house and grabbed his old wool jacket and hat. "It's freezin' out there. Make sure you keep the woodstoves burnin' hot. Don't want the pipes to freeze. And git this place cleaned up. Looks like a friggin' pigpen."

He dashed back to the truck and started out the driveway. He turned the heater on high and soon the cab was warm. However, the camper section had no heat and the girls had no coats, only the clothes they were dressed in. They shivered and held each other as they bumped along the long dirt road. They didn't know where they were going or where they had been. And for most of them, it really didn't make a difference.

43

Betty and Junie led Nadia out of the ell and into the main house.

"Check the stove, Junie, and I'll take Nadia up to the back room. When you come up, bring the first aid kit, some hot water, clean towels and the whiskey. We're going to have to take shifts between watching her and cleaning up."

Junie nodded. Then she said, "What if we don't git it all cleaned up in time, Betty? What if Nadia don't have her baby fast enough? What'll happen to us if the police come here before Oscar gits back? Will they arrest us? Will they think we're the ones who done it all?"

"Junie, there's no time to be thinkin' like that or for me to be answerin' all those questions. If you go about thinkin' and not doin', then we won't have enough time to do what we have to. And we'll get caught, if not by the police then by Oscar when he comes back. Me, I'd rather be caught by the police. You know what Oscar'll do if this place isn't to his likin'?"

Junie shuddered, nodded her head and hurried into the front room to check on the woodstove. Piles of split wood lay next to the big iron stove. She used a heating pad to open the stove door and saw that the stove needed filling again. She heaved six pieces of maple into the opening and laid one whole oak log on top. She slammed the heavy door and secured it.

"That'll last a while, I imagine," she whispered to herself. She ran into the kitchen and using an iron lift, raised the round iron burner on the big cook stove and peered down inside.

"Jeepers, this one needs a full load, too."

Junie hurried into the mudroom at the back of the kitchen where the kindling and smaller pieces of wood were stored for the kitchen cook stove. She gathered up an armful and opening the bottom door of the cook stove, threw the wood in.

"Not enough, darn it. Never enough. Two more. I got to git two more."

She scurried back to the mudroom two more times and filled the cook stove with wood, closed the door tightly and replaced the lift and the hot pad. She picked up the big iron teakettle, filled it with water from the sink faucet and placed it on top of the cook stove.

"There. Hot water cookin'. Stove's full. Now what? Bring in more wood? Can't leave the boxes empty or Oscar yells and hits. No. Somethin' else. Betty said to git somethin'. Hot water, yes. What else? Oh, hurry Junie, what else? Oscar's comin' soon."

She whirled around the kitchen looking for a clue to help her remember. She never could remember the simplest thing. She never could remember more than one thing at a time and Betty had told her lots of things. "Hurry, fill the stoves, hot water. That's three right there. But she said somethin' else, too. Oh my golly, what was it?"

Junie ran to the bottom of the stairs.

"Betty, Betty? What were the other things? I can't remember. You know I can't remember. Now I'm all nerved up. Betty?"

Betty appeared at the top of the stairs. "Calm down, Junie. I hear you. Stop yellin'. Stay calm. Don't go gittin' yourself all in a hysterical fit now. We don't have time for it. We got to git organized. We got lots to do."

"I forgot, Betty. I remembered three things, but you said more. I can't remember that much, you know that."

"Did you fill the stoves?"

"Yes. Both the big one and the kitchen one. But we need more wood to be brought in from outside. Did you tell me to do that?"

"No. We'll do that later. Did you heat water?"

"Yes, the kettle's on the stove gittin' hot. And I hurried, too."

"Good girl. Now, git the first aid kit, Oscar's whiskey bottle, and some towels. First aid kit, whiskey, and towels. Got it?"

"First aid kit, whiskey, towels. First aid kit, whiskey, towels. I think so. Can I yell again if I forget?"

"Yes, Junie. Now try to remember. We don't have much time."

"Okay. I'm hurryin'. First aid, whiskey, towels."

Junie scurried away, repeating her list over and over. Betty shook her head and returned to the back room.

The room was small, only eight by ten feet, and Betty's mother had used it as a sewing room. It was sparsely furnished. An iron cot stood pushed against one wall, its old mattress covered by a flannel sheet and a tattered patchwork quilt. A small bureau rested against the other wall. The pine floor was bare and the curtain-less window so frosted that Betty couldn't see out. Only a dim light filtered into the room from the hallway.

Nadia lay on the cot in a fetal position. She cried softly and tried to wrap the quilt around herself. When Betty came in, she looked up at her with wide frightened eyes.

Nadia spoke to Betty. Sobs interrupted her soft voice.

"No sense talkin' to me child. I don't understand a word you're sayin'. But listen to me and try to understand. You're havin' a baby. A bambina, a wee one, a baby, a baby. Do you know what I'm sayin'?"

Betty imitated a mother holding a baby and rocking it. Nadia stared at Betty. She started to talk to her again in some foreign language. Nadia pointed at her stomach and then bent over it.

"I know you're hurtin' girl. You're havin' a baby. You're gonna have to let me look at you. Down there. I gotta look and see what's happenin'. I'm not gonna hurt you."

Betty used sign language again. She pointed to her eye and then put her legs apart and pointed down between them. She bent to take the quilt away from Nadia, but Nadia clutched it and resisted. After a tug of war, Betty proved the more powerful. She yanked the quilt away and threw it on the floor.

She reached over to Nadia. Nadia moved back into her fetal position, moaning and crying. Betty slapped her face and then slapped it again hard. She turned Nadia over onto her back and bent down into her face.

"Behave. I'm just tryin' to help you. Do what I say or else."

Betty raised her arm as if she was going to hit Nadia again. Nadia just lay there. Her eyes studied the ceiling, watching the dim light move away from the corners, leaving them in dingy darkness. Nadia had taken herself somewhere else. Her little body with its swollen stomach lay stretched out on the bed, but her mind, her soul, had drifted away with the light.

Betty looked down at Nadia's expressionless face. "Just as well, dear. This won't take long."

Betty removed the girl's panties and pushed her legs apart. Using a flashlight, she peered at Nadia's bottom. She felt for liquid, she looked at her opening to see if the baby had started to come. Then she picked up the quilt and placed it gently over Nadia.

"That wasn't so bad, was it? I'm gonna have to do that a lot, so you'll have to git used to it. I'll bring you some tea soon. You rest."

Just then, Nadia jackknifed into a fetal position again. She groaned in pain. Betty felt her stomach and noted the time.

"That's a contraction. Pretty strong. I wonder how long you been havin' them. The number one girl was supposed to report anyone who goes into labor or gits sick. I bet you hid it from her, didn't you? That wouldn't have helped you any, Nadia. You know we take all the babies."

Nadia remained in her fetal position, but Betty could tell that the contraction had subsided in strength.

"I'll be back," Betty said as she opened the door and stepped out. She closed the door and locked it. "Damn. She's got to have this baby soon or Junie and me'll have to force it out. I don't want to do that. I hope we don't have to."

44

Betty ran down the stairs and called for her sister. Junie was standing in the downstairs bathroom, looking in the linen closet.

"I forgot again. Sheets, towels, washcloths, or pillowcases? Which one?"

"Oh Junie. Towels. Git four towels. Yes. That'll do. Where's the first aid kit?"

Junie looked bewildered. "I don't know, Betty. Ain't it where it's supposed to be?"

Betty sighed. She'd been taking care of her little sister all her life. She'd grown to accept her slowness, her inability to take care of herself, her forgetfulness. She protected Junie from Oscar's sadistic cruelty as well as she could, often taking the blame for Junie's ineptitude and receiving Oscar's punishments herself. She promised her mother she would look out for Junie because Junie couldn't do it herself. That was the only reason she'd stayed on the farm. To take care of Junie. She had wanted to leave so badly. But she couldn't leave Junie behind alone with Oscar. The Lord only knew what he might do to her. And, she couldn't go out into the world, work, and take care of her sister at the same time. She knew men wouldn't want to be with someone who brought such a burden into a relationship, so she gave up on marriage and a family of her own. She stayed on, taking care of the farm, the house, Junie, Oscar and then all these girls. As much as she hated it, she stayed for Junie.

Now, she had to accomplish an overwhelming task. She had to midwife the child upstairs and work with Junie to get rid of any evidence that the girls had been at the farm. Dusk had turned to dark. She was running out of time.

"Junie. Go to the ell. Turn on the light and go up to the girls' room. Get the buckets and carry them down to the calf barn. Empty them into the manure pile. Then bring them back here. Do you understand what I said?"

"Of course, Betty. You told me to go to the girls' room, git their dirty buckets, and empty them in the calf barn, in the manure pile. Just like every day. I know how to do that."

"Good. Then bring them back here. I need to clean them with disinfectant."

Junie started out the door.

"Wait, Junie. Put on your coat, hat, mittens and boots first. It's cold outside. Take my flashlight. It's dark now."

"Thanks for your flashlight, Betty. I'll take good care of it. I promise."

"I know you will, Junie. Now hurry. Git your outside clothes on, and then go get the buckets."

Betty took the steaming kettle of water off the stove and poured some of it into a teapot. Then she poured the rest into a galvanized milk bucket. She took the towels, the first aid kit, the half-filled bottle of whiskey from under the sink, the teapot and the bucket of water upstairs and placed them outside the back room as she unlocked the door.

Nadia appeared to be asleep. Betty left the first aid kit outside in the hall, brought the towels and water bucket inside the door and put them down on the floor. She placed the teapot next to Nadia's bed. She hadn't room to carry a cup up, but if Nadia wanted the tea, she could drink it from the spout. The room was very dark now. Betty brought in a small bed lamp and plugged it into the only outlet, next to the door. She placed the lamp on the little bureau and switched it on. It sent a dim circle of light down onto the pine bureau and spilled some light across the floor.

"At least you ain't in the dark, like in the girls' room. And you've your own bed and it's warm up here," Betty whispered as she gazed at the little form under the quilt. "I hope everything goes all right for you, dear."

Betty left the room, locking the door behind her. She went back to the kitchen, checked the cook stove and found it burning well. She stepped into the unheated mudroom and shivered into her cold boots and coat. She pulled her gloves on, walked back to the ell and up the stairs. She switched on the hall light, wondering why Junie hadn't turned the light on when she went for the buckets. She walked into the girls' room and looked around. What a mess. At least the slop buckets were gone. Junie had managed to do that.

Betty walked back out and into the clothes' room across the hall. She opened the small closet and removed a hammer and nail pincher from the toolbox stored there. She walked back into the girls' room and started tearing out the nails that held the pieces of plywood over the window. It was hard work. Soon she started sweating inside her heavy outdoor clothes. She removed her coat and continued working. Eventually, she removed all the nails and pulled the pieces of plywood off. She was just starting to push the old window up when she heard Junie yelling for her.

"Up here, Junie. I'm in the girls' room," she yelled as loud as she could.

In response, Junie just yelled louder, an edge of hysteria in her voice.

Betty sighed, dropped the hammer and nail claw and pulled on her coat. She walked into the hall, down the stairs, yelling as she went.

"Junie. I'm here. Here I am Junie. Junie."

Betty found Junie in the kitchen huddled over the kitchen table, weeping and sobbing with great gasps.

"I thought you'd left me here all alone, Betty. I was so scared. I thought the police would git me."

"Now, Junie. You know better. I ain't gonna leave you. I was just in the ell, startin' to clean up. It's okay. I'm right here."

Junie hugged her hard and didn't want to let go. Betty thought she'd never pry her hands off.

"Junie. I'm right here now. Let go. We got things to do. Did you empty the buckets? Where are they?"

Junie let go of Betty. "You're gonna be mad. Please don't get mad at me."

"Why would I be mad at you, Junie? What happened? Where are the buckets?"

"I don't know. I took them outside with your flashlight and I was followin' the light and then I didn't know where I was 'cause I was watchin' the light and not lookin' for the calf barn and all of a sudden I didn't know where I was. It was so dark and I was scared. I called you and you didn't answer. Oh, you're gonna be so mad. I dropped the flashlight, Betty. I ran for the lights in the house. I thought you'd left me."

"It's all right, Junie. I'll find the flashlight. Now come with me. We'll do this together and you can help me."

"Okay. If it gits dark you'll hold my hand won't you? I don't like the dark."

"I know Junie," Betty sighed. "I know you don't like the dark."

45

After the two sisters found the slop buckets out in the snow where Junie had left them, they dumped the waste on the manure pile in the calf barn. Then they carried the buckets back to the kitchen where Betty washed them out carefully with a soap, disinfectant and water mixture and put them away in the broom closet. Then they walked back up to the girls' room together. Junie started picking up the thin mattresses and scattered blankets while Betty pushed open the old window. Cold air rushed into the room. Junie and Betty started throwing the mattresses, blankets and anything else littering the room out the window. Junie, delighted with the spirit of the adventure, skipped around, picking up each scrap and heaving it out into the cold dark air with a giggle or cry of excitement as she watched it fall to the ground. Finally, the room was bare, except for the water bucket and dipper.

Betty went into the clothes' room to get the whiskbroom and pan from the closet and brought it back to the girls' room.

"Junie, you start sweepin' while I carry the clothes from the clothes' room in here and throw them out the window. Do a good job and git every little bit. You can sweep it into the tray and throw it out the window, too."

She watched Junie get started and then made trip after trip from the clothes' room tossing outfits out the window in huge heaps. She wasn't pleased to be handling the fancy clothes that the girls wore when they worked. They smelled of sex, blood and other things too horrid to imagine.

When they had emptied both rooms, Betty brought up the disinfectant, water bucket and mop. She followed Junie as she swept, mopping floors and closets, washing down the windowsills and sponging the walls as high as she could reach. Five times, she had to empty the dirty water out of the bucket and climb down the stairs to refill the bucket with more water and disinfectant. When she finished cleaning, the three rooms which had imprisoned the girls looked empty and unused.

Betty closed the window and sent Junie downstairs with the broom, water bucket, dipper, and mop. She remembered to shut off the radiator and take the toolbox from the closet. Then she went downstairs with the dirty water, sponges and cleaning cloths. In the kitchen, they rinsed out their cleaning materials and placed them back in the broom closet.

"What're we gonna do with all the stuff outside?" Junie asked.

"I'm hitchin' the trailer to the tractor and drivin' it up here. Then we're gonna load everything on and take it down to burn it."

"It's sure to be a big fire, won't it, Betty? It'll keep us warm."

"Sure enough, Junie. Now, you take care to bundle up and take this flashlight of Oscar's and go outside and start pilin' the stuff up. I'll be right back. I ain't leavin' for long, but you won't see me 'til I come back with the tractor. You'll see the lights when I come. Don't be scared. I'll be back."

They left together. Once Betty got Junie working, she set off quickly to the equipment barn, hitched the trailer to the tractor, grabbed the gas can, and started up the big old John Deere. It sputtered a few times in the cold weather, but Betty knew how to open the choke and slowly work the gas through the cold lines until the engine caught. She drove back to the house and the two sisters piled the trailer full, fitting everything on. Betty hauled Junie up on the tractor seat with her and they drove down behind the calf barn to the rusted oil barrels where they burned their trash. They stuffed the barrels full and Betty doused them well with gas.

"Back up Junie, this is gonna be a big burst."

Betty struck a match and lit the materials in the barrels. Flames flared high into the sky. As the fires died down, the sisters fed more material into them. When they had put the last of the plywood and clothes into the fire, they drove the tractor back to the equipment shed, put the gas can back and walked over to the house.

They stripped off their outer clothes in the mudroom, walked into the kitchen and huddled near the cook stove.

"Darn, we need more wood, Junie. I know it's dark, but could you go down to the porch at the ell and bring more wood back for the cook stove?"

"Can I take Oscar's flashlight?"

"Well, you can't carry much wood if you're holdin' the flashlight, too. Tell you what. This one time, I'll turn on the lights outside the ell. That'll give you enough light to see the way to the woodpile and back. Okay?"

"You ain't goin' anywhere are you, Betty?"

"No, Junie. I'm just gonna check on Nadia to see how she's doin'. I'm gonna take her some crackers and a little cheese and milk."

"That's nice, Betty. Maybe her tummy will feel better then."

Junie put her coat back on and left to get the wood. She pushed the wood cart slowly down toward the ell where she and Betty had stacked the wood on the porch. She watched the shadows warily and repeated the same words as she piled the wood into the cart.

"Betty said everything'll be okay and she won't never leave me. Betty said she won't never leave me. Betty said she won't never leave me."

46

Betty walked out of the kitchen and into her father's small office, which Oscar had taken over. She had to destroy the record book detailing the girls' health problems, menstrual cycles, blood types, and work records. She had maintained the records. As she opened the record book, she noticed one page was missing, the front-page summary. Oscar must have taken that with him to hand over to the people hauling the girls south.

Betty stuffed the book into the fiery woodstove and watched it disappear. Then she went back into the office and pulled up the braided rug. She lifted the loose board and started to remove the videotapes, client records and photo negatives stored there. She glanced at the labels on the videotapes as she picked up each one. She slipped the tape labeled "Wood, Preston, Sampson, Congressman Elliot and friends" into her apron pocket. All the others she threw into the woodstove. She tidied up the office, made sure she had all the information about the girls' business destroyed and closed the office door.

She patted her pocket and smiled. This tape was her insurance. Just in case she needed it. You could never be too careful her mother had told her. And she knew when it came to Oscar this adage was especially true.

She heard Junie come in and the thumping of wood being dropped in the mudroom. Then Junie left again to get another load. Betty climbed the stairs, unlocked Nadia's door and went in.

Nadia appeared to be sleeping. Betty lifted the quilt and gasped. Blood was seeping out between Nadia's legs and had soaked into the beige flannel sheet, making a big circle of dark red.

Betty shook Nadia and tried to rouse her. "Nadia, wake up. Come on, Nadia. Wake up now. You got to wake up and have this baby. Wake up."

Betty took Nadia by the shoulders and tried to sit her up. When she finally managed this, Nadia groaned. A great gush of blood flowed out of her, covering her legs and enlarging the soaked area of the sheet. Betty put Nadia down flat again and bent to examine her. The baby had clearly dropped down into the birth canal and she could see the crown of the baby's head through Nadia's enlarged opening.

Betty grabbed a towel, soaked it in the water bucket and quickly cleaned Nadia off. She bent Nadia's legs up, spread her knees out, and secured them with the extra towels. Then she ran downstairs.

Junie was just coming in with the next load of wood.

"Junie, quick. Take off your coat and wash your hands. The baby's coming and I need your help. Hurry."

Betty ran back up the stairs and bent over Nadia again. She felt for a pulse in Nadia's neck and found a faint beat. At least she was still alive, although the contractions seemed to have stopped. Junie ran in and stared at all the blood on the bed sheet.

"Oh, dear. Is it gonna be one of the bad ones?" she asked quietly. "I don't like the bad ones."

"Junie, just do what I tell you. I need you to put your hands here and here and when I say push, you push down and toward me, okay?"

"Yeah, but I don't like it when it's like this. I like it when they yell and the baby pops out itself."

"Me too, Junie. But Nadia's asleep so we got to help her.

So try a little push now while I watch to see if the baby moves."

47

Christie had no idea where she was. She vaguely remembered a long bumpy ride under a scratchy wool blanket, but that was all. She was in and out of consciousness so often that she could not even be sure of the time of day. Or night, for that matter. All she knew was that Stephen Scott had found her, just as she knew he would. And that the bumpy ride had ended some time ago.

She was very cold. She couldn't remember ever being this cold. The silence around her was deep. She couldn't hear anything, not a creak, the wind, or the sound of traffic. Nothing. Silent as the inside of a coffin. She couldn't see because she had some kind of wrapping around her eyes. She could taste and feel the tape tight across her mouth. She tried to yell, but made no sound. She couldn't feel her hands or feet and tried to wiggle them to get the blood flowing, but she couldn't move them. She was tied up, her hands behind her back and her feet crossed over each other and very tightly bound. She wondered if skin grafts were more susceptible to frostbite and hoped that her cotton gloves and the cotton wrapped around her feet would help to protect her. But for how long? How much time had passed since Scott grabbed her from the back seat of her car? Her shivers turned to shudders as the cold drove deep into her bones.

She had marched out of Bill's office, determined he had to be the first to apologize. She'd been so angry she neglected the safety measures she always took. She didn't take an escort with her. She didn't check the garage before she left the elevator. She didn't look around before she unlocked her car. When she got in her car, she didn't instantly relock the doors. She didn't check her rear view mirror. She did not immediately drive away. She had done everything wrong. She had left herself vulnerable for abduction. That Scott managed to catch her in her own car was nobody's fault but her own. If she were going to die, she had only herself to blame. And if she were to survive? She was the only one who could make it happen. There was nobody else.

Maybe Bill would call her to apologize. But what good would that do? She couldn't answer and tell him what happened. He would get her answering machine and probably assume she was too angry to pick up the phone. What if he was waiting for her to call him? When she didn't, he would probably think she was still mad at him. He might decide to wait her out until she got over it. He'd probably assume her silence was because of the argument. After a day of not hearing from her, he might start to worry about her, stop by to check on her. However, there wasn't any indication at her home of what had happened. Maybe he would think she took some days for herself, went to visit a friend or drove down to Boston for some fun. The idea that someone abducted her would eventually grab him, after he dismissed the myth that lightning never strikes twice in the same place. After he rejected the chance of the same perpetrator snatching the same woman twice in six months. Would he figure out Scott had taken her? Even if he did, how would he find her?

Alex had left early this morning for New York. No one was home to worry that she hadn't returned there. She tried to think if she had any appointments or scheduled meetings. Would someone be alarmed if she didn't show up? No, she realized. She had no meetings scheduled and had informed Stella and Celeste that she would be busy with Bill on the Cumberland County case all week. No one would even miss her. Except Tashie, of course. She had left the old dog all alone in the house with no one to let her in and out and no one to feed her. Christie felt tears forming in the corners of her eyes. Tashie had saved her from Scott before. She couldn't hope for that to happen a second time. If only she had agreed with Alex to have someone stay with her while Alex went to the city. If only her stubbornness about appearing so self-sufficient hadn't got in her way, someone might know she was missing.

She struggled briefly again to loosen her wrists and ankles from their bindings. Too tight. She couldn't get the ropes to stretch or loosen at all. All she succeeded in doing was rubbing her wrists raw.

She tried to turn over and found she was in a very tight, enclosed space. She pushed her head against the walls on each side of her. Then pushed herself up an inch and bumped her head against another wall. Terrified, she moved her body back down. Almost instantly her feet hit another wall. Horrified, she imagined a coffin, a box buried deep under the earth. For a moment, she could not breathe. There seemed to be no air. She was running out of oxygen. She started to hyperventilate. This was how she was going to die. Not at the knife of Stephen Scott after all. Instead, suffocated to death in a box under the earth where no one would ever find her.

48

Junie tentatively pushed her hands down on Nadia's stomach. Nadia groaned deeply. Betty saw the opening spread and more of the baby's head.

"Good Junie, you did just right. Now this time, push harder and longer, until I tell you to stop."

Junie pushed hard down and held her position. Nadia screamed and the baby's head crowned and then slipped outside.

"Junie, push down again, harder."

Junie complied, but the baby's shoulders didn't budge and a flood of blood passed out of Nadia.

"Junie, wait a minute. Now, this is gonna be like when the baby calf gits stuck in its mother. Remember? I gotta reach in and pull the baby out if it's gonna live. So when I tell you to push, push really hard and I'm gonna pull. Nadia may make bad noises, but she'll be better once the baby is out. Just like the cows, Junie."

Junie nodded. "Just like the cows, Betty. Then she'll be better."

Betty grabbed the baby's head with one hand, pushed her other hand into Nadia, and grabbed hold of one of the baby's shoulders. Nadia screamed, and then suddenly went silent.

"Now Junie. Push. Push real hard."

As Junie pushed as hard as she could, Betty pulled. With a wave of blood, the baby flopped out onto the sheet between Nadia's legs, the umbilical cord hanging down. The baby was blue. Betty turned it upside down and hit it on the back. No response. She hit it again, then one more time. The baby sputtered and then emitted a weak cry.

"It's alive," Junie cried. "It's a good one."

"Barely alive. Git a clean towel and wrap it around the baby. And rip up that cloth into little strips. I have to tie the cord off."

Soon, Betty had the cord cut and tied and the baby wrapped tightly in a towel. She checked that the baby was still breathing.

"Junie, this's very important. You done this before so I know you can do it. Take the baby downstairs into the kitchen and put it into the wooden breadbasket on the table. Make sure it's still wrapped good but that its mouth and nose are out so it can breathe. Then sit close to the cook stove and make sure you keep it warm."

"Is it a girl, Betty? Or a boy? What's its name? I want to call it something."

"It's a girl, Junie. You can name it if you want to. But remember. It's only here for a little while. Then we gotta say goodbye to it. What're you gonna name it?"

"Emily. After our mother, Betty. She'll be Emily."

"That's fine. That's real good. Now go down where it's warm. I gotta take care of Nadia."

Junie left and Betty kneaded Nadia's abdomen until the afterbirth presented. She cleaned Nadia up, put a clean towel under her to shield her from the bloody sheet, and packed some cloths between her legs to try to stop the bleeding. She tucked the quilt around her. She tried to pour a little tea into her mouth, but most of it just ran down Nadia's chin as she gagged and coughed. Betty held her up until she stopped choking.

"Now, don't you die on me, child. We got more than enough to worry about. I'll be back soon."

Betty gathered up the bloody cloths and water and took

them downstairs. Junie had followed directions and was holding the baby in its make-do cradle next to the cook stove. Betty threw the bloody cloths into the cook stove after she added a few more pieces of wood. She emptied out the bucket, cleaned it with soap and disinfectant and put it back in the broom closet.

"Now, I'm gonna make up a bottle of formula for the baby. If she cries, you can feed her a little."

"Do we have any left? I thought all the girls' stuff burned."

"I kept some things out the baby or Nadia might need. I put 'em in the pantry under the potato bin where no one would see them. Just enough 'til Oscar takes the baby to her new parents."

"Does Emily have to go, Betty? Can't we keep this one? I ain't never had a baby of my own. Emily could be mine. Do you think Oscar would let me keep her?"

"Junie, listen to me. I've told you before. These babies are for other people who ordered them. They cost too much for you or me. Plus, Oscar would git into trouble if anyone knew the baby was here. The baby has to go, just like the others."

The two sisters sat in front of the cook stove, watching the baby and resting. They were tired. Junie put Emily on the kitchen table and rested her head on the table next to her. Soon she was gently snoring. Betty held on a bit longer, but eventually laid her head back on the top of her rocker. Then she fell asleep as well.

49

After Bill spent an agonizing two hours with the clerk in Judge Howe's office, he finally allowed Bill to take the document into the judge's chambers for him to sign. After another wasted half hour, Judge Howe finally signed the warrant. Bill rushed for his car and called Christie. He got her answering machine.

"Christie, it's 10:10 and I just got the warrant from Judge Howe. I'm heading up to Little's with the full team. I'm sorry about what happened today in the office. I didn't mean to hurt your feelings. I'm sure you know that. Everything just seemed to get so hectic so fast. Frankly, I kind of lost it. All I could imagine was you getting hurt in some gun battle and I just couldn't handle the thought of losing you, so I took the easy way out and ordered you to stay out of the action. I've had some time to think and I admit I was wrong. You'll be a tremendous help with the Little sisters and the girls, if we find them. No, I mean to say, the truth is, I really do need you there tonight. You know far better than I do how to handle the Little sisters and the girls. I know you can take care of yourself. This whole damn thing was because of my issues; it wasn't about you or your competency. You are incredibly competent. So, please accept my apology, please forgive me and join us as soon as you can. We should be arriving at Little's around 11:00. Call me please call and let me know your ETA."

At 11:10, Bill drove up Little's rutted drive, followed by eight other vehicles. Two other task force SUVs held six investigators each. The Maine State Mobile Crime Scene Unit came next, filled with lab and forensic staff. Four patrol vans and another SUV, all filled with police, task force officers and K-9 personnel completed the convoy. Christie hadn't shown up yet. Bill was relieved she was late. He hoped to get everything safely secured before she arrived. Then he wouldn't have to worry about her.

The caravan jolted its way into the parking area in front of the shabby white farmhouse. Dark clouds covered the moon and stars. The vehicles' headlights cut through the black void, starkly illuminating the house. All the windows were dark. The house appeared deserted. No lights shone in any of the sheds or from the ell or barn. The men and women in the vehicles waited a few moments, coordinating on their phones, watching for any sign of activity.

Bill directed the communication from his vehicle. "They had to have seen our lights. The dogs certainly would have heard us, but I don't hear any barking. So, where is everyone? My guess is that if people are inside, they're laying low. Just to be sure, I want the K-9 team to set a man on every side of the house. They could let the dogs loose at any time. You know the routine. If you can't control and restrain the dog, then you'll have to shoot it. Sorry, but those are the orders. The rest of the K-9 officers will come with us and take the lead position."

The phone issued static then the voice of K-9 unit leader spoke. "Yes, sir, we understand. We're moving into position immediately."

Bill looked through the window and spotted four K-9 officers running low towards the house. When they reached the fence, they split up and three of them moved into place on the sides and back of the house. The fourth officer squatted outside the fence at the front of the house.

Bill continued. "Team 2. Split up into two-man teams and search the outbuildings, including the big barn attached to the ell, the equipment sheds, the smaller barn, the butcher shop, and any other sheds and buildings that you come across. We're only looking for individuals at this time. We'll start the evidence search when we have secured the site. Be careful. The dogs may be staked out there somewhere. If you hear or see any, call the K-9 liaison before you move in."

"Got it Sir; we'll spread out and cover all buildings, except the farmhouse."

"Good. Team 3. Stay in the Mobile Crime Unit Lab until you hear we've secured the site."

"Yes, sir."

"Team 4. You're with us. We'll approach the front of the house in exactly one minute. Headlights off now."

"Understood, sir. We'll wait until we see your doors opening and we'll follow and provide backup."

"Okay, everyone. On your toes. We could be dealing with some pretty bad people here. Be safe. Check in if you have any questions or problems. Let's go."

Bill opened his vehicle door, his gun in his hand, and started running toward the front gate, keeping low. Next to him, Sam Dorsey, electronics tech, pointed his flashlight at the gate mechanism. With a little maneuvering and a couple of snips of the wires, he was able to open the front gate. The team ran through the gate and moved into position at the bottom of the front porch steps. The K-9 officer led them up the steps and took his place in front of the door. Protective shielding bundled his right arm, chest and legs. A wire cage similar to a catcher's mask covered his face. He held his gun in his left hand.

Bill knocked sharply on the door and called out, "Police. We have a warrant to search the premises. Open up."

Nothing happened.

Bill banged on the door with his fist. "Open up now. This is the police."

No response.

Bill looked at the other officers. "Okay, we're going to have to break the door down. Tony, Dan, hit it with all you got and then step out of the way so Hank can lead, in case the dogs are waiting inside the door."

While the other team members shone their flashlights on the door, Tony and Dan put their strong bodies in position and then rushed the door, hitting it with their shoulders. Surprisingly, the door popped open, held only by a simple latch. Quickly, Hank took the lead, and then knees bent, arms out, he prepared for the onslaught of the attacking guard dogs.

Instead of dogs, the flashlights revealed two middle-aged women peering at them from around a doorframe that led off the hall. They were holding flashlights as well and shone them on the men.

"Go away. We ain't got no money. We're poorer than you. Go away or we'll call the police," shrieked one of the women.

"We are the police," said Bill as he shone his light on the women's faces. "We have a warrant to search the premises. Put down your flashlights and step into the hall where we can see you. Where are the dogs?"

Sam found the light switch and flicked it on. The hall was suddenly flooded with bright light. The two women squinted as they stepped tentatively into the hall and lowered their flashlights.

"If we drop the flashlights, they'll break," said the smaller woman.

Bill looked them over. They looked as meek as two house mice, startled by a gang of predator cats.

"Ladies, we're not going to harm you. We're the police and we have a piece of paper given to us by Judge Howe that says we have a right to search this house for evidence. Now tell me, where are the dogs?"

"You sure you got the right house? We don't have no

evidence," said Betty. "I don't even know what you mean by evidence. The dogs are out in the barn in their kennel where they should be, I imagine."

"Get Team 2 on the phone and tell them to check the barn for the dogs, first thing," Bill said to Tom Wilder. Turning back to the women he said, "We have a warrant to search the Little house, Rural Route 2, Dalton, in Cumberland County. Are you Betty and June Little?"

"Yep, that's us. But what're you lookin' for?"

"Where's your brother, Oscar Little?"

Betty answered, "I don't know. He left a while ago. He don't tell us where he goes."

"I'm sorry, but whether he's here or not, we're going to search your house. You two go sit in the kitchen. Okay, men, two of you start in the kitchen. The rest split up. Half work the downstairs and the rest go upstairs."

Betty and June backed into the kitchen and sat down at the table where they had been sleeping until they heard the cars roaring up the driveway. They watched while the men started opening up cupboards and drawers, searching wastebaskets and the mudroom, pantry and even the refrigerator.

"Where's this door go to?" asked Bill.

"The cellar. But there ain't no lights down there and nothin' else 'cept the fruit and vegetables we canned up last summer," said Betty.

"There's potatoes down there, too," added June. "And lots of mice and spidery webs."

"Two of you take a look down there," Bill said. "Be careful. Keep a flashlight in one hand and your gun in the other."

Two officers shone their lights down into the cavernous depths of the dark cellar. They cautiously descended the rickety staircase.

"Ladies, do you have anyone living in this house now?"

"Now? Nope. Just us and Oscar," said Betty.

"Is there anybody else here now? And you'd better be telling us the truth, because we'll find out when we search," said Bill.

"We gotta tell the truth," said Junie smiling. "We go to the Bible Church and it's a sin if you don't tell the truth."

Bill looked at her and smiled. "Yes, Miss Little. That's right. So you're telling me the truth, right?"

Junie turned to her sister. "We're tellin' the truth, ain't we?"

Betty said, "Of course, Junie. Nobody lives here now but us and Oscar. Go check it out yourself, Mr. Police Man."

"We'll do that," said Bill.

The two men returned from the cellar. "Nothing down there but dirt, some dusty canning jars, spiders and rats," they said as they brushed off their hair and clothes.

50

The kitchen and cellar search finished, Bill directed the men to continue searching the rest of the house. "All right. Finish the preliminary search of the house and attic if there is one. Then we'll go out to thc cll."

The group of investigators continued the search. They were looking for any suspicious or dangerous individuals. However, they also needed to find evidence connecting Oscar Little to human smuggling, prostitution, narcotics sales, abuse of minor children, or stealing body parts.

It didn't take them long to discover the loose board under the office floor.

"What was hidden under the floor board in the office?" Bill asked the sisters.

"We ain't allowed in the office, 'cept Betty, when she does the accounts," said Junie.

"I got no idea what Oscar did with his things," said Betty. "My daddy used to hide his whiskey under the floor in that hole, so my mother wouldn't know when he was drinkin'. Maybe Oscar did the same."

Bill wished Christie were here. She'd know how to handle these women. She was much more skilled at the interviewing process than he was. He wondered why she hadn't answered his call yet and decided to try her again. He stepped out in the hall and dialed her number. Nobody picked up the phone. He left messages on both lines urging Christie to travel to the Little farm. He assured her that they were making progress on securing the house and grounds. He informed her that he was having trouble interviewing the Little sisters and needed her help. He asked her to please hurry. Then he walked back into the kitchen, determined to make the sisters tell him something helpful. He decided to try a different approach.

"I get the feeling you two are covering up for your brother. Nice family loyalty. Oscar must be treating you really well, taking care of you, meeting all your needs. Is that right?"

The two sisters remained mute.

"Or maybe Oscar hasn't been so nice to you. Maybe he's threatened you? Are you afraid of him?"

The sisters darted looks at each other, but neither spoke a word.

"Or," continued Bill, "maybe you're partners in his nasty business. I wonder how two women like you had the stomach for what went on here."

The sisters looked at their hands, folded neatly in their laps. They remained silent.

"You better speak up for yourselves and forget about Oscar. You'll be in a lot of trouble if we find what we're looking for and Oscar disappears. Then, the blame's going to fall directly on you two, while he walks away free."

"I don't know what you're talkin' about," said Betty.

"Betty, maybe we better tell him the truth. God wouldn't like us to lie," said Junie.

Bill focused on Junie. "Tell me the truth, June. What is it?"

Junie twisted her hands and looked at Betty. "I don't want to go to jail, Betty. You said you'd stay with me. I don't know if they'd let us stay together in the jail."

"Don't you say a word, Junie. Not a word. We ain't goin' to jail. He's just tryin' to scare you. You don't got to talk to this man."

"But Betty, I want to tell the truth and the truth is we're scared of Oscar sometimes. If we don't do things right, he'd yell at us and hit us and that's the truth. We had to do things just like Oscar said or we'd be in trouble. Sometimes he locked me in my room, remember?"

"What else, June?" asked Bill. "Did anyone else hurt you or scare you?"

"Like who? I don't think so, just Oscar."

"Did Oscar have little girls staying here?"

Betty put her face close to June's and spoke very slowly. "Junie, don't you say another word. I'm warnin' you. I'll be very angry at you if you say another word. Do you hear me?"

Junie nodded.

"Don't you go takin' advantage of her. You can see she's a little different. It ain't fair to confuse her and ask her all them questions. She don't remember things too good and is, well, a little slow," said Betty, patting her sister's hand. "She don't know what she's sayin' a lot of the time."

Bill was just about to ask June another question when Tom Wilder yelled from upstairs.

"Bill, come up here. You'll want to see this."

The two sisters, startled and scared, jumped out of their chairs and tried to get through the kitchen door.

"No you don't, ladies. Sit back down. What're you so nervous about? What am I going to find up there?"

The sisters didn't answer. They sat down and held each other's hands.

"You two stay here and don't move. Ted, you stay here and watch them."

51

Bill climbed the stairs, staying to the side to avoid stepping where investigators had set crime scene markers, indicating evidence that forensic techs needed to photograph and collect. Bill saw drops of blood on several steps and along the middle of the hallway leading to three officers who stood on either side of an open door. They were looking into the room.

The little light on the bureau shone just bright enough for them to see the dark spot on the flannel sheet. They focused their flashlights on the spot.

Wilder said, "That looks like blood. Someone was bleeding heavily. Then the drops start right next to the bed, follow the hall and go down the steps. We've marked the drops all the way to the front downstairs hallway. We'll have to retrace our steps when we're done here and find where they go from the front hall. It looks like whoever was bleeding left the room and went downstairs and possibly out the front door."

"You know the rules, Tom. Don't touch anything and walk carefully to the side of the blood trail. Call the Crime Scene Mobile Unit and get them activated. I think the house is secure now. There's no sign of anyone other than the sisters here. Right? Get Jason up here with his cameras. We'll need samples of the blood as well as a complete photo set. Help them out with whatever they need, setting up the lights in here and outside, taping the perimeter and this room. Well, you know the routine. Follow it."

"Yes, sir."

"Nobody enters this room until they're booted, gloved and suited up fully. After Jason shoots it and Walt prints it, get everything on that bed into evidence bags. Search the whole room, vacuum, use luminal, the complete routine and do it right. I'm going downstairs and ask the sisters what happened here."

While the forensic team started work on the blood evidence and the bedroom, other investigators continued the secondary search for evidence, scouring drawers, searching though pockets in clothing, under mattresses, though sheets and in pillowcases, rolling up rugs, looking under pictures for hidden material. Bill hurried down the stairs and into the kitchen. He checked his watch and compared the time with the kitchen clock. Both read 12: 52.

He wondered again why he hadn't heard from Christie and whether she was on her way or not. For a moment, the thought of Stephen Scott flashed through his mind. He remembered when Christie went missing last fall; they had spent too much time assuming she was with friends or just didn't want to answer the phone. If he had only acted sooner, had guessed that monster had abducted her, he might have prevented some of the trauma she experienced.

He shook his head, bringing his mind back to the present. Scott wasn't the cause of Christie's absence; it was his own poor judgment and inappropriate dismissal of Christie's abilities. The last thing she said to him was that she quit. He thought she was just speaking impulsively, hurt and angered. But, could she have meant it? Did she really quit and that's why she wasn't answering his calls or showing up here?

He prayed that wasn't the case. If she quit the task force, when would he see her? Working with her meant he could call her, ask her to come to the office, spend hours with her, and be close to her without breaking the boundaries she'd set up. He needed to see her. He wanted to be near her, talk with her.

That last thought pushed him to dial her number again. He wanted to hear her voice and explain to her what a fool he was. He'd tell her again how much he needed her advice on confronting the sisters with the evidence found in the bedroom. She was the most qualified to evaluate their answers. He needed her now. The phone rang and her answering machine came on.

Impatiently he asked, "Did you get my messages? Are you all right? We're here at Little's and I need you ASAP. You didn't really quit, did you? Please say no. And call me," he added. "Even if you're so mad you really did quit, at least call me so I know you're safe and okay."

He dialed her home number and got the answering machine.

"Call me," he said. "I need to know you're all right, safe. I could really use you right now. We've run into some interesting evidence and I need you to talk to the Little sisters. Christie, I know we had trouble at the office, but this case takes precedent. I want you here now. At least call me and tell me you're okay, please."

Then he walked back to the sisters. "Time to tell the truth now. Who was bleeding in the upstairs bedroom? There's blood all over the sheet and towels on the bed and drops going down the stairs. What happened?"

Betty and Junie looked at each other with wonderment.

"Honestly, I don't know. Was anyone there?" asked Betty.

"No. Should there be? Someone had been there and recently. They're bleeding a lot. Who was it?"

Betty hesitated. "I don't talk about them things with men," she said softly.

"I want you to tell me right now. It'll go better for you if you tell me."

"It's private, woman stuff," said Betty.

"I can handle it," said Bill. "I was married and have two children. I know all about woman stuff."

Betty closed her eyes and moved her lips silently. Then she looked down and said very softly, "It's the monthly. It comes pretty hard sometimes. I had to lie down and I fell asleep and made a mess. I hadn't cleaned it up yet."

"That's your blood? That's what you're telling me?" Bill asked.

Betty nodded. She didn't look up. Her face was red with shame.

"We can test it, you know. We can tell whether it's yours or not."

"You can't stick me with a needle without permission or take my blood if I don't want you to, mister."

"You're partly right, Betty. I have to get permission. I might have to take you down to the police station in Portland to get permission, but eventually I'll get permission to take some of your blood and test it, so you'd better be sure you're telling me the truth."

Betty shut her mouth and sat with her arms crossed over her chest. "First you got to show me the paper that says you can take my blood. Until I see that I ain't doing nothin'. When Oscar gits back, he'll tell you. I'll git me a lawyer. I got my rights. Now git out and leave me and my sister alone. You go about your business of lookin' everywhere for whatever you're lookin' for, but leave us alone. We ain't done nothing bad and my monthlies ain't none of your business."

52

Bill could tell he'd pushed too far. Damn. He wished Christie would show up. Betty wasn't going to tell him any more and June looked like she was about to faint. His warrant didn't include the sisters. He had no right to search and interrogate them. He had hoped that they would open up and spill information voluntarily or under the pressure of his questions. His warrant stated the Little house, but specified Oscar Little, not the sisters. He would either have to get another warrant, find other evidence that tied the sisters themselves to a crime or arrest them on an authenticated charge. Right now, nothing indicated they had done anything criminal. Betty's menstrual blood was certainly not evidence of a crime. Without a sample of Betty's blood to test, they had no way to verify that the blood they found was or wasn't hers.

Several of the investigators checked in over the phone. They'd found some dogs and kenneled them without any injuries to the dogs or the officers. They would take them to the Humane Society until they completed the search, as it might take many days to complete the evidence search of the whole property. They could write Little up for animal abuse, for leaving animals in an unheated shelter during extreme weather, which validated taking the dogs. This charge was not a felony demanding Little's incarceration, but at least it would keep the dogs out of the picture until the search was completed.

The preliminary search of the ell found it empty and

unheated. No furniture, no clothes, no sign of people lodging in any of the rooms. Other than the split wood stacked on the porch, the only things uncovered in the ell so far were some splotches of blood here and there that the luminal spray had revealed. However, the blood patterns didn't indicate violence. Ironically, the strongest evidence was the lack of prints, dust and dirt in the upstairs' rooms. Suspiciously clean and smelling of pine sol, the rooms screamed cover-up. Tomorrow investigators would conduct an in-depth evidence search of the ell and send the photos of the blood spots to the blood experts. Otherwise, the ell hadn't revealed anything yet that would support charges against Little.

The newest looking shed housed the butcher shop. Filled with bloodstains and butcher tools, the forensic techs faced a nightmare of photographing, printing and collecting samples and evidence. They placed butcher tools into evidence bags for testing for human blood and tissue, then began the process of swabbing all surfaces for evidence of human blood. Three locked freezers were broken open. Packages filled the freezers, wrapped in butcher paper and labeled with numbers, names, addresses, and the part of deer, steer, moose, chicken, pig, sheep, or game the package contained. Every package would have to be unwrapped and tested to verify that internal contents matched the external labels. Finally, they would need to test the freezers themselves for any evidence of human blood or tissue.

The job was overwhelming and the teams would be working all night and probably most of the week collecting samples. Although the team Bill had assembled was highly skilled, it had not yet turned up any convincing evidence that criminal acts had occurred at the Little farm.

As the night moved into its darkest phase, Bill told the two sisters they could go upstairs to bed. He informed them that he and the others would be leaving soon, but would be back tomorrow morning. The upstairs back room where they had found blood and the butcher shop were the only areas sealed and off limits.

The investigators shut off the halogen lights and stored them in the Crime Scene Mobile Unit. One by one, the forensic techs loaded up their trunks with evidence bags and pulled down the driveway. Bill left two officers in a patrol car at the end of the driveway to apprehend Oscar Little when and if he returned and to stop anyone else seeking entrance. Finally, silence fell over the Little farm.

"Can we git the baby out of the potato bin now?" Junie whispered.

"Wait just a little while longer. We got to be sure they're really gone," Betty replied. "What I can't figure out is where's Nadia? How did she get out and where's she now?"

53

The funerals for the two officers, Hamlin and Tate, who had died in the line of duty, promised to be a huge event. The national media had picked up the story of the double death of Maine's finest and led the news with it over the last two days. The Maine turnpike was bumper to bumper with law enforcement vehicles. Police and sheriffs in their patrol cars, firefighters in their shiny-clean fire engines, paramedics in ambulances and emergency crews in trucks with flashing lights came from every township, village and city across New England. The law enforcement community was coming to honor two of its own.

Government and law enforcement officials were flying into the Portland jetport from all over the country. Some had come to perform their civic duties; others hoped that voters would see them as compassionate politicians, which might help in their upcoming elections. Mourners would follow the two caskets, each loaded on an antique funeral cart, drawn by a team of four matched horses from Congress Square down Congress Street, past the police station and Maine Task Force on Violent Crimes building. There they would pause for a prayer and a short talk by the mayor of Portland. Then they would continue up Munjoy Hill to the huge cathedral where a coalition of church leaders would lead the funeral services. The governor of Maine and several popular senators and congressional representatives would speak at the funeral. News helicopters would provide aerial views of the march for the national television stations.

Hotels and B&B's were full. Stretch limousines drew crowds in downtown Portland as both locals and tourists searched for celebrities and faces they had seen only on TV.

The FBI was present as well, sunglasses and dark trench coats giving them away as usual. Officers with rifles and scopes lined the roofs and upper floors of the buildings along the parade route and opposite the cathedral, protecting the governor and prominent members of Congress.

All eyes were on Portland. Therefore, late that evening on the eve of the funeral, no one paid any attention to the Silverado truck that waited in the parking lot at the run-down Budget Motel in the tired old town of Grant, Maine. In the darkness late that night, a tractor-trailer pulled in and parked. A man exited the cab of the truck and entered the motel office. A few minutes later, the truck driver opened door #17, carried his bag inside, flicked on the lights, closed the door and pulled the drapes. Little cursed the delay of the truck's arrival once more, then hopped out of his Silverado and unlocked the pickup's cap and pulled and pushed the twenty very cold girls to the tractor-trailer. He opened the back door and lifted them into the pitch-dark interior.

He clicked on his flashlight and pointed down a narrow aisle between the tall stacks of cardboard boxes. At the end of the interior of the truck, his flashlight lit up a little door. He pushed the first little girl down the aisle and whispered, "Git all the way down to the end. Git in that door. Hurry, hurry. Go on now."

The bewildered, frightened girls, still tied together, lurched toward the front of the truck and through the miniature door cut in the bottom of the front wall. When the last one had crawled through the door, Little shut it and latched it. He pushed a row of cardboard boxes over, hiding the door. Then he backed out, pushing the boxes together as he went. The aisle disappeared. He completed his delivery by shutting and padlocking the trailer's doors.

At room #17, he slipped a piece of paper under the door, followed by an envelope filled with cash and the key to the padlock fastening the back doors of the trailer. Then he turned, walked back to his Silverado, started it up and headed out.

The driver of the large tractor-trailer waited until he heard the Silverado leave the lot. Then he retrieved the paper and the envelope. He counted the money, smiling as he put it into his overnight satchel. He opened the folded paper and scanned the contents.

He noted that the load was twenty females instead of the designated 21. When he reported that to his boss, he'd be mad and right on the phone to the Maine bunch for a rebate. He scanned the list. A tattooed number on their upper right arms properly identified the girls. The age range was from six to 14 and most of the girls were in good health. That was good. He didn't want the cargo to die on him before he delivered them. That was bad for business. The cage would hold them, even though the behavior column indicated that several of the girls might be problems.

The status column confused him at first. Slowly he figured out that "live b" meant live birth. Eight of the girls had given birth to a live baby. Two more were pregnant. A good fertile bunch. That meant more money. And three virgins. That meant good business. There would be a lot of high bidding for those three. He guessed that the abbreviation "prem" meant that the girl hadn't started her periods yet. The numbers indicated the day the periods started for those they were watching for the proper breeding time. Overall, he thought they had got a good deal. Twenty young girls would bring in a lot of money with little expense. The Maine group's problems had become Boston's windfall. In addition, the Maine organization kept good records and delivered on time without causing any trouble for them. Today was their lucky day.

Cargo: 20 females: Tattoos on upper right arms

I.D. tattoo number	age	status	health	behavior
17	13	13th /1lb	good	watch
23	10	prem/v.	good	good
35	11	16th/v.	fair	good
42	14	17th/p/2lb	fair	good
43	11	prem/	good	watch
47	12	2nd/1lb	sickly	good
50	12	22nd/2lb	good	watch;some Eng.
56	10	prem/new	good	bad
59	13	16th/1lb	fair	good
63	8	prem/v	fair	good
68	11	21st/	good	good
73	9	prem/	good	good
76	12	20th/1lb	good	watch
77	11	12th/	fair	good
80	12	16th/2lb	good	watch
83	13	1lb/preg-6m	good	watch
86	10	2nd/new	fair	good
89	6	prem/	fair	fair
92	12	1 7th/1lb	fair	good
97	11	preg-4-m	fair	watch

54

Bill arrived home just a few hours before dawn. He took a long hot steaming shower and padded down to the kitchen to find something to eat. He rummaged around in the refrigerator and grabbed some bread, sliced ham and Swiss cheese. He put them together with a liberal dose of mustard and ate while staring at the shaft of light from the kitchen cutting into the darkness outside.

There were no messages from Christie on his answering machine or on the voice mail of his cell. He guessed she was still angry with him. So angry that she must have meant what she said about quitting the task force. He found it hard to believe that Christie would walk off this case, off the job, when working meant so much to her and her recovery. She was making such good progress, too. It wasn't like her to quit anything. Christie was more likely to work a case far beyond where anyone else would go, sniffing out the minute details, going over and over the files, calling more witnesses to see if she could ferret out any more information. So what was she doing now? Holding out for an apology? He'd given her that. What more could he do to bring her back?

It had been almost twelve hours since he had argued with her. He had called her; he had apologized. He had let her know the task force needed her. Something wasn't right. Christie wasn't one to hold a grudge. He tried her phone again. Nothing but the answering machine. If he weren't so tired, he'd jump in the car and drive up to her place. Just to check. Just to make sure she was all right.

He made another phone call. "Tom. Sorry. I bet you just got to sleep. Look, I'm a little worried about where Christie McMorrow is. She didn't come up to Little's tonight and I haven't been able to contact her. You don't live too far from her place. I wonder if you'd stop by on your way to Little's tomorrow morning. Well, actually that's this morning, now. Tell her we need her up there. Drive her up yourself if you can."

Bill listened for a minute. "No, I don't really have any reason to think something bad has happened. We had a miscommunication yesterday afternoon and I may have implied I didn't need her during the initial search. However, I need her there today to talk with those sisters. I did ask her to call me, just to let me know she was okay. But she didn't. That bothers me. That's not like Christie."

Bill listened. "No. No need to drive out there now. I appreciate your offer. But I think a few hours won't make that much difference. Get some sleep and check on your way up. I just want to make sure she knows the team misses her. Thanks Tom. See you in a few hours."

Bill was exhausted. He had only a few hours before he resumed command of the search up at Little's. Daylight and the search dogs would help them find any hastily dug gravesites or bodies hidden in the brush or woods. It was going to be grueling work, hard on the searchers, dogs and forensic team. In the sub-freezing temperatures, even walking a short distance was difficult.

They had a time limit today. They had to pack up and start their drive back to Portland by noon. Although the attorney general had excused the task force from attending the funeral parade this morning because of the importance of the case, he ordered them to attend the funeral service in the cathedral. Christie was required to be there with them.

Bill decided to lie down for a short nap. He'd call Christie just before he left and apologize again. He'd remind her of the task force obligation to sit together to honor the two dead law officers. He'd tell her to meet him outside the cathedral at 1:00, half an hour before the service began.

With this thought, Bill fell asleep.

The alarm beeped Bill awake. He forced his eyes open and saw that the clock read 5:00. He would have to hurry to make it to Little's so he'd be there when the others arrived. He dressed quickly and grabbed an apple on his way out to the car. He'd stop at the drive-through and buy coffee on the way up to Dalton.

Once he was underway, he dialed Christie's cell. There was still no answer. Strange. Even though it was early morning, he knew Christie slept with her cell phone on the nightstand beside her bed. She had to have heard the call. Did she see it was from him and decide not to answer? He called her landline and got the answering machine again. He was really worried now. This did not feel good. He left another message even though by now he was sure that something besides anger was stopping Christie from responding to him. Something must have happened to her. Thoughts of Stephen Scott sent shudders down his back. Was he back? Could he have taken Christie?

"Christie, Bill. Didn't you get my messages? I'm worried. Call me please. If you can't make it to Little's this morning, meet me outside the Sacred Heart Cathedral at 1:00 this afternoon so we can sit together at the funeral service. If you're not there, I don't know what I'll do. Probably put an all points bulletin out for you. Please be there."

The last statement was more a prayer than a request. If Scott had returned and abducted Christie, help from a higher power might be the only thing to save her.

Bill pressed down on the accelerator. He'd know soon from Tom if his worry was justified. Maybe Christie was just being difficult and he was over reacting from his fear of losing the woman he loved. Losing another woman he loved. He couldn't handle that. He had barely lived through the loss of Emmy.

Speeding up and needing to concentrate on the slippery road ahead of him helped Bill switch his thoughts from Christie to the job ahead. They could find anything this morning from a group of crying girls in a hidden hole in the barn floor covered by a trap door, to a mass grave of dead girls, hurriedly bulldozed over. Perhaps Little cremated the girls and mixed their ashes with manure to throw off the search dogs. Anything was possible. They might find nothing at all. And if that happened, and they found no evidence of any criminal activity? Bill decided he didn't want to think about that possibility just yet.

55

At daybreak the morning of the funeral parade, the roads were treacherous, covered with black ice. Cold air froze the windows of the vehicle as Bill sped north even though the heater was on full blast. It was going to be a tough morning for everybody at the crime site. His mind slipped back to thoughts of Christie. Was she feeling the cold, too? Where the hell was she?

Of course, he was the one who told her she couldn't go with the team to the Little's farm until they secured the site. He was the one who insinuated Christie wasn't tough enough or strong enough to accompany the group. Now, he was the one who regretted everything he had said. In the dawn light, everything looked different. There had been no gunfight, no danger to the team after all. They hadn't found any suspects at the farm, except possibly the sisters, who were far from a danger to the investigating officers. The situation with the dogs turned out fine, too. And obviously, he needed Christie to talk with the sisters. He had blown that interview. His thoughts stopped as he saw the convoy of law enforcement vehicles lined up by the side of the road, just before the driveway to Little's farm.

Bill rendezvoused with the others, looking for Tom Wilder, hoping for good news about Christie. Before he had a chance to talk to Tom, he realized that he needed to replace the two guards who had watched the road last night, give them a chance to warm up, eat, catch a nap before they could return to duty this morning. They would have to back their car out of the driveway so the others could move in.

Bill rolled up behind the patrol car blocking the driveway. Frost had etched all the windows so he couldn't see inside. The motor wasn't running. Bill honked his horn. There was no response.

Tom Wilder jumped out of the car behind Bill and walked up to Bill's door. Bill buzzed his window down. Frigid air raced in. Instantly, Bill felt cold to his bones. He looked up to Tom.

"What did you find out at Christie's? Was she there? Is she okay?"

"I stopped by Christie's house on my way up. No one was there. I could hear a dog barking inside when I rang the bell. All the windows were secured and there weren't any tracks in the snow around the house. I couldn't see inside because the drapes were all pulled. The garage doors were locked. There weren't any recent tracks in the driveway. You know we had that dusting of snow yesterday. Either Christie beat it home before the snow or didn't drive home at all because there aren't any fresh tracks."

"Where the hell is she?"

"I don't know. But it looks like she isn't home. Do you want me to have her friends checked out? Look for her car?"

"I don't know. Well, yeah. Call Jenny and ask her to call around and put out an APB on her car. I guess that wouldn't hurt. That is, if something's happened to her. Jenny has all the information on Christie's car, friends, and office numbers."

"Will do. She probably decided to stay in Portland for the parade and funeral service. Maybe Jenny can check the hotels, too."

"Good idea. You call and then let's get on with our business. What's with those guys in that patrol car? Why don't they have their engine on? That's odd. Maybe they froze to death last night."

Tom chuckled. "Or maybe they had a little too much

hot cider and didn't feel the cold at all."

"Go on up there and check them out. Be careful, Tom. I don't like the way this looks. Something's wrong here."

Tom walked over to the patrol car. He knocked on the window. Then he tried opening the door. It was iced over. He banged his gloved fist against the ice-covered door handle. Then he tried the door again. This time it opened.

Tom recoiled in horror. He turned away, bent over and retched in the snow bank. Bill and several others jumped out of their cars and ran over to the guards' car.

Bill looked in the car and then turned to the others crowded around. "It's awful. It doesn't look like they stood a chance. Oh my God. Dean and Stan. Dead. Blown away."

Frozen blood and brain tissue covered the two bodies, which were lying back against the front seats, the dashboard, the windshield and doors. Someone had blown both men's heads apart, apparently by several shots from close range. The men were unrecognizable, except for their uniforms and badges.

Bill waved to the Mobile Crime Scene truck and walked over to the forensic techs.

"Guys, we're going to need you to cordon off this road and start your work right here. Dean and Stan are dead. Shot in the head, both of them. Looks like several times, gangland style. Call the coroner, the sheriff's office and Atwood. You know the routine. You'll have to deal with this before you resume the work up at the house."

Bill walked over to the Mobile Crime Scene truck. "You park here and work with the forensic team. The rest of us are going up to the house on foot to see if anything else has happened. I'll call if we need you."

Bill gathered the rest of the men and women together. He was drawn and haggard. Too little sleep, too much pressure, too much worry over Christie and now the deaths of two of his team had almost wiped him out.

"I'm sorry to tell you, but we lost Dean and Stan sometime early this morning, after we left here. Someone shot them. The forensic team will stay down here and take care of this scene, but we need to get up to the house to see what else is going on. We're going to have to walk up the road from here. Lock your vehicles and carry your gear. We'll stay to the side of the road so we don't contaminate the scene any more than we have to. Put rubber bands around your boots so we can identify our tracks from others. Keep alert. Guns out and ready. We don't know who or what may be up there."

56

The teams walked single-file up the driveway. Where the road curved and the Little farm came into view, Bill stopped. Using binoculars, he panned the house and perimeter. Using the scopes of their rifles, several other officers also studied the grounds and buildings.

"See anything?" Bill asked. The others shook their heads no. "Then we'll go on. Be careful."

The officers walked up to the house, puffing misty clouds of breath into the frigid air. The crisp early morning light created shadows everywhere. The shadows were so deep in some places that the officers' eyes couldn't penetrate them. Their boots squeaked against the cold snow. The blue jays and chickadees were eerily silent this morning.

Bill waved a group of five over toward the outbuildings. He indicated to another group to stay put. Then he and eight officers walked to the house, staying just to the right of the trampled snow in the walkway.

The gate was still open, as they had left it last night. Bill stepped onto the porch and started to knock on the door. As his hand met the ancient wooden door, it opened with a squeal of its old hinges.

Pushing the door all the way open, Bill peered inside the dim hallway. It looked as it had last night. Nothing seemed disturbed. He stopped and pulled paper booties on over his boots. He slipped off his winter gloves and pulled on the latex gloves he carried in his pockets. The others behind him did the same.

He stepped cautiously down the hall and noted the temperature was the same as the outdoors, freezing cold. He looked carefully around him, gun ready. He pushed the kitchen door open and stopped.

"Oh my God," he whispered.

The others came up behind him. Lying on the kitchen floor, covered in blood, were Betty and June Little. Both had been shot in the chest and head. Frozen pools of blood surrounded the women. Bill carefully walked to each of them, trying to avoid stepping on the crimson ice. He felt for a pulse in Betty's neck. Nothing. She was dead. Then he moved to June and failed to find a pulse in her neck or wrist. "Their bodies are cold. No pulses. They've been dead for a while."

Bill looked back down at June. One arm was wrapped around what appeared to be a bundle of rags. Slowly he pulled it loose and unrolled the cloth.

"Oh no. There's a baby in here," he said. "Dead, too. But no blood. It doesn't appear to have been shot."

Bill rolled the cloth over the baby again, placed it back under June's arm, and stood up.

"Call the Mobile Unit and tell them we have at least three more dead up here in the house. As soon as they're finished with the preliminaries down there, we need them here. Tell the forensic team to divide. Send half of them up here to the house right now."

He turned to the officers outside the kitchen door. "Two of you search the kitchen. Maybe the killers left something behind. You others search the rest of the house. Be careful, they could still be here."

Bill looked around the kitchen. The cook stove was cold; the fire had gone out long ago. The sisters were dressed in flannel nightgowns and wool robes. They must have been sleeping when the killer entered the house. Was the killer Little himself, getting rid of all witnesses, even his sisters? Or would they find Little massacred as well, somewhere out on the farm? Where did the baby come from? It looked newborn and very tiny. He was sure that the sisters hadn't looked pregnant yesterday, so where was the mother?

He noticed the women's aprons hanging neatly on pegs in the kitchen wall. He remembered they both had worn aprons yesterday. He walked over and touched the old cotton cloth. There was something sad about the aprons, just hanging there.

As he rubbed the cotton, he felt something in one of the apron pockets. He pushed his hand into the deep pocket and pulled out a videotape. Quickly he read the names printed on the outside. He glanced around and saw that the other two detectives were busy checking the mudroom. Then he stuffed the tape into his coat pocket.

His cell phone rang. "Yes?"

"Bill, we found some more dogs up on the backside of the equipment shed. Somehow, we missed them last night. They're all dead. Shot. It's a mess."

"Okay. Cover the ground. Look for casings, tracks, anything that doesn't look like it belongs there. Put the crime scene tape around the area. Report back to me if you find anything. We'll have to determine if those dogs were killed at the same time as the sisters and Dean and Stan. The time line could be important."

Did Little come back and kill the guards, his dogs and then his sisters? He was cold enough to do something like that. Bill remembered him shooting the injured dog and then kicking it. What had happened here in the last few hours?

"The sisters' bedroom is pretty messed up, but no signs of blood. They must have put up a fight before they were dragged down here and shot. Other than that, everything seems normal. The back bedroom where we found the blood was still taped and closed. The killers aren't here now," reported Max Caswell, one of the task force investigators.

"Go back and search the ell and the attached barn. We have to cover it all and fast. Remember we're due to leave here for the funeral at noon and we should be there, full force, or at least as many of us as possible."

"We'll hurry, Bill, don't worry." Max added, "But we won't miss a thing, I promise you. We'll come back right after the burial, right? We can pick up then."

"Yes, we'll be here for days," Bill said. "There's a lot of territory to cover."

The front door flew open and Detective Dick Elliot ran to the kitchen, stopping at the door.

"Bill, we found someone. There's a girl up in the hayloft. She's in pretty bad shape, but she's breathing."

"Was she shot?"

"I don't know, but there's a lot of blood. She's unconscious. We wrapped her in some blankets and the paramedics are on their way."

"Show me," Bill said. "You two keep searching here in the kitchen, the cellar, the pantry. Then, meet us out by the barn. Put a tag on the door for the coroner and the forensic people. Indicate the body count, 3, on the tag. Put the tape across the door too."

Bill hurried out to the barn. Most of the other investigators were already there. Bill walked into the dark interior. The smell of hay, manure, dust and old wood hit him, reminding him of the visits to his grandfather's farm in Vermont, so many years ago. The barn had been his favorite place to play and he spent hours in the hayloft above the rest of the world, lost in his own dreams.

Little's barn was a mess. Piles of old horse harnesses, rusted tools and equipment were scattered around. Moldy burlap bags were tossed everywhere. Mounds of rotting manure filled the center of the barn.

Bill looked up. A female officer standing next to the wooden ladder that led up to the loft waved down to him. He started to climb. The rungs were splintered and loose. He held tightly to the sides of the ladder, afraid that one of the rungs might snap under his weight.

"She's over there, sir." The officer pointed to a pile of hay bales in a dark corner. Bill had trouble seeing what the detective was pointing to.

"Where?"

The officer flashed her light in the corner.

"See the officer kneeling over by the wall? The girl tucked herself down in there, between two loose boards. She covered herself with hay. It was a miracle that I stepped back there and caught a glimpse of her leg with my flashlight. She had hidden herself very well. I guess that's why she managed to escape what happened here last night."

Bill made his way over bales of hay to the corner. He bent over the officer sitting on the floor. There in a nest of hay, lay a little girl. She was as pale as a winter moon and not moving.

"Is she still alive?" Bill asked.

"Yes, sir. Her pulse is weak and she's bleeding. I wrapped her up really well and I'll stay here with her until the emergency folks get here. Detective Walker would like to stay, too, if it's all right. Just in case she wakes up and wants a woman around."

Bill thanked the two officers and climbed carefully down the ladder. He could hear a siren in the distance and hoped it was the Cumberland County's ambulance speeding toward the farm. He prayed they made it in time.

He glanced at his watch. They would have to secure the site and leave for Portland in less than two hours to make the funeral service. Whoever massacred two officers, eight dogs, two middle-aged sisters, and possibly a newborn baby was probably far away by now. He didn't think the killer or killers would return. Nevertheless, Bill wanted to be ready for anything. He would leave six men on guard, four at the driveway and two near the house. He wondered how the girl had escaped and what her story was. He prayed that she lived long enough to tell him.

57

Back at the empty task force building in Portland, the fax spit out the final autopsy report on the Jane Doe from last summer, adding details to the preliminary report that Christie had been looking at yesterday.

Although severely burned, the corpse still gave out information about herself. Evidently, Atwood's substitute had failed to lay out the bones to determine if the coroner's people recovered the full skeleton. Atwood found she was missing both leg bones. She could not determine, due to intense charring, whether the killer had removed the girl's skin prior to setting her on fire. However, she was able to ascertain that last summer's Jane Doe had delivered a baby some time before she died. Atwood also concluded that the killer removed the heart, kidneys and liver from the body before burning it. The links Bill and Christie hoped to find between the two Jane Does existed.

The next report spilled out. Atwood's autopsy report stated that Bobby Hamlin had died of a gun shot to the head that could not have been self-inflicted. He had been murdered, up close and personal. Pages detailing the full autopsy followed. Then the fax paused.

The fax sputtered again and the preliminary autopsy of William Tate slipped down onto the paper holder. William Tate's method of death was homicide. Atwood had found enough fentanyl in his blood stream to kill him three times. She surmised from his stomach contents that the fentanyl had been added to his coffee. Investigators had recovered his stainless steel thermos and Atwood found fentanyl in it also. Testimony documented that Tate filled his thermos at state police headquarters before leaving for his regular patrol on the Maine Turnpike. Atwood concluded based on the fast activation rate of fentanyl, that as Tate turned onto the turnpike and established his patrol speed, he most likely took his first drink of coffee. Almost instantly, he would have felt dizzy, lost muscle control and control of his car and then lapsed into unconsciousness. Whether the tractor-trailer was there or not, whether he had hit a tree or veered off the side of the road onto the safety lane, Trooper William Tate would be dead within minutes. Cause of death: fentanyl poisoning.

Atwood added a postscript that the killer probably orchestrated the car accident as well, using the tractor-trailer to ensure severe injuries to Tate. No autopsy required. Death by accident. Tox screens and lab work would be unnecessary. There would be no reason to explore further. Therefore, the real cause of death, poisoning, would remain hidden.

Her last sentences said it all. "That miserable s.o.b. planned it all out so well, except for one thing. He forgot I'm compulsive when it comes to determining cause of death. Not many people fool me. Investigate the state police. Check out that tractor-trailer driver. How did he just happen to pull alongside Trooper Tate shortly after he left the office and took his first drink of coffee? Hope this helps you catch the bastard. Fry him. The final report will be in your hands in a few days. Next up on my calendar is the dump Jane Doe." E. A.

58

Dave Hadley called the Maine State Task Force on Violent Crimes the morning of the funeral parade. No one answered the phone. No one was there.

Jenny had done her best to contact everyone who might have seen Christie, but she didn't have any success. No one on Christie's call-list knew where she was. Jenny reached Alex in New York, who immediately canceled her trip and headed home. She would be calling everyone she could think of on the way back.

Jenny then called the state police. Because of the possible threat of Scott, Christie had provided them with the security code and keys to the house. They reported that the house was locked and undisturbed. No one was there. The garage was empty. They had let the dog out for a few minutes, fed her and then reset the security alarms. No tips had come in about her car, even though the APB had been out for hours. Jenny contacted hospitals, hotels, inns, and airlines, all with the same result. No one had seen or heard from Christie. It was as if she had just disappeared.

In the memo she left in Bill's mailbox, Jenny suggested Bill file a missing person's report. She had attempted to contact Bill several times by cell phone, but could only leave him the messages that she, the state police, and Christie's contacts had not located her. She had done all she could. Late already, she dashed off to attend the funeral proceedings. Everyone else was in the field or had already left for downtown to participate in the funeral parade.

The recording Hadley heard was, "We're sorry, the task force offices are closed until 4:00 today. All personnel are attending the funerals of Officers William Tate and Sheriff's Deputy Robert Hamlin. You may leave a message. If you are calling with an emergency, please call the Portland police department at 207-908-3344. For other options, please listen to our menu."

Hadley impatiently waited until he heard the message option for Bill's voice mail. "This is FBI agent David Hadley. I need to talk with you immediately. It's urgent. Call me on my cell."

Dave had already called Bill's cell, but received no answer. He called again and left another message.

"Hadley calling. We're focusing on Boston. We expect to wrap that up and when we do, we'll take over the ongoing investigation in Maine. Cease all action on the Cumberland County case, as of now. I repeat. Your orders are to cease all action on the Cumberland County case immediately. Call me to verify that."

Hadley hung up. He tried Bill's home phone again and the answering machine picked up. He didn't want to leave a detailed message in case the line wasn't secure, so he simply said, "Your orders are to cease all action on the case we discussed. Extremely vital. Call for more information. Hadley."

Hadley was nervous. If the task force uncovered and revealed the names of VIPs involved with human trafficking of children in Maine, the publicity would forewarn others. Stings directed at operations in seven cities would blow up. Then, who knows what disaster would happen. The FBI might be pulled out of the investigation, accused of politicking, of trying to ruin the reputations of senators and congressional representatives. They might lose funding. The people who had taken the lead roles in the investigation, who pushed for prosecuting these men, might lose their jobs and far worse.

The major players in the criminal ring, some of whose faces appeared in the newspapers nationwide for their good works, their diplomatic successes, their civil rights legislation and their political and economic wisdom, would be safe. Their part in enslaving and abusing thousands of victims would remain a secret. Instead, these power-driven men would continue to hide under their public images while they sought revenge, tightened up their operations, and spread their filth and destruction. They would continue to receive millions of dollars as their rewards. And thousands more children would be sold into a world so evil that dying would seem the only way out.

59

Bill rushed into Portland. He had stopped at Christie's house and verified what Tom had told him. She wasn't there and hadn't been there last night or today. He checked for messages on his cell phone. He ignored the messages from Dave Hadley, but listened intently to the brief message Jenny had left and then called her at the office. She had already left.

He tapped in his office voice mail number. He had messages from Hadley ordering him to close the Cumberland County case down immediately and directing him to call him back ASAP. He deleted the messages; he'd deal with him later. He had another message from Jenny about her unsuccessful attempt to find information about Christie, the state police visit to Christie's house and her suggestion to file a missing person's report. There were no messages from Christie.

Bill was more than worried now. He was frightened. He quickly called the Portland police and explained that he didn't have time to stop and file a missing person's report at the station, but he wanted one put out immediately for Dr. Christie McMorrow and briefly detailed the circumstances. He explained that they already had all Christie's information on file and an APB had been issued for her car earlier. The sergeant on duty agreed to prioritize the missing persons report and procedure, but reminded Bill that only a skeleton force was working on incoming cases, due to the funerals. Bill could expect no more from the police until after the activity surrounding the funerals ceased. He hung up the phone.

He realized he couldn't do anything right now to find Christie. Maybe by some chance, she was all right and would show up at the funeral, unaware of all the worry she had caused. He tried to hold on to this thought to keep his fear from destroying him. His heart was beating too fast; his hands were trembling and his mind jittering from one idea to another, one image to the next. He remembered how Christie looked when he found her last November. Naked and blue with cold, feet and hands charred to the bone, curled into a fetal position and tied to a pine tree in the woods behind her house. He thought she was dead. He shook his head to dislodge the image.

By now, he was really running late. He didn't really care any more; his mind was focused on Christie. His task force, the ones he needed to help him find Christie were all at the funeral service. He'd have to go there and yank them out. He left his vehicle parked illegally on a no-parking side street. He placed his task force parking permit in the center of the windshield and hoped the parking authorities would not tow his car. He walked briskly several blocks toward the cathedral. As he neared the huge church, the crowds became almost impossible to push through.

Huge satellite trucks formed a block of their own in the Hannaford's grocery parking lot across from the cathedral. Reporters were talking rapidly into microphones, identifying the attendees of the funeral service as they arrived.

Bill thought the scene looked more like the Academy Awards' red carpet show than a funeral for two men who had died in action. Except for the American flags that were waving everywhere and the absence of balloons, it could have been any huge celebration in Portland.

Bill looked around for Christie, but he didn't see her. It would be nearly impossible to find anyone in this crowd. Perhaps she had already entered the church. If Christie didn't show up for the service, he would know that the worst had happened to her. Tears started to well in his eyes as he moved through the crowd.

It became even harder to push through the crowd as he neared the cathedral. People were queued up trying to get a good view of the famous people allowed inside while they waited out in the cold. The crowd was not happy about Bill trying to force his way through to the front and several people jostled him as he passed by.

He felt a sharp pain in his neck, then another under his arm. He tried to turn to see what was happening. Had someone stabbed him? His vision blurred as he tried to spot his attacker. Then he was hit again with a shockingly painful jolt that dropped him to his knees in the middle of the crowd. Another powerful shock hit his chest just before he lost consciousness. As everything turned black, he heard someone yelling.

"Give him room. He's having a heart attack. I know this man. Step away. Someone help me carry him out of the crowd. Hurry."

Bill felt someone grab his arms and legs and lift him up. He couldn't open his eyes. He heard someone far away say, "Make way, make way. We have a sick man here. Step back."

60

Bill slowly became aware that he was waking up. He was confused. His mind didn't seem to be working right. He couldn't open his eyes. He tried to lift his hand to his face and found he couldn't move it. His hand was underneath him and when he tried to move it again, he realized it was tightly bound to his other hand.

He tried to roll over, but couldn't. He couldn't move his legs either. They were tied together and then fastened to something else that immobilized them. When Bill finally opened his eyes, he couldn't see anything. Blackness surrounded him. He couldn't even distinguish shadows or outlines against the black background.

Where was he? What had happened to him?

He remembered going to Portland. He recalled trying to push through the tightly packed crowd. He felt again the sharp stabs into his back, neck and chest, and then nothing. He must have passed out. He thought he recollected someone carrying him away. But who and where?

He tried to move his head around to see where he was. His head wouldn't move. He tried to rub his head on whatever he was lying on and detected that he had something hard around his head. Sharp edges pushed against his scalp.

Bill tried to calm down and assess his situation. Someone had obviously abducted him. They must have stuck him with a hypodermic needle or stunned him with a taser. If the taser hit him at least three times, the shock could render him unconscious.

He listened. He heard nothing. Not a sound. Perhaps he was alone. He was cold, bitterly cold. He couldn't remember ever being so freezing cold. Yet, he had a sense that he was inside. Inside what? He tried to sense his environment. He was lying on his back on a hard surface. His stiff, numb fingers moved against the surface. Wood. Splintery old wood. So was he in some sort of a building with a wood floor?

He tried to call out to test sound bouncing off walls. Then he realized with a start that a gag filled his mouth. Why didn't he notice the gag earlier? What was the matter with his thinking? Now that he realized he had something shoved into his mouth, he grew worried about breathing. He'd have to be careful. He tried to move his tongue around the cloth in his mouth, push it away from his throat. He was unsuccessful.

He felt panic rise. He was thirsty. How was he going to get water? Even in the cold, a person could die after three days without water.

He forced his mind back to the present moment. Maybe he could make some noise with his hands and feet on the floor. He tried lifting his legs again. It was as if they weighed a ton. He couldn't get them to leave the ground.

He wiggled his fingers and knocked them against the floor. He could barely feel the contact; his hands were so cold. He tried again. There was a soft tapping; his clothes and body muffled it.

Whoever had tied him had done a professional job. He couldn't move his head, body, arms, or legs at all. He was gagged and couldn't make a sound. It was so dark; he might as well be blind. Only his fingers had the tiniest bit of movement. With the intense cold and the lack of blood flow to his hands, how long would they keep moving?

Was it Little? Was it someone from the trafficking operation? Could it be the same man responsible for the massacre at Little's farm? Was it the FBI, trying to stop his investigation? Why hadn't they just killed him? Why truss him up like this? What did they want from him? What could he do? Eventually he stopped asking questions and tried to think of a way out.

After a while lying immobile in this dark silent tomb, Bill started to lapse into an uneasy sleep. He was exhausted, terribly cold and his mind was still not functioning normally. In the place between awake and asleep, he remembered that people who were very cold, who suffered hypothermia, often fell asleep and never woke up. It would be so easy to do. He wondered if he would ever see light again.

61

A white ball of blinding light burned into Bill's eyes. Automatically, his eyes squeezed shut. He heard a man laugh and a woman call his name.

"Bill. Bill, are you all right?"

It was Christie. He tried to answer, but the gag in his mouth prevented him from doing anything but groaning deep in his throat. He tried opening his eyes again, but the light was too bright.

"Bill, it's me. Christie. He's here. He's got us."

Bill heard laughter again. "Tell him who, Dr. McMorrow. Don't leave him in suspense."

Christie called again. "It's Scott. Stephen Scott, Bill. He grabbed me in the underground parking lot. Yesterday, or was it the day before? I've been so confused. He's kept me in a box. Are you hurt? Are you okay?"

"That's enough, Doctor. You don't need to go into every detail. We have some work to do."

Bill was shocked. His abductor was Stephen Scott. Not Little, a mobster from a syndicate, an old enemy or the FBI? Stephen Scott had kidnapped Christie and then went after him? While he had considered Scott a possible suspect in Christie's disappearance, he hadn't let himself believe it. Bill had still hoped he'd see her in the cathedral as he was making his way through the crowd.

He tried to get his mind around the idea that Scott had

captured both of them. Bill felt he was swirling in a surreal world, lost in a frightening nightmare. He tried to say something and ended up choking. He felt his face turn red from the struggle to breathe and the effort to stop the choking in his throat. In spite of the cold, drops of sweat formed on his forehead and started running down his face. Finally, he got control of the coughing and deeply inhaled the cold air through his nose. His racing heart began to slow.

"Bill, are you okay? Help him. Don't let him choke to death. Do something,"

"Oh, I'm going to do something, you can be sure of that. He'll be just fine. See? He's already stopped coughing. Are you ready to listen, Detective Drummond? I've explained everything to Dr. McMorrow already. Now you can learn about our events for today. Today we are going to finish what we started last November. With the added element of you, Detective Drummond. I'm going to release you along with Dr. McMorrow. Now, I've never completed a mission that released a man before, let alone a man and a woman together, so this is pretty exciting. Wouldn't you say so? This is a first for me. A departure from the rules, the ritual and my Uncle Luke's training. I've had to be inventive. I've even had some fun being creative."

Scott laughed again. Bill wanted to ask Christie if she was loose or tied up. He wanted to know if she could move at all and could maybe maneuver over to him and untie his hands. He needed to see. He would just have to open his eyes and get used to the light, no matter how painful. Then maybe he could signal Christie in some way.

Bill tightened his eyelids and then forced them to open a slit. The white light poured into the openings and protectively his lids closed. Tears dripped down his face. He tried again. And again. Finally, he could tolerate the light for a few seconds, especially if he looked out the corners of his eyes and not directly into the light.

The trouble was that even looking out the corners of his eyes, he couldn't see anything. The rest of the room seemed to be in total darkness. He imagined that he lay on the floor in a glaring spotlight and around him, all was dark. He was on stage and the intense lights hid the audience from his view.

Then he noticed that his vision was cut into pieces by something very close to his head. Instead of focusing away from his position, he tried to see what was so close to him.

The wire stretched as far as he could see, up over his head. The metal wire was what he felt pushing into the back of his scalp when he tried to move his head before. Wire. Wire formed into a cross hatch, like a cage. He looked out the other side of his eyes. It was the same there. Wire caging as far as he could see. He closed his eyes and tried to picture himself.

He was lying on an old wood floor, spotlighted by a blinding light. His arms were tied under him. Scott had bound his legs and then fastened them to something so he could not move them. He was gagged, but not blindfolded. In addition, a wire cage surrounded his head, tightened painfully around his neck. A small square in front of his face looked like a door, with a latch to keep it locked. Christie and Scott watched him from the other side of the glare.

What the hell was going on? Scott said he had told Christie what his plan was. If only Christie would tell him. Why doesn't she just yell it out so he would know what Scott was going to do next? Heaven knows what Scott had already done to Christie. At least she was alive and able to talk.

Bill closed his eyes to rest them from the penetrating light. He had to figure some way out of this horrible situation. He couldn't yell. He couldn't signal Christie by voice or by action. He couldn't even communicate with Scott, let alone try to barter with him for their lives. Bill searched his mind for solutions. He couldn't overpower Scott because he couldn't move anything except a few fingers. He had no weapons within reach. No way to reach the outside world.

He knew Tom Wilder and the task force members would miss him at the funeral service. His colleagues would guess that something unexpected had happened. They would find his car. They would search for him and question witness after witness until they found someone who saw what had happened to him. And then what? Would they be able to identify the vehicle his abductor put him into? Even if they got that far, how would they know where that vehicle had gone? An APB for the vehicle would most likely be too late. Scott had already reached his destination and probably had the car hidden away. What would the task force do then?

Bill's whirling mind took him for a few brief seconds into another world, the world he was familiar with, the world that brought him some comfort because he knew he would be the object of a massive search. However, thinking about that world did him no good. Reluctantly, he returned to the reality of the bitter cold room and the blinding light, sore wrists and ankles and the wire cage that encircled his head. What was that cage for? How could he prepare himself for what Scott had planned?

Bill was at the mercy of a madman. He had never felt so frustrated, so helpless and so frightened for his life.

62

Scott unplugged the light from the large battery that charged it, plunging the room into total darkness. Bill opened his eyes wide but all he could see were white circles where the lights had previously been. He blinked and blinked, trying to erase the impressions left on his retinas. He hoped his eyes would adjust quickly to the dark so that he could see what was happening and where he was. Before his eyes had a chance to recover, he felt Scott move close to him. He heard a distinct click.

Bill turned his head in the direction of the sound. He grew excited as he realized he could now move his head. Evidently, Scott had unsnapped a line attached to the wire at the top of the cage around his head. Scott pushed Bill up into a sitting position. Then he secured the line again with a click, jerking Bill's head up as high as possible. Now Bill was sitting straight up, his hands tied behind him. The change of position relieved the pressure from his weight on his hands and he could feel blood beginning to move down into his fingers again. That was better. He could move his arms slightly away from his back. He had gained some mobility there. Nevertheless, he couldn't move his head at all. His neck stretched as far as it could, keeping him rigid. A tether immobilized the cage around his head.

Bill's eyes were beginning to adjust to the change of light. He could see the shape of the man who must be Scott move away in the darkness. Bill heard the click of a lighter and then saw the glow of a kerosene lantern. Slowly the room filled with a dim light.

Now Bill could see Christie on the other side of the small room. She was sitting on the floor, leaning against the log wall. Her hands and feet were tied and cords bound her to bolts screwed into the wall. As she shivered, her teeth chattering softly, she stared at Bill and then smiled weakly. "I'm okay," she mouthed behind Scott's back.

Bill studied the room that imprisoned them, searching for something that could help. The inside of the cabin was unfinished; the logs of the structure served as the interior walls and were dark and unadorned. The room could not have been any bigger than 12' x12' and appeared windowless. Either that, or the windows were boarded up, or it was night, as no light from outside entered. The room held only a battered table, two rickety wooden chairs and an old iron woodstove. Bill had only limited vision because of his restricted head movement, but his hopes faded as his eyes scanned the room. He couldn't see anything they could use to free themselves or overcome Scott.

He looked back at Christie. At least she looked okay. He couldn't distinguish any blood or wounds on her and thank heavens she was still fully clothed, although she had no shoes on. He didn't know what he would have done if Christie had been naked or wounded. It would have been too much to bear. His heart went out to her. She had been through all this once before. How could she bear it a second time? She must be terrified. He took a deep breath. He wished he could just touch her, let her know he would do anything to save her. That he loved her. He took another breath to clear his feelings. No time for emotions now. He needed to think about how to get them out of here. Then he realized his shoes were missing too. No wonder his feet were so cold.

Bill stared at Scott standing by the door holding the lamp. He was grinning, obviously delighted with the results of his scheming.

"So you two meet again and are obviously glad to see each other. Fine. You can see that I've not harmed either one of you. I'm hoping you'll cooperate so I don't have to punish you. Of course, if one of you misbehaves, then the other will feel the pain the disobedient one deserves. Remember that, Detective Drummond. You wouldn't want to be responsible for me having to hurt Dr. McMorrow, would you? Of course not.

"Now we're about to begin our truth-telling session," Scott continued. "Telling the truth is the first thing a child learns to do. Truth is the ethical base from which humankind operates; truth is critical for humans to learn how to trust one another in this world. From truth comes faith. Unfortunately, too many people learn to lie as they grow up and continue to do so, losing their faith and integrity to the detriment of themselves and others. Just as in Eden, when Eve lied to Adam and started all the misery of the world."

Christie had been mouthing words to Bill behind Scott's back while he paced up and down the small room, lecturing. She indicated that she was not hurt, but she didn't know what to do. Should she harass Scott? Get him angry and off track? Bill blinked his eyes rapidly, trying to tell her yes.

Suddenly Christie interrupted Scott. "What does this garbage you're spouting have to do with us? Look, it's too cold in here. We can't listen to you when we're shivering and getting frostbitten. It's a waste of your time. Before you can even begin to carry out your plan, the cold will freeze us to death. That wouldn't further your mission any, would it? Light a fire in the stove and get us warm enough to pay attention. Fix us some hot tea. We're freezing just sitting here without moving. At least untie our feet and let us walk around a bit to get our circulation moving."

Bill understood that Christie was trying to distract Scott and at the same time establish a bit of control. It was a good move, but it didn't work.

"Shut up and listen. You want Detective Drummond's feet cut off? Then he wouldn't have to worry about frostbitten feet. The cold's the least of your worries, slut."

Scott pulled a knife out of his pocket and took a few steps toward Bill. Christie shook her head no and looked down at the floor, as if submitting. Scott hesitated, walked back in front of Christie. He pushed the kerosene lamp close to her face. Bill struggled to move, fearing that Scott was going to set her hair on fire. Finally, Scott withdrew his hand.

"You've already experienced how flesh feels when it burns, Dr. McMorrow. Perhaps after I cut off Detective Drummonds feet, I'll cauterize them with fire. If you want Detective Drummond to share your experience, interrupt me again."

Scott drew his hand back and started pacing again. He put the lamp on the floor and the knife back in his pocket. Eventually, he continued talking in a slow, modulated voice.

"As I was saying, women have brought evil into the world and continue by their actions to be she-devils, trying to take over the world. First, they brainwash children's minds, then they take over the work force, while men go unemployed. They run for political office or control their political spouse. Women are even in the process of controlling the churches. Think of it; some churches let women become priests or ministers to the congregation. Devils as pastors. This sacrilege must be stopped. My missions spread the word, the truths about the evil women do and what must be done to rid the world of them."

Scott paced faster and faster around the small room, enjoying the sound of his own voice. As he got lost in his rhetoric, Bill and Christie attempted more silent communication. Christie mouthed, "Should I talk to him again?" Bill blinked yes.

"The critical point is for women and in our particular case today, for you Detective Drummond, to tell the truth before being released. That way you could go to a better place after death and may have a chance at redemption. That's up to God. I'm only his chosen one here on earth to get rid of evil."

"But Stephen," Christie interrupted. "Not every woman is evil. What about Sister Teresa? Or Saint Joan? Or women who have dedicated their lives to teaching kids, treating the sick, or taking food and medicine to those who need it? These are good women. There are millions of good, kind, honest women. You're wrong."

"THERE ARE NO GOOD WOMEN!" Scott yelled at her. "There is not one good woman. They may pretend they're good. They may seem to do good deeds. But that's all show. Down deep, the demon lurks in them, ready to destroy the world with sexual perversions and pain. I know. I have endured the wickedness of such a woman. I endured it and endured it."

Christie said softly, "I'm sorry that happened to you, Stephen. But whoever taught you that all women are bad or evil was not telling you the truth. They twisted the truth into something dark and disgusting. You don't have to believe them anymore. You can break free of that way of thinking. You don't have to serve those people ever again."

Scott looked at Christie. "You lie," he said. "You all lie. You're telling me lies, hoping that I'll change, turn away from my Uncle and Mother Luke's lessons. Turning the child away from his family is the work of the devil. It is evil to strike against the God-given family. You are evil. That's why you have to die."

Christie started to say something, but Scott yelled, interrupting her. He walked close to her, towering above her. He reached down and slapped her face so hard that her head cracked against the log wall. Blood started to drip from her mouth, where her teeth had cut into her lips.

"Shut up. Shut your filthy mouth. If you say another word, I'll cut your boyfriend's throat. You will watch the blood gushing from his throat and know you killed him. You will watch him bleed to death. He'll die unrepentant and suffer in hell forever. Then I'll take care of you. In every way I want to. Do you want that?"

Christie shook her head. She would have to find another way to stop him. Words didn't work. Pleasing him didn't work. Fighting him didn't work. She failed at trying to trick him. The only way to save them both was to kill him. She shivered at the idea of her hand being the one that took a life, any life, even Stephen Scott's. She could see no other way out. However, how could she kill him when she was trussed up and tied to the wall?

She looked at Bill. She was terrified just seeing his situation. The ropes that tied his legs were bolted to the floor, in the same way she was bolted to the wall. He was sitting up with his hands behind him. She assumed they were tied as well. He had a wire cage over his head. Bolts held the top of the cage to the ceiling by several long cables, so that Bill couldn't move his head. His neck was pulled taut. The cage was only a little bigger than the circumference of his head, maybe three or four inches of space between Bill and the wire. A small hole in the front of the cage opened into a flat area that ran to his chin. The wire fit so tightly around his throat that she could see indentations and spots of blood where it pushed into his skin. Scott had gagged him. She had never seen Bill look so frightened, so helpless. She couldn't count on him to help her to overcome Scott. She'd have to do it herself. But how?

"Now that we're quiet again, I'll continue. I've decided that the ritual to release a man will involve some of the same rites that I use with women. First, a man must tell the truth. He must tell all his sins and beg for forgiveness. That's the first step. We'll get to the other steps in time. Detective Drummond, will you tell the truth?"

Bill could only look at Scott. He had no way to answer him.

Scott walked over to Bill and opened the small door in the front of the cage. He reached in and removed Bill's gag, threw it on the floor and closed the cage door.

"There. Now you can answer my questions. Will you tell the truth?"

Bill tried to speak but his mouth was too dry from the gag. Finally, he managed to say, "Water. I need water."

Scott stared at him. Then he picked up a cup and threw the contents at Bill through the wire cage. Bill caught some of it in his mouth and licked up drops he could reach with his tongue. "Thanks.".

"Now answer me. Will you tell the truth and list your sins and ask for repentance?"

Bill said, "I'll tell you what. If you undo my hands and let me out of this contraption, I'll tell you anything you want me to. I can't feel my hands anymore. I think they might be frostbitten. Will you untie them? If you do, I tell you all my sins and more."

Scott hit the top of the cage hard with his hand. The wire cut into the crown of Bill's head and punctured his skin. Bill cried out in pain and blood started to drip down his face. On the other side of the room, Christie gasped.

"Please Stephen. Don't hurt him. Bill, say what he wants you to. If you don't, he's only going to get angrier."

"No conditions. I will have no conditions, Detective Drummond. Tell the truth. State your sins. Beg for repentance. If you refuse, I'll have to move to step two and I don't think you'll like that."

Bill said, "If you won't untie my hands, then let Dr. McMorrow go. I'm not doing anything you ask until you release Dr. McMorrow. Untie her hands, you shit bag. Let her go. Let her go now! You know I'm with the police, but did you know they're on their way here right now? I have a tracker on me. They know exactly where I am. So, either let us go, or you had better get out of here right now. If you don't, you'll end up with a bullet in your head."

Scott laughed in Bill's face. "Angry, Detective? Don't want to tell us your sins? I thought it might be more difficult to convince a man to cooperate than a woman. Women like to cooperate; they beg to cooperate, so they can be released. I can see you're going to need some convincing. By the way, I searched you both very carefully. There's no tracking device; you're lying. Your guns are in my possession. I threw your phones in the woods. I kept some of your personal belongings. Interesting, Detective Drummond, the photos of your wife that I found in your wallet, next to the picture of your kids. Look, here are her pictures. This one must be the before picture. Such a pretty thing she was. And this, must be the after, when she was riddled with the cancer of her sins. She must have had a very slow, painful, horrible time dying. I can just imagine the agony she must have gone through. So painful. Do you remember her moans, her screams of pain, Detective? Were you with her when she took her last breath? How did it feel? Huh?"

Scott rubbed his fingers slowly over the picture of Emmy, fondling her. "If only I had been there. I could have released her and ended her eternal suffering. Something you couldn't do."

63

Scott walked to the corner of the room and fiddled with something on the floor next to the wood stove. Christie whispered very softly to Bill,

"Are you okay? Don't let him get to you. Remember he's crazy, operating out of delusions. We can't talk him into anything. It's obvious that getting him angry is just putting us into more jeopardy. Just pretend to play his game until we can figure something out. Got any ideas on how to get out of here?"

Bill whispered back. "He's such a bastard. I don't care if he's crazy or not. If I could just get my hands on him. But I can't move anything. Even if I did have a gun, I couldn't reach it or get it to you. Can you move at all? How's your head? That was quite a slam he gave you."

"A little headache, but I'm okay. I've been working on the ropes around my wrists for a while. I've managed to loosen my hands a little. He tied the ropes over my cotton gloves, so if I can just slip these cotton gloves off, the rope will loosen up some. Maybe enough for me to get my hands free. I've got my fingers out of one glove and I'm working on pulling it down off my hand now."

"Great. If you get your hands loose, then start on your feet. Do you see a taser or our guns? I think Scott got me with the taser. Put me right down. If you could get hold of that, Scott would be paralyzed for a while and you could free me."

"I don't see anything like a taser. But it's obvious he has

something in his pockets, the way they bulge out."

"Maybe the guns and taser are in there. The knife is. If you get untied you'll have to try to get anything you can."

"I don't know how, but I'll try. How's your head, Bill?"

"It hurts pretty badly, but I think the bleeding's slowing down. Quiet, he's turning around and coming back."

Scott walked back toward Bill. He was carrying a wire cage, similar to the one on Bill's head. He held up the cage so the light hit it. Inside, three large white rats were scurrying back and forth, trying to keep their balance.

"Do you think I didn't hear you two whispering? You want a gun so that you can kill me. Don't you realize yet that I can't be killed, or captured? God has chosen me. All these years I've been releasing women, and no one even had a clue. That's because God was protecting me. Even when your people shot me, I survived and escaped. You can plan all you want but it won't do you any good. Look, I'll take the guns out of my pocket and put them right here on the floor. If God wants you to kill me, he'll untie you and let you get to the guns faster than I can."

Scott put the rat cage on the floor. He fumbled in his pockets and then pulled out two guns. He pulled the taser from the other pocket. Placing them on the floor next to the chair, Scott stepped back and smiled confidently.

Minutes passed. He looked from Christie to Bill.

"Well? I don't see anyone moving. Do you? The guns don't seem to be flying into your hands, do they? Does that prove it to you? I'm satisfied with the outcome. God is satisfied with his choice. He just demonstrated that. Now, let me get on with His work."

Picking up the rat cage, he took another step toward Bill and said,

"These are my persuaders." He smiled at the rats. "I had two more but unfortunately they died. I don't know whether it was the cold, they starved or the other rats killed them. However, it doesn't matter. I think three are enough to persuade Detective Drummond to tell the truth."

Bill and Christie stared at the cage. "No, you can't do that," Christie cried. "Please don't do that."

Bill just kept his eyes on the rats. Now he understood the reason for the cage on his head.

Scott approached Bill. He opened the door on the front of Bill's cage and smiled in at him. "I think they'll like the blood, Detective. Nice and fresh. Are you sure you won't follow the rules to be released?"

"Fuck you, Scott, you crazy bastard. You think you're so high and mighty, chosen by God. Bullshit. You're nothing more than a delusional nut case. God wouldn't bother to spit on you, let alone listen to you. And He will get you, if I don't. Just you wait. Your turn's coming. You're no better than those rats. In fact, the rats are higher evolved you are. Get away from me, you scum. Take your rats and run back into your crazy delusions. Get away."

Scott stepped back. He carefully opened the door of the rats' cage.

"I take it you're refusing right now to tell your truth and be saved. You'll get another chance in a little while. That is, if you're still alive."

He grabbed one of the white rats by the tail and held it over the door to Bill's head cage. Slowly he dropped it in and closed the door.

The rat just sat there, whiskers twitching, eyes darting, watching Bill's face. Bill stared back at it, only inches away. He could smell its stench; see its pink tongue and sharp teeth. The rat's long sharp nails grasped the wire tightly. Bill wondered which part of his face would be the first target.

Then Scott removed the second and third rats, dropped them into Bill's head cage and closed the door. He stepped back, pulled up a chair and sat down.

He turned around and addressed Christie. "I'm not blocking your view, am I, Dr. McMorrow?"

She had her eyes closed. She didn't respond.

Scott jumped up and walked over to Christie. "I think you need a front row seat, Doctor. This is going to be fun to watch and, I think, very educational."

He quickly slashed the ropes around her wrists and released the straps that held her bolted to the wall. He left her feet tied. He dragged her over to his chair and flung her down on the floor. He sat down and then grabbed a fistful of her hair and pulled her head up. Bill was right in front of them, only a few feet away.

"Can you see real good now? It's going to be quite a show."

The rats snarled at each other. This was new territory for them and they smelled food. The coppery smell of Bill's dripping blood worked them into a fury. They charged each other, clawing and biting, forgetting the food in front of them, lost in the age-old instinct of might is right. The honor of claiming the first bite always goes to the victor.

Bill remained absolutely still. Cold sweat mixed with warm blood dripped down his face and off his ears. Even when the rats bumped into his nose or mouth in their battle with each other, he did not move or twitch. He was frozen, waiting until one of the rats emerged victorious and turned to him to claim its reward.

64

Tom Wilder was talking with several other detectives on the task force. The funeral service had just ended and they were standing outside the cathedral in the middle of a throng of people.

"It's not like him, or Christie either. They wouldn't miss honoring an officer of the law. They said they'd be here."

"What do you think happened?" asked Sam Green, a task force investigator.

"I don't know, but I intend to find out. Bill was worried about Christie. She didn't answer his calls and didn't show up at Little's farm as she was supposed to. Jenny's checked everywhere, but no one's seen her. The state police and I both checked her house. No sign she's been there. An APB has been out on her car for hours with no result. And the last time anyone saw Bill was at Little's this morning. He was definitely coming here for the funeral."

"So what now, Tom?"

"We'll have to check everything out. Start with their homes. Check them out thoroughly. Look for a note, a map, anything that might point to where they are. Check their closets. See if there are any empty hangers, missing suitcases. Check airports. Put an APB on both their vehicles. Alert all officers to be on the lookout. Maybe they're together, maybe not. Check all their friends, family, hospitals, and accident reports."

Sheriff Wood walked up to the group. "So where was

your director? I expected he'd have enough respect to honor Bobby Hamlin, at least. I didn't see him during the parade either, or his assistant Dr. McMorrow."

Tom glanced at Wood. "Dr. McMorrow is not Bill's assistant. She's a forensic psychologist consulting with the task force. Bill would have been here if he could. Believe me, both of them would have. They were stricken by shock and grief at losing both Hamlin and Tate, just as we all are. We believe they're in danger. Something has happened to them."

"Like what?" Wood asked. "Maybe they're in front of some warm fire someplace making whoopee."

"You're out of line, Wood. They're colleagues, not lovers. Moreover, they would never disrespect a fallen officer or his family. If you could be serious for a moment, we'd like your help trying to locate them. Can your deputies patrol Cumberland Country and check around? The last Bill was seen was at Little's farm."

Skip Preston and Frank Sampson joined them. "I heard that, Tom, and it's not true. I saw Bill here, right before the service. He was trying to get through the crowd," said Skip Preston. "I guess he didn't make it."

"What?" Tom said. "You saw him? Where? Was Dr. McMorrow with him?"

Sampson piped up. "Skip and I were just at the top of the cathedral steps heading inside. We turned around to look at the crowd and all the television cameras. We both spotted Bill plowing through the crowd, making his way here. McMorrow wasn't with him that I noticed. Since he obviously changed his mind and skipped the funeral service, he'll have some explaining to do. The governor didn't like that his director of the Maine State Task Force on Violent Crimes didn't put in an appearance when all the dignitaries here expected to meet him."

"I'm telling you. Something went wrong." Tom turned to Sam. "Check with crowd control officers and paramedics.

Get someone to talk with the people who were up on the roofs and top floors with binoculars or scopes. See if they saw anything unusual in the crowd near the cathedral just before the service. Check if any surveillance tapes were taken of that area where Preston spotted Bill."

"We'll be glad to help out. Just let us know what you want, Tom," said Wood as he, Preston and Sampson moved away, shaking the hands of voters and smiling into television cameras.

Sam clicked off his cell phone. "Bill, the paramedics had several calls before the service. The crowd was so packed that it was easy to slip or get bruised by an elbow and such. They took several people to the hospital, but not Drummond. Someone did call with a report of a man down with a suspected heart attack in the area around the cathedral, but when the paramedics checked it out, the man was gone. Witnesses told them that his friend carried him away with help from somebody in the crowd. The Red Cross tent had no record of him showing up there. The paramedics never made contact with that case again. They assumed his friend got him to a hospital."

Tom said, "I have a bad feeling about this. Maybe someone was out to get Bill and stop the task force's investigation. We haven't found Little yet. He could be gunning for Bill. Or that person reported with the heart attack could have been Bill. Check the hospitals. Find out more about the incident. Find some witnesses to the heart attack episode."

Detective Evan Gunther interrupted Tom. "Tom, Bill's task force vehicle has been found, about three blocks from here. Locked, illegally parked, and empty. Looks like he did come down here."

"And then disappeared," finished Tom. "Let's get back to the office and start the ball rolling. Two missing task force members. Four officers killed on duty. Two women and a baby dead. Four Jane Does, three dead. A bunch of missing girls.

We'd better get some help on this. I don't mean from the state police or Sheriff Wood's office either. I'm going straight to the Attorney General on this one. Let's go."

65

Standing by their cars, Preston, Sampson and Wood talked as the crowd thinned and the media vans packed up and left.

"Do you think Little did it?" asked Preston. "Would he have the balls to kill two cops, his sisters and then kidnap Drummond?"

Wood answered, "I don't know Skip, but I'll tell you this. He's cold enough to have done it all. At least he got rid of those girls and all the evidence in time. One of the task force guys told me that besides those unlucky police guards who were blasted to death, they didn't find anything but Little's two dead sisters, a dead baby, dead dogs, a bloody bed, and some kid, half dead, hanging out in the barn. I wouldn't be surprised if Little pulled all that off."

"Was the kid one of ours?" Sampson asked.

"Looks like it. We're going to have to take care of that, and soon," said Woods.

Preston jumped into the conversation. "Sampson, did you hear from Boston?"

"Yeah, twenty arrived. One short, but they took what they got, so it's off us now. They got all their equipment back from Little, too, a few days ago. So, the task force couldn't find any evidence about what Little was doing with the ones who didn't make it. They didn't say anything about Little or Drummond. Do you suppose Little joined up with them?"

Sampson said, "More likely, they killed him after he took

care of everything at the farm. The task force just hasn't found his body yet. Do you think he killed his own sisters? Or did the Boston group do that? I'm betting on Boston. Unless it was you, Wood."

The three men laughed. Then Preston said, "Hey, maybe they took Drummond, too. Unless it was you, Wood." Only Preston and Sampson laughed.

Wood replied, "Okay, enough of that. Of course, I didn't take Drummond. And, I don't think they'd risk taking Drummond, either. Killing him would just get them more attention than they want. You know I didn't like the idea of Little roaming around, knowing all he knows. Moreover, if he took Drummond and the task force found him, we would be in a real mess. Right now, we don't know where Little is. If Boston didn't put him down and he shows up, I'm going to have to do it. If you hear from him, let me know. I'll take care of him. But right now, I'm more worried about that kid they found. What if she talks?"

"I know," said Preston. "I'm with you. As far as that kid goes, I'll nose around and see what I can find out about her. Our Crime Scene Mobile Unit was at the farm with the task force. Some of my guys will have some information about the kid. She must be one of ours. That's why the number was off one on the cargo count. If she lives, we'll have to do her in, too."

"If Little contacts any of us, set a meeting with him and ask about Drummond. Whether Little has him, killed him, or not, Wood has to take Little out. Damn it all to hell. This keeps getting more and more complicated," griped Sampson. "I don't like it. I don't like it one bit. We clean up one mess and another pops up."

"Well, the Tate thing worked out as far as I know," said Preston. "The truck driver followed Tate from our office. I had fixed Tate's coffee and it was just a matter of time. When he started losing control, the trucker smashed into Tate's side door.

That's all it took. Dead and really smashed up. No reason for an autopsy."

"You did a good job with that one, Preston. Tate dumps the body, shoots the deputy and then you get rid of Tate. Just the way I like it, no witnesses. What about the truck driver? Can we trust him?"

Preston answered, "We don't have to. He's on his way to Alaska now with a load. I have a friend up there who's going to take care of him for us. No questions asked."

The three men nodded. Wood and Sampson took deep drags from their cigarettes.

Wood said, "Sampson, if you hear anymore from the Boston group or Judge Howe or, well, you know who, let us know what's going down. I think I've found another place to use for the next shipment of girls. It's remote and I know the law in the area. Whenever that next shipment of goods comes, we can be ready. I hope it's not too long. I sure could use the money. My wife's been nagging me for two months to get our summer camp remodeled."

The men laughed. "I hear you, Woods. I'll see if I can find out more about Little, too."

"Well, that should do it. I think we have a plan. See you later."

The men shook hands, got into their cars and lined up for the funeral cortège to the burial sites at the Portland Cemetery. They maneuvered their cars close to the governor's limousine. After all, the community considered them important enough to take one of the privileged places in the line of mourners' cars. They represented their fellow law officers and were doing their civic duty by honoring them.

66

The rats had determined dominance. One huddled against the door to the cage, licking his injured foot. Another rat lay dead next to Bill's chin, one eye ripped out; its neck chewed open. Bill could smell rat urine and feces, released during the battle. He worked hard not to gag.

The alpha rat, the largest of the three, sat just inches from Bill's mouth and studied him. His white whiskers twitched as he sniffed Bill's scent. Without blinking, his red eyes scrutinized his prey. Bill saw hunger and menace in those eyes.

The rat moved an inch closer and stood on his back legs, tail erect. He was preparing to attack, to take his spoils of war from the hunk of warm flesh and wet blood in front of him.

"Noooo," Christie screamed.

The rat skittered back against the wire, turned and looked for the source of the loud screech.

Scott jerked Christie's hair back brutally. She shrieked in agony. She managed to say, "Stop it. You can't do this to him. Please stop it."

"Scream like that again, Doctor McMorrow and I will just slit Detective Drummond's vital areas and let the rats eat him alive while he dies slowly and painfully, like his wife. Do you want that? No? Then don't make any noise. Do you understand me?"

He tugged viciously on her hair again. Christie mumbled a quiet "yes".

Silence fell in the room once more. The lamp flickered as the wick grew smaller. Bill continued to stare at the big rat as it turned and slunk closer to him again. He could see it trembling slightly. Bill hoped it was hurt or scared, but he feared the quivering resulted from its frenzied anticipation of fresh food. The rat drew closer, his whiskers brushing Bill's chin. Then the rat stopped, motionless. Bill held his breath.

Suddenly, with a guttural squeal, the rat leapt at Bill's face open mouthed and teeth bared. He chomped onto Bill's upper lip and sank his teeth as deeply as he could. Bill screamed. The movement of his mouth flung the rat upward and tore its razor-sharp teeth out of Bill's lip. The rodent landed on the floor of the cage, a bit dazed. Blood poured out of Bill's upper lip, which was hanging by a flap.

"Enough Detective? I can stop it here. All you have to say is you're ready to tell the truth."

Christie was sobbing; her head down, she was terrified to watch.

His injured lip distorted Bill's voice, but he managed to growl out,

"Tell you what, you son of a bitch. The real truth is that you're a loser, a victim of your uncle's abuse. Your uncle used you for his own sick reasons. God didn't choose you. Your uncle chose you. He chose you so he could use you, rape you, torture you, any way he wanted. Nobody ever loved or wanted you. God didn't want you or he would have saved you from your uncle. Your whole story's a lie, only you're too dumb to realize it. You're nothing but used, sick trash."

Scott released Christie's hair and rose out of his chair in rage. "How dare you say that to me? You don't know anything about my uncle or me. He loved me and so did my Mother Luke. They did everything for me. They trained me. They showed me God and taught me his wishes. God's protected me on every mission. That's why no one ever caught me. Never even came close. You're going to die, detective and you'll go straight to hell."

When Scott jumped out of his chair, Christie slid away from him. Bill could see her moving towards the guns that Scott had placed on the floor beside his chair. If he could just keep Scott focused on him for a few more moments, Christie would reach the guns.

Bill yelled back. "Keep believing your dirty little lies. They're nothing but the delusions of a mad man. You're a fucking nut case, spoiled goods. Don't you get it? You're nothing but a deranged killer, just like every other murderer. An ordinary killer. That's all you are. You're the one going to hell, not me. You might think you're something special but you're not. You're a worm, a Goddamn fucking sicko and you're too crazy to know it. Everyone laughs at your perverted beliefs and the way you were fooled by your uncle."

The rat leapt at Bill's face again. It ran up his chin, past his nose and bit at his eye. Bill closed his eyes and squeezed them tightly together to give the rat less purchase. The rat bit into Bill's left eyelid and pulled. A tear of skin ripped off and the rat ran down to the floor of the cage and started chewing on it. Blood and tears poured from Bill's eye.

"Oh God," he cried.

"There," Scott gloated. "God got you for that. Too bad the little persuader didn't get the whole eye, detective. However, with your lid partly gone, my friend won't have any trouble getting to your eye the next time he tries. He'll be munching your eyeballs soon."

Scott stared at Bill's face with great interest. He reported what he saw. "You have blood dripping from the top of your head, your lip is almost ripped off, and your eyelid is repulsive. I wish I had a mirror so you could see what how nauseating your rat-bitten face looks. Really quite stomach-turning, if I do say so myself. Perhaps you're getting closer to confessing your sins."

"Don't you think so, Doctor?" he asked as he turned to Christie.

67

Christie sat on the floor, her feet still tied. She held Bill's gun in her hand. She pointed it at Scott.

"Get that cage off him, now."

"Christie, don't bother with that. Shoot Scott."

"Oh Doctor, remember the oath. First, do no harm. Aren't you bound by that?"

"Shut up Scott. Take the cage off him, right now, or I'll shoot you."

"Christie, listen to me. Don't barter with him. Just disable him. Shoot him in the leg, Goddamn it. Shoot him before it's too late. Then you can help me."

Christie flipped off the safety. She aimed at Scott's left leg. The gun was shaking.

"I'm going to give you just one chance, Stephen. If you do what I say, I won't shoot you. You'll go away to a place where they can help you. I'm telling you. Take that cage off Bill's head and do it now."

"Now this is interesting," said Scott. "A lover's quarrel between the two people I'm going to kill and position in a lover's sex knot. Now stop your quarreling. I want you two mooning over each other, like adulterers in an office. Then when they find your bodies, they will discover how the wicked doctor fornicated with the detective. And they both seemed so pure." Scott laughed.

"Shoot him, Goddamn it. Shoot the bastard."

"Stephen, I'm warning you for the last time. I don't want to have to shoot you. Do what I told you," said Christie. "I'm pulling the trigger back now."

Scott continued, "Fascinating. A woman I was ready to release, to kill, as you put it, giving me a chance. How very interesting . I didn't give you any chances. Why are you giving me one? Is my God controlling your hand, refusing to let you shoot his chosen one? Why don't you just shoot me, as your lover begs you to? Aren't you mad about what I did to you, how I touched you? Don't you want revenge for your burned fingers and toes? What about making me pay? Don't you want justice for what I did to all those other women? Maybe, Dr. McMorrow, just maybe you liked what I did to you. Is that it? Did you get off on it and want some more? I'd be glad to oblige you. Your boyfriend here could watch while he's being munched on."

"Shoot him, Christie, don't listen to him. Shoot him. You're not shooting a man; you're shooting a murderer who's going to kill us. Goddamn it, shoot him now."

The rat was licking up blood that was dripping on the floor of the cage, slowly making his way closer to Bill's face again. The yelling from the humans around him no longer frightened the big rat. He had savored the piece of skin ripped off Bill's eyelid. He wanted more. Limping behind him, the injured rat licked at the blood the alpha rat had missed. Eventually, the two rats stood by Bill's chin, whiskers flicking and tails held erect.

When both rats jumped onto Bill's face, he screamed. At the same time, Christie shot the gun, Scott yelled and lunged at Christie. He landed on her hard and smashed her to the floor. She dropped the gun. She felt an immediate pain in her chest. Then she couldn't breathe. Scott's weight had forced all the air from her lungs. If she couldn't move him off her, she would fall unconscious. Already, darkness was closing in on her.

Christie jammed her legs upward as forcefully as she

could. Since her feet were tied together, her legs worked in unison, providing more thrust into Stephen's groin. He cursed once as he spun off her into a ball, holding himself between his legs. Christie rolled over and over away from Scott, toward Bill, gasping for breath.

She reached up and opened the door to the cage. Bill had passed out. The rats were ripping at his face, feasting on his flesh. They ignored Christie. She stuck her gloved hand into the cage, tore one of the rats off Bill's face and threw it across the room. Just as she was reaching for the other rat, she felt a cold hand around her neck.

68

Christie whipped around and shoved the alpha rat onto Scott's face. The frightened rodent dug its claws deeply into Scott's face so it wouldn't fall. Scott dropped his hand from Christie's neck and groped at the rat. The more he pulled, the deeper the rat dug its claws into his skin.

"Get him off. Get him off. I'll tell you everything. Get him off me. Please."

Scott fell to his knees, clutching at the rat. His face was bleeding badly and his hands, slippery with blood, couldn't get a hold on the determined rat. He started to cry, sobbing like a child.

"Please let me out. Please. I'll be good. I'll do anything, Uncle Luke, I promise. Please let me out. Get it off me. Please."

Triggered into regression, Scott curled up into a ball on the floor. He wet his pants. Wrapping his hands around his body, he no longer saw or felt the rat chewing on his cheek. His huge blue eyes rolled up into his head. He was lost in the past.

Christie looked for the guns, but couldn't find them or the taser. The weapons must be under Scott's unconscious body. She turned back to Bill. She managed to get to her knees. She studied how Scott had fastened the cage. She untied the wire twists holding it together along three seams and spread the pieces apart. Bill's neck looked like it had been garroted. The cuts were deep and they encircled his throat. She felt his throat for a pulse. It was still strong. However, his face brought tears to her eyes. Ripped to shreds, bleeding and puffing up around the angry looking wounds, Bill's face was practically unrecognizable.

Christie's eyes welled with tears. If only she had shot Scott when she first got her hands on the gun. She might have saved Bill's face from the vicious rats' attack. It was her fault that Bill was injured so badly. Why hadn't she just shot Scott when Bill first warned her? Why had she hesitated?

Christie knew the answers to the questions she asked herself. Scott was mentally ill. Shooting a delusional person, one who was insane through no fault of his own, no matter what he had done, felt wrong to her. He was sick and she was a doctor. At first, she wanted to handle the situation so she did the least harm possible. She had tried to be true to her values. However, when he didn't do as she asked, she realized she would have to shoot him to save Bill and herself. Her finger pulled the trigger. She shot at him. She shot him because she had to. She didn't know if she actually hit him or not and then he landed on her, knocking the breath out of her lungs and the gun out of her hand. If she could do it all over again, she would choose to shoot him first and deal with her ethics later.

She looked over at Scott. He was still unconscious, lying in a fetal position. Drool trickled out of his mouth and mucus dripped from his nose. She didn't see any sign of a bullet wound. Perhaps she had missed him, although at that short range, a miss seemed impossible. The rat had dislodged itself from his face and was sniffing around Stephen's shirt collar. Then it disappeared inside his shirt.

While keeping a close watch on Scott, Christie worked on the knots tying her feet together. Her hands were cold and stiff, but she finally got the ropes loosened and off. She pushed herself to her feet and limped a few steps, getting her blood moving through her legs and feet again. Then she worked on Bill's bonds. She untied his hands, pulled a chair over and stood on it to release the fasteners holding the cage. She jumped back down and pulled the whole cage away slowly so that Bill wouldn't fall back suddenly and bump his head against the floor. Then she untied his feet. She looked for something to cover him, but there was nothing.

She walked over to Scott. She could take his parka and put it over Bill. She knew she had to tie him up, but she didn't want to touch him. Even though he was unconscious, she didn't want to get too close to him. She forced herself to kneel. Gritting her teeth, she stripped the coat from him as quickly as she could. Using the ropes she had untied from Bill and herself, she tied Scott up as tightly as her cold hands would allow, then stood and backed away. He offered no resistance. His mind had escaped to some other place. He was catatonic. She had forgotten about the rat that had slipped into his shirt and the weapons that lay somewhere under his body.

She covered Bill with Scott's parka. She found a bucket of water in the corner of the room and carried it over to Bill. She removed her cotton glove, dipped it in the water, and then gently placed it on the wounds and welts on Bill's face. She rinsed it out in the water and put it over another wound. She continued with the cold-water treatment until Bill began to come around. He moaned and moved his head. He tried to open his eyes, but the one the rat had bitten was already swollen shut. The other eye was barely visible in his puffy, engorged face. He looked at Christie from his one good eye.

The blood crusted on his mouth and the swelling around it made it hard for him to talk. Nevertheless, he managed to get out a few words.

"Did you get him?"

"Don't worry, Bill. I've taken care of him. You're going to be okay. As soon as you feel up to it, I'll help you get out of here. Do you think you can walk?"

Bill didn't answer. He had lapsed back into unconsciousness. She tried rousing him, but couldn't. She tucked

Scott's coat in around him then walked over to the woodstove. Maybe if she built a fire she could warm him up, get his circulation going. Hypothermia was a threat for anyone in Bill's condition and could be more dangerous than rat bites. She found some wood piled beside the stove, but when she searched for matches, she couldn't find any.

"Damn it. Scott had to have some matches or a lighter."

She looked around the old cabin for matches, a lighter, a flint, anything that could help her light the fire. There was no electricity or phone. The windows were all boarded up. Maybe she could find something outside. She walked to the door and tried to open it. It was locked. No key in the lock. She walked to the door on the side of the room facing the pond. She turned the knob. It opened. She took a step outside.

It was pitch dark outside. She looked up. The sky was overcast; she couldn't see the moon or any stars. Walking away from the cabin and back to civilization, wherever that was, would be very difficult especially without any light or any way to determine direction. She turned back into the room, trying to think of what to do. Bill needed immediate medical attention. She knew she couldn't carry him, but perhaps she could get him onto a board or one of the chairs and slide him out.

First, she needed to find some way to get some warmth in here, or they'd freeze to death. She thought about going through Scott's pockets to find a lighter or matches. She shivered just imagining herself getting that close to him again. She didn't know if she could actually force herself to slip her hand down into one of his pockets. But she knew their lives depended on it, so she would do it.

Perhaps after she built the fire, she should leave Bill and Scott behind and walk out herself, try to find a road or another house. But it was so dark; she had no shoes and no flashlight. She didn't want to leave Bill alone with Scott. What if Scott woke up, got untied? No, she would either leave with Bill or stay with him until he could be moved.

She thought about the battery Scott had used to charge the spotlights. Could she rig that to spark a flame? Or reattach it to the bright lights? The lights might produce some warmth. However, she had no idea how to wire the battery to the lights or how to light a fire from a battery. Outdoor survival skills hadn't been part of her training. Her mind was quickly sorting through options, rejecting most, but holding onto some ideas that might possibly work.

Just then, the kerosene lamp flickered out. Total darkness swept away every recognizable shape. Christie cursed as she realized she could have used the lamp to start a fire. What was wrong with her brain? How stupid she was. Now it was too late. As she stood wondering what else she had overlooked, she heard footsteps coming slowly toward her.

69

Christie squatted behind the table. She didn't dare call out. Perhaps Bill had revived, but if Scott had managed to free himself and was moving toward her, any noise would give her location away. Where was the gun? She had dropped it after she shot at Scott, when he jumped on her. The other weapons were somewhere on the floor. She cursed herself again, silently. Why hadn't she picked up one of the guns or the taser when she had a chance? Her only advantage now was the dark that hid her. She held her breath and waited as the steps came closer.

They stopped. Silence spread across the room. Christie could hear the breathing of the man who was no more than four feet from where she crouched. His breaths were ragged, uneven, and harsh.

A breeze rattled the door Christie had left ajar at the front of the cabin. A cold stream of air rushed in. The man must have felt it, too, because he turned in that direction. His steps started up again, following the path of cold air, moving toward the door.

Christie stayed frozen, her head turned in the direction of the uneven footsteps. She heard the man step outside. Why would Bill do that? Could he do that in his condition? How would he know where he was going? Wouldn't he call out for Christie?

Scott wasn't likely to leave the cabin, either. Even if he came out of his catatonic state and managed to untie the ropes around his hands and feet, he wouldn't just leave the cabin. He'd make sure Bill was dead. He'd be searching for Christie.

Who had left the cabin? Christie decided she had two options. She could check the body left on the floor, determine whether it was Bill or Scott, and at the same time find one of the guns. On the other hand, she could follow the man who left. Christie decided on the floor search.

She crawled around the table. She crept on hands and knees in the direction where she had left Bill. She moved stealthily, not wanting to bump into something that would give her position away. As she crawled, she searched for the guns with her hands. She touched an object. Not a gun. It was a foot.

A foot without a shoe. That had to be Bill. Scott had removed their shoes when tying them up, making it harder for them to escape. Christie edged up alongside the body, past the arms that were not tied up like Scott's had been, and with her hand found a shoulder, then a head. She whispered in his ear.

"Bill, it's me. Wake up. We need to get out of here. Scott's gone now, outside. Come on, Bill. Listen to me. It's Christie. Please wake up."

Suddenly the body sat up, cracking Christie's head back in the process. Two hands grabbed her throat and started squeezing. Christie fought back with all the strength she had left. But Scott was too strong for her. As she struggled, she wondered where Bill was and tried to call his name. If he had been strong enough to walk out the door, maybe he could help her.

"This is the last time you wake me up, you witch. I'm not doing anything you tell me to do anymore. You're not my mother. You never were my mother. You're just a freak, Mother Luke. You need to die. You've taught me so well how to kill. Now it's your time."

Scott kept one hand squeezed tightly around Christie's neck. She continued to fight him. She tried to pull his hand from her throat. She began to feel dizzy from the lack of air. She felt him fumble with his other hand in the front pocket of his pants. He pulled something out. She heard a click and a butane fire lighter sent out a flame. The light from the flame was bright enough for Christie to see his face. She realized that Scott could see her as well and would recognize who she was, that she wasn't his Mother Luke.

But Scott didn't recognize her. He put the flame so close to her face that she felt her eyelashes and eyebrows crisping from the heat. She struggled and pulled back as far as she could. He glared at her and then spit in her face. He thrust her down flat on the floor and held her down with his knees while he reached into his pocket again and pulled out the knife he used for his rituals.

"Mother Luke, you're going to die the same way you taught me to kill evil women. You're an evil woman. I should have known that a long time ago."

Scott stopped, lost in thought. "I did know that, didn't I? I already killed you, didn't I? I ALREADY KILLED YOU!"

He moved back from Christie, holding the knife in one hand and the fire starter in the other. Christie sat up, rubbing her throat and catching her breath. Scott pointed the fire starter at her.

"Stay away from me. I should have known," he said pointing at Christie with the knife. "You're the Devil herself. You can't be killed like humans. That's why you're back. I have to do it right this time."

Christie got to her knees. She stared right into Scott's enormous blue eyes.

"You can't kill me Stephen. I am your Mother Luke. You couldn't kill me then and you can't kill me now. I'll call your uncle and he'll punish you the way you deserve. Now put down the knife. Put down the lighter. Do as I say."

"I can't," Scott screamed. "You're the Devil. You speak nothing but lies. I'm supposed to fight you. I have to kill you. I'm not supposed to listen to you. God chose me to kill you.

Don't you remember what happened to me when I did what you said last time? It hurt so much."

Scott sobbed. "Please don't hurt me Mother Luke. Please don't. I'll try to be better. I promise. I'll do just what you want. Don't tell uncle. Don't make me do it again. Please. Please. Please."

Christie stared at Scott as he screamed in fear. He was hallucinating, lost in a past world of pain and confusion. He was terrified. He was terrified of her. He thought she was his Mother Luke and he crumbled before her. The strength of Scott's intimidation, the power of his madness over her burst and shrank, shriveled until it disappeared. Before her sat a victim of trauma, caught in the terror of reenactment. This man who had haunted her dreams and controlled her life for five terror-filled months had no more power over her than the helpless child into which he had regressed. No matter what horrors he had committed in his life, right now he was a wounded, vulnerable child.

Christie stood up. "Give that to me, Stephen." She took the lighter from Stephen's hand. He gave it up willingly. She looked around, using the lighter to try to locate a gun or the taser. She spotted one a few feet away in the corner.

"Put the knife down, Stephen. You don't need it anymore." Christie stepped back, closer to the gun.

Scott hesitated. He looked at the knife as if it were an old friend. A friend he could depend on.

"Can't I keep it?" he asked.

"No, Stephen, you can't," Christie answered. "If you don't give up the knife, you will be severely punished. Put it down on the floor."

Scott started to comply when suddenly he screamed. "A demon. She's got me. Oh. She's stabbing me. She's killing me."

Christie ran to the gun and grabbed it. She held it in her

right hand and the lighter, the only source of light, in her left hand. She pointed the gun at Scott. She was ready to shoot him, to kill him.

He jumped up, slapping at his body with the knife, trying to reach his back, screaming and wild-eyed. He paid no attention to Christie. She didn't understand what he was doing. She feared he was up to some new trick. She tightened her grip on the gun.

"She's got me. Help me. The Demon's eating me alive."

Scott started stabbing at himself with the knife. First his chest, then his side, then over his shoulder and into his back. Dark spots of blood began to appear all over his shirt as he stabbed himself repeatedly.

Christie was bewildered. What was happening to him? Scott was completely out of control. He had forgotten her in his anguish, so she lowered the gun and slowly backed away from him. Then she remembered the rat that had disappeared down his shirt. Stephen's erratic movements must have frightened the rat into defensive behavior; it was biting and ripping at Stephen as it scurried around, trapped beneath his shirt.

Stephen ran past her, out the open front door and jumped into the snow bank outside. Christie lit a piece of kindling on fire and then dashed out the door. The torch was strong enough that she could see Scott racing down through the snow toward the pond. He crashed through the thin ice along the bank and then heaved himself up on the thicker ice over the deeper water.

Christie looked around for Bill. She found him at the corner of the cabin. He had fallen down and lay motionless in the snow. She knelt by him and felt for a pulse. It was weak, but it was there. The snow around his face was bloody. She turned him over, put her hands under his shoulders and pulled him up the stairs. She laid him on the wood floor and turned to close the door.

Christie's eyes caught movement out on the pond. She watched as Scott slipped on the ice. She thought of yelling out a warning, but she clamped her lips closed.

Scott couldn't hear her, even if she called. He no longer could understand what was happening or where he was. He was running from the devil, the woman he called mother. He felt demons eating at his body. Christie saw him slip on the ice. He got up and then stumbled. His feet broke through the ice when he was thirty feet from shore. He sank down into the icy black water as if a giant monster were pulling him under.

Christie watched from the front porch doorway. She waited for Scott's head to appear from the hole in the ice. She saw him pop up once again. He screamed pitifully.

"Help me. She's got me. I promise, I'll tell the truth. Hel…" and then his head went under. She didn't see him surface again. She turned to help Bill.

70

Christie called the state police three days later, inquiring about the search for Scott's body.

"We're sorry, Dr. McMorrow," answered the dispatch officer. "We've had to delay searching the pond until the ice goes out. That should be fairly soon, according to the meteorologists."

"What will you do then?"

"We'll put the divers in. The water will be pretty hazy, but they should be able to find his body. Don't worry, he's not going anywhere."

Christie thanked the officer and looked at the calendar. March and April were always iffy months when it came to weather. Some years spring would come early. More often, winter held on into May. She hoped this year was an early spring year. She knew she wouldn't be able to rest until searchers found Scott's body.

A week later, she called again. The ice was still holding although it was melting more quickly now due to warmer temperatures.

The ice went out the next week. At the same time, a tremendous spring storm brought four inches of rain, enough to flood the lakes and ponds, sending their waters crashing down streams to rivers heading for the sea.

When Christie called the state police, the dispatcher said,

"Dr. McMorrow, we can't conduct the search along the

shores until the flood waters recede. It's just too dangerous. But the water level will be down in a week or so, as long as we don't get any more rain."

"Isn't there anything you can do? Can't you put boats in the pond to at least look?"

"Sorry, Dr. McMorrow. We did put out several boats after the ice broke up, but we didn't find anything. His body might be hooked on something along the bottom. Or now that we're in flood stage, there's a possibility that his body got washed into the Royal River and on down to the sea."

Christie sat silent, feeling the sweat fusing her hand to the phone.

"Dr.McMorrow? Are you there?"

"Yes, sorry. Are you saying that you may never find his body?"

"That's a possibility. It would be unusual, but it happens. We're doing all we can."

Christie hung up.

Over the weeks, each Monday she performed the ritual of calling the state police. Each time she called, she heard the same information. No body had been found.

71

Six weeks later, at a ceremony presided over by the governor, speeches praised the outstanding work of the Maine State Task Force on Violent Crimes to a full house at Portland City Hall. Detective William Drummond and Dr. Christie McMorrow were awarded special badges of honor, especially created for them by a Maine silversmith. The circular silver badges displayed the raised letters MSTFVC around the edges. The silhouette of a single gold acorn rose from the center. The motto underneath read:

For Exceptional Merit
Every Positive Act No Matter How Small
Can Produce Enormous Growth and Good.
March 2007

Bill stepped to the stage, his left eye and face terribly swollen and partially bandaged. Plastic surgery on his eyelid and lip was still in the initial phase. More operations were scheduled throughout the next months. His hair had started to grow over the scars on his head. The abrasions around his neck had paled to a thin pink line. With a crooked smile, he accepted the award from the governor and nodded his thanks to the task force team who occupied the front rows. A thunderous round of applause filled the auditorium.

When they called Christie's name, she climbed the five

steps to the stage without using her cane. She walked with only the slightest limp to the center of the stage and shook the governor's hand as she received her award. She no longer wore her white gloves. Another huge response from the audience produced a big smile from Christie as she bowed to the members of the task force.

Next, the governor recognized the entire task force team. They stood up and turned to acknowledge the applause and cheers from the audience. The governor handed each of them a lapel pin in the shape of an acorn, with the letters MSTFVC etched across it.

It was a good day.

After the awards ceremony, at the reception, task force members informally shared pieces of the stories about the Cumberland case: the prostitution ring, the sorry ending to the lives of two middle-aged sisters and four officers, and the evidence found that would have put Oscar Little behind bars forever. There was enough verification to conclude that Oscar Little had killed the Jane Does, skinned them and removed their body parts in his butcher shop. The evidence also proved that Little killed the two police officers guarding his driveway and then his two sisters shortly afterward, just a few hours before he himself was murdered.

The tale of how Tom Wilder and task force searchers, using cadaver dogs, found Little's body in the woods behind his farm made the rounds as well. He had been shot six times: once in each leg, then once in his abdomen, followed by a bullet into his right shoulder. M.E. Atwood was certain Little was still alive when the fifth bullet drove through his left eye. The final bullet, through his right eye, was post-mortem. Little's death was slow and painful, typical of a gang killing. There was no evidence found that pointed to the killer of Little.

State police officers congratulated task force members. The task force praised Sheriff Wood and his deputies. All three groups cheered the FBI, District Attorney's office, Judge Howe, the Attorney General and the governor.

The account of Stephen Scott's death, ending the vicious serial killer's years of murdering women, highlighted the conversation. The report describing the drowning of Scott moved around the reception. The fact that his body had not yet been recovered was the cause of great speculation. Could he have escaped once again? Was he was still alive? Forensic experts argued that no one could survive water that cold and that Scott had to be dead.

The crowd applauded Bill and Christie for outsmarting the psychopath and surviving. Their courageous efforts caught everyone's imagination. The nightmarish tale of horror, Bill tortured by the attacking rats, was on everyone's lips. Christie was urged to recount every detail of their long, dangerous walk through that bitter cold night that brought both of them to the edge of death before they reached the nearest house and help.

There was discussion of a made-for-TV movie, portraying the final actions of the serial killer. Deciding which Hollywood stars would play the leading roles brought chuckles, alleviating the undercurrent of horror and disbelief that the previous story telling had aroused.

No one spoke about a dead baby. Nor about a young Eastern European girl, now residing in a safe house, the only known witness to the crimes the human traffickers had committed. Not a word was said about twenty girls, stolen or bought from their families, who were now missing, and that someone higher up on the chain must have been involved in Little's operation.

What the papers reported, the speeches repeated and the talk at the reception reiterated was that Oscar Little was the instigator of a rural prostitution ring in Cumberland County. Officials believed the girls he used were runaways who had showed up at local churches for food and a place to stay. The

Little sisters offered to put them up, determined to reform them so they could return to their families. They were doing God's work. The girls stayed at the Little farm, cared for by Little's two sisters. Somehow, the story went, local men approached Little offering to pay for sex with the girls. It was assumed that he imprisoned the girls, began charging for their sexual sevices, running a profitable sex and porno ring for the local pedophiles, none of whom were ever identified. If a girl became pregnant, he had arranged with a lawyer, who had since disappeared, to sell the babies for $10,000 each. The girls reportedly managed to escape sometime before the task force searched the premises.

The task force arranged for the burial of the bodies of the Jane Does in the Cumberland County cemetery after a short service. Although Interpol continued the search for their identities across Europe and Asia, no one positively identified any of them. The FBI confiscated all of the files containing the detailed information about their autopsies.

Law enforcement agencies had arrested, tried, and imprisoned no one, although at least twelve people had been murdered. Most of the murders were attributed to Little, who was himself murdered. Editorials in several newspapers speculated that some of the murders might have been gangland or syndicate kills, but no name or syndicate was implicated.

Wood remained sheriff of Cumberland County. Preston commanded the state police and Sampson continued as the County District Attorney. They were still playing golf together every weekend. Judge Howe sat on the bench and dispensed justice to all who appeared before him. The Attorney General remained an enigma to most people and politicians.

72

Christie visited Nadia at the safe house where she was cared for by a hard working and kind couple who had emigrated from Romania ten years ago. The foster mother served as an interpreter for Nadia and Christie as they talked in the warm kitchen of the old house in South Portland. Nadia, who was learning English at a fast rate, would soon have no need for a translator.

"You look very pretty in that red dress, Nadia," Christie said.

Nadia looked at her foster mother who repeated what Christie had said in Romanian.

Nadia smiled at Christie and smoothed down the red wool jumper. "Thank you," she said softly. Then Nadia launched into her native language.

Her foster mother translated. "She says she likes your pin. There are acorns where she lived, too."

Nadia was very bright and answered Christie's questions with very little hesitation.

Christie learned that traffickers picked up, lured, bought or kidnapped Nadia and twenty-one other girls from all over Eastern Europe. They herded them together into holding places, often basements, shacks, barns or the back of a truck as their captors made their way to the coast. They fed the girls very little and told them that they would die if they didn't do exactly as they were told.

When they arrived at the coast, they brought the girls to the back of an old pub and told them to undress. They shot one girl who refused. The others followed the traffickers' orders. They were examined from head to toe, internally and externally, amid jeers and sexual jokes. Many of them were too young to understand and just sobbed. After their physical examination, the traffickers smuggled them aboard a trawler, hid them in a small room in the hold and took them to Canada. They stayed in the hold for three weeks, sick and starving. They gave the girls only water and some crackers and cheese to eat. By the end of three weeks, they and the hold smelled like a latrine.

Finally, the traffickers took them to a house in Canada where they showered, changed into clean clothes and ate some decent food. Again, the traffickers stripped them naked. A doctor examined them internally and externally, a terrifying experience for the girls, whose mothers had trained them to be modest.

The next move was over the Canadian border into Maine hidden in a secret compartment in a truck. From there their captors transported them to Little's ell room. There Wood, Sampson, Preston, Tate and others showed them what they were to do when the customers came. Nadia cried while she talked about the painful training and the terror when well-dressed men would come and pick one of them.

She skipped on to when the first girl became pregnant. The sisters treated them all to some good food for a while. Then only the pregnant girls got the good food. The two sisters took the girls away when they were ready to deliver their babies. They brought them back later, without the babies.

She didn't talk about her own pregnancy and her experience giving birth, nor did she ask about her baby. She quickly switched topics.

Nadia described the girls' life. They had no books, no TV, no exercise outdoors, no games. They would sleep, fix each other's hair, talk about home or fabricate stories about being rescued between parties or private clients. Little beat them if they misbehaved or resisted.

Christie listened attentively, absorbed in Nadia's story. Then slowly, so the translator could keep up, she told Nadia the story of a girl much like herself, who had been hurt very much while she was young. When the girl had grown up, a man kidnapped and hurt her very badly again. Christie said that she was that girl and that after all the hurt she hadn't believed that she was worth very much and would be better off dead.

Nadia nodded with understanding.

Christie continued, saying that she had recently discovered something very important about herself. Something that she hadn't known before. She wanted to tell Nadia that underneath all the hurt was something very strong. That Nadia had it, too. Christie called it, in English, the will to survive. Nadia repeated it in English, "The will to survive."

"Yes," Christie explained. "Somewhere deep inside, where hurt cannot reach, is the bright star of our souls. No matter what happens to us, the soul is there. Often, it is hidden or hard to find, but it is always there. Someday, you will do something, maybe just a tiny thing, perhaps look at a beautiful sunset or watch a baby bird fly for the first time, and you will feel your soul warm inside you. Then you will know that you survived all the bad things. And that you have the capacity, the gift of knowing beauty, the awe of innocence and love again."

Nadia looked at Christie. Tears welled in her eyes. Nadia believed her.

Christie bent close to Nadia. "I promise you, Nadia. You will see yourself. And who you see will be wonderful."

73

"Hello Roberta. This is Doctor McMorrow."

"Yes, thank you, Roberta. I missed you, too. I understand you talked with Dr. Stella?"

"I see. And what do you think about resuming our sessions, just to have some closure between us?"

"Well, I'm happy about it, too. Would 5:00 on Wednesday work for you?"

"Excellent. My office number is 3443. That's on the third floor."

"Yes, that's right. Just one floor up from Dr. Stella's. So, you know where to come?"

"That's good. I'm really looking forward to seeing you again."

"Yes, you, too, Roberta. Wednesday at 5:00. See you then."

Christie smiled as she hung up the phone. She looked around her office. She decided she needed to hang some nice artwork on the walls to brighten the place up a little. She'd bring in the picture of the loon that Alex had painted for her. The handmade clay mugs that Bill had given to her last year would be great to use for tea.

Christie glanced out the window of her office at the setting sun. The days were getting longer now. March was gone and April had come in like a lamb and the days warmed even more in May. Soon she'd be working in her gardens again. She'd better order her seeds right away. She was already late in starting them, but she'd do it anyway, just as she always did. She would start them indoors by the kitchen bay window where they would sit in the warm sun most of the day. The little seeds would burst into sprouts in no time. In another month, when the true leaves were strong, she could harden them off. Then, it was up to them. With care, they would grow full and beautiful. She thought of Nadia. Christie would order some seeds for her, too, and help Nadia care for the seedlings as they grew into their fullness.

74

Christie picked up her office phone. "This is Dr. Christie McMorrow. How can I help you?"

"Christie, it's Bill. Do you have time to meet with me today? Something's come up. I have to talk to you."

"Regarding what?"

"Well, I'd rather not say on the phone. Can you meet me?"

"Let me see. My schedule has filled up much faster than I expected. I was planning on half time, but I almost have a full load of clients now."

Christie turned the pages of her schedule book, looking for a free time slot. "How about tomorrow morning for breakfast? Would that do?"

"No. This is rather urgent. Can we meet today sometime?"

"Today? Hmmm, let me see what I can do. How about at six o'clock tonight? I had plans to meet Stella for dinner, but I'll call her and cancel."

"Thanks. I wouldn't push you like this, unless it was important."

"I know. Could we meet at that little restaurant we both like? The Italian Bistro on Fore Street? Say at 6:15?"

"Perfect. See you then."

75

Christie found a parking space just big enough for her sporty red Saab outside the Bistro. She took her briefcase and purse, locked the car doors and walked into the restaurant. She didn't need her cane anymore and her limp was hardly noticeable. Immediately, the warm spicy smells of oregano, tomatoes, onion and garlic tickled her nose; visions of eggplant parmesan caused her stomach to rumble softly. She spotted Bill at a corner table and headed over.

He stood up and hugged her. His face was mottled and still puffy in spots, but other than a few red scars from his surgeries, he was looking better each time Christie saw him.

"You look great. It's so good to see you. I've missed you. How've you been?" Christie smiled at Bill and touched his hand. Bill squeezed her fingers.

"I'm fine, for the most part. I'm sorry I didn't call you earlier this week for our movie outing. I missed you too. I was looking for another case that we could work together on, just so I could see you on a more regular basis. I like having you in my life."

Christie smiled. "I like it too. I've been so busy at work that the time has passed really fast." She reached across the table and held his hand. "But I've been thinking about you a lot. I'd like to see more of you."

Bill put his other hand on top of hers. He smiled. "We'll make that happen. I couldn't wish for anything more. I've been busy, although things have slowed down at the task force. You know how it goes; warm weather gets people outside releasing built-up energy and tension. They feel better. Therefore, the violent crime rate dips for a few months until it starts getting hot in August. Anyway, I've been busy with all my plastic surgeries that I'm happy to say are finished for a while. In a few months, I might need some refining. My doctor said in time I'll be as good as new. I tried to convince him to do a full-face conversion, but he just laughed and said the insurance wouldn't pay for it. So, I guess I'm stuck with the same old version."

"Which is very nice, Bill. I like the way you look."

The server took their drink order and returned shortly with two glasses of the house red wine.

They clicked glasses. "To us," Bill said.

Christie hesitated a moment then she said softly, "To us."

They sipped their wine in silence. Then Christie asked, "What was so important that we had to meet tonight? You've really piqued my curiosity."

"Besides wanting to see you, something happened last night. Something really important. I need to ask you to keep what I'm going to tell you in strict confidence, Christie. No one, not even your therapist, Stella or Alex can hear this. It would just put them into potential danger."

"Danger? Bill, what's going on? What danger?"

The server returned to take their order and to leave a basket of warm bread sticks.

When he left, Bill started to explain, talking very softly as he leaned across the table toward Christie.

"I haven't told anyone about this. I haven't really known what to do about it. However, after what happened last night I decided that I wanted to tell you. I know you'll feel the same way about it as I do."

He stopped to take a drink of his wine.

"Go on. Don't make me drag it out of you."

Bill's eyes suddenly filled with tears. "Nadia's gone. Her foster family called me last night and said someone from the FBI came and just took her away. They wouldn't say where she was going or how to reach her. Nadia didn't want to go. They had to pick her up and manhandle her into the car. The foster family's very upset. So am I. I called Hadley and he wouldn't return my calls."

"I can't believe it. That's awful. How could they do that? Isn't she still under task force jurisdiction?"

"Evidently not. I think someone decided that she was a loose cannon. She knew too much. She'd seen too many people. She was too great a danger to too many. So they took her."

"But where? Would they send her back home?"

"I doubt it. I found out that Nadia was living with a second cousin in Romania before they grabbed her. The cousin never reported her missing. The rest of her family's dead. There's no one to stand as her guardian so I don't think they'll send her back there."

"What will they do with her? Are they trying to protect her? Has there been a threat?" Christie leaned back, rigid in her chair. "Oh God, they're going to kill her, aren't they?"

"I don't know. But that thought occurred to me too."

"What can we do? Is there someone we can call?" Christie was wiping at her eyes with the napkin and grabbing at her purse as if she planned to take some action that very moment.

"Christie, wait. I have to tell you something else. This is confidential as well."

"Yes? Tell me. It can't be any worse than what you've already told me."

"When I was searching the Little's kitchen, after we found the two sisters dead, I came upon something. I was looking at their aprons hanging on the pegboard on the kitchen wall. They reminded me of my grandmother's. Every night when she finished with her work and was ready to go to bed, she'd take her apron off and hang it up. When I visited, she always played a little game with me. She'd tell me she had forgotten something and it must be in her apron pocket. Would I get it for her? When I put my hand in that soft cotton apron pocket, there was always a treat, like a cookie or a jaw breaker or a piece of gum."

"That's a sweet memory. But what does it have to do with what you're trying to tell me?"

"Hold on, I'm getting to it. The memory of my grandmother caused me to reach up and feel the cloth when I saw the sisters' aprons. Instinctively, I put my hand in one pocket and there it was. My treat."

"Your treat? What do you mean?"

"I found a tape. A videotape. The label read Wood, Preston, Sampson, and others. Nobody was watching me. I just stuck it in my pocket."

"You put it in your pocket? You didn't process it?"

"No. I just hid it in my coat pocket. I guess I was afraid that after the massacre at Little's, the FBI would take over and that tape would just disappear. You remember what Hadley said would happen if we uncovered any evidence of important people being involved with our case?"

"Yes, he said he'd shut us down and the FBI would take over. And you didn't want that to happen?"

"No. I guess something you said about Hadley and the FBI got to me. I know now you were right about there being a conspiracy that is protecting certain people. The tape's proof of it. The tape alone would be enough to bring certain people up on charges. And with Nadia as a witness? The whole operation would go down and everyone in it sent away for a long time."

"Did you watch the tape?"

"Yes. It was so painful. I had to fast forward most of it. You can see Wood, Preston and Sampson clearly, no mistaking them. Judge Howe, Congressman Elliot, and some other men that are well-known shakers and movers in Washington are on the tape, too. There's one scene. It's so horrible. It's sickening. Nadia's shown with some old person. That's why when she disappeared, I just knew it was time to do something about this tape. Maybe it could help to save Nadia's life or some of the other girls."

"Why did you wait so long to tell me? We could've done something sooner."

"First, I was so involved in my surgeries, I wasn't in any kind of shape to accuse people and cause a major media event. Then, I was afraid that if I revealed the tape, something bad would happen. Like the tape would disappear. Some so-called accident would destroy it. Or I might suddenly die on the surgery table. This tape's dynamite. It's dangerous and we could use it to blow this human trafficking organization sky high and take everyone who's involved with it."

Christie thought a moment. "And it could blow us up with them, especially if they find out you have it and I know about it now, too. Look what happened to Nadia."

"You've got that right. I didn't want to endanger you, Nadia or anyone else. So, I didn't tell you. I kept everything quiet, trying to figure out what to do."

Christie leaned over the table to close the space between them.

"Bill, I don't know what to say. However, what's happened to Nadia is morally unacceptable and appalling. We have proof on tape that the horror of the traffickers really did occur and probably is still occurring right now somewhere else. We have to do something. I just don't know what action we can take."

"That's why I wanted to talk to you. I need your help. I have a few ideas of what we can do. I want to run them by you. I don't know if there's anyone else we can trust, someone we could get to help us. However, I've decided I'm going to do something, even if I have to do it by myself. I have to take some action that might help Nadia and others like her. I thought I might try to trade the tape for Nadia. Then hide her where no one would ever find her."

"Look Bill, I'm with you. Knowing what I know now, I can't stand by and do nothing, no matter how dangerous it may be. However, trading the tape for Nadia may not be the best course of action. First, you can't trust that the traffickers will follow through on the trade. They could decide to go after you, kill you and destroy the tape. I hate to say it, but they might have already killed Nadia. If so, then we'd lose the tape for nothing."

"I know. I'm afraid she might be dead. How terrible."

"I can't bear knowing traffickers are stealing, torturing, using these kids as sex slaves and baby breeders. Then killing them. Selling their body parts. It's even harder understanding why government officials across the world do almost nothing to stop it. Token funds, a few activists, a couple of conferences and statues directed at the problem are not enough. Maybe making this tape public would help."

"I think you're right. Listen to plan B. We'd have to do it pretty much ourselves, with just a few people who we trust and are willing to work with us. We'd need someone to go undercover. If we could infiltrate a trafficking organization and start leaking information back to an well-known investigative reporter who feels the same way we do and writes up the story, we might just be able to raise enough public anger and outrage. Revealing the tape would be the climax. Officials will be forced to do something."

"Undercover? Infiltrate? Bill, I've never done anything like that before. I don't have the least idea how to pull that off. Isn't that terribly dangerous?"

"Yes, it's dangerous. I wouldn't let you do it. They'd recognize me, so I can't do it. We'll use someone who's experienced in that line work. If you can think of another way, tell me. I'm open to any idea."

Christie thought. "Give me a little time, Bill. I need to do some research and find out what we're getting into. I'll have to limit my clients, so I'll have time to work on this. I just finished setting my new schedule. It's complicated."

Bill stared into her eyes. "You don't have to take part in this. The truth is I just wanted you, someone I trust, to know what I know, just in case I disappear or, well, you know. I've made several copies of the tape and hidden them in locations that I've mailed to you, an old friend from my FBI days, and put into my safety deposit box. I've arranged to take a leave of absence from the task force for a few months. The attorney general approved the time as a medical leave, so no one will wonder why I'm not around. I know I can't change everything, but maybe I can make a dent in the human trafficking business in the United States, at least. Then I might be able to sleep again."

"Bill, you're a good man. It's an honor to know you. Thank you for caring so much. Maybe we could plan an undercover operation. I think the idea of linking to an investigative reporter is great. We definitely will need some more people in on it with us."

"Like who? Whom could we trust? And who would be willing to risk so much?"

The two bent their heads together in the warm candle lighted Bistro, forgetting their dinners. To the other patrons, Christie and Bill appeared to be affectionate lovers. In actuality, they were making plans to expose a systemic operation of human trafficking in the U.S. that could save 20,000 lives each year. They shared the same hope: that once citizens of the United States became aware of human trafficking in their own country, they would insist on eradicating it, making sure that such despicable crimes against humanity would never be ignored again and certainly never forgotten.

76

Spring in Maine comes and goes very quickly. One day the ice breaks up on the lakes and ponds; the daffodils flower with the crocuses and forsythia. The next day snow blankets the terrain again. The spring snow melts quickly, replaced by wild thunderstorms and rain that never seems to stop. Snowmelt and rain fill lakes and rivers, which overflow and flood, pushing ice, flotsam, jetsam and debris with them on their way to sea.

Christie called the state police again.

"No, Dr. McMorrow. No sign of the body yet. We've had the divers in the pond several time since the ice went out. The K-9 unit took cadaver dogs, specially trained to detect bodies under water, out in the boats last week. If his body were still in the pond, those dogs would have found him. They didn't find anything. We're still searching the shores of the Royal River, leading from Yardly Pond. Right now our best guess is that spring overflow swept Scott's body downstream. By now it's somewhere in the ocean. That current runs pretty fast and carries a lot of stuff from up land down into the estuaries. Truth is we may never find it."

"Are the estuaries and ocean shore line being searched as well?"

"The Coast Guard's in charge of that. We've notified them and I'm sure they're conducting searches as well. You'd have to call them. Of course, if they did find his body they'd report it to us. We'd call you."

"Thanks." Christie clicked off her cell. She had been inquiring about the search for Scott's body ever since Bill and she escaped from him last March. First, no one could search the pond until the ice melted. After the ice went out, rains and flooding made searching the pond and river shores nearly impossible.

Christie had been looking forward to spring hoping that the searchers would finally turn up Scott's body and confirm his death. She was the only witness to his drowning. Sometimes, she questioned her recall. The memory of the time Scott had held them in the cabin was so hazy. She wondered if she could have missed seeing him climb out of the hole in the ice. Could she have repressed that memory? Maybe he came up one more time when she turned her back to take care of Bill. Did he crawl out over the ice and make his way to shore? She knew that until they found his body she wouldn't ever really rest. It was now May. Over two months had passed.

Christie wandered out to her garden and began pulling weeds under the warming sun. She enjoyed pulling weeds, freeing the small sprouts, and uncovering the dark fertile soil. Earth smells rose as she made her way down the row where the peas were already starting to climb the mesh fence she provided for them. Her thoughts in the garden were always pleasant. Today she thought about Bill and wondered where he was and what he was doing. She hadn't heard from him yesterday. Maybe she'd give him a call and invite him up for dinner tonight.

Christie's cell phone rang. Hoping it was Bill, she clicked it on.

"Hello. Hello."

No one answered.

"Is anyone there?"

She listened. The line sounded open, connected. Was that static she heard? Or was someone breathing on the other end?

THE END

CRITICAL ACCLAIM FOR TWISTED TRUTH

"Clarey utilizes her background as a psychotherapist to present realistic interpretations of complex internal conflicts. She does an outstanding job of presenting a portrait of a sadistic killer, without all the cliches or sterotypes...She also constructs intricate relationships between the central characters...Clarey's profession has obviously informed her characters, and it adds credibility and realism to the novel.

Christie is a terrific protagonist and Stephen Scott is terrifically terrible. A novel of this depth and magnitude, written very much in the tradition of James Patterson's Alex Cross series, is writing we would like to see more of."

——— Writer's Digest

Printed in the United States
78891LV00003B/1-48